Praise for
Kiss and Hell

"A fun, lighthearted paranormal romance that will keep readers entertained. Ms. Cassidy fills the pages of her book with nonstop banter, ghostly activity, and steamy romance." —*Darque Reviews*

"Delaney, with her amusing sarcastic asides, makes for an entertaining romantic fantasy with a wonderful mystery subplot . . . Readers will relish this lighthearted jocular frolic."

—*Genre Go Round Reviews*

"Cassidy has created a hilarious lead in Delaney Markham. Readers will run through all types of emotions while enjoying laugh-out-loud moments, desperate passion, wacky and fun characters, pop-culture references and one intense mystery. The book's charm is apparent from the first page, but the twisted mystery tangled throughout will keep the pages turning." —*Romantic Times*

The Accidental Human

"I highly enjoyed every moment of Dakota Cassidy's *The Accidental Human* . . . A paranormal romance with a strong dose of humor." —*Errant Dreams*

"A delightful, at times droll, contemporary tale starring a decidedly human heroine . . . Dakota Cassidy provides a fitting, twisted ending to this amusingly warm urban romantic fantasy."

—*Genre Go Round Reviews*

continued . . .

"The final member of Cassidy's trio of decidedly offbeat friends faces her toughest challenge, but that doesn't mean there isn't humor to spare! With emotion, laughter, and some pathos, Cassidy serves up another winner!"
—*Romantic Times*

Accidentally Dead

"A laugh-out-loud follow-up to *The Accidental Werewolf*, and it's a winner . . . Ms. Cassidy is an up-and-comer in the world of paranormal romance."
—*Fresh Fiction*

"An enjoyable, humorous satire that takes a bite out of the vampire romance subgenre . . . Fans will appreciate the nonstop hilarity."
—*Genre Go Round Reviews*

The Accidental Werewolf

"Cassidy, a prolific author of erotica, has ventured into MaryJanice Davidson territory with a humorous, sexy tale."
—*Booklist*

"If Bridget Jones became a lycanthrope, she might be Marty. Fun and flirty humor is cleverly interspersed with dramatic mystery and action. It's hard to know which character to love best, though: Keegan or Muffin, the toy poodle that steals more than one scene."
—*The Eternal Night*

"A riot! Marty's internal dialogue will have you howling, and her antics will keep the laughs coming. If you love paranormal with a comedic twist, you'll love this book."
—*Romance Junkies*

"A lighthearted romp . . . [An] entertaining tale with an alpha twist."
                                        —*Midwest Book Review*

More praise for the novels of Dakota Cassidy

"The fictional equivalent of the little black dress—every reader should have one!"
                                        —Michele Bardsley

"Serious, laugh-out-loud humor with heart, the kind of love story that leaves you rooting for the heroine, sighing for the hero, and looking for your own significant other at the same time."
                                        —Kate Douglas

"Ditzy and daring . . . Pure escapist fun."
                                        —*Romance Reviews Today*

"Dakota Cassidy is going on my must-read list!"
                                        —*Joyfully Reviewed*

"If you're looking for some steamy romance with something that will have you smiling, you have to read [Dakota Cassidy]."
                                        —*The Best Reviews*

Berkley Sensation titles by Dakota Cassidy

KISS & HELL
MY WAY TO HELL

THE ACCIDENTAL WEREWOLF
ACCIDENTALLY DEAD
THE ACCIDENTAL HUMAN
ACCIDENTALLY DEMONIC

my way to hell

dakota cassidy

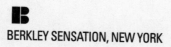

BERKLEY SENSATION, NEW YORK

THE BERKLEY PUBLISHING GROUP
Published by the Penguin Group
Penguin Group (USA) Inc.
375 Hudson Street, New York, New York 10014, USA
Penguin Group (Canada), 90 Eglinton Avenue East, Suite 700, Toronto, Ontario M4P 2Y3, Canada
(a division of Pearson Penguin Canada Inc.)
Penguin Books Ltd., 80 Strand, London WC2R 0RL, England
Penguin Group Ireland, 25 St. Stephen's Green, Dublin 2, Ireland (a division of Penguin Books Ltd.)
Penguin Group (Australia), 250 Camberwell Road, Camberwell, Victoria 3124, Australia
(a division of Pearson Australia Group Pty. Ltd.)
Penguin Books India Pvt. Ltd., 11 Community Centre, Panchsheel Park, New Delhi—110 017, India
Penguin Group (NZ), 67 Apollo Drive, Rosedale, North Shore 0632, New Zealand
(a division of Pearson New Zealand Ltd.)
Penguin Books (South Africa) (Pty.) Ltd., 24 Sturdee Avenue, Rosebank, Johannesburg 2196,
South Africa

Penguin Books Ltd., Registered Offices: 80 Strand, London WC2R 0RL, England

This book is an original publication of The Berkley Publishing Group.

This is a work of fiction. Names, characters, places, and incidents either are the product of the author's imagination or are used fictitiously, and any resemblance to actual persons, living or dead, business establishments, events, or locales is entirely coincidental. The publisher does not have any control over and does not assume any responsibility for author or third-party websites or their content.

PRINTING HISTORY
Berkley Sensation trade paperback edition / July 2010

Library of Congress Cataloging-in-Publication Data

Cassidy, Dakota.
   My way to hell / Dakota Cassidy.—Berkley Sensation trade paperback ed.
      p.   cm.
   ISBN 978-0-425-23443-3
   1. Demonology—Fiction.   2. Chick lit.   I. Title.
   PS3603.A8685M9   2010
   813'.6—dc22   2010005993

PRINTED IN THE UNITED STATES OF AMERICA

10 9 8 7 6 5 4 3 2 1

With never-ending thanks to my BFFs, Renee George, Terri Smythe, and Michele Bardsley. Dudes, for serious, you rule. Also, my test readers and pals, Vicki Burklund, Amy, Qwill, Kaz, and Erin—your input is invaluable.

My agent, Elaine Spencer, who knows when I'm riding a good freak and tells me to shut it. That, in an agent, is invaluable, people.

Cindy Hwang because she lets my crazy run hog wild.

My Yahoo! groups—the Accidentals and the Babes. You're priceless—don't evah change. I love you more than my facial cream. You all know what moisturizer means to this old broad. And to a special member of our group, Bill. You've been there since the beginning, babe, and you're all kinds of awesomeness.

My pal Kaz, who flies in for my book signings and answers my e-mails when I need a naughty word in Spanish.

Rob, my soul mate, who suffers my greasy-haired, unwashed-laundry, unwaxed-eyebrow whines—I love you—like a buttload.

But most especially to the lovely Pat Richardson from the DFW Tea Ladies—because everyone deserves big, honkin' hooters and a hot pair of legs, sistah!

acknowledgments

www.brainyquote.com
www.famousquotes.me.uk
www.tshirthell.com/hell.shtml

Please note, any and all mistakes regarding the quotes, dates, and/or history of the sports icons and celebrities used in this book are entirely mine.

one

"Your breath smells like the stench of a thousand rotting souls, *muchacho*."

"And your dress is no more a designer label than I am a perky Bichon Frise."

"At least if you were a Bichon you'd be easier on the eye and drool less."

"But you, my little cheesy enchilada, would still be just as tacky."

Marcella Acosta pointed the Rottweiler's—the *talking* Rottweiler's—muzzle away from her nose with one finger. "If I were you, Darwin, I wouldn't point fingers. Oh, wait, I mean paws. Because you have no fingers, do you?"

Darwin reared his head out of her reach, letting his tongue loll from his wide mouth. "Nope. But I still have excellent fashion sense—even fingerless. I don't need those to tell me your dress is horrifying, darling."

"I don't need fingers to slap you in the head, *mijo*."

"True that. But you do need them if you're ever going to make contact with anyone other than me. Something you sincerely suck sweaty balls at since you were allegedly banished to this hot mess. Mock all you like, but at least I can travel from plane to plane. You?" He gave her a pointed doggy look. "Not so much."

Anger, sharp and stinging, seared her gut while she slid down the trunk of a leafless tree. "Fuck. You."

"Not even if you were a fluffy French poodle who was leash trained, potty mouth." He turned his chocolate brown eyes on her and gave his "so over this" look, then yawned, revealing his big, white teeth.

Marcella leaned into him, nudging his black, squat haunches. "You know, Darwin, each day I spend with you on this godforsaken plane I've been banished to is like shopping for Jimmy Choo shoes at Payless. Im-fucking-possible."

His big rust and black head cocked to the left. "You're just cranky because you've been wearing that hideous dress for three straight months. You do realize, now that you're doomed to roam this plane, with only occasional relief when some half-baked medium mistakenly summons your spirit to Earth, that shopping trips are a thing of the past for you, yes? That is, unless you get off your vivacious, tight ass and do something about it. Too bad, so sad. Guess you'll be in the wrong color for the rest of your nonlife. Your nonlife being *eternal*, and all."

Marcella flicked a finger in the air aimed at his wet, cold nose. "Care to tell me again how it is you, a dog, can *talk* on this plane? Just until I figure out how to rip your esophagus from your throat, that is."

"Care to tell me how it is that you, a one-time not even level-one demon, thought you could throw down with Lucifer and win?"

Marcella smoothed a hand over her wrinkled, torn dress and stuck her tongue out at him despite the fact that it was childish and petty. "Go to hell," she muttered out of the side of her mouth, letting her head rest on her knees. She'd thrown down with the horned one for one reason and one reason only.

Her closest friend, Delaney.

Okay, so she'd been her only friend.

In seventy-six years of demonicness.

And since that infamous, albeit totally humiliating, utterly defeated smackdown with the aforementioned king of evil, she'd been in her own special hell.

The one without a Pier 1.

Appalling.

Because she'd defied Lucifer in the name of her best friend of over ten years, he had banished her once demonic butt from Hell. Seeing as she was now considered "the demon formerly known as," hitching a ride on the elevator upstairs was simply out of the question, because ex-demons, no matter how ex, weren't offered the light option package. There'd be no light for her to walk into.

Like, ever.

That wasn't something she hadn't known for decades now. But at least as a demon, she'd had earthly privileges. She'd wandered around as though she were still human. Here? Not likely.

So that meant she was shit out of luck. If she couldn't go up, and down was no longer a possibility, in between was all that was left. Now she was doomed to drift endlessly, roaming a plane that was as mortifying as a trip to the Dollar Store.

But her arrival on this very plane meant Delaney had survived, and she'd won Clyde, the man of her dreams. That was all that mattered to Marcella. She'd smile for a hundred eternities spent right here in this dreary, colorless place because Lucifer'd lost that fucking battle. Delaney was safe. *Alive.* Lifting her head, she saw that Darwin remained rooted to her side, so she repeated, "Didn't I tell you to go to hell? Where in there did I slur my words?"

"I'd much rather stay with you—here on Plane Dismal. It's much less humid, don't you agree?"

A chilly, raw wind whipped at the edges of her torn dress. The tree at her back shivered from the gust. "Isn't there a light you should be chasing a cat into?"

"Oh, I've no question there is. But who in their right mind would want to walk into a light when they can hang out with the fucking ray of sunshine that is all you, peach pit?"

Her intake of breath was ragged with defeat. She was so done with their banter for today. So over the injustice that a dog, her friend Delaney's *dead* dog, could not only *talk* on this plane but travel between planes with the ease of a 747. Done with feeling like she'd fallen through a black hole smack-dab into the Mad Hatter's tea party. Done-da-done-done. "Just go the fuck away, Darwin. Go off to the plane where unicorns jump over goddamned rainbows in herds and showers of dog biscuits rain down on you every day at three sharp, and leave me the fuck alone."

"And let you stew in the stank of that disgraceful dress? Not on your unlife, sweetheart. If I didn't do my part to at least find you a change of clothing that's more suited to your complexion, what kind of faithful companion would I be to Delaney? Stop being such a candy-ass and figure this out."

They'd only been over this a thousand times. Okay, so she'd only been over it once with Darwin—out loud and all—but she'd been over it in her head at least a thousand times. "You're a *dead* companion to Delaney, one that she can no longer see or hear, to boot. And what's there to figure? I'm being punished for defying Lucifer. He has me tethered here somehow, the mother-fucker. I'm sure of it. My eternal punishment is this plane, where the in-betweens roam with restless dissatisfaction or some such depressing, melodramatic crap. Oh, and you. You *have* to be part of some kind of damnation."

"Tsk-tsk," he growled, then he snorted, making his sagging jowls tremble. "This is so not the Marcella I know. The Marcella I know wouldn't take this kind of crisis lying down. Well, not unless there was mancake involved and a bed with silk sheets to do the lying down on. The Marcella I know would be kicking and screaming her stilettoed feet until she found a solution. Scarier still? She'd be putting that one brain cell she has left to good use by figuring this out. If the other undecided and doomed souls can make contact with the living, if they can leave this plane at will, then why can't you?"

Marcella jammed a hand into her tangled hair with tense fingers. "The Marcella you know is ass-fried, pal. How many people in an afterlifetime can lay claim to the fact that they've been not only a demon but now . . . this? I'm tired, Snausage breath. Bone weary, *chico*. And what about *damned* escapes you, mutt? Every time I try, I'm slammed right back into this dump. Satan jacked me up but good. The other souls on this plane seem to have some kind of magic transmission juju I just don't. Don't think I haven't tried, either."

Because she had tried. She'd even resorted to using the Heavenly Medium Administration's approved list of mediums to attempt to contact a ghost whisperer so she could send a message to Delaney. She'd also blown chunks at it, but she was only halfway through the HMA's list. Though, she hadn't tapped that Sylvia Browne or John Edward yet. There was still hope.

Or not.

"What happened to the Marcella who would have *Matrix*ed her way out of here? Are you saying you're going to let a wee thing like the fear that Satan has tethered you here keep you from making contact with Delaney? You do realize she's been worried sick about you, don't you? Just the other day I heard her and Clyde discussing it. She feels incredible guilt because of your sacrifice. She's beyond frantic over your fate. If you were any kind of friend, you'd find a way to send her a message that would console her."

Marcella flipped him the bird with the harsh whip of a finger. "Wee this, you ASPCA reject. You weren't there that night with Delaney and Clyde. You have no clue what that was like. There was nothing *wee* about it." A violent shiver slipped up her spine just recalling it.

Thunder, lightning, locusts, snakes—all the happy-clappy things true nightmares are made of. Marcella had no desire to dredge that night back up.

Evah.

Darwin yawned, revealing a gaping black hole filled with miles of pink tongue. "I know, I know. That night was dreadful times a million. Old Lucifer whipped you like so much cream. That still doesn't mean you just give up, Marcella. Other souls from this plane manage to make contact. You could, too. If you were willing to break a nail, that is."

"Don't you think I'd send Delaney a message if I could, you antagonistic shit? I've tried everything. I just suck at this." And she did. Suck at it, that is. She just couldn't get a feel for the whole deal. No matter how many times she tried to connect with a medium, she ended up crapping out with a fizzle. She'd even gone so far as to attend this shitty plane's therapy sessions and more self-help classes than she could count, like it was her new religion. Yet thus far, she'd tanked in "Medium + Ghost = Happily Ever After for Eternity," and she couldn't even begin to express her dismay over the "Limbo Doesn't Have to Suck" class.

The one last earthly thing she wanted to do was let her friend know that she was all right. That the choice she'd made that night in a hospital room in Nebraska was made with no regrets. Not one.

What made being doomed here that much more doomish was the idea that knowing Delaney like she did, she knew guilt was chewing a hole in her gut. Delaney was the kind of friend who'd never have allowed her to give up what she'd given up that night. In fact, she'd have probably rather had a limb hacked off in lieu of. The least Marcella could do was let Delaney know she'd survived. Her friend would never have complete happiness if she didn't have peace of mind about Marcella's fate.

"So?" Darwin prodded. "What are you going to do? Whine or take charge?"

"Here's the problem, mouth, and you know the rules as well as I do, Darwin. Because I was *banished* to this plane, I can't leave unless someone summons my soul or unless I can find a medium to connect with and send signs to—which seems to be about as difficult as getting hold of the date for the second coming of Christ. Maybe some of the mediums on the approved list they gave me are just a bunch of shysters. Delaney always said there were more fakes than the real thing. And seriously, do you really think a place called the Spirit Shack—where, I might add, they offer five séances for five hundred bucks, get the sixth one free—is the real deal?"

"The Spirit Shack just helped that Andre, didn't they? He'd been here for eight years, Marcella. They can't all be hack mediums if they helped a hard-core plane dweller like Andre. That's just a convenient excuse for you not to get off your keister."

"Oh, bullshit," she snorted, enraged that he was goading her. "Andre's the perfect example for why I think I was *banished* to this plane instead of just *dumped* here. He crossed without the use of a real medium. It was just his time to go, I guess. I tried hitting up the Spirit Shack and got nothing out of it other than watching some lying piece of shit who called himself Jean-Franc perform a séance then pretend he could see some guy named Marlon from

Hoboken who wasn't even there. He couldn't see me any more than Delaney can still see you. If that's not enough proof for you, then I got nuthin'."

Darwin scratched his underside with a rapid thump of his paw. "While I'm certain some of the mediums who manage to make the approved list are just as you claim, full of shit, they aren't *all* full of shit."

"Look, the only friggin' medium I knew for sure was the real deal was Delaney, and she's no longer a medium, remember? Or are you forgetting the reason she could see the dead in the first place? The contract with Lucifer. You know, that crazy contract her freaky half brother Vincent had with the horned one that gave him all that evil power he abused the shit out of while he was alive? The power that, upon his death, was passed to his next oldest living relative? That relative being Delaney—who used the power for good instead of evil, by crossing souls. Do you also remember the clause in there that I mentioned to you? The stupid loophole that said the power would stay in Delaney's bloodline for as long as there were living relatives to be had? Which would have been great had Delaney not actually died that night in the hospital."

She shivered with remembrance all over again. When Lucifer had used Marcella as a human catapult, launching her body full force at Delaney, her friend had fallen hard and hit her head against a solid porcelain sink, essentially killing her from the impact to her skull.

Yet Clyde, the whole reason they'd had the big smackdown with Satan to begin with, had resuscitated Delaney, saving her life. Though Marcella'd been weak and battered beyond the point of moving, she'd seen everything, lying on that hospital room floor before she passed out and ended up here.

Darwin peered at her with an intent gaze. "I remember this tale

as if you told it just yesterday. In fact, I believe it was just yesterday when you *finally*, after three months, decided to leave your
entrails at my feet. What does that have to do with you getting off
this plane?"

"The contract. It has to do with the contract. Because Delaney
died, she lost the power. That means she no longer sees dead people. I am, for all intents and purposes, the former. You know—
dead people. Her medium days are ovah. No one's going to
summon me because no one but Delaney cares that I'm dead . . .
gone . . . whatever I am. And if Delaney's the only medium I
know—knew—then color me all kinds of screwed. I've tried doing
what the others do when they set out to send messages to their
family members via a medium. You do remember me following
that moron Ivan to Psychic Saul's in the West End, don't you?"

What an ass-sucking disaster that'd been. She'd ended up
crossing Ivan's signals with her own and confusing the ever-loving
shit out of poor Saul. Ivan had been so pissed because she'd messed
up his big moment, a moment that had taken him four years to
get the nads up for, he'd made sure no one, not a drifting soul,
would sit with her during their "Decisive Decision Making in the
Afterlife" class.

"Ah, yet the others, who're lesser women than you, have managed to make contact. Slacker."

For the love of all things shiny. "The others aren't here on
the orders of Satan, smart-ass. They're just lost and undecided
for the most part. They're not bound here by anything other than
their own pathetic lack of the take-charge-and-face-up-to-your-
obligations gene. The light is still an option for the others once
they figure out what they want and settle things. We both know,
and I don't need to be reminded, the light isn't an op for me. I lost
all hope for a choice years ago when I didn't go into the light upon
my death. Maybe that's why I keep running into roadblocks when

I try to contact a medium. Whoever's in charge just thinks there's no point in allowing me to send a message, because I'm not worthy. So get off my back, Lord of the Kibble, and go chase cars. A lot."

If it were still possible for her to be nagged to death, she'd be six feet under, and Darwin would win all kinds of awards for all the poking and prodding he'd been doing since she'd hit this plane. Yet, he was right. She'd once been a take-no-prisoners kind of girl. But since she'd arrived here, her energy points had been dwindling by the hour—and the Marcella of three months ago would've been fucked before she'd allow even Satan to get one over on her.

"I can't tell you how disappointed I am in you."

Marcella snorted and looked Darwin in the eye. "I'm all kinds of broken up over it, too. I'm just good at hiding my complete devastation. You can't see it, but really, I'm crying on the inside." She let the sarcasm in her words ring crystal clear.

The pair remained silent for several moments. Marcella lost in her misery, Darwin flopping down beside her to roll on his back with a carefree wiggle.

"So riddle me this," he said, interrupting any further wallowing.

"No."

"Oh, stop being so negative, whiner. I have an important point to make. Something that's been bothering me since you landed here on Chez Drab."

"Make it—and then go awaaay."

He eyed her from his upside-down position with glassy, dark brown eyes. "How do you know Satan *personally* banished you? I mean, did he actually raise his fist to the sky and dramatically declare you dead to him while you displayed weak emotions like tears and begged him to spare you from the pit?"

Now that made her pause. Huh. Not that she'd have begged for anything from that puke to begin with. No one was more yippyskippy than she was when someone managed to keep that freaka-zoid from wreaking more havoc. She'd gone into it knowing full well she might end up in the pit for eternity. She hadn't been a demon for seven and a half decades without knowing the risk she was taking by trying to best Lucifer and protect her friend. She'd never asked to be a demon to begin with, so rebellion of any kind would receive only kudos from her. In fact, nothing got her rocks off more than interfering with Lucifer and his fucked-uppedness.

Nothing.

She'd laid low during her demonic stint, and she'd managed to slip through the cracks of Hell going virtually unnoticed, for the most part. Marcella had ridden Hell's fence for a very long time—but when she'd jumped off that fence, she'd jumped big.

When she'd landed—she'd landed here.

But no. The devil hadn't handed down an edict for any kind of punishment . . . not that she was aware of. Fancy that.

Darwin pawed her dirty, partially shredded sandal. "So?"

"Fine. No. No, he didn't, but if you'll recall, after that night with Delaney—you know the one, right? The one with locusts, and flames licking at my pert butt? The one that in general is the shit nightmares are made of? The one where I tried to stop him from taking out my best friend? What happened after that was *this*." She spread her arms wide. "This was where I woke up. I as-sumed, because I no longer had earthbound privileges, that he was the one who dumped me here. Or one of his ass lickers did it. Why else would I be *here*?" If picking planes had actually been an op-tion she'd been aware of, this gray dive wouldn't have been high on her list of plane picking.

"He may have banished you from *his* domain, genius, but he didn't necessarily banish you to this plane. Believe you me, there are plenty of planes far worse than this, and if Lucifer was as hacked off at you as I think he'd be because you interfered and kept him from exacting revenge on Delaney for stealing a soul that was supposed to be his, I have to think he'd have left you somewhere much more horrifying. You know, a place where your worst fears come to life. Like maybe the plane where there are never any sales at Pier 1. This is like Candy Land compared to that for someone like you. You know, hit a girl where it hurts and all. He's not as omnipotent as he'd have you think. Only the Big Kahuna has that kind of power. Satan only has control over Hell, Marcella—nothing more, nothing less."

Only. "Then why don't you explain to me why I can't make contact with anyone like the other spirits can, Wonder Dog."

"Okay, I'll give you this much. Yes, you've tried. Yes, you've failed. Boo-hoo. But to believe Satan could tether you here when he has absolutely no jurisdiction to do so is an easy out, if you ask me. That would take stupid to a whole new level. Do you really believe that?"

"Yes. No. I mean, I don't fucking know. It wasn't like I made it a practice to learn every rule in the demon handbook. I have mentioned a time or two that I didn't choose the demon lifestyle with the intent of actually being demonic."

"You have, and that puzzles me, too, my Spanish rose—"

Her head shook back and forth while her lips thinned. "Forget it. That part of my eternity is over and done. All I know is I had no one but Delaney when I was a demon, and she can't see me anymore if I'm a ghost—which is, for the second time in this conversation, what I am now." Marcella stuck a finger in her eye, pushing it through her skull and out the back side of her head with a dramatic flourish to emphasize her point. "See all the freaky stuff I can do on this plane? I can't touch anything anywhere else but here. That makes me a ghost. So one more time for posterity: Delaney doesn't see ghosts anymore. I have tried to do what everyone else here does and sucked so much wind for doing it. Try not to forget that. End of. Now go dig holes or gnaw on some mailman." To rag on her because she was just no good at this ghost thing, probably worse at the ghost thing than she'd ever been at the demon thing, was heinous. And mean.

"Oh, Marcella," he said, disgust seeping into his words, "I always feel as though I'm the only one who puts any effort into our relationship. Weren't you the one who just told me, for the second time in as many days, that the gift of sight Delaney once had was passed to her because she was her half brother's oldest living relative and when he died it was transferred to her? Very soap-opera-ish when you say it out loud, don't you agree? Anyway, you said it yourself. Satan whipped up some crazy contract with that scum-of-the-earth Vincent, and in that contract there was a clause that kept the power within Delaney's family for as long as there was a *living* relative, right?"

Irritation prickled her skin. "Point, Darwin. Make it. Soon."

"Didn't you just get through telling me that Delaney actually *died* the night that she faced off with the pitchfork lover? Yes, yes, you did. With a dreamy-eyed, wistful look on your face, you told me Clyde resuscitated her. Oh, and then you sighed—also wistfully, I might add, leading me to believe you're a bit of a romantic, despite the fact that you'd like everyone to believe your heart is nothing more than a shriveled-up piece of beef jerky. Again, I don't want to be redundant, but might I point out the *contract*. The bit about the power staying in the Markham family for as long as there was a *living* relative . . ." He trailed off with an expectant look in his large, brown eyes.

Jesus Christ in a miniskirt.

Her jaw might have scraped the floor if she hadn't the fortitude to clamp it shut with a clenched fist.

Darwin sat back up and peered into her eyes—eyes that were wide with disbelief. "I feel a defining moment approaching," he drawled.

Marcella grabbed his jaw, cupping his muzzle. "Kellen . . ." she muttered. It was all she was able to manage.

Blowing out a breath that made his jowls flap, Darwin nipped at her finger. "Survey says . . . Right on, sistah. Kellen. When Delaney died that night, the gift of sight passed to her brother. Your favorite person in the whole wide world. If the trouble really is that all the mediums you've tried to reach so far are hacks—we know of at least one who's anything but a poser. Kellen's your target."

Her grip on his muzzle tightened. "And you didn't tell me this sooner, why? I've been here for three bloody months and you knew all along Kellen was the medium I should target." She spat the words out at him through clenched teeth.

He let his wet nose graze her hand before jerking out of her grip. "Ahem. As I recall, you were playing the post-traumatic stress disorder card and just couldn't bring yourself to talk about that night until *yesterday*. I wasn't privy to all of the details, just bits and pieces I heard via Delaney and Clyde's conversations. Oh, and the stray, lip-trembling comment from you. Until yesterday. You do remember our conversation, don't you? It involved a tear or two staining your pretty, chiseled cheekbones. One even fell on that train wreck of a dress. Then you whined—which became a rather awkward moment for me. So I ditched your sissy ass and skipped off to the plane where Milk Bones shower me at regular intervals to give what went down that night some thought. When I was all thought out—which, P.S., took all of ten minutes, in case you're wondering—I rushed over here to brain you with my genius discovery. 'Cause I haz skillz."

"Kellen . . ." she whispered. His name on her lips, rolling off her tongue, made her knees weak and her hands shake.

"Bingo, darling. You remember him, right? Never mind, of course you do, sugar. He's the man you secretly lusted for but never put the old Marcella moves on because he hated demons. The man you went to extreme lengths to rile with your sharp tongue because it kept him at arm's length, and that way he'd never know your libido sang a chorus of hallelujahs whenever he was around. Indeed. He's your man."

Color rose in her cheeks, because Darwin was right. She hated that he was right. So she reacted with appropriate venom. "Fuck you, Darwin."

"And again, not if you were a fuzzy Pomeranian who lived in a villa high on a hilltop in the French countryside and dined on canned food every day. Now, get over your shock and dismay, and get off your ass and do something."

Marcella swallowed with a gulp, fighting the well of tears in her eyes. Jesus. Was she really giving even a little thought to crying? Her only defense was the frustration that knowing Kellen could see ghosts created for her. Yeah. She was frustrated. "I can't."

"Because?"

"Because Kellen hates—hated—my guts." Hoo, boy, had he hated her guts, and she'd done everything she could to stoke the flames of his hatred due to her fierce attraction to him. He was the one man in all her years as a demon who'd made her wish she had just a week to be human again. A week that included a bed, some silk sheets, a bottle of expensive champagne, and not a stitch of clothing. Delaney was the one who had kept her from crossing the line during the ten years she'd known Kellen. No matter how much Delaney had loved her, treasured their friendship, she'd have never been comfortable with Marcella making a move on Kellen.

Her demonicness, even though it'd been a choice made out of sacrifice, would never fly, considering the Markhams' past history with Satan. Though there'd been plenty of times when Kellen was sending daggers of death at her with his eyes that she'd wanted to throw him on whatever surface she could find and have her way with him. Have a big way with him. "Kellen hates me. Period. He hated that I was a demon. He hated that I was Delaney's friend. He hated. Game over."

Darwin huffed. "I hate you, too, but look at me now all making nice. And why do I make nice with you? It certainly isn't because you have good fashion sense. It's because of Delaney. Because she loved you, whether we all thought that was a total waste of emotion or not. I love Delaney. It's why I won't cross over. I can't bear the idea I'd never see her again. Kellen loves Delaney, too. We both want whatever makes her happy."

Darwin's confession stung just a little, softened only by the notion that the hatred they felt for her was likely because of misinformation. If only Darwin and Kellen knew how misinformed they truly were. Still, there'd never be a time when she'd ever regret doing what she'd done to become a demon, no matter how much disdain and scorn was heaped on her.

"Do you honestly think he hates you enough to keep you from reassuring his sister that you survived that night? Kellen isn't that kind of man, Marcella. You know that as surely as you know you wanted to get a good freak on with him. Stop stalling, pansy, and get on it."

Energy surged through her for the first time in three months, making her jump to her feet. It was true. Kellen would never refuse to send a message to Delaney for her. He might not like it, but he'd do it.

But it meant she had to see him again. Be near him. Smell his cologne. See his hazel eyes fall on her with the same old contempt. Pathetically long for his sculpted fantasticalness all over again while he gave her the evil eye. Being here, thinking she'd never see

Kellen again had almost been a comfort. Knowing she just might be able to connect with him shook her up.

Darwin nudged her thigh with his back end. "C'mon. Hike up your big-girl panties, and let's get 'er done. You've stared Satan in the eye. Kellen's easy-cheesy compared to that."

Snapping her fingers together under his nose, Marcella narrowed her gaze at him. "Shut it. I need to think."

"About what? If you think too long, you'll set this plane ablaze from one end to the other. You've done nothing but think for three months. Clearly you did a half-assed job in the thinking department to begin with. It wasn't you who figured this out—it was me. I know you're gaga over Kellen, but I also know nothing can ever come of it, and so do you. Get over your case of lust long enough to let your best friend know you're well. All you have to do is show up, state your case, and bounce. Simple."

Right.

She sagged to the ground again, leaning back against the tree, strangely deflated.

Fuck.

The zing she'd felt just moments ago petered out and died.

"Get up, Marcella. If not for anyone else, then for Delaney," Darwin urged, but his voice, growly and low, grew distant and warbled.

She reached for the base of the tree with fingers that sought to anchor her body to it. The odd sensation that she was being dragged grew. Yet she remained immobile, still clinging to the tree.

Her stomach began to swell, rising with sweeping surges in an odd concoction of butterflies and anxious rumblings. Marcella put a hand to her head, rubbing to alleviate the light, airy feel to it. Forcing her limbs to move, she struggled to stand, shimmying against the trunk of the tree for support. But her legs were like soft butter, caving and twisting beneath her, refusing to acknowledge the signals her brain sent to them.

Closing her eyes, Marcella swallowed hard to diminish the nausea assaulting her, the kind of seasicklike nausea she'd experienced when she rode the Teacup ride at Disney World.

Then the sensation shifted so suddenly and so swiftly, she had to take a deep breath. It was like someone had turned her inside out, then outside in. Reaching behind her to find a tree that was no longer there, she teetered on unsteady legs.

Her eyes fluttered open for a mere moment, scanned her surroundings, then closed in disbelief.

A surprised gasp slipped from her lips.

And then another surprised gasp slipped from someone else's lips.

Which totally made the surprise-gasping thing a declaration of symbolic unification in astonishment.

Marcella forced her eyes back open and found herself face-to-face with Kellen Markham.

Standing right in front of her, holding an old scarf she'd once lent to Delaney.

Under his nose.

Huh.

two

The scarf he'd been holding fluttered to the floor in a heap of designer hues of gold and blue. Kellen cocked his dark head in what Marcella would guess was a coupling of surprise and confusion.

Of course, due to the nature of their relationship, those emotions were almost instantly replaced with narrowed hazel eyes and sour lips.

Her lower lip warred with her over a good tremble. Kellen's utter contempt for her wasn't without merit. She'd never let either him or Delaney believe she deserved otherwise. She wasn't going to start now.

All she had to do was have him take a message to Delaney, and that would be that.

Even if *that* was complete suckage.

Instead of looking him directly in the eye, Marcella scanned her surroundings. She was in Delaney's bedroom, but it was different. Her king-size bed was gone—the one that bedded those creatures she was always saving—replaced by a queen, and her cramped closet was virtually empty. Kellen's cats, Vern and Shirley, had chosen a sparse corner to curl up in together, undisturbed by her abrupt entry.

After giving the room a good once-over, she lifted her head.

Their eyes met again and held.

Formalities were in order. "So, what's good?" she asked, like she'd just asked him about his well-being only yesterday.

"Good?"

"Yeah. You know, like wha's up? What's happenin'? What's goin' awn?" She made pistols of her fingers, shooting them at him.

"You're kidding, right?"

"Say again?"

"I said, are you kidding me?"

"About?"

Kellen's cheeks sank into his face with an inward suck of air. His anger was so flagrant, if she stuck her tongue out, she might taste it. Like the first falling snowflake of the season.

"You have some set, Marcella."

She couldn't resist. She looked down at her breasts, hovering enticingly over the top of her dress, then captured Kellen's eyes with a sultry, knowing glance. "That's what all the boys say."

He didn't even flinch. "Ever mouthy, I see. Three months didn't change that."

Marcella blew him a kiss with the pout of her red lips.

"So. Explain yourself."

She'd bristle if his demand wasn't so exquisitely hot it sent a ripple of pleasure straight to her passion parts. "What am I explaining?"

"You did not just pop in here after that vanishing act you pulled and ask me how it's going like you haven't been missing for three solid months."

Her eyes swept over her very unghostly form. Well, it hadn't been easy as popping went. But that sort of fit the bill. *"Au contraire."*

Kellen's disbelief was written in the thin set of his usually full lips and in the tight pull of his black sweater across his pecs when he squared his shoulders. "Where have you been?"

No way was she spilling where she'd ended up. If she knew anything, she knew Delaney and the kind of guilt only her BFF could work herself up over if she had even the tiniest of inkling about where Marcella had been these last months. Delaney was better off thinking she'd gone off to some exclusive spa to recuperate after their bitch slapfest with Lucifer. She looked down at her dress but said nothing. One of the hardest things for her as a demon had been lying. She'd never been deft at deception. Sometimes you said it best when you said nothing at all.

Cocky and Kellen became one when he crossed his arms over his wall of a chest and widened his stance. "Wait. Let me guess. You were so booked with social engagements in the afterlife that you couldn't take the time out to let Delaney know you were safe, right?"

Out of the blue, eyeballing his clear disdain for her, a disdain she'd allowed, nay, cultivated for years, made her bone-weary. Suddenly and unmistakably, she was just plain whupped. They'd been at each other's throats for a decade. If this was the last time she'd ever see him, the need to keep her cover wasn't nearly as important as it had once been when she was earthbound, but it was crucial if he were to believe she'd just been selfishly off doing Marcella-like things. All the snipes she'd taken at him over the years were to keep him at arm's length. Not only did it solidify Kellen's hatred of demons, it kept her from ever having to worry that he'd succumb to her charms should a weak moment arise and she give in to the mad crush she'd had on him forever.

Knowing she should be angry at his assumption that she'd

been doing nothing more than flitting from party to fucking party went without saying, but that required work. She was too tired to put much effort into arguing with him. It was a merry-go-round she didn't feel like getting the pukes from riding.

Instead, Marcella scanned his hard-planed face in thought before running a hand down the skirt of her torn dress. Apathy was so totally not her thing, especially if she was called out, and Kellen was definitely calling.

But who knew how long she could sustain herself on this plane before she had to go back, and if she went back, what if she couldn't return? For once in her forever-and-a-day-long life, she wasn't going to be impulsive. Time management was prudent. Rather than cocking both barrels, she loaded just one with a curt, but evenly voiced reply. "Here's the skinny. I don't care a whole lot what you think about where, who, or what I've been doing since that night in Nebraska, Kellen. Just do me a favor. Tell Delaney if I could have come sooner, I would have. *Nothing* would have kept me from reassuring her I was okay."

A dark eyebrow rose in skepticism. "Except something did."

Oh, an assload of "somethings" did. "Yep."

"And that's all you have to say? After three months, that's all you have to offer?"

Her nod was stiff. "Yeah. I think that covers it."

Or not. "Where the hell have you been, Marcella, and how could you have waited this long to get word to Delaney? Jesus, she's been sick about you, and you show up here after three solid months of worry like it's no big deal."

Hah. In the scheme of deals being big, getting here had to be bigger than the one made for the Brooklyn Bridge. But why waste the effort of explaining that to him? After ten years of beat-down after beat-down because she was a bottom-feeding demon, she was officially all outta piss and vinegar where Kellen and his demon scorn were concerned.

It dawned on her that Darwin was right. She was giving up. Or had she already? But was that such a bad thing? She'd fought the good fight for seventy-six years, and it had landed her on a plane with a bunch of souls who didn't know where they wanted to spend eternity.

There were pluses to that. The king of evil was no longer a threat to her earthbound privileges. She didn't have those anymore because she'd been dismissed from his army of ass lickers. He couldn't take away what she didn't have. She didn't have to keep her goings-on on the down-low anymore, either. If the price of peace and quiet was a shitload of whiny souls on said plane while she rested up after her madcap demonicness, it was no big thang for her. She had no torturous choices to make like the others did. Thus she could soul-watch and kick back.

So now what she really wanted was to crawl back to her plane and be left alone. If her answer was anything less than passionate, so be it. "It's like I said, Kellen. If I could have contacted her, I would have, okay? But despite the fact that it's been longer than the allotted time you would dub suitable, I'm here now. Just tell her I'm fine. Everything's fine. And that I love her, and hope that she and Clyde have one baby for every mutt she owns."

The left corner of his mouth lifted with an almost smile. His hands, hands that had been clenched, relaxed. "She's doing really great, you know."

That thing in her chest Darwin had called shriveled jerky shifted, and she knew it wasn't just because Delaney was faring well. The right corner of her mouth lifted, too. "There isn't a single thing in this entire world that could make me happier than hearing D's doing great. She deserves great. The greatest. And now I have to go." She frowned. The trouble was, *how* did she go? When she'd been a demon, hopping from place to place was the matter of a snap of her fingers. Fuck. Ghosts had different protocol. And had she attended the "Don't Find Yourself Stranded" class, she'd know exactly how to get back to her plane. A dramatic exit might be out.

"Hold the hell on. Why won't you tell me where you've been, for Christ's sake? She deserves to know. Despite that Uriel's reassurances, Delaney's spent three months worrying Lucifer had his way with you and you landed in the pit."

"Pit" wasn't an undeserving term to describe Plane Drab. "I'm not in the pit." And who was Uriel?

"Then where are you?"

"Not in the pit, and that's all you need to know."

"Afraid you'll reveal where the supersecret Bat Cave is?"

Because all the cool kids wanted to know. "Nope."

Kellen moved closer toward her, past the box between them on the floor. The muscles in his thighs bunched through his stone-washed jeans with each step he took toward her, menacing and bomb-diggety hot. "Marcella, what the hell's going on? You aren't the woman I once knew. You were once fully capable of slinging zingers that were entire sentences whether your input was welcome or not. And you float," he remarked. "I don't ever remember you being able to float."

Shit. "Just a little something I picked up while I was on sabbatical." She pointed her toes in midair. "You like?"

Kellen cocked an eyebrow of disdain. "Lay it down, Marcella. Why haven't you been around for three months?" His eyes narrowed with a gleam again. "Are you in hiding from that prick Satan?"

Taking a step back, Marcella heaved a sigh that whistled. "No. I'm not hiding."

"Then why aren't you popping in and out of here, annoying the shit out of me like you've done at least once a week for ten years? Why haven't you gone to see Delaney and Clyde?"

She couldn't help it. The question was out of her mouth before she could stop it. "Where is Delaney, and where's all of her stuff—the creatures?"

This time he grinned, as rare when in her presence as the Hope Diamond. Marcella fought the zing of pleasure it brought her to cock an ear when he answered her question. "Long Island. She and Clyde bought a house and a backyard for the creatures—er, dogs."

A tear stung her eye. That meant her best friend was finally getting her slice of Americana. Her deepest wish. A husband and a family. Good on D. Marcella's head bowed to her chest to keep the glimmer of tears that welled in them from spilling, because seriously, her dress didn't need any more catastrophes to befall it.

And she'd rather be thrown in the pit than let Kellen see her cry.

She swallowed hard before speaking, searching for a balance of nonchalant and carefree. "All her dreams come true, huh? The whole 'you're the footprints to the sand in my heart' thing. That's hard-core." Pausing for a moment, a million questions on her tongue, Marcella bit them back. "Okay. So good, then. And now, I'm out. You give that crazy afterlife aficionado a big hug from me, and for the love of all that's frizzy and unmanageable, tell her to condition that hair. See ya, Kellen."

Closing her eyes, blocking out the man she'd wanted since the day she'd met him, Marcella willed herself to be gone, hoping it worked in similar fashion to her grand exits of demon days gone by.

Only it wasn't exactly working out.

There was no allover body tingle, a one-time sure signal she was hoofing it on out of wherever it was she no longer wanted to be.

Scrunching her eyes tighter, she willed once more.

Nothing. Maybe she hadn't given it enough time to work. Count. She'd count. It had never taken more than a minute twelve to get gone when she was in her earliest stages of demonicness.

One Mississippi, two Mississippi, three Mississippi . . .

Oh, come the fuck on.

A warm hand was at her upper arm, closing around it and gripping it with firm, lean fingers, the heat of them shooting thready zingers of warmth to her shoulder. "Where do you think you're going, Marcella?"

Pier 1, silly. So I can get one last shop on. She let her eyes flutter open to gaze into his with cool regard. "Let go, Kellen. You're breaking my concentration."

"Nope. You're not going anywhere until Delaney sees for herself that you're just fine. And I swear to you, if you don't make up a good story about where you've been that doesn't leave her as pissed off as I am right now, I'll hunt your ass down."

A thought occurred to her just then. Looking down at Kellen's fingers wrapped around her arm, she realized something. Something big. He could touch her . . .

Hold—the—phone. Delaney had never been able to physically touch the ghosts she'd communicated with. Not in all the time she and Marcella had been friends, anyway.

Leaning in, Kellen's breath blew the stray strands of her dark hair by her ear. "Did you hear me, Marcella? If you hurt D any more than you already have, you'll answer to me."

Mmm-hmm. His overprotective statement on behalf of Delaney was so hot she almost purred her approval.

But again, don't touch that dial. Didn't Kellen realize the only person who could see her was him? Why would he, when he could touch her? Just as she suspected, he thought she was still demon.

Perfect.

"Let's go, Marcella. I'm putting your ass in my car and we're driving out to Delaney and Clyde's."

Fear twisted her intestines. No way was she letting the cat out of the bag. If Kellen didn't realize she was no longer demon, she wasn't giving it up. Delaney would only be more upset at the idea that she was doomed to roam a desolate plane of undecideds.

In order to keep up appearances, she had to summon up her inner demon. If she was the bitch she'd always been to Kellen, he'd never suspect.

Marcella yanked her arm from Kellen's grip. "I have a hair appointment I can't miss. Just pass the message on to D." Stepping around him, she headed for the doorway, but he blocked her with his bulk. Bulk that smelled so good that if her nostrils had to withstand any more torture, they'd ignite.

"I'm not letting you leave."

Honestly, now would be the perfect time for a fireball. Just a little one to let him know she meant business. No one was allowed to even consider "letting" her do jack shit. "Ask yourself something, Kellen. When was the last time anyone ever told me I was going to do anything other than what I wanted to do?"

His eyes grew dark.

"Exactly. Now move or I'll move you myself." She hoped just the threat of her old demon powers would deter him, because threats were the only thing filling up her menace account at this point in her spectral existence.

"You're not the typical woman, Marcella—"

"So I've been told," she retorted with a wily smile and a pouty lower lip.

"That's not what I mean. What I mean is you're as strong as I am, demon that you are. I'll take you down before I'll let you leave."

"You'd hit a woman?"

"Nah. I won't hit you, but I will restrain you."

Heh. "I didn't take you for the kind of man who dug hand-cuffs, but I will give you this—it's always the science teachers who get off on the kink."

His nostrils flared. "I'm done playing."

Bummer. He was hot when he played. "Yeah. Me, too. Now *move*."

"Not a chance."

"You know what I think, Kellen?"

"You think?"

"Not often, but when I do, it's all bright and shiny. So, know what I think?"

"What do you think, Marcella?"

She winked one green eye at him, smoldering. "I think you just want to cop a feel."

His cheeks sucked inward.

"You're losing your patience with me, right?"

"I think that's fair."

"Then move and impatience will be a thing of the past."

"The hell."

Arching her back, Marcella let her body align with his, allowing him to have the full impact of her prowess. She hadn't been out of the game so long she didn't remember the kind of sexual vibe she threw out into the universe in sensual waves. It was one trick that, demon or ghost, she'd always be able to use. Walking her fingers along Kellen's chest, she stopped just under his arms. Lovely, strong, capable arms. "Don't throw the word 'hell' around in vain. It hurts my demonic feelings." She let her lower lip fall open again, this time with an extra-enticing pout.

Kellen ran his index finger over it, making her flesh sing corny Air Supply songs. "You need ChapStick. Wherever you skulked off to, it must've been dry, because it hasn't been kind to your big mouth."

That was it. Like applying a fresh coat of lip gloss, the need to best him came with ease. Marcella snatched at his finger with her teeth, chomping down on it and catching him by surprise. When Kellen yelped his pain, she tickled him under his arms, making him lurch forward. As he fell away from the doorway, she skipped out of it as fast as she could in her tattered sandals and floated directly through a stray chair that might have kept her from getting to the front door had it not been for her ghostly skills.

Like the hounds of Hell were nipping at her heels, she made a beeline for the front of Delaney's East Village store and, without so much as a twitch of fear, hurled herself headfirst through the glass, spilling out the other side without a mark on her.

Booyah for ghostie powers.

Ducking, Marcella headed for the alleyway, zigzagging to avoid hitting people strolling along the sidewalk. Though she found, via the portly man in overalls, she had no need to take care that she didn't bump into anyone. Not when she could walk right through them.

Wheeling into the alley, she pressed her spine up against the brick structure and almost fell into it. Like literally. While she righted herself, a little boy with an older woman Marcella was sure she recognized sauntered past her. Their hands were entwined, swinging between their bodies.

The child looked up at her, all big, green eyes and gangly limbs, and smiled, raising his free hand to wave at her with a coy glance.

Yet the old lady looked right through her. "Come, Carlos. You must hurry. You are always daydreaming," she chastised, though the reprimand was tempered with a warm, indulgent smile.

Heavy footsteps thudded against the pavement, forcing her to set aside her curiosity in order to make a quick getaway. Without even realizing how, Marcella floated down the alleyway and through the building at the end of it to pop out on the other side.

One block away from Delaney's store.

While it was a crazy-cool ability to possess, it still didn't beat disappearing and reappearing at Pier 1. When she'd been a demon, she could still shop.

So now what?

Fuck-all. She should have at least peeked at that snob Irvin Epstein's test when they'd had a pop quiz on how to give your afterlife direction.

Asking for directions back to Chez Dreary wouldn't make her feel like less of a man at all right now.

"You saw her?" Delaney's face was fraught with myriad emotions. Her eyes filled with worry as she poured herbal tea into mugs for the three of them. The tinkle of her bracelets jingling together soothed Kellen, who made a point of hiding his reaction to Marcella with a cool glance at his sister.

"I did. Just like I'm seeing you," Kellen offered. "She said to tell you she was fine." He'd relayed almost word for word his conversation with Marcella, while Delaney listened intently.

Dropping onto the sofa, his sister grabbed her husband Clyde's hand, bringing it to her chest. "Did you hear that, honey? Kellen *saw* Marcella!"

Clyde's eyes met Kellen's over the top of his new wife's head.

They passed an unspoken message between them, one that had a big question attached to it. Then he looked down at Delaney, warming his gaze when it fell upon her soft red hair, wild from the damp, cold rain they'd been having. "I did. So do you feel better? Knowing she's okay?"

She shook her head, falling back on the couch next to him and dragging an old afghan over her legs. "Uh, no. And what do you mean she's fine? That's *all* she had to say after disappearing and keeping me up every night worried sick? *Why* didn't she tell you where she's been? What the shit is that?"

Kellen's lips pursed. *Because she's the most difficult, disagreeable full-on pain in the ass I know.* A pain with the sweetest ass he'd ever seen, but still a boil on his butt. "She was pretty reluctant to tell me anything, D. And shouldn't she be? She's been off screwing around for all this time and never once came to tell you she was all right. I'm pretty sure she was just too embarrassed to tell me where she's really been." That Marcella had been off having a good time while his sister had worried herself sick over her tripped his trigger. Not even her smokin' hot bod could make him forget that.

"Nope. Sorry. I know you'd like nothing more than to believe Marcella's been off on some tour of Neiman Marcuses around the globe—"

"Pier 1. I thought she liked Pier 1," Kellen interrupted without realizing he'd given away the details he knew about Marcella. Details he'd heard in conversations she'd had with Delaney over the years while he'd try to focus on anything other than her seductive presence in the room. In fact, he knew more about Marcella Acosta than he did almost any other woman outside of his sister.

Clyde reached over and slapped him on the back with a grin that Delaney had once said melted her heart. "For someone who once told me he'd rather be flayed alive at high noon and have vinegar poured on his open, bleeding wounds than to ever have to see Marcella Acosta again, you sure know her deets, don't you?"

Delaney snickered when Kellen grumbled, "She was always talking about it. I'm just pointing out how much she loved to shop." *Niiice cover, Markham. Caught red-handed, dumb-ass.*

Delaney shook her head of long, golden-red curls again. "Nope. You'd love to believe Marcella was a selfish, superficial demon, but I knew her. She was the only friend I had for ten damn years, Kellen. She fought with the devil himself to help me save Clyde. The hell I'll believe she cared so little about me that she blew me off all this time. If you remember, I didn't want her involved in the mess with Clyde in the first place. She just wouldn't take no for an answer because she was looking out for me. She was the one who helped us figure out the whole reason why Clyde ended up in Hell. After that night in Nebraska, you can't convince me she'd take off without a word even if I saw her skipping through the aisles of Pier 1 in her party dress with my own damned eyes. So, brother, if you're going to Marcella bash—blow. I'll find some other way to find her." His sister's eyes flashed at him, hot with anger.

Yeah. There was that. As much as he disliked Marcella, Kellen had to admit she'd taken one for the team. Her reluctance to tell him where she'd been had even had him wondering what the frig was going on. Kellen gave his sister a contrite glance. "Okay. I apologize. She did go to bat for you, but that doesn't explain why she hasn't come to see you, yet she did come to see me."

Delaney's slight gasp had all seven of her dogs, sprawled in various parts of their living room, and Clyde at attention. "You don't think Lucifer threatened her, do you? Like maybe told her she had to stay away from me? Uriel promised me she'd be safe. He didn't promise that safety would come without strings attached."

Kellen's nod was curt. Uriel, an archangel, had been a part of that night with Clyde. If not for him, no one would have ever known Clyde's soul had been improperly damned to Hell in the first place. Due to a delay in Uriel's soul collecting, he'd forgotten to catch Clyde's soul as it left his body. Clyde had wrongfully ended up in Hell as a result. When Uriel stepped in to prevent Lucifer from claiming Clyde, he'd born witness to the lengths Marcella had already gone to keep Delaney from harm.

As a favor to Delaney, Uriel had promised that he'd try to keep Marcella out of harm's way. Because she was a demon, there wasn't a lot he could do. He did play for the upstairs team, so his power would be limited. "I imagine that's a possibility. I think we both know what Lucifer's capable of."

"God damn it! If only I could still see the dead. Maybe I could put some feelers out. I don't believe everything's all rocking horses and rainbows. If that were the case, Marcella'd just rearrange her schedule so she could shop here with me in Long Island instead of the city. Something's not right, Kellen."

That brought to mind her departure earlier. She hadn't just snapped her fingers and disappeared like the old Marcella. She'd trampled *through* chairs and the front door to the store—floating. It had nagged the shit out of him during the entire drive to his sister's. "I was wondering. Do you ever remember Marcella being able to walk through objects? Like doors? And float?"

Delaney rocketed upward off the cushiony sofa she'd been sitting on with Clyde. "Walk through doors? Explain."

"When I told her she was coming with me to see you, she got angry. Typical Marcella, is what you're thinking when it comes to anyone telling her what to do, right? I thought so, too, at first, but when she took off out of the store, she blew right *through* the door, Delaney. I know she had a power or two, but I don't remember her walking through solid objects or floating, which she did during the course of our entire conversation."

Delaney jammed a hand into her flowing skirt and popped her lips. "You're right. She could lob some fireballs. She was crazy talented at disappearing. She even managed to summon snakes, but she never walked through solid objects and rarely levitated. Maybe she acquired some new powers in the last few months."

"But that doesn't explain her dress." Kellen spoke the thought, unaware he'd said it out loud.

"Her dress?" Clyde repeated from the couch.

"Yeah. It was a hot mess, torn and wrinkled. So were her sandals. We all know Marcella never went anywhere unless her clothes were all but spray-painted on her, and her hair was never anything less than perfect."

"Said the man who hates the lady demon, but remembers details about what she was wearing," Clyde taunted with a deep chuckle. "It's the little things, pal."

Kellen ignored his brother-in-law's poke at him. What he did know was that, at the beginning of his encounter with Marcella, her almost defeatist attitude was totally out of character. For whatever reason, it had taken her a few rounds to warm up. Couple that with her rumpled clothes and ripped shoes, and something didn't add up. "Maybe Lucifer damned her to a life of off-the-rack clothes and thrift-store shoes. That's like dying a thousand deaths every day for someone like Marcella." Kellen volleyed the thought back at Clyde—even if he didn't one hundred percent believe it.

"Was anyone else with you when she showed up, Kellen? Like Mrs. Ramirez, maybe?" Mrs. Ramirez was the woman Delaney had hired to help at her herb store. She'd been with Delaney a long time, and she had a modicum of understanding when it came to his sister's former gift of sight.

"Nope. I was alone."

"I have a thought," Delaney said, making her way through the pack of dogs at their feet and heading to her sprawling kitchen, where she did far more herb-oil making than she did cooking. She flung open the door of the pantry, which housed hundreds of herbal remedies and books on communicating with the dead.

Carrying back a pile of books she almost couldn't see over the top of, Delaney clunked them down on the distressed wood coffee table she and Clyde had just recently bought. "So tell me, little brother. How's the ghost whispering going?" she asked with a sinisterly sweet smile.

Kellen gave her a dubious look. "I did just take a sabbatical from teaching because of it, didn't I? I'd say it's going the way of the country's economy as of late. To shit. I can't get a handle on this the way you did, D. Maybe I'm not patient enough. But I gotta say you were much better at putting the pieces of some ghost's story together than I'll ever be. I spend more time ducking the shit they throw at me than I do understanding what they want. Remember the last guy who showed up and wanted me to pass on that message to a woman, only I didn't know the woman was his *wife*?"

Both Clyde and Delaney winced. "I do," she said.

"Do you suppose I deserved to be slugged because I found said wife with his old boss—in bed? I thought he just wanted to know she was happy. I told him she seemed pretty happy with the whole glow thing she had going on."

Delaney shook a finger at him as she settled back onto the couch. "I told you, you have to be careful what you relay to them. They're crafty and some use their afterlife to gather information so they can exact revenge. You're a conduit now, but you have to be a sensitive one. What I still don't get is that they're able to touch you . . . I never . . ."

But Kellen wasn't listening. It helped to rant about this gift, which had been thrust on him without warning, to someone who understood. "Oh, yeah. It's a real perk. I had a black eye for two weeks from that bastard. That's without even mentioning the craziness that ensued in my classroom." Between dead sports heroes and singers showing up and the mayhem when an angry ghost had chucked the globe of the world at him, just missing a student by a hair, Kellen had had to make the choice to take a sabbatical so he could figure out this ghost thing. Delaney had offered to let him run the store with the help of Mrs. Ramirez.

Business had picked up since Delaney's showdown with Lucifer. So when she and Clyde had decided it was time to start a family and move to Long Island, they'd offered it to Kellen as a way for him to at least have some income while he got his gift of sight under control.

Delaney hopped back off the couch again and paced. "Wait. Did you touch Marcella?"

He shifted in the big, poofy chair he sat in by the couch. "Touch her?"

"You know what I mean, Kel. Did you touch her? Did she touch you?"

"I grabbed her arm." *Threatened to take her out.* So, yeah. He'd touched her. And yes, she'd touched him. The fire she'd created with just her fingers had left a burning imprint.

"Oh. My. God," Delaney yelped. "I know why she wouldn't tell you where she's been, Kellen. And if I'm honest, I have to say, we have a shitload of work to do on your ghostie antennae. She's a ghost, Kellen! Don't you see? She walked through the store's door. You touched her and I'd bet she touched you. I'd also bet my new AeroGarden only *you* can see her. Oh, shit. How the hell did this happen? We have to find her."

"How am I supposed to find her, Delaney? None of the ghosts you were once buddy-buddy with will give me the time of day, much less help me locate Marcella. I don't even know how she got to the store in the first place."

"That's because you keep stomping all over them with your size elevens. You're just a big Neanderthal when it comes to being a sympathetic ear. And she got to the store because I'd bet my last case of Saint-John's-wort you were thinking about her." When Kellen made an effort to dispute her claim, despite the fact that it was dead-on, she threw up a hand. "Don't bother. You're only kidding yourself if you think we don't know you thought Marcella was hot. She needed a conduit to call her from the afterlife—which means you were doing some heavy breathing in the thinking department." Her smile was smug.

"But I've thought about her before," he defended, only to realize he was just digging a bigger hole. He slumped down in his chair, clamping his mouth shut and shooting Clyde a dirty look for snickering.

Delaney scrunched her lips up. "I'll just bet my bippy you have, brother. But despite your crappy medium techniques, you're getting stronger, and your will to see Marcella in person must've been strong."

Narrowing his eyes, he sank further into the chair and compressed his lips tighter.

"Now," Delaney said, "I know exactly what we need to do."

"You want me to get the chimes, honey?" Clyde rose, running a loving finger down Delaney's nose.

"Why do we need chimes?"

"A séance, bruiser. We're going to summon Marcella from the other side. So go hone your vibes, brother. Make sure they're properly greased. We have a hot Latina ghost to catch."

three

"Does this feel just a little ridiculous to either of you?" Kellen asked Clyde from across the kitchen table. The table they all held hands around. Chimes hung from the stained-glass ornamental light above, and candles scattered the room, their flames whispering soft orange and blue.

Clyde cleared his throat. "If I were you, my friend, I wouldn't mock your sister. I've been to that rodeo and I came out of it bruised and battered. Nothing feels ridiculous after what I've been through. A séance was how I found Delaney in the first place. So don't hate."

Delaney cracked an eye open and flicked his wrist with her fingers. "This is exactly what I mean, Kellen. What ghost would want to enter this realm with the kind of negative vibe you put out? You can't guide anyone if you mock their very existence while you do it. You know they exist, so I just can't get a handle on your problem with inviting them to a warm, nurturing environment created by you, the newbie ghost whisperer. It's so important you make them feel welcome and secure. Now, get in touch with your spectral side and help me out. You're the only way we'll reach Marcella, and if I don't find her, it's you who'll end up with knots on your head from the noogies I'll give you."

Kellen sighed. Negative vibe, his ass. It wasn't like he wasn't trying to get a grip on this thing. When Delaney had the gift of sight, he'd seen some pretty whacked stuff. It wasn't that he didn't believe, either. He believed. He'd just liked doing it from the outside looking in. Adjusting to this had been a challenge, to say the least, and Delaney could only do so much now that she no longer had this thing she called a "gift." "Sorry. Okay, so what do you need me to do? Chant? Taunt her with Pier 1 sale circulars?"

Clyde snorted but quickly buried his mouth in his shoulder when Delaney's brow furrowed in admonishment.

His sister sighed, this time long and aggravated. "Just think of her. It's not like it's a hardship. You've watched her ass swivel out of a room more times than I can count on all our fingers and toes put together, and that glassy-eyed look you used to get said it all. Get a visual of her in your head and go with it."

Kellen closed his eyes as much to block out his sister's accusatory glance as to bring up the mental image of Marcella. The one he'd had when he'd found her old scarf in the box at the store. It wasn't the purest of thoughts, he'd be the first to admit, but it was the one that had haunted him since she'd taken off. "Marcella? C'mon. I know you're out there somewhere. Gimme a break and make an appearance. Delaney's here and she won't get off my back until she knows you're okay."

"Ugh. Very nurturing, Kellen. And you wonder why these ghosts leave you with black eyes. I'd give you one myself if it weren't for the fact that I've seen more than my fair share of violence this last year. Now, get on board or the next ghost that fancies clocking you one is going to have my utter and complete support."

He knew that tone. It was the one that said he'd better stop thwarting the process Delaney had spent fifteen years cultivating. To mock would be to deny the good his sister had done in the past. "You're right. I'm sorry. I'm in. Here we go. I'm visualizing . . ."

Once more, the image of Marcella in an innocent, yet hotly seductive baby-doll nightie he'd seen in some store window popped into his head. Her hair, black and thick, fell over her shoulders and streamed down her back in loose curls. It framed her face, wisping across her high cheekbones while her eyes glowed green and smoldering. Her lips were full and glistening with that pink lip gloss she was so fond of. Olive skin shimmered smooth and clear beneath the frilly, pastel pink of the material, tucking around the smooth skin where her hip met her thigh.

This was exactly how he'd conjured her up earlier today, by smelling her perfume on that scarf she'd left behind. Kellen shifted uncomfortably in his chair when his jeans grew tight, guiltily waiting for Delaney to tell him to knock it off and get serious.

When she didn't, he relaxed a bit. No one had to know what the image of Marcella he'd called up was.

A low thrum of vibration began at his feet, traveling along his calves and upward until his ears hummed with a buzzing that grew almost uncomfortable. The air around them became its own living entity, thick and oppressive. The candles fluttered and the chimes sang . . .

"I would never wear a cheap nightgown like that, Kellen Markham. How dare you create a visual image of me in cotton? I'm a silk girl, through and through."

Marcella's laughter tinkled in her ears when Kellen jumped, knocking the table with a jolt of shaking teacups. She was only guessing at the visual he'd used to summon her. Clearly he was as much a man as he'd ever been, with the lingerie creativity of a kindergartner. Though, the very idea that he'd fantasized about her in anything but a headlock was titillating—and best left alone.

Unfortunately this meant the cat was out of the bag. There was no way to hide the fact that she was now spectral versus demonic. That Kellen had called her up with such ease didn't just disturb her because it would upset Delaney, but because she'd been ensconced in trying to figure out how to pick up objects, and he'd interrupted. She knew some ghosts could do it. She just wasn't one of them. Again, another class she might have spent more time listening in instead of sulking while she slumped down in her chair like a two-year-old in a time-out.

"She's here?" Delaney leaned in Kellen's direction with a hopeful look.

God, she looked fantastic. Marcella grinned a watery smile, letting her hand hover over her friend's hair, remembering the feel of it so soft and unmanageable. Marriage had been just what the heavens had ordered, apparently. At least from the looks of the cozy house she and Clyde had chosen. Braided area rugs in deep greens and burgundies scattered the floors. Seven cushy dog beds lay by an old woodstove in the living room. Scarred paneling, worn and well loved in a deep brown, traveled from floor to ceiling. Little pieces of Delaney's old life, like her prism meant for demon catching, sat on chunky wooden end tables with multicolored tiled surfaces.

The kitchen, where everyone was seated, was almost exactly as Delaney had once described the one she wanted if she ever married and could afford a bigger place. Rustic white cabinets, distressed to match the rest of her furniture, lined nearly every wall, and drying herbs hung from their tops in tied bundles of sage and mossy green. An antique stove Marcella was sure she used to whip up herbal remedies rather than cook with took up a good portion of the back wall. Paned windows hung over the steel basin sink, allowing a view of a big backyard with pine and maple trees. Whimsical bells and chimes hung from hooks next to lush green spider plants. Every corner of each room screamed Delaney's dream come true.

Marcella scrunched her eyes shut before looking to Kellen, leaning in to let her lips press against his hair. "You can tell her I'm here, and that I think the house is beautiful." Her voice caught on her last words. How in all of fuck she'd become so weepy these days befuddled her.

"She's here," Kellen confirmed, jamming a finger into his ear and wiggling it.

Delaney rose from her high-backed chair and scanned the warm room with eyes that squinted. "Damn you, Marcella Acosta, where have you been? What happened after that night that left you like this?"

She floated in front of Kellen. Because it was a nifty little power, because she could, and because it left her feeling like she was just a little in charge of a situation that had gone careening out of control. "Okay, so I wasn't entirely honest with you earlier today. I'm not a demon anymore. I'm a ghost, and I would have been happy continuing on as a ghost if you'd left me alone instead of sucking me like a milk shake through a straw here to Delaney's. I'll have you know, it's uncomfortable, to say the least."

Kellen's lips thinned again, the signal he was about to protest, but Marcella threw up a hand with the most pathetic excuse for unmanicured nails he'd ever seen. "And before you get that thing called indignation you have so cornered going, I didn't tell you because I figured you'd be more likely to buy a story like that I was off partying far easier than you would my ending up a ghost." While that hurt, she never expected anything less. She'd refined her party-girl, livin'-on-the-edge persona over the years, knowing full well Kellen found women like that despicable.

She noted the fleeting look of guilt on his face before it hardened in a defensive expression. Marcella planted her hands on her hips. "And I see I was right. Now we have a problem because Delaney's going to be very upset and start whining about sacrifices—which we both don't want, amigo. I did what I did because my future has no end. Delaney's does, and when it ends, I want it to end with Clyde and a dozen kids surrounding her. So let's keep the drama to a minimum, okay? Between the two of us, I just know there's something we can cook up that'll make her believe I'm happy right where I am. Got it?" She had him by the short hairs, and he knew it.

He didn't look thrilled about it, but he nodded curtly while Delaney and Clyde looked directly through her, waiting. "Good. Tell D I don't know how I ended up a ghost. One minute we were trying to take down that candy-ass Satan, the next I woke up on what I lovingly call Plane Drab. I don't know how I got there, and I don't know why. I would have contacted her sooner, but contact isn't as easy as it seems. So tell her she's right when she said there were kooks out there who couldn't really see ghosts. I know because I attempted to use their services and failed dismally.

"And on that note, you, Kellen Markham, can shove your speculation on my whereabouts right up your tight, stuffy ass. Believe me when I tell you, there's nothing I'd have liked more than to have spent the last three months shopping and partying in Rio. But that wasn't exactly the case, as evidenced by my dress." Jamming her face in Kellen's, she rolled her neck on her shoulders in a "take that" gesture.

Delaney gripped the sleeve of Kellen's sweater. "You don't look happy. What's she saying?"

"She said she doesn't know how she ended up a ghost." He passed on the rest of the message, omitting the part about his tight ass.

Delaney's eyes filled with tears just as Marcella had known they would. "Uriel promised me he'd look out for her! I don't understand how this happened. But I do know it had to be Lucifer who took her earthbound privileges away. That has to be what it is. That fuck! There has to be something we can do."

If only. And who was Uriel? Never mind. She didn't want to know. Marcella put a hand to her head to massage her temples only to find that, if she didn't use a light touch, her hand shot straight through to the other side of her head. Why she couldn't bring her skills from Plane Drab with her here was just another fun ghost factoid. "Here's where you'd better pony up, Kellen, and make it convincing because we both know our Tenacious D. Tell her I *like* being a ghost. In fact, I'm so in love with the idea of skating through walls and being invisible, my world is all sunshiny colors and kick-ass rose-tinted glasses. So it doesn't matter who took what from me. I'm golden. Now hurry. Before she snowballs and we're in the middle of her glacial path."

Kellen tightened his grip on Delaney's hand, his gaze sympathetic and warm. "Marcella said to tell you that she likes being a ghost much better than she ever liked being a demon. It has its sacrifices, but Lucifer isn't dogging her anymore, and for the first time in a long time, she feels safe. She said she misses you, and she loves you and she wants you to stop worrying."

Delaney rolled her hazel eyes with a grating snort before crossing her arms over her woolen sweater. "Tell her I said she's full of so much bullshit. Wait. Never mind. I'll tell her." Delaney looked to Kellen. "Point me in the general direction."

Kellen stabbed a finger in front of him, pointing toward the ceiling while fighting to keep his face emotionless but leaking a smug look of satisfaction for the shit Delaney was winding up to give her.

Delaney looked upward, unaware she'd actually captured Marcella's green gaze. "You're full of horse puckey, Marcella Acosta. Don't you try to snow me. I know you. You've been my best friend for a long time and there's no one who lives louder than you. To be shipped off to some plane that's dreary and desolate, sans shopping and foot massages, is its own special hell for someone of your ilk. So knock off the brave front and let's figure out how you can become a demon again because Pier 1's going to have a sale that'll blow your mind, and you'll miss it with all this self-sacrifice bullshit. Not to mention the employees who'll have to apply for food stamps because their commissions are in the crapper."

Marcella fought a smile. Delaney was as loyal and as dedicated as ever. Though no way was she giving in. Delaney had better things to do than to try to find a way out of this for her. There were babies to make with her geeky/hot husband. No more mixing it up with the paranormal.

She cocked her head in Kellen's direction. "Tell her this is one ghost who doesn't need her to 'fix' anything. I don't need help. There's nothing she can do anyway. I already know crossing over isn't an option, but we've always known that. That's what her specialty was, and it isn't even hers anymore. It's yours. And you suck at it, if what I heard is right. So tell her I said to go make babies—loads of 'em, so I'll always have an influx of fresh meat, not jaded by adulthood, to haunt."

Kellen laughed now, too, but immediately straightened when Delaney asked, "What does she have to say for herself?"

"She said stay out of it and go make babies. Loads of them. She doesn't want you to fix anything for her."

Delaney's eyes narrowed. "Oh, I'm not going to fix it. You are, little brother. I mean, I'll help, but ultimately you're now the one with the connections."

"No!" Marcella yelped in Kellen's direction, reaching out and gripping his arm. "Kellen, you've got to keep her from stepping in any more shit than she's already been in. I don't want Lucifer chasing after her again and neither do you. Especially now that she doesn't have the kind of help she once had from the other side. She has Clyde to consider, too. And the children they may have— I'd rather rot in the pit than let Satan touch them. Just tell her to let it be, for the love of Christ. Please. Maybe not as much for her sake as for mine now. I'm tired. I've been around a long, long time avoiding Satan.

"Being on this plane I've been on has given me the chance to finally stop running. I didn't realize I wanted that when I was earthbound, but I've found peace in not having Hell breathing down my neck for the first time in more years than I care to count. I didn't realize how exhausting it was until I didn't have to do it anymore."

And it had been. Maybe resting up would be just what the doctor ordered. If she could get back, that was. She'd tried all day with no success, and yet again, it wasn't like she'd paid a lot of attention when they were doling out advice on that hovel they called a plane. But she definitely wasn't dragging D into anything that even remotely threatened to trigger Satan's awareness.

Kellen cupped Delaney's cheek, giving her a sympathetic smile. "Honey, she said she's tired, that she just wants to rest now. She can do that on the plane she's been relegated to, and she begged me to tell you not to get involved."

"*What?* Are you sure this is Marcella? *My* Marcella? Because my Marcella would be spitting fake fingernails and shredding fine linens to get back here to Earth!" Delaney's eyes danced with fiery determination when she looked into her brother's.

"I'm positive, D," Kellen assured his sister with no hint of crack-ing. "She's been doing this a long time. Eternal life has to have its drawbacks. I think I get what she's saying."

"Oooh, better duck. Rapture's headed your way," Marcella quipped, chuckling in his ear. While she was so close to him, she inhaled deeply, breathing in the spicy cologne he wore. Mingled with his own unique blend of man scent, it left her dizzy.

Kellen waved a hand at her. "Look, D. It's been a long ride for her. She's, what, a hundred and fifty—"

"Seventy-six—which explains why you teach science and not math." Marcella swiped at a lock of his dark hair, only giving brief thought to the fact that although she sure as hell wasn't able to pick up that bottle of Chanel No. 5 she'd lusted for while she floated about in Macy's earlier, she could actually touch Kellen.

"Right. Seventy-six, a hundred and six. Either way, you're old. She's old. Whatever. Point is that's a long time to run from Satan. And I seriously don't want you to get involved in anything that has to do with that prick, Delaney—*ever again*."

Tears filled Delaney's wide eyes, trickling along her creamy-peach-highlighted cheeks. Instantly, Clyde was up and beside her, rubbing soothing circles along her shoulder blades while their dogs, in various states of one ailment or another, stirred in aware-ness of their mistress's upset. "I can't believe she won't even try," Delaney sobbed against Clyde's shoulder with a dramatic heave.

Tears. Delaney'd never been much for waterworks unless she was backed into a corner and frustrated. Marcella squirmed her discomfort. Fuck. Now what?

When all was said and done, she'd give Kellen this much: there was no denying the bond between him and Delaney. From the look on his face, the tears Delaney noisily sobbed were obviously almost physically painful for him to watch. "D, don't cry. How about if I promise to try to keep in touch with her? In fact, I have a great idea. Maybe Marcella can help me feel my way around the afterlife. It would definitely help because not only can she *see* the ghosts I'm dealing with, she can communicate with them, too. You can't anymore, and that only makes it more difficult for you to guide me. We'd sort of be cutting out the middleman and getting straight to the source. She'll be the guide you can't be."

Because really, who didn't want to be Julie the Cruise Director to all of the afterlife? She would not let him suck her into this. There was no way she could deny Delaney anything, and if Kellen gave his sister hope she'd stick around, she was doomed to help him cross souls indefinitely. "Kellen! Don't make promises you can't keep. I can't figure out how to get back to where I came from, which means I can't even help myself. How do you suppose I can help you? Man up, you candy-ass. Resist the tears and don't give in. She's working you like a breast implant salesman at an Itty-Bitty Titty convention."

The look he shot her said to can it, but he replaced it with a smile for Delaney's benefit—sweeter and more angelic than a choirboy. "Marcella said she thinks it's a good idea, too."

And he dared her to say otherwise. As if she could even if she wanted to.

As quickly as they'd come, Delaney's tears passed, leaving Marcella very suspicious of her friend's motives. "I guess I don't have a choice, seeing as Marcella's turned into the mother of all pansies, now do I?"

Marcella gasped. Hovering above Kellen, she gave him a glimpse of her hard eyes. "A pansy? Moi? A pansy? Oh, she'd better be glad I don't have the gift of fireballs anymore or I'd set her whole stash of wheat germ on fire! You tell her—"

Kellen grinned wide, then bobbed his head, obviously pretending to be pleased with her answer for his sister's sake. "Marcella says she understands you're just upset and it's going to take a while for you to come to terms with her decision. Until then, she said for you, she'd be honored to help me. In fact, she said she'd rather help me than have her hair and nails done." He rolled his tongue along the inside of his cheek and jammed his hands under his armpits.

Honored schmonored. God damn it. If she still had the ability to lob a fireball, she'd flame his forked tongue.

Delaney curled her lower lip in skepticism, letting her head fall back on her neck when she gazed up at her brother. "Are you sure you have the right Marcella? Maybe she's just someone who looks like Marcella. The Marcella I know would rather have her head shaved bald than do anything for you, Kellen Markham."

Marcella nodded her agreement, cooling off a bit. Yeah. *True dat.* Yay for having your BFF's back.

Kellen shrugged his shoulders and sighed with a mockingly forlorn breath of air. "Maybe this ghost thing's given her a new outlook on her eternity. There are no parties to go to where she is, no places to shop, and it's obvious there's no place to get her nails done. Doing something productive with her time, especially because it's for you, her *best friend in the whole world*, is something I think you'd support . . ." The way he let his sentence trail off in superior satisfaction, the sheer glee he was taking at taunting her, made Marcella's fingers itch to lodge right in his esophagus.

Clyde, his dark blue eyes rooted firmly to Delaney, cupped her chin. "Maybe Kellen's right. Marcella does have an edge you don't, sweetheart. It's been nothing but frustrating for you to try to help Kellen."

Delaney gave a wistful sigh as though she were considering giving in. "Maybe you're right. I mean, if Kellen can work with Marcella, her being *the most difficult, hot-tempered, infuriating ex-demon, pain in the ass ever*"—she paused, looking upward with a devilish glint in her eyes—"then there's hope he'll be able to help the more difficult lost souls." She nodded her head with a firm shake. "So, yeah. I say this could be a good thing."

Kellen smiled indulgently at his sister, saving his look of relief for when she reached up to pat Clyde on the cheek. "You feel better now?"

Delaney nodded at her brother, using the edge of her sleeve to wipe away her crocodile tears.

Oh, if she could ever pick up, say, a heavy piece of wood again, she was going to make the back of her BFF's head one with it. "You are the biggest suck-ass ever, Kellen Markham!" Marcella thundered. "You played right into her hands!" Throwing the back of her hand over her forehead, she sighed dramatically. "Oh, Kellen. Boo to the hoo. All I have to do is let my big, innocent eyes get all watery and I can wrap you right around my widdle finger."

This time Kellen looked directly through her, ignoring her taunts and rising to give Delaney a hug and a kiss on top of her head. He made a big deal of looking around the room. "I think she's gone now. So I'm gonna hit the bathroom before I hit the road." Strolling out of the kitchen, a smug smile on his close-to-perfect face, he made a hard right for the guest bathroom, with Marcella right behind him.

She stopped just short of smacking into Kellen's wide back as she fell through the door of Delaney's mosaic-tiled bathroom. "Hey!" she called out with a sharp snap that bounced with the acoustics of the bathroom walls.

He cringed before pivoting on his heel, his expression playful. "Is privacy too much to ask?"

"Like you have anything that impressive to see," she taunted.

Crossing his arms over his chest, he stared her down, his expression thundercloudish.

"Pay attention, noob. You and me? We're not doing anything

together." And not just because it would make her yearn for all the things she couldn't have all over again. While she'd restlessly roamed today, she'd realized the distance between herself and her mad crush had been good for her. There were no more earthbound nights spent wondering what if she'd been just some human girl who was friends with Delaney and not a sullied demon? Would Kellen have been as attracted to her as she was to him?

On Chez Dreary, though she'd thought of him often, she'd been able to let some of it go due to the fact that if she couldn't have pursued him before, she definitely couldn't now. There was a comfort to finding that kind of peace. And now he'd gone and fucked it all up by promising something to Delaney he had no right to promise.

Kellen's eyes held no apology and only a smidge of sheepish when they pinned her to the door. "Look, she was crying. What can I say? I can't stand to see her cry."

Marcella clamped her fingers together in an open-and-shut motion. "Blah, blah, blah. She played you like a Stradivarius, buddy. All you've done is bought her the time she needs to figure this out. Now, instead of focusing on what she's wanted most of her adult life, she's going to be up until the wee hours of the morning, reading those stupid books for a clue to help me that doesn't exist. In the meantime, I'm stuck with you. That makes for a very unhappy Marcella. If I'm unhappy, you can count on the fact that you'll feel my back draft."

Kellen's laughter pinged off the walls, and his half grin caught her off guard. "I don't doubt it, but I'm willing to suffer if it makes Delaney happy, and knowing where you are apparently makes her happy. So get over yourself and explain the part about not being able to get back to this plane you've been on."

Marcella paused. That had been an egregious admittance on her part. Had she kept her big mouth shut, she could have slunk off somewhere until she figured it out. "Like you'd have a solution? You're no John What'sHisFace. And there's nothing to explain. I don't know how to get back."

"How did you get here to begin with?"

Marcella popped her lips. "Oh, now, c'mon, Kellen. Don't play shy. I think it had a little something to do with you and your *visualization*." She shot him a kittenish smile, fluttering her eyelashes. "I guess because you're a legit medium, and you knew me when I was earthbound, you had the power to conjure me up. It doesn't matter how I got here. How the hell do I get back?"

Kellen's gaze swept over her torn dress. "You obviously haven't been able to achieve the high level of maintenance you had when you were here. So why would you want to go back?"

"Because that means I'm not stuck here with you?"

"Could we be serious here?"

"No. The only thing that's serious is how damned dumb it was of you to tell Delaney I'd help you. You took advantage of me because I have no voice, and that's low, pal. I don't want to help you." *Because if I help you, I'll have to smell your cologne, hear that sexy rasp of your voice when you're yelling at me all het up about something. Keep my hands off you while I'm reminded I can never have you.* Why it was so hard to deal with now, when she'd been doing it for ten years, left her puzzled. Maybe the answer lay in how disconnected she now was from the only two humans she'd known so personally.

"That's unfortunate" was his bland, disinterested answer.

Fists clenched, she narrowed her eyes in anger and hissed, "Look, you ghost whisperer by proxy, here's what's unfortunate—" Just as her windup began, Marcella experienced that odd tugging sensation she'd felt earlier, rippling along her body in short jolts. Her legs grew weak and her vision blurry. Reaching behind her for an anchor, she stumbled backward with a gasp.

"Oh, lay off the drama, Marcella," Kellen rumbled, but his warning was watery and filled with static. "You're not going to get out of this with one of your infamous hissy fits."

Marcella wanted to strike back. In fact, if he didn't knock it off, she'd definitely put striking back at the top of her list of things to do the next time they tangled. However, as of this moment, she had no power to do anything but go with the strange tug and pull of whatever was sucking her out of Delaney's bathroom and dumping her into what looked like a small child's room.

That was, if the toy soldiers and tanks littering the floor were any indication.

Just when she saw a boy sprawled on the bed, its dark blue bedspread showing various stages of the moon, he looked up as though he sensed she was in the room. Green eyes, wide and innocent, scanned the far wall until he located her.

Marcella winced, waiting for him to freak. She had just appeared out of thin air. When silence greeted her ears, she popped one eye open to find the young boy staring at her. His grin was toothy, his expression not even a little surprised.

There was no fear when he looked directly at her.

There was no tremble in his voice when he said, "I saw you today. I'm Carlos. Who're you?"

Uh, totally not the tooth fairy.

four

Delaney smiled happily at Clyde from across their kitchen table, threading her fingers through his while they listened to Kellen bellow. Anyone who didn't have the gift would think it was just him lovin' up the sound of his own voice. "Aw, listen. Hissing and spitting has occurred. It's only been a couple of minutes since I forced them to forge a bond made in Hell, and already they're playing well in a team setting," she doted. "Bet Marcella's pissed. All that crap Kellen fed me about how happy she'd be to help him is just that. Crap."

Her husband grunted. "Honey?"

"Clyde?"

"You did a bad, bad thing."

She lifted her eyes just enough to chance a quick glimpse at his handsome face. "Well, some might call it bad. I call it innovative and acting fast on my feet."

"Honey, you can't force Marcella to stay where she doesn't want to be."

"Do you really believe she wants to be on some plane where the undecideds roam? Do you remember that plane?"

Clyde's right eye twitched from behind his glasses. "I do, and it had its ugly moments. But you're taking matters into your own hands for both Kellen and Marcella. And if you're being honest with yourself, it isn't because you want Marcella to be able to shop again."

"Okaaay, okay. I admit it's selfish, but if she helps Kellen, it'll buy—"

"You time to figure out how to get her back here. Maybe she really does just want some peace."

"Really, is there any other kind of inner peace like a shopping spree and a spa day for someone like Marcella?"

"Delaney . . ." Clyde's voice, the practical though indulgent one, sent out a warning.

"I'll be careful. Promise. Besides, it'll do them both some good. It'll teach Kellen to hone his communication skills with the dead, and it'll force Marcella to realize how much she wants to be back here on Earth."

"Just a thought, but how do you suppose Marcella's bickering with your brother is going to make her pine for her old demonic life?"

"Oh, honey. Haven't you paid attention to me—even once? Marcella's hot for Kellen. She always has been. Kellen's hot for her, too. The more one-on-one time they spend together, the more Marcella will want to find a way back—to Kellen, and me as a by-product." Delaney gave him a satisfied grin.

"But I thought Kellen hated demons."

Her expression was sweet and full of innocence. "But Marcella isn't a demon anymore. She's a ghost."

Ever contrary, Clyde replied with, "But if she manages to get back, won't she be a demon again?"

She waved her hand with a dismissive gesture. "Technicalities. Look, all I know is this. Kellen, whether he'll admit it or not, has always been attracted to Marcella. The demon thing is a problem, yes. But I'd bet my whole stash of valerian root he'd change his mind if he could just experience the woman I know. Not the one who hurls insults at him, but the one who kept us together at all costs. Remember her? We're the reason why she's wherever she is."

"I do, and every day I'm grateful to her for the second chance she gave me. Gave us." He nibbled at the tip of her finger then frowned. "Did she ever tell you how she became a demon anyway? I've always wondered, especially since she wasn't anything like the freaks I ran into during my stint. Becoming a demon happens via choice, unless she did something really shitty and was left with no choice."

"Nope. I never asked and she never told. But I just know it had nothing to do with her being evil. I know it here." She pointed to her chest in the general vicinity of her heart.

"Could it be that you're just wrapped up in the romance of it all?"

Sticking her tongue out at him, she said, "Could it be you're just wrapped up in the überlogical? I don't think I'm romanticizing this at all. I just know my friend and the woman who saved us couldn't—*wouldn't*—have done anything heinous enough to have made her final destination Hell. And that's that."

"You can see me?"

"Uh-huh." Carlos bent his dark head to gather up a plastic army man.

Her thoughts came in choppy rushes. He could see her. He

wasn't screaming for his mother in terror. Oddly, he'd hardly missed a beat while playing with the plastic toys on his bed. In fact, *she* might scream for his parents because she was so freaked out that he wasn't freaking out. How the hell had she landed in the bedroom of a kid who couldn't be more than eight or nine? "You're not afraid of me?" She'd be afraid of her.

His glossy head shook. "Nuh-uh. You're just a lady."

Yeah. A lady. In. Your. Room. How had this happened? She didn't even like kids. She had no idea how to relate to them. "I am, at that. Just a lady. Nothing to be afraid of. So, your name's Carlos? I'm Marcella."

"That's a weird name." He giggled on his words, scrunching his nose up.

Like Carlos was a top pick.

"You look sorta like my mom, but her hair's shorter."

Marcella almost snorted. She did not either look like *anyone's* mother. Moms didn't look like this. Her boobs were too frisky, her belly too flat and concave. "That's nice. So what are you playing?"

He held up an army man and gave her an impatient roll of his eyes. "Duh. Army."

Duh. Okay. Painfully, and ever so obviously, small talk and kids weren't her thang. Figuring out how he'd gotten her here was. Because she wanted out before she got caught scaring tweens. "Do you know how I got here, Carlos?"

"Nope."

What a fount of helpful information. Marcella frowned.

"You wanna play army with me?"

Like her ass wanted cellulite. "Maybe another time."

"I'll let you have the general."

Superfly. "I think I'll have to pass."

"But the general's the best guy in the army."

"I thought colonels were the big guys."

Carlos giggled again, strangely sweet and almost infectious to her ears. "That's stupid. The general's the biggest guy in the army. Mine has five stars," he gloated.

So? I can walk through walls. "I'll try to remember that. But no, thank you. Don't you have some friends you can play army with?"

For the first time, he looked away, casting his eyes back down at the green figures while his slight shoulders shrugged. "No."

It wasn't as much the word "no" as it was the flat tone of his response that made her heart jerk. "You don't have any friends?" Didn't eight-year-olds hang out together in grimy, snot-nosed packs, playing video games and soccer?

"Not really."

"I know how that feels."

"You don't have any friends either?" His face brightened—like they'd just bonded over their social ineptitude.

"Nope." Not any that could see her, anyway.

"It sucks sometimes."

The impulse to reach out and soothe him by ruffling his hair grew intense with a rush of lonely sympathy. Marcella fisted her hands at her sides instead. "Sometimes."

The skitter of fingers against Carlos's bedroom door made her jump. "Carlos? Dinner. I make you tamales. Hurry so dey don't get cold." Footsteps, light and brisk, made their way down what Marcella supposed was a hallway.

Carlos slid off the edge of the bed, his legs clearly reluctant. "I gotta go eat. Will you be here when I come back?" His gaze, dark and longing, was so hopeful, Marcella almost couldn't breathe from it.

She bit the inside of her mouth. At the rate she was going, who knew where she'd be by the time he had tamales splattered down his crisply clean shirt? Yet she didn't have the heart to tell him no.

The thought actually hurt. Hurt. "I'll try, but I can't promise. I sort of just show up, you know?"

He placed a small fist around the doorknob. "Yeah. I know. 'Bye, Marcella," he said, the flat tone of his words returning. Carlos let the door close with a soft hush against the red carpet covering his floor.

"'Bye, Carlos," she whispered. Watching his bright-orange-clad back disappear from view gave her an inexplicable pull, a sad throb of her heart, making more tears well up in her eyes.

Jesus. What was it with all the crying? Was this some kind of afterlife payback because she'd skipped through menopause with nary a night sweat to her credit?

Swiping at her eyes with her thumbs, Marcella gave one last glance around Carlos's bedroom. The bright primary colors that graced the walls, the mobile of army planes that hung from the fan on the ceiling all beckoned her to sit at the edge of his bed, making her want to take the knitted blanket on the bedpost and hold it to her nose so she could deeply inhale this child's scent.

Since when was she into snarfing up the sweaty, toe-jammed odor of some kid she didn't even know?

Fuck-all if she didn't need to get back to Plane Dismal and head straight for some of those classes she'd been too busy moping in the first time around to garner any helpful information.

Surely, in one of them, there was an answer to this pathetic melancholy she was experiencing—this rush of hormonally imbalanced fucked-uppedness.

Maybe they had afterlife estrogen patches.

I'll take a full body one, please.

"Joe, I don't get it. I want to help. I really do, but I'm lost. You show up here, throwing around random words and euphemisms, and look at me like I should know how they translate to what it is you need. This is the second day in a row you've done it. So, care to explain in complete sentences how exactly I can help you?" Kellen dragged another box straight through the fluttering image of Yankees great Joe DiMaggio. He bounced a transparent baseball from hand to hand, grinning. "What does monkey business have to do with anything?"

"You're always so warm and snuggly, Kellen."

Kellen glanced up at Marcella, cocking a dark eyebrow at her. "You're back."

Yeah. How or why had no rhyme or reason, but she was back. "Live and in the transparent."

"Look, Joe. It's Marcella. *The ghost.* I bet if you take her with you, she'll give Marilyn a run for her shopping money."

Time and some thought had made Marcella decide to try to make this thing work for Delaney's sake. Even though Delaney had forced the two of them together with her lame attempt at getting them to do what she wanted with tears, she really had nothing else to do, nowhere else to go. But if he kept up the asshole-ish behavior, she couldn't be responsible for the fallout. Delaney knew their relationship was antagonistic at best. If Kellen lost a limb in the ghosting process, shit happened.

Her hands fidgeted near the hem of her torn dress. She'd feel much more like herself if she at least had on something cute. "Look, I've learned a thing or two being on that plane with those undecideds, if you care to hear where you're going wrong. I know it'll be a blow to your ghost-whispering ego, but I do know some things you don't." Not many, but some. And she'd heard all about how disorienting and difficult it was for a ghost to come back from the afterlife and try to explain what message he or she wanted to send. It was all the undecideds moaned about day in, day out.

Dragging an X-acto knife across the tape that secured the box, Kellen shook his head. "I don't know how Delaney did this. I heard all the stories. I even saw a crazy thing or two when she was communicating with them, but to have dead people, especially a legend like Joe DiMaggio, show up in the middle of your bedroom is just this side of insane. Worse, they never make any damned sense."

"It's just about putting together the pieces of a puzzle."

"So hit me, Jigsaw Puzzle Queen."

Her hands went to her hips in cocky fashion. "Don't tempt me, you epic ghost-whispering failure."

Dragging a hand through his hair, he narrowed his eyes at Joe, who let loose a chuckle and repeated the words "monkey business." When his gaze returned to Marcella, he asked, "Did you just come here to razz me? Or was there something you needed?"

Oh, if only you knew how I needed . . . "I came here to do what *you* promised your sister I'd do. Help you. You have no one to blame but yourself for that, now, do you?" Her smile was smug.

His lips first thinned, then gave way to a scowl. "Fine, then help. Explain to me what Joe wants. Maybe the two of you can find some common ghost ground I can't."

Marcella winked at Joe and smiled before addressing Kellen. "Some ghosts can't communicate the way they did when they were human. Sometimes they're stuck on something they left behind at death, but the only way they can relay information to you is in bits and pieces because they're disoriented when they get sucked back to this plane. Truth be told, it's like being thrown into a blender and sucked out through a straw."

"Then how is it you're not at all disoriented? Your communication skills, while still crass and littered with bad language, are still intact."

"Blow me, and I have no idea. Maybe because I didn't actually die? I was technically already dead when I was dumped there. So my guess is Joe here's got something to say."

His look of irritation said he'd heard this same song and dance before. "Anybody ever tell you how intuitive you are?"

"Anybody ever tell you how cranky you are?"

"Forget it. You're not telling me anything I don't know already. Color me an ass for even suggesting to Delaney that you help me."

"What's your favorite color?"

His teeth clenched together in a delectable snarl. "Christ, you're the most difficult woman. What the hell was I thinking when I told D I'd have you help me?"

Marcella cocked an eyebrow at him. "That's easy. You were pacifying her because you're a man, and men hate to see women cry. You gave her exactly what she wanted. Now she's just buying time until she can find a way to fix something that's unfixable. Job well done, Mr. Great Beyond."

Crouching down beside the box, Kellen raised his hands in white-flag fashion before leaning his elbows on his knees. "You're right. I'm sorry. I put you in a shitty spot. I did this. So let's just try to get through it until . . ."

"Until you can get me out of your hair."

The door jingled to the sound of one of Delaney's old chimes, making Kellen rise with a grunt. "Customer," he said with a brisk tone, taking care to slip by her without touching her.

"Kellen? Hey, you back there?" a woman's husky, seductive voice almost growled.

The hair on the back of Marcella's neck bristled and her nostrils flared. Floating to the bedroom entryway, she peeked out into Delaney's old kitchen to find a woman, dressed in low-rise jeans, a figure-hugging black T-shirt that said "The Devil Made Me Do

It," and work boots, leaning against the countertop as if she were very comfortable doing so. Her straight hair fell down her back in ripples of a deep chocolate brown, healthy and clean, that shone under the lights in the kitchen.

Marcella's eyes narrowed in the direction of Miss Tortilla as her nostrils once more flared. She could still smell and she knew that scent. Demon.

"Some like it hot," Joe whispered with a chuckle of evident glee.

Marcella waved him off with an irritated hand over her shoulder. "Shut up. She's not that hot." With Kellen's raging dislike of demons, she had to wonder why he was all up in this chick's demonicness.

"Some like it hot," Joe repeated in her ear, chant style.

"Yeah, yeah. And some can't see lukewarm for the trees in the forest. Don't you like needy blondes? Never mind. Be quiet and let me listen." Joe drifted away, dissipating into a fluttery white haze as he did.

Kellen's easy grin as he bobbed his dark head and his hazel eyes took in every lithe inch of Ms. Thang made Marcella want to wrap a fistful of that perfect hair around her hand and drag her out of the store. *And you might be able to do that had you attended the classes, dipshit.* For now she'd just have to settle for eavesdropping.

"Did you get it from your sister?" she asked.

He smiled, genuine and warm. *Warm.* Since when did Kellen do warm when it came to a demon? What disturbed Marcella more was his face; it was lighter somehow, with none of the brooding hardness he bestowed upon her whenever she was in the room. "I did. Hang on a sec and I'll get them from the front."

Marcella followed him to the front of the store, slipping past "some like it hot" without notice. She appeared beside Kellen, startling him. "Could you not do that?" he rasped, rolling his shoulders and slamming the cash register drawer shut.

"Who the hell is that?" She fought to keep the jealous tinge of her question to herself. It just wasn't working out the way she'd hoped. Not if her ears were set on truthful.

"Why the hell do you care?"

Argh. This man. "She's demon."

"Yep." He dug around under the cash register, peering beneath the shelf below it.

"Yep?"

"Uh, yep."

"That's all you have to say? Did you hear me? She's demon."

"So?"

Her mouth opened in disbelief. "So? *So?* Excuse me, but don't all demons have the cooties as far as you're concerned? Or was it just me?"

Kellen's head popped up and he smiled at her, all foxlike. "You definitely have something. I wouldn't rule out cooties."

Her teeth clenched. "Who is she and where did she come from?"

"Her name's Catalina Gutierrez, and does she look at all familiar, seeing as all demons come from Hell? Maybe you passed each other in the halls. Shared a story or two by the water cooler?"

"You know what I mean. What does she want?"

"This." He held up a small brown box. "It's bat shit from Texas, and don't ask."

"Bat shit."

Placing the box on the counter, he tapped the top of it and smiled again. "That's what the lady asked for."

She wanted to sock him for how much he was enjoying this. "Okay, so care to explain why all of a sudden you're best friends with a demon? You know, evil incarnate."

"She's a customer. That means money. Something I really need since quitting teaching. She's also a customer who's waiting. So go practice ghost things. I'm busy." He stepped around the counter, skirting her once more, and went back in the direction of the kitchen. All too eagerly, if you asked her.

Marcella tried to stay rooted to the storefront. But curiosity, and okay, maybe some green-eyed monster, just wouldn't let her. She drifted to the corner in the living room, skulking like some weird stalker.

"Kellen, you're my knight in shining armor," this Catalina crooned, all seductive and breathy. Even Vern and Shirley liked her, swirling their tails around her calves and meowing for attention.

When Kellen bent down to mutter something in what Marcella was certain was a perfectly shell-shaped ear, she had to fight not to gag so she could hear what he said, but she missed it.

Then Catalina giggled.

Giggled.

Bleh.

And then she did this slinky thing, tilting her shiny head and placing a hand on his arm, positioning herself even closer to Kellen as he hauled her close, arching her slender spine. His head lifted but for a moment, making Marcella shrink back into the wall.

The playful crack of his hand against Catalina's round, shapely ass stunned her so, she tipped backward.

Into the backyard.

She let out a scream of rage when she tripped over her tattered sandals. Since when had Kellen Markham jumped into the demon-loving pool?

That self-righteous, pious fuck. All that talk about hating de-mons. Years of making her feel like she was just one step up from a serial killer, and all of a sudden, Mr. Do-Gooder had a hard-on for one?

The thought stopped her in her tracks.

That meant it really had nothing to do with his despising demons and everything to do with Kellen just not liking her. Unsettling realization sunk to the pit of her belly.

Ow, ow, ow.

Clearly he could forgive a woman for being a demon. Just not *this* woman.

And then came the tears that clarity brought, streaming down her face in frustration and pitiful longing.

She absolutely had to find a way out of this. Not even for Delaney could she keep up this façade, and especially not with a woman Kellen coveted in the picture.

Not even for Delaney.

"Is she gone?"

"I can't believe you can't see her, too. I thought everyone from the great beyond, including you demons, could see each other."

"Some of us morally bankrupt worked harder at our demon skills than others. I never made it to the 'Don't Be So Self-Centered— You're Not the Only Paranormal Species' class. If I focused long enough, I'd probably be able to see her, but ghosts don't give me any trouble. It's demons and their shenanigans that burn my britches. So I stick with what I know." Catalina looked around again surreptitiously. "So are we clear? Because," she whispered up into his face, "my fucking back hurts."

Kellen eyed the room and sniffed. Marcella's perfume had faded along with her voluptuous curves and her fresh mouth, leaving him with a moment of concern for her safety. He brushed it aside in favor of the idea that Marcella was tough as nails. If she'd survived being a demon, other ghosts had to be cake. "Yeah, I think we're clear."

"Good, then let me make one more thing clear. Like, really clear.

If you ever touch my ass again, Kellen Markham, I'll set your ninnies on fire. We good?"

He threw his head back and laughed, not at all threatened by her warning. "Yeah, we're good."

Catalina's face softened and she smiled. "So how about you tell me why you're behaving like a spiteful five-year-old for a woman no one can see but you?"

"You want honesty?"

Her sigh was ragged, the pull of her slender shoulders beneath her T-shirt tense. "From just one man in my life, yeah, I'd like some honesty. It's rarer than hen's teeth in my world."

Hearing the thread of bitterness in her response, Kellen considered asking where it came from, then refrained. "I can't let her get too close."

"Reason being?"

He gave her a brief overview of what had happened to Marcella and Delaney, their friendship, and the ensuing battle with Satan. "Marcella and I go way back. She was friends with Delaney for ten years and for every single one of them, we fought. It's just easier that way."

"How does fighting with her make anything easier?"

"More honesty?"

"It's hella fun for me. I actually think my faith in men might be in for a big comeback. So, yes, be honest."

"It keeps her at arm's length. When we're arguing, I'm not busy thinking about things I shouldn't." Like how she'd look naked. Shit.

"Like?"

He opted for evasive. "Like the things men and women do."

"Ah. Fucking."

Laughter came from deep in his throat. If there was one thing he admired about Catalina, it was her no-bullshit policy. "There's that, along with a multitude of other issues."

"So you've been hot for her for ten years and never made a move?"

"Nope."

"Why?"

"Because she was a demon. My experience with them wasn't exactly something I ever wanted to go through again. I let what happened to Delaney and me fester for a long time. As far as I was concerned, all demons were the bottom of the barrel. I grudged, despite the fact that she and Delaney were best friends."

"And what changed your mind about we of the wicked and immoral?" she teased.

"What Marcella did for Delaney and Clyde. That, and you, and this mission you seem to be on to prevent teen possession, among other things."

Catalina scoffed, giving him her best hard look. "Please. Don't let me fool you. I'm as amoral as they come."

"Right. That's why you paid three thousand dollars for someone to collect bat shit for you in Texas so you can mix potions and save kids who have no idea the can of worms they've opened with their Ouija boards. All I'm saying now is I get that not all demons end up demons because they made the choice to be one. If I learned anything from what happened with Clyde, I learned shit goes down and it sometimes has nothing to do with what you intended." The problem was, he'd realized it much too late where Marcella was concerned. He'd been too blinded by his rage and by the chaos his half brother, Vincent, had created in the name of Satan. His hatred of anything remotely related to Lucifer hadn't left him with a lot of gray areas where Marcella was concerned. Thus, their relationship had been clouded by his prejudice.

"I heard about what happened to Delaney, how she got the gift of sight and passed it on to you. Can't say I can hate on you for not buying into the idea that not all demons want Hell to rule."

"Can I ask you something?"

Her grin was withholding. "You can always ask."

"How did you end up a demon? I know damned well it wasn't a choice."

Catalina's eyes became evasive, her spine rigid. "Yeah? Says who?"

"Not who. What. I ordered you bat shit. I think that says it all."

The vague, haunted glint in her eyes came and went, replaced with that cocky gleam she wore more often than not. "It's a long story, and if honesty's what we have going on here, it's personal and painful—even after all these years. But I can tell you this, your Marcella may well have been in over her head when she chose Hell. If what you say is true, she sacrificed her earthbound privileges to save your sister. She can't be all bad."

"Or maybe, after experiencing Hell, and the reality that it isn't all it's cracked up to be, she decided to try to win favor with the man upstairs?" He spoke his favorite mantra about Marcella's six degrees of separation from the devil, but the more he said it out loud, the less he believed it.

"Yeah. Maybe. But here's the catch. There is no winning favor once you choose Hell."

"You know that because?"

"Because I'm high-IQ demon. I know just because I know. There's no going back without some serious divine intervention—*ever*. So whatever she did to get there, I'm going to suppose she did it for a reason if she's altruistic enough to save your sister's life."

"Like you?"

Catalina waved her hands in the air, dismissing him. "You so want me to be a good guy, don't you? Forget me and focus on the woman you've possibly judged unfairly."

Once more, he had to shove down the uneasy feeling that there was far more to Marcella than she let on. "There's nothing to focus on. She's not demonic anymore. She's a ghost."

"Now, that's something I know very little about. If Lucifer shunned her, I don't know if that works the same way as when the big guy does it. But I can ask around. And don't bother to tell me you don't want me to. Then you'd be lying and my resurgence of pathetic hope in the male species would be dashed."

Kellen didn't bother to beat around the bush. He wanted to know. No, he wasn't being honest. He *needed* to know. "Okay. Ask around."

"Done. I'll also see if I can get any background on her."

"You'd do that for me? A knuckle dragger from the barely evolved?"

She pointed to the counter. "You did hook me up with some fine Texas bat shit."

"That's just how I roll."

Catalina chuckled, scooping up the box of bat feces, and gave him a waggle of her fingers before she slid into the shadows of the living room and disappeared.

He stood for a moment in the kitchen, fighting the unwanted anticipation of hope that Marcella wasn't what she'd pretended to be all these years. Yes, she'd saved Clyde and Delaney, but she'd done it as a demon. But what if she'd become a demon for reasons that were just as selfless?

If she turned out to be one of the good guys, that'd be some error in judgment on his part.

That would mean he was a chump of the worst order. He'd always been able to keep himself from her sultry charms when he thought about what one had to do to become a demon. It never failed to stop him short, no matter how often she popped into his lusty dreams.

If the choice that led her to opt for Hell had loopholes, it would also mean ten years of not allowing himself to give in to his wild attraction to Marcella had been foolish time wasted.

Worse, she was further out of reach as a ghost with no earth-bound privileges than she'd ever been before, leaving him feeling a deep hunger.

Like, deep.

five

Marcella sat on a bench in the park, watching the brittle leaves of winter skip over the pavement while she fought more tears of embarrassed outrage. The sun faded with a fell swoop, leaving her in the pinkish dusk of early evening. The dark purple-and-blue-streaked sky settled into a chilly midnight blue as another day came to an end. Letting out a long sigh, she glanced up at the sky.

Like the end of a day made a bit of difference. They rather blended.

Her head fell to her hands, and she noted with mild surprise that she was now able to keep it from going directly through her palms. She was also sitting on the park bench versus falling through it to the cold ground. Little by little, she was apparently acclimating.

"You savin' thisss ssseat fer some . . . one?" A leathery, weathered hand slapped the place beside her on the wood bench.

The pungent stale scent of hard liquor wafted to her nose, filling her nostrils. Putting the back of her hand over her mouth, she shook her head, cocking her eyebrow with disdain. Somebody'd had a little drinky-poo.

She saw from the corner of her eye, rather than felt, the shift of the bench as the boozer weaved, then settled beside her with an uneven plunk.

"So how'sss it goin'?"

Marcella paused, turning to face him. His navy blue knit cap was almost threadbare in places, and bushy thatches of wiry gray hair spilled from the sides of it. Layers of clothing in various colors lay beneath his dark green coat, moth eaten and heavy with the odor of sweat and urine. He held a bottle of amber liquid openly, not even bothering to disguise it with a brown paper bag. But none of that mattered—he could *see* her.

"You can see me?"

His head bobbed forward then back while he fought to focus. "Not ssso goo-good."

"But you can see I'm sitting next to you?"

He hacked a deep, crackling cough before he spoke. "Yeahhhh," he said on a hiccup.

Why was it that boozers and kids could see her but not like a personal shopper? "How is that possible?" she muttered, more to herself than to the homeless man.

His body tilted sideways, his head landing right on her shoulder. He could touch her, too? He smiled up at her with a blackened grin. "Don't be sssilly. I could always sssee you."

Marcella fought her gag reflex. Beggars couldn't be choosers and seeing as she had but two allies, one who hated her, and one who wasn't old enough to remember to change his own underwear, she figured one more, albeit plastered and stankified, couldn't hurt. "What do you mean you could always see me? Have we met?"

"Yesss," he slurred. "But gimme a minute. I can't"—he shook his head, creating a wave of more noxious air—"remember who I am. Oh, this was cleeearly a mistake. How agre—egr—eegious egregious."

Marcella's eyes popped open. She stared down into the goofy grin he gave her. No drunk had a vocabulary like that. "Jesus Christ—Darwin, is that you?"

He bolted upright. "Yesss! Tha'sss who I am. Darwiiin. I know my name. Darrr—wiiin. 'Sa good name. Lubs it. Nice lady give it to me."

Giving him a hard shove, Marcella knocked him off her lap with a grunt of disgust and surprise. She could touch him, too . . . Then why the fuck couldn't she touch the cute outfit at Macy's? "Ugh. Sit up. Good God. What the hell were you thinking, possessing a homeless, drunk man? One who smells like a Porta-Potty, to boot. I remember the 'Possession Is Nine-tenths of the Law' class, and they distinctly tell you to be very careful about who you possess, you moron."

Darwin reared upward, then slammed back down on the bench. His head lolled at awkward angles. "My head. It keeps falling."

Using her palm, she pushed it back upright then snatched her hand away. "That's because you possessed the body of a goddamned alcoholic. And what are you doing here anyway? Isn't there some big bowl of Chuck Wagon you should be shoving down your gullet?"

Letting his head fall back on his shoulders, he stared up at the sky with glazed red eyes, one hand clinging to the bench rail, the other precariously holding on to the empty bourbon bottle. "Ugh. The ssspin is parking."

"I'll bet the spin is parking, and that's because the empty is bottle." She tried to yank the bourbon from his hands unsuccessfully and resorted to pointing to it so he could see it was barren.

He scrunched his red-streaked beady eyes shut, then reopened them with apparently no success in focusing. "I mean the park. It's spinning like a—a ghastly amusssement park ride. Around and a . . . round . . ."

"What are you doing here, Darwin? Did you come to gloat about what a failure I am because I can't get back to Chez Gray? Because I can't, you know. So if you're not here to help me, go away. I'm not up to another round. I've done my time in the ring for today."

"No, I have to talllkkk to youuu." He held up a hand covered in a glove with no fingers and shook it back and forth, pausing for a moment as the motion mesmerized him.

She swatted at him. "Knock it off and focus, Darwin. Talk to me about what? I can't think of any other reason you'd be here other than to snark me."

"Nooo. Tha'sss not why I'm here. Ssswear it. I'm here to—to— tell you someting. Yesss. Tha'sss what I haf to do."

For a moment, even though the body he'd possessed was distasteful, it was Darwin. As ridiculous as that was, feeling as alone as she did, he was like comfort food. Granted, it was comfort food that was bad for your glutes, but it still comforted. "What do you have to tell me that's so important you had to possess Jack Daniel's?"

"I dooon't knooow," he whined. "Can't think ssstraight, an' I have fery few teef to work wif."

She was just too tired. Marcella gave him a consoling pat on the knee accompanied by a long sigh. "It's all right. You probably just missed razzing me. Everything's always exaggerated when you booze it up. Your emotions get all out of whack. Believe me, I know. I'm a crier when I'm snockered."

He shook his rolling head with a dizzying nod. "No. No. No. 'S important. I know it. Gimme a sec to tink."

"Okay, you tink, *chico*. Mind if I destress while you do?"

"I can't tink if you yak."

Twirling a lock of her hair, Marcella ignored Darwin's fight to keep his head erect and his indirect protest for silence. She had to get this off her chest. "So I can't get back, Darwin. I don't know why, but I can't get back. I tried, because God knows I don't want to stay here after what I just saw, but I can't do it. What happens to me if I can't get back? Do I just drift here forever? Shit. I never thought I'd say this, but I want to go back. At least on Plane Dreary there's peace." And no women named Catalina who swished their round, pert asses while they made even a plain old T-shirt look like an advertisement for Big Breasty Babes.

"Oh!" Darwin hollered. "I 'member. Uh, re—mem—ber," he enunciated. "You haf a problem."

She frowned, grabbing him by his bearded, shaggy chin. "What problem?"

"I can't reeemember."

"Bah. Let me tell you about problems, pal. First, Delaney. I made contact and she knows I'm okay, but she twisted that horndog of a brother around her little finger and convinced him it would be a good idea for me to help him with his ghost whispering while I'm stuck here. Which leads me to the problem with Kellen and his mistress of malevolence. Can you even believe when I tell you that two-faced, self-righteous shit is hot for a demon? Yeah. I saw her today. Right there in Delaney's shop, just like she'd been there before. Verrry comfortable, I tell you. All rubbing up against him like some cat on a kitty condo laced with catnip. It was vile. Disgusting. Shameful."

His giggle, high and sharp, echoed in the empty, open space of the park.

"How's that funny?"

"Do you haf a twin?"

"What?"

"A twin. She sssounds jusss like you."

Marcella bristled, knocking her shoulder with his. "Oh, shut up. I was never so blatant."

Darwin let go of a gurgling snort. "Blatant should be your ss-surname. But tha'sss not why I come, er came. I haf to tell you sometink. So shhh."

With a roll of her eyes, Marcella leaned back, crossing her ankles and arms.

"Okay, I tink I got it. I heared, damn—*heard* sometink."

The hairs on the back of her neck stood up. "About?"

"Aboutchuuu."

"Big deal. Like everyone on that godforsaken plane hasn't talked about me at one time or another. I'm not winning any popularity contests because they think I'm unsociable."

"No. No. No. Was about sssomebody you know."

"I know lots of people, Darwin."

"Thisss one is bad. So, so, sooo bad."

Goose bumps crawled along her arms. Maybe he was just exaggerating because he was drunk.

"Calvin! Yesss." The wrinkles in Darwin's forehead deepened. "Wait. No. Not Cal . . ." His knit-capped head dropped to his reed-thin chest, his lips blew out puffs of air, and he began to snore.

She gave him a jolting shove. "Wake up! Who is Calvin, Darwin?"

His groan was long. "'S not Calvin."

She squinted. "Sounds like . . . ?"

"I don't knooow," he whined. "The only sound I can hear is the voice that tells me to dink more and tink less."

"Get out of this body, Darwin, right now, you canine calamity."

"Nuh-uh. Can't. On this plane I can only talk if I possessss."

"Remind me of that the next time you're hounding me."

"Carlos!" he bellowed, pitching forward with a wobble. "Yep. Tha'sss right, babyyy. Carlos."

A shiver of dread walked along her spine, stopping at her intestines. "Tell me right now what you know about Carlos. Now, Darwin, or I'll see to it that you never see another beef-basted pig ear again!" Oh, Christ on the crapper. What did Carlos have to do with anything? He was just a baby. An innocent child.

"I can't tink," he moaned.

Alarm bells shot off in her head. "Well, you'd better get to tinking, pal. Carlos is a little boy. Maybe eight or nine. If you heard something about him, I want to know what the fuck it is and I want to know now. So let's go get coffee or something to sober your lame ass up. I need to know what you know." She poked Darwin with a ragged nail, but he'd resumed his slump while long, choppy breaths escaped his chapped lips.

Leaning into his ear, she lifted the cap and winced, her nose wrinkling. Jesus, he was ripe. "Daaarwiiin! Wake up!"

His head snapped up, crashing into her jaw. She grabbed him by the shoulders, scanning his red-rimmed eyes. "Damn it, dog, what do you know about Carlos?"

"They want him."

Chills coursed along the back of her neck. "Who wants him? *Who?* Why?" she yelled, her throat tight.

Darwin began to drift again, his eyelids making a slow descent, but just before he slumped into three-sheets-to-the-wind oblivion, he managed, "They know he can sssee you."

As Darwin slumped to the left, splaying his upper body over the arm of the park bench, she jumped up, panic-stricken.

Who could possibly want Carlos that knew her? Oh, good Christ.

Except for Delaney, Clyde, and Kellen, the only people who knew her were bad, bad fuckers. Why would they want a little boy? Because he had the gift of sight?

She didn't even know how she'd been summoned by him—or where the frig he lived. One minute she'd been in Carlos's room, the next she'd been sucked back to Kellen's place. Damn it all. How could she possibly look after a little boy she couldn't find? Her demonic contacts were long gone—there were only two people in the whole world who could see her, and to make everything that much worse, she was always crying these days.

As evidenced by the big fat droplets falling from her eyes, splashing to the cold, cracked pavement below.

Jesus, soon she'd have to start stuffing her bra just to keep tissues on hand.

"Hey, Carlos. How's it goin'?" Kellen asked over his shoulder as he unpacked yet another one of his boxes.

The little boy shrugged his shoulders and gave an answer so hushed Kellen had to strain his ears to hear it. "Okay, I guess."

"Cool. You wanna help me unpack? I have lots of science stuff in these boxes from my old school. Bet there's a lot of stuff in there you'd be interested in," he suggested, keeping it light. Since he'd met Mrs. Ramirez's grandson, he couldn't help but wonder if he was either being ultrasensitive because he'd worked with children for so long, or if Carlos really wasn't just a quiet, introspective child, but troubled.

Uncertain as to whether Mrs. Ramirez felt comfortable enough to confide in him yet, he tried not to pry. She'd been Delaney's long-standing part-time help, and when he'd taken over the store, he'd inherited her along with it. She brought him food, she helped him take care of the ever-growing clientele Delaney somehow had managed to develop before she'd left for Long Island, and she never questioned the odd conversations he had with what appeared to be himself.

Yet, when her eyes fell on her grandson, they grew dark with concern—which, in turn, concerned Kellen. She was a proud woman. If there was trouble with Carlos, she might not be ready to confide in him just yet.

In that moment, he realized how much he missed the routine of his classes. How much he missed his kids. How strange it was that now that he had the time to deal with the afterlife, it was eerily quiet, with the exception of Joe showing up. It meant the spirits of the afterlife felt they couldn't trust him, and as much as the spirits drove him to want to hit a six-pack, he found he wanted to do right by them. Like Delaney had. He wanted to do it as well as she had.

Mrs. Ramirez blew past him, rubbing her hands together. "Ees—" She stopped short, correcting herself and the broken English she worked so diligently on three evenings a week at the high school. "*It is* cold in here, Meester Kellen. You turn on de heat today?" She smiled a beaming grin at him, clearly proud that her hard work was paying off.

Kellen gave her the thumbs-up sign then glanced at the digital thermostat. It read forty-two degrees. Jesus, if one more thing needed to be replaced, he was going to give D back the store and live in a cardboard box—they were warmer. Kellen frowned, rising to get a closer look. "It was just seventy about an hour ago." He tried to reset the temperature, but it wouldn't budge. "Damn. I'll have to call the landlord. Mrs. Ramirez, do you know where his number is?"

She shivered, her round face pensive. "I think Meess Delaney, she leave it in de flippy thing."

The Rolodex. He headed for the cash register, grabbing for the flippy thing, but it slid away, as though an invisible hand were trying to snatch it from him. And to think, just moments ago, he'd been pondering the afterlife peace he'd been granted.

Kellen waited a second, then grabbed for it again, capturing it just before it got away. He gave Carlos and his grandmother a hooded glance, hoping they hadn't seen the Rolodex move of its own accord. He flipped it open, trying to remember the landlord's last name.

The index cards began to shuffle, spinning slowly at first then gaining momentum until they began to frantically flip. Kellen threw his body at the countertop, hoping to land on it, but it zig-zagged away out of his reach.

By now he should be used to this kind of madness, but it still never failed to make the hairs on his arms stand on end. "Look," he muttered into the air, "do me a favor. Can it until the kid's gone, okay? Whoever you are, I'll try to help, but you're gonna have to wait. Now quit before you scare him."

But it was too late.

Carlos, dark eyes wide, was frozen in place by the boxes he'd been helping unpack.

Fuck. "Carlos? It's okay, bud. I know this is kind of weird, but I promise you, it's okay. I'm here. Why don't you come stand next to me?" He held out his hand, but Carlos refused to budge, though if Kellen had judged his line of vision correctly, he wasn't even looking in the direction of the Rolodex.

Kellen followed Carlos's eyes to the ceiling.

Holy. Shit.

His eyes opened as wide as Carlos's. Whatever the fuck it was, it was no ghost.

Kellen looked to Mrs. Ramirez, who hadn't batted an eyelash.

She continued to dust the shelves that held bottled herb oils with the feather duster as if a slimy creature wasn't crawling along the ceiling right above her head.

Each step he took, his clawed, webbed hands and feet dragged a gooey substance, leaving long strings of it dangling from his appendages. The creature was small, but spry. His red eyes scouting the room, spying Carlos, he paused in definite recognition. With a screech so high the bottles on the shelves rattled, he opened his mouth wide, leaving a cavernous black hole in its place. The quake of the bottles made even Mrs. Ramirez turn around.

Carlos trembled, fat tears filling the corners of his almond-shaped eyes, his thin chest rising and falling with sharp intakes of breath.

Kellen was beside him in an instant, pulling him to his side, feeling the violent shivers that rocked his slight body. Before he could speak a soothing word to Carlos, everything went dark.

"Meester Kellen. I think you better hurry and call the landlord!"

Somehow, he didn't think the landlord was going to be able to fix what was happening now.

Streaks of lightning pinged across the room, sizzling and crackling with their appearance. In the shard of one arc of light, Kellen saw Mrs. Ramirez, now holding her purse high over her head, ready to strike their invisible attacker.

The chimes Delaney had left behind began to sway violently, their musical clattering far from soothing. They shivered with an angry, intensely fevered pitch.

Yep, it was time to make a break for it. Whatever that thing was on the ceiling, it was far too interested in Carlos for his taste. Kellen hurled Carlos up over his shoulder like a sack of potatoes and made a run for Mrs. Ramirez, who swung her purse just as he made a dash for her, clocking him in the eye. "Ow! Mrs. Ramirez!

Hold still. Give me your hand!" He held his free hand out to her, but as suddenly as she reached for it, she snatched her own back.

"Oh, *madre santa*!" she whispered with a terrified tremble, making the sign of the cross over her chest.

Whenever she made the sign of the cross over her chest, it meant bad shit was anticipated and she was thwarting it by calling on the big guy. Forcing himself to turn around, he fought to mentally prepare for whatever he was about to find.

But there was no preparation for what his eyes fell upon.

For as long as he lived, he'd probably never be able to tell the kids he taught there was no such thing as the boogeyman with any kind of conviction.

Oh, my, my, my. What a beast.

The demon Marcella encountered when she was dragged back to Kellen's wasn't winning any tiaras for drop-dead gorgeous. For sure, he wouldn't win Miss Congeniality if his attitude were any indication.

He lingered in the far end of the room, roaring and making a godawful mess with his blasts of lightning. Using his fingers as if he were controlling a puppet on strings, he plucked the air, creating shock waves of colorful light.

He'd presented himself with a skull face, the eyes hollowed out but for the red glow that pierced the room. Long, pointed teeth protruded from his wide mouth, wiggling each time he roared. And goo dripped from his hands and feet.

Why was it that demons, when choosing their demonic overcoat, went out of their way to pick the form that drooled and had sticky shit all over its feet? It had to be a male demon. They loved the gore. Demons of the female persuasion never opted for those attributes. Scales? Yes, because they were a little scary. Horns? Sure. Horns carried an imposing threat. But for the love of all things salivating, only the male demons opted for drool.

Ick. Marcella shuddered, thankful she couldn't touch it. That would mean she'd have to aid Kellen in knocking this mother-fucker off, and if she got goo on the only damned dress she had, DEFCON 5 would have a whole new meaning for this particular demon.

And he was scaring poor Carlos—the bastard. She cocked her head in confused thought. What was Carlos doing here? Another roar from the minion kept her from pondering any further.

Something inside of her lurched like a twisting knife to her gut, making her wish now more than ever she still had her demonic powers. "Get the salt, Kellen! Get it now!"

Kellen whipped around, catching a glimpse of Marcella's trans-parent form before the thundering bolts of lightning calmed and, in their place, the room began to vibrate, knocking bottles off their shelves, sending shards of prickly glass across the old, wood floor. "I don't know where it is!" he bellowed over the thunderous rumbling.

"In the cabinet in the corner—top shelf!" she screamed back. "I can't help you. I can't pick anything up!"

Kellen put his head down, running for the corner hutch where Delaney had always kept a Costco-sized box of Morton salt. Pray Jesus it was still there. Icy fingers clutched at her heart as she watched Carlos's head bob up and down, his slight weight bounc-ing against the breadth of Kellen's chest, his eyes glassy and wide. He must be petrified. She wanted to run to him, drag him from Kellen, and hold him to her chest.

Which, even in the midst of all this chaos, freaked her the fuck out. Since when did she want to hold little kids with filthy hands and runny noses?

With a holler of pain, the cabinet doors slammed against Kellen's fingers, but he managed to fling them open against the roaring wind. They ripped from their hinges, crashing against the wall and breaking apart in splintering, cracking chunks.

Marcella might have breathed a sigh of relief at the sight of that salt, if not for the dark, ominous figure approaching Kellen and Carlos from behind. "Kellen! Throw the damn salt! Hurry! Throw it over your shoulders *now*!" she screamed.

And then a glimpse of the demon's face made her take pause. She knew that face—knew the form he'd taken because he'd once fought with another demon over it. *Abbadon*—a demon that rather enjoyed destroying everything in his path. "Wait, Kellen! Abbadon! You son of a bitch, knock it off now!"

She floated directly toward him, suspended in mid-air so they stood, er, hovered, face-to-face. She shook a finger under his nose. "There's a little boy here, you piece of shit! How dare you come here and frighten him. If he has nightmares, I swear to you, I'll hunt your gooey ass down and make you miserable for as long as I have to wear this ugly dress. I hate to be the one to tell you, but it looks like I'm stuck with this frock for eternity. It would so suck to be you, if that's the case. Vengeance *will* be mine."

His ominous form staggered backward, swaying like one of those big blow-up ghosts people tethered on their front lawns at Halloween. "Fuck off, Marcella. I'm just doing my job," he spat with scorn, his words echoing with eerie vibrations.

She opened her mouth in disbelief, her eyes wide with fiery admonishment. "Did you just swear in front of *a child*?"

His skull face went instantly sheepish, his nearly lipless mouth pouting. "You did it first."

Rearing up in his face, she jabbed a finger into the socket where his red eye glowed. "I don't give a shit. You watch your mouth around the kid. Feel me? And might I suggest a breath mint. Just because you have to be scary, it doesn't mean you have to reek like the bowels of Hell while you do it."

His nod was contrite, his sigh aggravated. "Fine. No more swearing. Now go away. I have a job to do."

Marcella's ears pricked to the tune of information. "Yeah, about that—who sent you and what's the job?"

"You know the rules, Marcella. I ain't tellin' you nuthin'."

"Listen here, you ass licker, spit it out." For all the threatening she was doing, she was thankful he was too dense to realize there was absolutely nothing she could do but verbally knock him for a loop.

A mere second later, from the sudden clarity on his face, she realized that was a mistake. It was in that second that he laughed, all deep and demonic. Just like they'd taught them in class when they'd watched all those old *Omen* movies. "You can't hurt me, Marcella. You're not demon—now back off, bit—"

"Uh, uh, uh—you watch your mouth," she warned with the click of her fingers.

"Back—off!" he thundered, sending her transparent form across the room with the whistling blow of his stagnant breath.

But Kellen, stunned to silence in the moments while she'd lectured the demon, sprang into action, hurling the entire box of salt at Abbadon.

From the far corner of the room, Marcella admired the lean mass of muscle in Kellen's arm when he lobbed the salt, all while still protectively holding Carlos. When she had seen women cooing over a man holding a child and saying how sexy it was, she'd never understood it. But she did now. It was rather late in the game, but she got it.

Squeals of agony nearly raised the roof as the fine crystals showered over Abbadon, the salt leaving gashes of deep, oozing welts all over his body before he sizzled to the floor.

Carlos buried his head in Kellen's shoulder, fisting his hands over his ears until the screams were nothing more than a hushed moan of pain.

The woman who'd looked familiar to her when she'd seen her walking with Carlos lay slumped in the corner chair, her big, square, multicolored handbag clenched to her chest.

Silence, in all its bliss, settled over the trashed remains of the store.

Marcella fluttered to Mrs. Ramirez, whose chest rose and fell with a—thankfully—easy rhythm. "Is she okay?"

Kellen bent beside the older woman, pressing a fingertip to her neck. "I think she just passed out."

Marcella was instantly beside Kellen and Carlos, tipping her head at an angle so he could see it was her. She smiled. "Hey, Carlos. You okay?"

Kellen's sharp eyes took her in. "You know Carlos?"

"Sort of. Let's just say we're acquainted, right, Carlos?"

"He can *see* you?"

"And you thought you were the only one with divine passage to me. How is it that you know him?"

"He's Mrs. Ramirez's grandson. She's the woman who helped Delaney out here, remember?"

Huh. She didn't have time to think about it now, but it was too weird that Carlos was connected to Kellen and they'd both been able to summon her. "I laid low, remember? My visiting hours were limited due to my bad-assedness. Though, I remember D telling me Mrs. Ramirez was very religious and she didn't want me to run into her in case she whipped out her rosary. So this is her grandson . . . Does she know he has the gift of sight?"

Kellen ruffled a hand over Carlos's head with a soothing hand. "Well, if she didn't know before, I think she might have some indication now."

"Shit. What a way to find out." Smiling down at Carlos, who'd lifted his head, she asked, "Carlos? Remember me?"

He nodded, but his lips made no effort to move.

"Are you okay, little man? Don't be afraid of stupid old Abbadon. He's just a big bully. I'll make sure he doesn't bother you again. Promise."

Carlos shivered, but once more nodded, his fists clinging to the collar of Kellen's shirt in tense balls. Fuck, fuck, fuck. If she ever had hellbound privileges again, she was going to kick Abbadon from here to Sunday. "Carlos, has this ever happened before? I mean, have you seen other things besides ghosts?"

When he finally spoke, it was staggered and hushed. "Some . . . sometimes."

Marcella sent Kellen a look of deep concern.

"You wanna talk about it?" Kellen asked against the side of Carlos's silky black hair.

His head moved from side to side.

And who could blame him?

Kellen pulled out a chair that hadn't been ruined from the corner where Delaney had once held story time for the neighborhood children. He sat, planting Carlos firmly on his lap. "I have a secret, Carlos. Wanna know what it is?"

Marcella's heart shifted in her chest when his shoulders shrugged, but he'd stirred, meaning Kellen had caught his attention.

"I can see ghosts, too."

She held her breath, waiting for Carlos to react, intentionally shoving aside the kind of grateful she felt for Kellen's experience with children. Finally, he lifted his head. "Really?"

Kellen smiled, warm, reassuring, and heart-stoppingly sexy. "Yep. It's true. That's why I can see Marcella just like you. So I just want you to know, I understand what it's like to feel different from everyone else and not want to talk about it. But if you do decide you want to talk about it, anytime day or night, you just have your grandma bring you over here. Okay?"

Carlos said nothing, but his eyes cleared a bit, most likely in relief. Then he laid his head on Kellen's shoulder and closed his eyes once more, sending Marcella one last sleepy gaze before he yawned and fell asleep.

"You're really great with kids," she remarked, fighting a stab of jealousy.

"My job required it."

Her eyes softened when she saw his jaw stiffen. "You miss it, don't you?"

"Every day. But this ghost gig's made it almost impossible to function."

"Because they can touch you."

"Yeah. I can't very well preach to the kids about talking things out if I'm showing up to class with black eyes and lumps the size of Detroit on my head. The PTA just wasn't buying my bullshit about boxing lessons," he said with a sarcastic tint to his words, tucking Carlos closer to him.

Marcella bit the inside of her lip. So maybe the sexy man baby-holding thing had merit. Kellen was like a different person with Carlos. He related to him in a way she not only admired but aspired to.

Oh. God. She had not just wished she could relate to a child. *Ah, but you did. In fact, you felt a feeling quite natural for all women. Say it isn't so, Marcella. Say you're not growing a sensitive bone.*

The hell. She was just being decent. Yet when she looked at

Carlos, snuggled against the hard muscle of Kellen's chest, she wanted to throw her arms around them both, take protective measures so no one would ever harm them. Feed them milk and cookies she'd baked, watch them throw a baseball back and forth in the park . . .

Out, out, out! She needed to get the fuck out of here.

As she pondered what to do about Carlos, and how to do it before she could run back to Plane Dismal as fast as her ghostliness would allow her, someone burst through the door of the store.

"What the hell happened?"

"Oh. Look. G.I. Joe Demon," Marcella remarked with wooden sarcasm.

Kellen's face brightened in the way it had when he'd seen Catalina earlier, piercing Marcella's heart as though he'd shot an arrow directly through it. "How did you know anything at all happened?" he asked, clearly surprised.

She stomped in her work boots, none too ladylike, Marcella noted, toward Kellen and Carlos. "I told you how it works, Kell. I get this sort of eerie vibe going. Sometimes it wakes me up out of a sound sleep. I can sense the intent for"—she leaned in to Kellen's ear and whispered, for Carlos's benefit—"demonic possession. So what can I do to help?"

Move to the Ukraine? Marcella rolled her eyes upward.

Catalina gazed down at Carlos and gave a half smile, ruffling his hair. "So what happened?"

"I think Carlos has the gift. In fact, I know he does because he can see Marcella, too. Though I haven't exactly pinpointed when he saw her."

Catalina gave Kellen a cocky grin. "Isn't it funny how just about everything in your life leads back to Marcella? Before, I might have been inclined to think it just had to do with your fantas—"

Kellen was up and on his feet in a split second, interrupting Catalina. He cocked his head in Marcella's direction. "She's here," he said, and it sounded like a warning.

"Oh. Cool." Catalina's mouth clamped shut, but her gorgeous eyes scanned the room. "So, uh, heyyy," she called out.

Yeah. Hey. Marcella flipped her the bird from behind the hutch.

Kellen gave her his stern teacher's face before returning his attention to Catalina. "Anyway, it seems Carlos can see ghosts, but what just happened here was no ghost. Marcella called him Abbadon."

Catalina's tongue clucked. "Hoo, shit. He's a scary bastard, but mostly a minion. He appears in the most disgusting of ways, but he's not winning any contests for most demonic. I will say this was probably some kind of warning. What about or why they'd be stalking a little kid, I have no clue."

"Do you think you can find something out?"

"Oh, I'm definitely in. None of those fuckers'll be scaring little kids on my watch, if I can help it."

How philanthropic. Mother Teresa demon. She had a closet full of hats. But in the interest of helping Carlos, Marcella decided she was all about sharing info. "Tell her I got a warning from another ghost earlier, too, about Carlos. All he said was they want him. I don't know who they are or what it means."

Kellen relayed Marcella's words to Catalina while she listened with a frown marring her beautifully smooth forehead. "Who gave you this message, Marcella?"

"He's someone I know on the plane I've been forced to roam and very reliable. The problem is, when he's earthbound, he can't talk unless he possesses a body. Unfortunately, he possessed a drunk and couldn't get a whole thought out without falling into a drunken stupor."

As Kellen passed the message on, he swayed to and fro, rubbing Carlos's back with the palm of his hand in a circular motion. Marcella found herself swaying with him, fighting a sigh of contentment.

Catalina swung her arms back and forth, smacking her fists together, her mouth becoming a thin line. "Okay, then. I'm on this. Let me see what I can see. In the meantime, keep track of the kid. Abbadon is a clear message. He showed up and no one summoned him. Carlos has something those ass lickers in Hell want. That, my friend, scares the shit out of me. So I'm out. I'll be in touch." Jamming her unmanicured fingers into the pockets of her jeans, Catalina disappeared.

Marcella's stomach sank like a rock thrown carelessly in a pond. Catalina obviously knew her way around the demon world and, just as she'd surmised, Abbadon showing up was a bad sign.

Kellen nudged her from her worry with his shoulder. "You okay?"

"I'm fine. It's not me we should worry about. It's Carlos here. What could Lucifer want with a child?"

His look was fierce when he returned her gaze. "I don't know, but I can tell you this much, I'll be damned if I'll let him get his hands on him."

"I'm right there with you," she agreed, her eyes softening when they fell on Carlos's sleeping form.

"So the ex-demon has a heart."

"No. Having a heart would mean I cared, and we both know your views on that, now, don't we?" She knew she was being petty and spiteful, but it was what worked for them. There was no reason it shouldn't keep right on working.

But Kellen didn't fire back. "Views change. Opinions do, too."

How deflating. "Did you find Jesus?"

"I don't get your meaning."

"Have you gone all spiritual on me?"

"No."

"Drugs? Pharmaceuticals?"

"Not today. Though I think after what just happened, I wouldn't knock drowning myself in a bottle of booze."

"Are you doing some sort of lame find-your-center exercises, like yoga?"

"Get to the point."

"Lay off the do-gooder crap. It's knocking me off balance, and I think it's obvious"—she spread her arms wide, looking down at her sandal-clad feet hovering two feet above the floor—"I could use some balance."

"I'm just pointing out that time and perspective can change an opinion."

Where was this coming from? This sudden understanding? "Thank you, Gandhi. Now lay off the introspective malarkey. It's born out of pity, and I don't need your pity."

Kellen's hazel eyes pinned hers, but they didn't have the usual hint of malice in them, making her insides go all marshmallowy. "I don't pity you, Marcella."

Well, I pity me. Who wouldn't pity this hot mess? "I'm elated. And now I'm out. I'm going to see if I can find out something more about what's going down with Carlos—so stop dreaming me up. And if you can't manage to keep from visualizing me, can I at least have on something in silk when you do?"

Those eyes, which had a softer shade to them a moment ago, once more narrowed.

Nice.

They were back on the path of mutually satisfying mutilation.

With that, she floated out of the store and away.

Yet as she slipped through the front of the store, her last look at Carlos sleeping on Kellen's shoulder grabbed at her heart once more. If she had to pinpoint the emotion eating a hole in her heart, she'd call it longing.

She'd also call it ridiculous. Marcella Acosta didn't long.

Wouldn't.

Ever.

six

Catalina stomped through the ultraswank men's clothing store, leaving a trail of muddy work boot footprints in her wake, oblivious to the snobbishly outraged gasps and stares that followed her.

She eyed her mark at twenty paces and went in for the kill with a hand to the gun at her belt. "Got any thoughts on where Dameal is?" Catalina asked her sometime nemesis, sometime ally, all-around burr in her saddle, Vassago.

He brushed the shoulder of his immaculate black suit, pretending he wasn't intimidated. "Oh, silly. How should I know where Dameal is? And why, pray tell, do you care?"

Her jaw clenched as she rounded on him, cornering him against a rack of men's silk trousers. "I don't care about *him*. I care about what he knows."

Vassago wrinkled his nose at her and gave her a deliberately facetious smile, cocking his carefully waxed eyebrow. "Oh, you do, too, care about him. Don't play coy with me. Are you planning on reconciliation? How romantic. But wait. You can't reconcile. You do remember that little clause in your relationship, don't you? Of course you do. Though, I have to say, not having the two of you screaming down the halls of Hell has been a blessing. So what gives? Spill, sister."

Her right eye twitched in irritation. "V, I'll only warn you once and then I'll start at your knees, and while I might not kill you, I'll jack you up so you won't be attending any possessions for at least a month. So spew, demon."

He held his hands up in resignation, his human form turning a chalky white. "What do you want to know?"

"Dameal is Abbadon's level boss, right?"

He nodded his sleek, black head while he straightened a pair of gray slacks. "Yes, indeedy. So?"

"So I need to know why he ordered him to terrorize some little kid."

"Oooh," he cooed with twisted glee, clapping his hands together. "Who's the kid?"

She snorted, startling the few patrons in the cool interior of the store with the sharp escape from her throat. "I'd rather be bathed in salt while prisms are dangled over my eyeballs than tell you. Just tell me if you've seen Dameal, and I'm off your back."

"Will you stay out of my possessions?" he baited.

"Not likely. But I will set your superfly man-pants with the perfect crease in 'em on fire right here in front of everyone in Barneys if you don't tell me."

He looked down at that very perfect crease in his trousers and cringed. "Fine. The last time I saw him was about a month ago. I don't know what good knowing where he is will do you anyway.

Didn't we just go over this? He can't talk to you. Like, literally, and that's no one's fault but your own."

Fuck. That was true. In her anger over little Carlos, she'd forgotten her predicament with Dameal. The predicament that had left her a demon. The one that that lying, cheating, Lucifer-loving fuck had left her in. "Then send him a message—tell him to tell his freaky fucks if they come near the kid, they'll deal with me and my righteous indignation."

"Shhh, Catalina!" Vassago warned. "We're in public. Behave as such. Do you want to get me fired?"

"Since when do you need a job?"

"FYI, Miss Traitor, do you have any clue the kind of corruption you can find in a clothing store of this caliber? It's a virtual playground of sin and iniquity with jaded monkey bars and a seesaw just dripping with wickedness. You'd know that if you were a proper demon. I won't let you spoil it for me because you have no class." He flapped a hand in the direction of the exit. "Now go stalk some other demon just trying to get ahead on the ladder of success. Your trail of muddy footprints will lead you back to the door."

Standing on her toes, she whispered up at him, "You remember what I said. Tell Dameal to order his lackeys to back off, or the next possession I thwart won't be with some prissy box of salt."

"Very *Terminator 2*," he said dryly. "I'll tell him. Now go away."

Catalina stomped her way back out of the store with an angry growl at anyone who dared to look in her direction.

Dameal was her only connection to this mess with Carlos. He ran the ninth level of Hell, and Abbadon was most definitely on his watch.

To her knowledge, as vile, despicable, and bathed from head to toe in scum as Dameal was, he never fucked with the heads of little kids.

But maybe he'd sunk further than even she could have anticipated. And while that shouldn't still sting—it did.

It damned well did.

"Marcella?"

"Surprise."

"Do me a favor, would you?"

"I'll take it into consideration."

"Could you not hover? It's unnerving when I'm trying to sleep."

"Could you not keep visualizing me every time you close your eyes? But thank you for at least putting me in something better than cotton while you do it."

He grunted from beneath his pillow, muffled and low.

"Is Carlos all right? Did Catalina get back to you with any information?" She hadn't been able to breathe since leaving him behind earlier. This foreign emotion troubled her even more than crying did. But she had to know.

Moving the pillow aside, he gazed up at her with heavy-lidded eyes. Sleepy, and yummily sexy. "Everything's okay for now, I think. He was pretty shook up, but I told him Catalina would make sure no one bothered him. She offered to keep an eye on him for me while I figure this out. But Mrs. Ramirez . . . I don't know. I think she wore a hole through her rosary in blessings alone."

For someone without the gift, and who was as religious as Mrs. Ramirez, something as devastating and frightening as a demon showing up meant a surefire trip to church to light candles. "Does she understand what's happening with Carlos? Is she a believer? Or is there going to have to be some serious convincing on your part?"

"She's always known Delaney 'thought' she talked to ghosts. I know she's seen some odd things because Delaney told me she has, but they were ghost things—cute pranks, moving stuff around the room—not lightning-hurling, red-eyed glowing monsters showing up out of nowhere. Today I think she became a whole lot less skeptical. Though she attributed none of what went down today to Carlos's having a gift. She's put that blame squarely on me, and I didn't tell her otherwise or she'd be dragging Carlos to the nearest church to have a proper exorcism before you could say 'enchilada.'

"I'm not hip to the idea that we should give her the big picture just yet. At least not until we can figure out what a demon wants with Carlos. He's frightened enough as it is. His grandmother's reaction may only make an already dramatic situation that much scarier for him. Right now my priority is to find out why a demon showed up with the specific intent of getting hold of Carlos."

Marcella's head shook, still in disbelief. "I wish I had more to give you than I did earlier, but I don't. My contact has apparently dried up, and I can't summon so much as a good manicurist, let alone some of my old demon acquaintances. If they were reluctant to talk to me before, they'll definitely stay as far away as they can once Abbadon tattles like the candy-ass he is." Her sigh was forlorn. She'd been unable to find Darwin again, the only hope she had for more information at this point. "So have you been able to find anything out? Any ghosts showing up to maybe pass on a message from the great beyond?"

"Nope. It's been eerily quiet."

That statement irritated her. If he were the sensitive medium D had been, ghosts would be showing up left and right to help, thus allowing her to grill them mercilessly. "That's because you're no Delaney. If you were more like her, we'd have a leg up on helping that poor child."

Kellen eyeballed her from his place on the bed, letting the covers fall to his waist as he rose on his elbows, stirring Vern and Shirley who lay curled together in a big ball of multicolored fur. Instead of taking the shot she'd so graciously offered him, he said, "You're right. D was a much better medium."

Damn right. Wait, had he agreed with her? Wasn't that the second time in a matter of days? Oh, God. For sure they were doomed.

"Are you okay after today?"

And now he was inquiring after her? Her head tilted to the right. "I've never been better. There's nothing like drifting aimlessly with absolutely no purpose and no way to get back home in a dress meant for Holly Hobbie while I look for clues as to why demons are literally hunting a small child. But that doesn't trouble me nearly as much as this. I want to know what the hell's gotten into you. You've never asked me, in all the time you've known me, if I was okay. Has communicating with the dead made you go soft and squishy, or what? You're not nearly the snark-o-rama you once were."

His response, easy and calm, left her worried. "I'm not nearly as motivated as I once was."

Her glance was skeptical and discomfited. "Because?"

The shrug of his taut shoulders covered in nothing but his ruddy skin made her mouth water. "Like I said, things change. People change."

She didn't like this new Kellen. The old one was less of a mystery and way more fun to rile. "Well, stop it. I don't like change, and I definitely don't like you asking me if I'm okay. It screws up my natural order of things. I like you much better when you're being a toad."

"Did you know that a toad can catch as many as ten thousand insects in one summer?" He smiled, all friendly and conversational.

"I think I've waited all my life to know that, Bill Nye."

"Then it's been a long time coming, eh?" he teased, but again, without the hard edge to it of snarks gone by, thus baffling her. What could have happened in just a couple of days to change an opinion he'd had for a decade?

"Yeah. And I'm pretty hot for seventy-six. You know it, and I know it. Which is why I'm here, I'm guessing. Because I'm hot and you obviously can't stop thinking about me."

"That's true," he admitted, folding his arms behind his head without a hint of malice.

His statement left her crashing to the bed. A bed she didn't fall through, but instead landed directly on top of. She'd only been bluffing because it soothed her ego to make him uncomfortable. He might think she was hot, but he *liked* that floozy Catalina. The like in the equation had become more important to her than the hot.

She clenched her fists against the cool cotton of his broadly striped bedspread. The feel of Kellen's sheets was euphoric and not just because they were his, but because she could touch them, run her fingers over the stiff cotton.

Heh.

Things were looking up.

Sliding up to the head of the bed, Kellen moved over to allow her room to sit beside him. He patted the edge of the bed, where she planted her doubtful ass. Cocking his head, he acknowledged her fists clenched around the sheets. "So I see things are improving."

"In leaps and bounds. Soon I'll be able to clutch a Pier 1 candlestick in my grubby paws and clobber you over the head with it," she drawled, letting her eyes go all challenging.

"I'd deserve it."

Such a givah. Her jaw lifted. "Did Delaney threaten you?"

"Why would she threaten me?"

"Did she tell you you have to play nice until she can figure out how to get me earthbound again or she'd take away your Discovery Channel privileges? Maybe your Bunsen burner?"

His chuckle came out in a husky, sleepy rumble, lifting the sheet that was rapidly falling to his tapered waist. "Nope. I haven't spoken to Delaney since we saw her the other day."

"Then what's with all the understanding, sympathetic mumbo jumbo? You hate me. I hate you. Like Barney in reverse. We go a few rounds, retreat, only to do it again in the future. Fight back, already."

Raising his knees, he laid his elbows on them and shook his head, the chestnut gleam of his hair highlighted by the moon spilling in from the bedroom window. "I'm not interested in fighting anymore, Marcella."

How unfun. She couldn't keep her distance if he was nice. "We always fight, Kellen. It's what we do. I call you an old, cranky man. You call me a whore with fireballs. It's what defines us." She circled the circumference of their space with a finger.

Kellen leaned forward, pinning her with his gaze. "That's not what defines you, Marcella. And if it's what defines *us*, our relationship, then that's going to change. At least on my behalf."

"Weenie."

"Are we free-associating?"

Now it wasn't just important to rile him, it was her mission. Whatever had brought about this change in his attitude toward her was unsettling her to the core. If he was kind to her, generous even, she'd never be able to go back to Plane Dismal and summon up the kind of hatred she'd need to sustain her for eternity. Unpleasant memories were always much easier to grudge with. Though she'd crushed on him, she'd taken solace in the idea that he despised her, and there was no changing that. This new, gooey soft center he'd acquired would leave her with visuals of his smile, warm and with perfectly straight teeth. It would make her heart ache if she had to remember his eyes going all gentle and understanding instead of hard like chips of granite.

And she wouldn't have it.

Marcella knelt on the bed, pushing his knees down, bracketing his shoulders with her hands until they were eye to eye. "Whatever this is about, knock it off. You know as well as I do it can't last. I'll do something so heinous you'll only end up disappointed. So let's get it on. We had a rhythm of snark. I don't want to miss a beat."

His steady intake of breath hitched when she sunk the heels of her hands into the bed, leaving her cleavage just beneath his chin. She sent him a cocky glance as if to prove she had him right where she wanted him.

But then his hands wrapped around her wrists in a steel grip, twisting them behind her waist, and he flipped her to her back with the ease of a trained wrestler.

Kellen was on top of her before she could catch her breath, laying his solid weight against hers, her nipples brushing against the hot skin of his chest. When he moved closer, it was to let his lips hover so near hers she grew dizzy from the need to lift her head but an inch and clamp her mouth to his. "I say we talk about who you really are, Marcella. The real you. Not the one you've let everyone believe is you. And I can wait—all night if I have to."

Marcella struggled beneath him, but it only made her thrusting against the hardness of him that much more unbearable. The muscled length of his legs, lying flat out on hers, the fine hairs that sprinkled his upper thighs, tickled her flesh. "Get—off—of—me, you buffoon!"

"Or what?" he teased, his eyes flashing all sorts of challenges.

"I dunno, but it'll be bad," she heaved. "Uglier than ugly."

He chuckled again, the vibrating rumble spreading from her chest to her toes. "Talk to me, Marcella. Tell me how you ended up a demon."

Her chest tightened at his request. No. She never spoke of it. Never. And she wasn't going to start now. It made her hands clammy and her mouth dry.

Raising an eyebrow, she gave him a bored look. "Well, that's easy. I was swayed by the dark side. You know—money, fame, fabulous boobs for all eternity. The norm. It paid off, don't you agree?" She wiggled her body beneath him to express just how well it had paid off.

"Nice. Now the truth," he demanded with a hint of the old hard-edged tone he'd always reserved just for her.

"That is the truth, ignoramus. You know what it comes down to when you die. You make a choice. I made mine."

"How did you die?"

"Neiman Marcus fire sale. I was trampled in the rush to get to the half-off designer shoe rack. A pity, too. I would have rocked those heels. I have great legs." To emphasize her point, she ran a calf along the length of his leg, wrapping it enticingly around his waist.

Kellen lowered his head, grazing his lips against her ear. "Did Neiman Marcus have fire sales in the dinosaur age?"

Jerking her head away from the hot, sweet feel of his breath against her ear, she spat out of the side of her mouth, "They were woolly mammoth–skin wedges with these cute little strappy things that went up over your calves. All the rage way back when, in the days of yore."

"And in the days of yore, what was your life like? How old were you when you made this choice you seem so determined to prove you made?"

She bit her tongue—hard—and it wasn't only because she didn't want to dredge up the kind of pain her past wrought, but because this brick shithouse of a man was putting the kind of hurt on her that set her skin on fire and her toes curling. Not to mention her girlie bits. They, too, heard the sweet strains of violins playing.

"I've got all night, Marcella," he crooned against the column of her neck.

"Yeah? Well, I've got all of eternity," she shot back with dry sarcasm.

"Then we'd better get comfortable," he offered, settling on top of her with a grunt. "Because you're not going anywhere until I have some answers." Plopping his head on her shoulder, he inhaled deeply.

Fury tickled her spine, and other things tickled her ovaries. "Why the fuck do you care how I became a demon or what my life was like before I was dead? What difference does it make now?"

Kellen's head popped up again, his hazel eyes playful. "You know, when you swear, it's a little hot. Add in that accent you try so hard to hide, and you're officially smokin'. I'm just throwin' that out there. Now, there's a reason you've kept your death and afterlife a secret. I have every intention of finding out what it is."

"For what purpose?"

"Call me curious."

"I'm much more at ease with fucktard."

His lips whispered over her shoulder, making her jump. "The way you roll your *r*'s is hot, too."

"The way I roll you won't be hot at all if you don't get off me!" She lifted her hips with a hard shove, only to encounter the rigid line of his shaft, hard and pulsing. A groan slipped off her tongue before she had the chance to beat it into submission.

Kellen heard the hiss of it and acknowledged her yearning by rolling his hips into hers.

The awareness between them became thick, as though it had a life of its own, swirling in the air they inhaled with shuddering breaths. Lifetimes passed in the still of that moment. Her heart thrashing inside her chest, her eyes clung to his, knowing he felt the spark, too.

She watched Kellen war with his lust, turn it over in his mind, measure the consequences, just before he lowered his lips, so full and delicious, to hers.

That was his first mistake. The second was the notion she was going to let him plant those decadently fine lips on hers and get away with it. She'd never survive that memory. Marcella let her body go slack as if acquiescence was something she could no longer fight. When he sank into her, relaxing his body, she shoved him with a jolt of her palms against his shoulders. The slap of her hands against his flesh was enough of a shock for him to move just enough for her to wiggle out from under him and rise to the ceiling. "I don't owe you explanations, Kellen, and you have no right to ask for them," she seethed. "You never bothered to ask before, don't bother now!"

Rising up, he sat at the edge of the bed in nothing but his boxer briefs. She had to avert her eyes to avoid the memory of all that luscious man just waiting for the taking. "Would you have told me if I'd asked?"

No. She probably wouldn't have. Score one for the living. "That point is moot after all this time. And quit with the counselor-type questions. What happened to me, my choices, they're no one's business but mine. Now go to sleep and stop thinking me up in your perverted little fantasies about naughty demons gone wild. I can't get away to try to find anything out if you keep dragging me back here. We have to figure out how to protect Carlos."

There was no shame in his gaze, no hint that he was embarrassed. In fact, he smiled a wide grin, infuriatingly so. "Teachers."

"*What?*"

"My fantasies have nothing to do with demons."

"I believe I've pointed out the scholarly ones are always the kinkiest."

He chuckled before sliding back between the sheets, Vern and Shirley curling up against the shelter of his side. "'Night, Marcella."

"Good night," she whispered, disappearing into the bedroom wall and out into the storefront before she threw herself at his mercy and sang like a canary.

Melancholy struck her when she passed Delaney's herb catalog, lying open by the cash register. She missed her friend. These conflicting emotions about Carlos and Kellen were worthy of a good BFF powwow.

She lingered but a moment before clearing the front door and whisking her way to the park. Her favorite place to sit and think and wait in the hope that Darwin would reappear.

The wind was brisk when she slunk down onto what she'd dubbed her thinking chair. It whipped her hair around her face, whistling through the deep plum-colored night.

Maybe if she made the rounds of some of her old haunts, she could get someone to squeal like the wee little piggies they were. But that was a dangerous proposition without any demonic power to back her up. She didn't know a whole lot about ghosts, but risking being banished somewhere that wouldn't allow her to get back here would be foolish.

"Yo, yo, yo, babyyy," a voice cackled from behind her left shoulder.

Marcella froze.

"Wha's good, mama? Hey, you got any cash you could spare?"

Turning around, her gaze leveled at a young boy. Maybe no more than twenty. His gold-capped teeth flashed in the streetlamp when he gave her a malicious grin. The fist he'd propped on the top of the bench held a shiny knife. His eyes were wide, scanning the park wildly, and his pupils were dilated.

She sighed. "Darwin?"

"Tha's right, my sistah. In somebody else's flesh."

"Where the hell have you been?"

His jittery, evasive response made her wince. "Around, and I ain't been nowhere near that Rodriguez dude, copper. And tha's all I'm sayin'. I ain't no narc."

The guilty response and paranoid sweep of his eyes made her roll hers. With two fingers, she opened his right eye wide and gazed into it. "Are you high?"

"As a fuckin' kite, *chiquita*. I don't mind sayin', i's aaa'ight, too. Crack's underrated. E'rebody should do it. Just e'rebody. World would be boot-i-ful. No doubt."

Flicking him in the side of the head, she pursed her lips at him. "Pull your pants up right now, you heathen, and come sit down. I need your help. And put that knife away before you hurt someone."

Hopping over the back of the bench, he took his place beside her, using the knife to dig dirt from beneath his greasy fingernails. "So wha's up, pretty lady?"

"Why do you keep possessing only chemically dependent bodies? It's disgusting, and stop leering at my hooters. Isn't there a nice little old lady's body you can find?"

"Not at this time of night. Only druggies and drunks hang out here this late." He flung an arm around her shoulder with an awkward, jarring thunk, pulling her flush to his side.

"If you don't take your arm off me, I'll gnaw it off with my teeth. Now try to get past your crack-induced delusions to pay attention. I need your help. A little boy needs your help."

He made a smacking noise from between his chapped lips. "Yeah. I know dat, fo sho."

"What were you going to tell me before you passed out yesterday? I need to know what you meant when you said they want Carlos."

A metaphoric light went off over his stained do-rag–covered head. "Oh, snap—yeah. Tha's some badass crap gonna go down."

Fear shot through her veins. "With Carlos?"

He sat up ramrod straight, rocking back and forth as he slapped his fingers on his thighs to a rhythm only he could hear in his head. "Dude, yeah. I don't know the particulars. Just know what I told ya. I heard rumblings from some demons, and they say the little boy's important to someone. I heard the kid's name, but I got the hell outta there before they saw me. I don't need no demon shit breathing down my back."

Important? Because he could see dead people? "I don't get it, Darwin. There are plenty of legit mediums, and demons aren't beating down their doors to stop them from doing anything."

He threw his hands up, palms forward. "Heyyy, quit puttin' the heat on me, sistah. I told ya what I know. Now, about that cash . . ." His eyes lowered to the front of her dress again.

"Darwin?"

"Yeah?"

She wrapped her index finger and thumb around his nose and lifted his head, forcing him to look into her eyes. Eyes that held a plea she hoped would penetrate his hyperawareness. "Stop looking down my dress and get out of this body. Go back to that hell-hole plane and get me some answers. Do it discreetly, and do it now. Meet me back here tomorrow night when no one's around, and for the love of Christ, try to find a nice, clean, *sober* hooker to possess. I *need* you to do this for me, Darwin. Please. I'll never ask you to do another thing again, but we need your help. Kellen needs your help."

Darwin popped up from the bench as though he were going to make his exit, but he whipped back around. "Sheee-it! There was something else I heard, too."

"What? What else did you hear?"

Bending at the waist, he cupped his head in his skinny hands—hands that trembled. "Hold on. Lemme think. Fuck if this shit doesn't make your brain move at warp speed."

Marcella sprang to her feet, placing a comforting hand on Darwin's back, reflecting on how touching things on this plane had become easier and easier. "Tell me how I can help."

"There's a box. A box, a box, a box!" he yelled triumphantly, frenetically.

"A box? A box that has to do with Carlos?"

"Yep, that's it. A box with something bad in it. Tha's what I heard. Tha's *all* I heard, lady. Don't try to squeeze me for nuthin' else. You can't make me talk, copper!" He began to back away, slinking into the dark night thick with the smells of the city. The sound of police sirens off in the distance left her with nothing but the echo of his sneakered feet, beating a frantic path away from the park.

What could he possibly mean? A box. A box with something bad in it. It made no sense to her. Where was this box?

Maybe the crack was confusing him.

But then a glimmer of a memory from long, long ago whooshed through her brain like a freight train out of control.

A box.

There was once a box. A box with something bad in it.
Oh, holy mother of all things unholy.
No.
Jesus, please.
No.

seven

Marcella flew through the doors of the store the moment day broke, surprised to find Kellen awake and pacing in front of a man who was vaguely familiar. She'd battled the remainder of the night over whether she should tell Kellen what Darwin had shared last night. She couldn't even be positive what he'd shared was accurate due to his drug-induced state. But that message about the box had scared the ghostly shit out of her. How it related to Carlos had her baffled, but she intended to find out if it meant anything at all.

She peered around Kellen's shoulder, fighting the impulse to inhale his freshly washed hair curling over the back of his neck. His hooded sweatshirt and low-slung jeans, comfortable and worn, gave bow-chick-a-wow-wow a whole new meaning. That lingering sharp jab her heart experienced each time she saw him as of late returned full throttle. "Fashion consultant?"

When he turned to face her, he smiled. It had a welcoming glow attached to it that left her breathless. "Hey, how was your night?"

Marcella scowled in return. "You care why?"

"Because it's nice to inquire after someone when you're maintaining a healthy relationship." As the words left his mouth, Marcella saw the tic in his jaw jump. Just a little, but jump it did. He could still be egged on if she just kept pushing.

Good times.

She'd decided last night she wasn't going to make her stay here on this plane easy for him. They weren't going to be friends. They weren't going to smile fondly over old times as they forged new ones. The further she pushed him away, the less likely he'd be interested in dragging her past out of her. "How sunshiny. My nights are all the same, thanks to you, you suck-ass. That translates to, I have no nights, and no days either. I don't sleep. I don't eat. I just drift. So thanks. Buttloads. If you hadn't thought me up, I'd be off spreading my cheer and goodwill to a bunch of lame undecideds."

"And unable to help Carlos."

"I wouldn't know Carlos existed if you hadn't sucked me into this mess."

"Then accept my deepest, most heartfelt apologies."

Cocking an eyebrow, she tilted her chin up and gave him a haughty glare. "No."

His wide shoulders shrugged affably. "Suit yourself. Right now I have bigger problems." Pointing to the agitated ghost in the corner, Kellen ran a hand of frustration through his hair. "He's been here for over an hour, dancing around, repeating something I can't make head or tail of. I don't even know who he is. The only thing I can pinpoint is he definitely has that John Travolta move down to a science."

"That's because you're a child." Marcella eyed the man and his outfit, a metallic copper shirt, open to his waist, tucked into tight, white pants.

"Compared to you, Methuselah, I suppose some might see it that way."

She almost grinned—because this was familiar, welcome even. A warmth spread through her, but she managed to contain her smile of fond familiarity. "You really don't know who that is?"

"Not a clue."

"You know why that is, Kellen?"

"Why is that, Marcella?"

"Because you spend too much time watching the Golf Channel."

"That's not one hundred percent true. Sometimes I get cagey and watch entire marathons on the Food Network."

"It's Maurice Gibb. You know, the Bee Gees?"

"The who?"

Her sigh was put-upon. "The Bee Gees. 'Stayin' Alive'? You know, the aforementioned John Travolta?"

His handsome face was blank. Still beautiful, but blank.

"Forget it. Did you ever do anything fun, or did you spend all of your teenage years dissecting poor frogs and studying the Earth's crust?"

The spot on the right side of his jaw began to pulse, meaning he'd begun to simmer. "Excuse me. I'm an assload of fun."

"Do they tell you that at the senior citizens' center?"

The twitch of his jaw came as fast as it went. His hard face relaxed again, and he slapped a placid mask on. "Every Wednesday at eight when I give my dissertation on global warming. You don't know what you're missing. Standing ovations as far as the eye can see."

The giggle that fled her lips burst out before she could stop it. "Whatever. The Bee Gees were huge in the seventies. I'll chalk up your not knowing that to your youth and the fact that you come from another dimension, where music and dancing are considered frivolous and the work of the devil. So let me see if I can figure out what he wants."

"You go, Dancing Queen," Kellen quipped, sweeping a hand in front of him to signify Maurice was all hers.

From a distance, she could see Maurice's lips move fervently, but she couldn't make out what he was saying while he jabbed a finger up in the air, then plunged it down to his waist to the music in his head. His copper shirt, unbuttoned to the waist, and his tight, white pants made Marcella grin. "Maybe he'd be able to communicate better if his pants weren't so tight. It's got to make it hard to think." She sighed wistfully. She'd done her share of the Hustle in clubs all over New York back in the day. "I so miss platforms and picking out my hair." She tugged a tendril, letting it curl around her finger.

Sauntering toward him, Marcella watched his lips move more closely. She gave him a saucy wink as he twirled. "So, Maurice. What brings you to our corner of this plane?"

When she caught his attention, Marcella couldn't help but wonder at the look of relief on his face at seeing her. Maurice looked as though he'd been waiting on her forever by the way he threw his hands up in the air in a gesture that said "it's about damned time."

He gave her a sad gaze, filled with pity, and pointed a finger at her chest. "How can you mend a broken heart?"

Marcella clapped, pulling her hands to her chest with a smile. "That was a good one, but by far my favorite from that soundtrack has to be 'More Than a Woman.' In fact, I'd venture to say it could've been my theme song. I was quite the viper until just recently."

Maurice shook his head in exasperation that bordered on angry. Once more, he pointed a finger that smacked of accusation. "Jive talkin'," he spat out.

She experienced a jolt of defensiveness when he threw the song title out with such a bitterly harsh ring to it. "Hey! Don't get all huffy with me, crooner. I'm just trying to help. You know, I was a big fan of the Bee Gees, and I had an übercrush on Andy. Don't be so cranky."

Kellen hovered near her ear, his lips but a fraction from touching the outer shell of it. "Well, Miss Sensitive and Nurturing, do you see what I'm up against? You don't have the patience for this any more than I do."

But then a thought hit her. She held up a finger to Kellen's lips. "Wait. Maybe what he's trying to tell us has nothing to do with him, and everything to do with what's going on right now. I remember D telling me that while the whole thing with Clyde was going down, ghosts kept showing up and giving her clues that they didn't realize pertained to Clyde's predicament until later. So maybe what Joe was spewing—the monkey business thing—and whatever Maurice wants have to do with Carlos."

Maurice began to jump up and down with a frantic gesture that made his comb-over flap. "*'Tragedy'!*" The syllables echoed around the room, ominous, anxious, coming in stuttering waves.

Marcella blanched, barely able to find the words to speak. "There's going to be a tragedy?" she squeaked. "With Carlos?"

His head bobbed up and down with furious jabs.

Fear clutched her heart. "I need more than that, Maurice. I need you to tell me what's going to happen to Carlos. Who's jive talkin'? For that matter, whose broken heart needs to mend?"

While Kellen grabbed a pen from the counter and scribbled the titles on a piece of stray paper, shoving it into the pocket of his jeans, Maurice's image began to flutter.

"No, wait!" Marcella shouted, chasing after Maurice's disappearing form. "Come back! God damn it, I'll never watch *Saturday Night Fever* again if you don't get your ass back here!" She stomped her foot when he slipped away completely. Kellen came to stand behind her, placing his warm hands on her shoulders with a reassuring touch. She so wanted to curl against him and sob in the shelter of his broad shoulder.

"We'll figure it out, I promise," he said, though he didn't sound like he believed it. Pulling the paper back out of his pocket, Kellen ran his fingers over his wrinkled brow as he stared down at the song titles. They sprawled across the paper, menacing and ugly. Tragedy. What did it mean?

"Fuck. I don't like the sound of this. I'm worried about Carlos." Marcella let go of a shuddering breath, wrapping her arms around her waist. "Me, too."

Brushing a chunk of her hair over her shoulder, he asked, "Who'd have thought, Marcella Acosta?"

She didn't like the sentimental tone to his voice or the way her heart went soft like room-temperature butter at his touch. "Thought what?"

"That you'd get so wrapped up in a frightened little boy."

Certainly not her . . . She bristled. "Please. I'm not wrapped up. I'm involved by proxy and because you couldn't help but be a pansy-ass where your sister's concerned. I have nothing better to do with my time. God knows I can't shop, so I may as well try to help Carlos."

His pessimistic glance made her harden her eyes. "Right. I saw how indifferent you were to his snotty charms while you cooed at him over my shoulder all sweet and maternal. And that brings me to a question. How did you end up meeting Carlos? In the chaos, we never got around to establishing that."

She shrugged her shoulders in what she hoped appeared as indifference, brushing his heated hands away as she did. "When you were kissing Delaney's ass at her house and I disappeared—I ended up in Carlos's bedroom. I have no idea how it happened. It seems I have no control when I'm sucked from one place to another. If only someone would suck me into the nearest designer boutique."

"This means something, Marcella. So far you've only been summoned by someone with the gift of sight who's been thinking about you."

"I'd venture to guess Carlos wasn't thinking about me in cheap lingerie," she said dryly.

He gave her a shameless, lascivious smile. "Touché."

She rolled her eyes. He was back to not biting again. "Then explain why a kid, one I don't even know and never saw before a couple of days ago, is thinking me up."

"I don't know, but somehow you're involved in this."

"That brings me to why I'm here at the butt crack of dawn. Last night I hooked up with my contact again—"

"Who is this contact, Marcella?"

"If I told you, even with all the ghosts and demons that run amok in your life, you'd never believe it. Anyway, he said there's some kind of box involved in this thing with Carlos and it's bad." Stopping there, she watched him assimilate the information. She couldn't—*wouldn't*—let herself speculate on this box until she had solid proof of its existence.

Kellen frowned. Leaning against the counter, he steepled his hands over his lips. "A box? Do you know what that means?"

The ringing of the phone saved her from answering his probing question. No one needed to panic until it was absolutely necessary.

After a brief conversation, he clicked the off button on the phone with a grimace. "That was Mrs. Ramirez."

Instantly, fear clutched at her gut. "Is Carlos all right?" She knew her tone only verified his earlier statement, but she didn't care. This strange pull, this odd connection to Carlos left her with no room to hide her emotions.

"He's fine, but his mother's in some serious shit."

Marcella had never given thought to his mother. "His mother?"

"Mrs. Ramirez says she's in jail. She asked if I'd watch Carlos for her so she can go bail her out."

Jail? How could a sweet woman like Mrs. Ramirez have a daughter capable of landing in jail? "That poor kid," she muttered. It wasn't bad enough that the boogeyman was hot on his heels, but now his mother was locked up. "Did she say why his mother's in jail?"

His face was grim with concern. "Solicitation of an undercover cop, and according to her, this is totally out of character. Mrs. Ramirez rambled on and on about what a good girl her Solana is—was."

Good girls didn't offer to wonk for cash. "Jesus. Is she bringing Carlos here?"

"Yeah. You wanna stick around?"

She couldn't look at him for fear her eyes would give her away. Instead she let her eyes drift to the world globe Kellen had set out on the table in the story time area. "Are we baking cookies and finger painting? There's nothing I love more than ruining a good manicure as I add ten unwanted pounds to my thighs while I amuse a child who surely has some icky diseases." How's that for maternal? In reality, there was nothing she wanted more than to hang around and just be near Carlos. See that he was safe. Protect him.

Gak.

"I was thinking maybe we'd do something fun like play Xbox 360 games. Maybe Guitar Hero or Rock Band. But what do I know about fun—me being such a snooze and all?" he teased.

"An assload of snooze," she reminded him with a smirk.

Kellen chuckled over his shoulder, heading to the back of the store while Marcella fretted. Spending any more time with Carlos and Kellen than was necessary was treading on dangerous territory. Already this peculiar affinity for Carlos was burning a hole in her heart, and it frightened her far more than going back to Plane Dismal for eternity. What alarmed her even more was the possibility that she'd end up sucked back there and not be able to stay here and help. For all the good she was doing at this point.

The jingle of the bell on the door, and the sound of a harried Mrs. Ramirez rushing in with Carlos in tow, interrupted her worry.

Carlos, running behind his grandmother, backpack in tow, caught sight of her and gave her a shy smile.

And then her heart sang.

Jesus Christ on the crapper.

She gave him a little wiggle of her fingers and slipped behind the pair to listen to what Mrs. Ramirez said to Kellen. Kellen sent Carlos into the living room, where he'd set up the video game and told him to wait for him so they could rock out together.

When he turned to Mrs. Ramirez, he placed a reassuring hand on her shoulder and listened to her frantic explanation. Her dark hair, smattered with gray, usually so neat and tidy, flew in stray strands about her head. She clutched her large, multicolored purse to her chest like it was her lifeline. Her words shot from her mouth in chunks filled with anxiety. "I am so sorry, Meester Kellen. I don't know what to do. My baby, she is a mess! This is *not* like my Solana. She *is* a good girl. But since Carlos's father die, she never been de same."

Kellen looked over her shoulder to catch Marcella's gaze momentarily. Their questioning glance synchronized. "I had no idea Carlos's father was dead. How long ago did it happen?"

Tears filled her large, almond-shaped eyes. "A year ago. He die in car accident. Ohhh," she moaned, "it was so bad. So, so bad. My Solana, she cry and cry. Me and my husband tell her to come home from California. We help with Carlos while she work, but she no work. She always with the going out at night. She gone all the time. Poor Carlos, he so sad, and now, bad things happening with him, too. You see yesterday. You know, Meester Kellen, Carlos, he like you and Meess Delaney."

"So you understand?" Kellen asked, his voice hesitant.

"I think I do, but I am scared."

Kellen's nod was calming, his words caring and gentle. "It's okay, Mrs. Ramirez. I'll help as much as I can."

She shook her head, obviously overwhelmed. Digging a wad of tissues out of her purse, she pressed one to her nose and sniffed. "I have to go now. The bail man, he say I have to hurry. You look out for my baby, yes? I could be gone a long time." The worry in her eyes tore at Marcella.

"You have nothing to worry about. You go take care of Solana. Carlos and I will be just fine."

Mrs. Ramirez hurled her portly body at Kellen, wrapping her arms around him and squeezing. "I make you enchiladas when this all done. I promise. Carlos," she called to him where he sat in front of a drum set. "You be good boy for me, okay?" Her fond smile, so obviously riddled with worry for her grandson, melted when he nodded his consent.

Kellen kissed the top of her head and set her from him, encouraging her to go get her daughter with a gentle nudge. The bell on the door chimed, signaling her departure.

Both Kellen and Marcella breathed simultaneous sighs of relief. Mrs. Ramirez's fear and anxiety were like a heavy weight. Her burden was clear. Her love for her family, more so.

Marcella knew that kind of love.

She knew that kind of pain.

She knew.

"Hey." Kellen gave her shoulder a nudge with his, pulling her from her reverie. "You wanna play drums or guitar?"

Her nose wrinkled. "Don't be ridiculous. I don't want to play anything."

"Wow. You're an assload of fun," he whispered with a wink.

"C'mon, Marcella," Carlos coaxed. "It's fun." His smile, so different from the wide-eyed terror of the day before, yanked at her poor heart. A heart that wasn't accustomed to so much use.

"Fine. But you both do know I may not be able to pick anything up, don't you?"

"You can sing," Kellen offered with smug satisfaction. "I even have a microphone stand. You don't have to touch a thing."

Carlos waited with excited expectation in his twinkling green eyes. Those eyes. There was just no resisting them. Throwing up her hands, she gave them both a mock pained look. "Okay, but just remember, I'm warning you. I sound like I've been dipped in acid when I sing. You'll both be a pair of sorry, deaf men when we're through."

Kellen watched Marcella's pert, round behind sway to the music as she lent truth to her earlier statement. She blew chunks as a vocalist. But that hadn't stopped them from doubling over with laughter as he and Carlos razzed her about how Russia had called and asked her to stop all that caterwauling.

Out of glee-filled spite, she'd smiled that sly, seductive smile of hers, with a tilt of her lips; thrown back her head; and begun to sing even louder, leaving Carlos almost unable to play the drums due to his fits of giggles. Giggles that made Marcella, the allegedly vain, shallow demon, glow with such apparent joy, Kellen was left dry mouthed.

Her long, curly hair fell in waves down the back of her ruined dress, so enticing he wanted to drag his hands through it before securing her full lips to his in a kiss that would demand she submit. Her voluptuous curves, swishing to and fro, left him planting his guitar firmly on his lap to hide his obvious arousal.

But what had caught his attention, beyond her obvious beauty, beyond her sultry charms, was her interaction with Carlos. The connection was clear between the two as they joked and laughed when she failed a song.

This was a woman who had more facets than a diamond. The woman he'd always thought was cold, calculating, and heartless was warm, funny, and bonding with a little boy she'd known for just a few short days.

It made him want her all the more.

He wanted her so much he ached with it. Ached in places he hadn't known existed. Last night, when her curves had been so molded to his, he'd pressed her for answers about her past mostly because he truly wanted to know who Marcella was, but also to distract himself from finishing off that trashed dress of hers by tearing it from her body.

He wanted to explore every blessed inch of her, and now, knowing she wasn't who she'd always claimed she was made it that much harder to stay away from her.

"Fire awwwaaayyyyyy!" Marcella howled into the microphone, finishing with a curtsy when Carlos fell off his chair and pretended to pass out from her ear-bleeding screeching.

Kellen smiled when she knelt beside him and said, "Excuse me, mister. Are you making fun of my velvet pipes?" She reached out to give him a poke under his arm, failed miserably by sticking her finger right through his armpit, then giggled with abandon when they both realized she couldn't touch him. This scene that played out right before his feet was one he'd often hoped for—maybe not with a ghost and a nine-year-old who was being hunted by demons, but similar if not as desirable. When they'd bent their heads together while Carlos explained the rules of the game, it had done something totally unexpected to his heart. Unexpected and he'd like to claim unwelcome. But he couldn't. Damn it all, he couldn't.

Yet, soon enough, it would all go up in a puff of smoke.

Marcella couldn't drift here forever unless Delaney found some sort of answer. Carlos would have to go home to his grandmother and his wayward parent.

He had to get a grip. Setting the guitar aside, he rose and said, "Okay, rockers. Whaddya say we break for something to eat? Hard-core musicians need to refuel."

"Awww." Carlos chirped his protest. "Can't we play just a little bit more?"

Carlos's obvious need for any kind of attention showed in the way he preened when praised and tried harder when corrected. He was a classic case of unintentional neglect. More than likely, Mrs. Ramirez was too overwhelmed by his mother's behavior to devote as much time to him as she'd like, and his mother's lack of interest since her husband's death all led to a cry to be heard. Add into the mix his father's death, demons, and ghosts, and it made for a mess of emotions on overload.

Marcella held out her hand to Carlos and gave him a teasing grin. "C'mon. Kellen's right. Little twerp rockers need nourishment if they hope to rock another day."

Carlos grabbed for her hand, knowing full well he couldn't hold it, but playing the game with her anyway. She led him into the kitchen by holding her hand out to him, then yanking it back as they laughed their way into the kitchen.

Kellen paused for a moment in the midst of their instruments' electrical cords and discarded drumsticks, listening to the sounds of their laughter, straining his ears to catch the words Marcella spoke in Spanish.

And for the first time, he understood why his sister was so happy now.

He understood the ache she'd once described when she'd talked about children and a husband, a home. The fear she'd never have those things because of her gift. The relief he sometimes saw in her eyes when he relayed an encounter with a particularly surly ghost. He suddenly understood the soft hush to her tone when she spoke of Clyde and the love they'd fought for.

He understood.

Carlos dug through his backpack, pulling out his treasured army men to show Kellen while Marcella hovered, feeling far too cozy. Familial.

Really, how long did bailing someone out take? The longer the hours grew while they waited for Carlos's grandmother to come back, the more Marcella never wanted their time together to end.

Seeing them together, Kellen listening with interest and patience to Carlos, left her wanting both to escape and to join them, all at once. When Kellen placed his large hand over Carlos's to show him how to draw a three-dimensional box, her heart got all warm and syrupy. Carlos wasn't at all upset or fearful of her presence. He didn't flip a nut because she couldn't touch him. He didn't seem to find anything about her, besides her name, strange at all. Which led her to wonder when he'd begun to experience the afterlife.

"Hey, Marcella. Do you still hate my army men?" Carlos asked with a giggle that swelled her heart.

She rolled her eyes with intended exaggeration. "I never said I hated them, young man. I said I didn't want to play with them. I think I'm just more of a Barbie Dream House kind of girl. Or maybe Malibu Barbie, ya know, wisenheimer?"

"Barbies are stooopid," he chanted on a laugh, ducking his head to dig in his backpack.

"Hey"—she pointed a finger at him—"you calling me stooopid?"

Carlos shook his head immediately. "Nuh-uh. My grandma'd yell at me."

"Hey, I've got a question for you, little man. You mind?" she asked, floating toward him.

Green eyes became hesitant.

But Marcella sought them, winking. "It's no big deal. I was just wondering something, but you don't have to answer if you don't want to." She kept her request easy and as though it were no big thang if he didn't want to answer.

Relaxing back into the kitchen chair, he nodded.

"Do you know how I ended up in your room that day, bud? I was just wondering because I was thinking, if you need me, you can just call me back the way you did the first time, you know?"

Carlos gazed at her with uncertain eyes. "I don't know how come you came to my room. I just remember I saw a picture of you in my head, and then you were in my room."

So how in the fuck did a virtual stranger get a picture of her in his head? She and Kellen exchanged glances with questions attached to them. Kellen chucked him under the chin. "Has it been a long time since you started to see ghosts?"

He shrugged his shoulders, the blue of his sweatshirt bunching while he fidgeted. "I dunno. For a little while, I guess."

"Do you remember who the first ghost was?" Kellen asked. "I

totally remember the first one I saw. He wasn't scary or anything. Just really loud," he said as though he were confiding in Carlos, telling his deepest secrets.

"Yeah. I remember. It was my dad."

Marcella fought her gasp. If she could grip the faded countertop for support, she would. Instead, she wobbled in midair. "Did he come to tell you he loved you, *chico*? I think that makes you pretty special if he did. Crazy cool."

Carlos's lower lip began to tremble. "I miss my dad. He played army with me. He told me he loved me, but he said other stuff, too."

Kellen held his breath along with her. Kellen reached across the small table and ran his hand over the top of Carlos's head. "You wanna talk about it?"

"He just said I was going to have to be a five-star general soon. I think he meant I have to be brave."

Oh, sweet mother. "Did he say anything else?" Marcella fought for calm, to beat down the squeak in her voice.

Pulling his backpack toward him, Carlos shut down. "I don't wanna talk about it anymore. I just want to play with my stuff." Burying his head in his backpack, he withdrew. Gone was the impish grin. Gone the squeals of delight. Back was the solemn, intimidated little boy.

Marcella's heart shattered into a thousand sharp pieces, each shard cutting her as though it were made of glass. She swallowed hard when Kellen's eyes once more sought hers. Silent messages passed between them.

So much baggage for such a slight set of shoulders.

Bowing her head, she fought those ridiculous tears once more. When she lifted it, a silver gleam dragged her eyes front and center. Her hands went ice-cold. Her vision blurred, then cleared, only to return with a dizzying swoop.

Calm. Calm and steady. She battled for it. Refused to be anything but, in front of Carlos.

Yet her intestines tangled in knots. Her head rang with a piercing buzz. Wave after wave of panic thrust at her with vicious jabs.

Darwin had been right.

Carlos did have the box.

Terror rose like a flood of bilious waste, sticking in her throat.

Oh, Mary, Mother of God.

He'd opened the box that contained the fetid, vile, tainted soul of her dead husband, Armando.

Once locked away seventy-six years ago.

Now?

Not so much.

eight

Oh, fuck. Fuck, fuck, and fuuuck! Jamming a finger into her mouth, she fought her scream of horror.

"Marcella?" Kellen tipped his head in her direction, his concerned eyes falling on her.

She held up a hand to silently ask for a moment, turning from him and gasping for breath. Her head swam. How could Carlos have the box? It was supposed to be buried—years ago. How had he figured out how to open it? He was nine, for the love of God! She had to know where he'd gotten the box. *Who* he'd gotten it from. Shaking off the initial shock, Marcella turned back to face the pair, forcing a serene smile to her lips. "Hey, Carlos, where'd ya get the cool box?"

Holding it up, he smiled with pride. The silver interlocking sides were askew, no longer precisely aligned like they had once been. It shone, menacing and ugly. "My grandpa gave it to me. He's in Puerto Rico visiting his cousins. But he said he gave it to me because I was sad he was leaving for a month. I unlocked it. It was really hard, like a puzzle, but I figured it out."

Booyah for high IQs. Fine hairs stood up on the back of her neck. She had to try to see inside it. "You are seriously smart," she complimented him. "Can I see inside the box?"

He twisted the top open, revealing the burgundy velvet lining and nothing else. Wrapping her arms around her waist, she bit the inside of her cheek to fight the onslaught of fury that rose like vitriol to settle in her mouth.

Kellen stood, pushing away from the table, and cornered her with eyes that held fear and hands that pinned her shoulders in a light grip. "Tell me that's not what I think it is."

"I can't," she squeaked, swallowing hard.

"It's the box that you said your contact told you about?"

"Yes," she hissed on a harsh breath.

"What was in the box, Marcella?" he demanded, keeping his voice low, but apparently unable to hide the harshness in it.

Pressing a fist to her lips, she spoke around her hand. "Something horrible. Vile. Heinous. Oh, Jesus, Kellen. How could a kid like Carlos have that box?"

"Tell me what was in the box."

Over Kellen's shoulder, she saw Carlos's eyes taking them in. The last thing he needed was more turmoil. "Not now. Not in front of Carlos. I have to go, Kellen. I'll be back, and I'll tell you. I promise I'll tell you."

The tight line of his mouth expressed his aggravation at having to wait, but she pressed two fingers to his lips. "*I promise,*" she whispered. Clenching her eyes shut, she forced herself to smile once more.

"Carlos, *chico*? I gotta blow. So I'll check ya later, okay?"

"Aw, how come?"

His question, laced with such disappointment, made her chuckle.

"Dude, I'm a ghost, and it's getting late. Ghosts work at night. We have important ghostie things to do like houses to haunt and doors to open and close so we can freak people out. We can't spend all night playing Rock Band," she joked. "So I gotta roll. I'll catch you soon. Now remember what I said. If you need me, just think me up and I'm in, okay?"

He sighed, clearly resigned to her leaving. "'Kay. 'Bye, Marcella."

"'Bye, Tommy Lee." She blew him a kiss and sent Kellen a meaningful glance before floating to the front of the store and out the door.

She literally flew to the park, rushing to the bench where she'd told Darwin to meet her. The bench was devoid of anyone, hosting only dead leaves scattered along the seat from the tree above.

"God damn it, Darwin. Where the fuck are you?" she yelled into the brittle chill of the wind. "I need you to get your hairy ass here now!" As if yelling was going to help.

"Gurrrlll, shoot. You don't gotta yell."

Whirling around, she came face-to-face with a woman, a very large woman, with garish makeup, overblown lips, and so much frosted blue eye shadow she'd surely keep those women who sold that ridiculous Bobbie-Sue Cosmetics in business for life. Her platform boots wobbled beneath her enormous feet, and the pink boa she wore, covered in glitter, ruffled in the breeze, creating a gaudy halo around her neck.

Marcella expelled a huge sigh of relief, then paused. "Darwin? Please tell me you're not three sheets to the wind. I swear, I'll neuter you myself if you're under the influence."

He bent his hand at the wrist, placing the other at his hip. "Oh, honey, I'm not under the influence, but I've decided I wish I were. This she-male's thoughts are insidious. What would ever possess her to want to have her Mr. Peabody turned inside out surgically so she can finally make the 'big money'? It's unthinkable."

Marcella would laugh, if she didn't want to cry. "*Ay chihua-hua, chico*. Could you have found anyone uglier?"

Darwin rubbed his Rubenesque ass, his long, gleaming red fingernails getting tangled in his boa. When he responded, for a mere moment he sounded like the old Darwin. Her Darwin. "Have pity. I've been violated."

Reaching for his large hand, she clasped it between hers. "Listen to me. Did you go back to Chez Dreary? Did you find anything out?"

His lips curled in disgust. "I went back, I did. I didn't find out a friggin' thing. Gurrrlll—I mean, girl, that shit's tighter than my goddamned frilly thong. Which, I'm not ashamed to tell you, is unforgiving, if you know what I mean."

Marcella would laugh at Darwin's war with the transsexual hooker's clothing and mental processes if everything weren't such a blessed mess. Tears formed in her eyes again, and she swiped at them with angry fingers. "Oh, God, Darwin. Something horrible's happened."

His overly made-up eyes cast her a look of confusion. "Worse than that dress you got on, sugah?"

She eyed his pleather miniskirt and cropped corset where the bushy hair from his belly puffed out in dark tufts. "You should be throwing stones?"

He looked down at his breasts, overflowing from his corset like the doughy dinner rolls you bought in a can and opened by cracking it on the side of the counter. "Noted. So what's happenin'? Tell old Brittany all about it, honey."

Her eyes bulged. *"Brittany?"*

Cocking an eyebrow at her, he stuck his neck out, circling his head. "From what I hear her tell the younger, less experienced girls, Brittany says that using a younger, uh, *stage* name makes men feel virile when they scream it out during the, you know"—he winked—"passion making. I don't choose the names of the prostitutes and addicts I possess. Cut me some slack, girlie."

Hearing his voice, even embodied in this heifer of a transvestite, pushed her over the edge. Fat tears streamed down her face, disappearing before they ever hit the ground. Sinking to the bench, she gripped the edge of the seat on either side of her legs and drew in ragged breaths. Her shoulders sagged as the weight of seventy-six years seeped into her bones. "Darwin, oh, Jesus, Darwin. This is so bad. Everything's gone to shit."

Cupping her chin, he pulled her eyes to his. "Who the fuck are you, sister? The Marcella I know sure don't"—he sighed in clear exasperation—"*doesn't* cry. She's a hard-ass from way back."

Yeah. Who the fuck was she? "I don't know!" she yelped in helplessness. "I don't know what the fuck's wrong with me. All of a sudden I have all these weird bodily functions. Like, I'd swear my heart beats, and I can't stop crying over everything."

"Phantom pain, sugah. The heartbeat thing, breathing, a pulse is what the souls call phantom pain. Like when you lose a limb and your brain tells ya it's still there."

"Those shitty-ass souls have an explanation for everything, don't they? Can anyone explain why I'm a shitwreck all the time? Why I'm getting attached to a little boy who's in some serious dookey? I mean, me, Darwin, *me*—attached to a nine-year-old child. Kellen's behaving like he's found the meaning of life with Tibetan monks, so he won't fight with me anymore, and now there's the box." Tremors of anxious panic swept up her spine.

"The box . . . Christ almighty! I remember talking about the box—but damn if I can remember what I said, I was so trashed. What's so important about the box?"

Marcella began to wail. Highly uncharacteristic and so out of the blue, even she was surprised. "Carlos has the box, Darwin," she sobbed.

His garish lips formed an O. "What's in the box, sugarplum?"

"My d-d-dead husss-baaand."

His O-shaped lips fell open. "You had a husband?"

She sprang up from the bench, clenching her fists and yelling to the sky, "Yes! God damn it all, yes! I had a husband. He was a disgusting, filthy, lying pig, but he was mine! It makes me want to vomit just saying it, but yes, yes, *yes*! I had a husband." It shouldn't feel good to say that out loud, but it did. Fuck-all if it didn't feel good to finally spew her hatred for that monster out loud. Sinking back onto the bench, she inhaled deeply.

Darwin also took a long, shuddering breath, and when he released it, the condensation of warm breath hitting cold air created a puff of cloudy steam. He dropped down beside her in a slump. "Why didn't you ever tell me you had a husband?"

The disbelief that settled on her face went straight from her brow and out her mouth. "Why would I tell you anything, you mange-riddled mutt? You hate my guts. Everyone hates my guts because I'm a bad-girl demon. I've found peace with that. We're not friends. I don't confide in you unless you make me. I wasn't always a demon, you half-wit. I didn't just hatch. I once had a life and I shared that life with a husband."

"Easy there, girlie. Okay, so we weren't friends. Did we have to be friends for you to tell me you had a husband? One that's in a box . . . Wait. Did you put him in the box?"

Oh, indeed she had. "You bet your ever-lovin' ass I did, and I'd do it again, that fucking prick." Her eyes narrowed just thinking about that day. The betrayal, the urgency, the horrific choice she'd had to make in a matter of moments.

He peered at her from beneath his false eyelashes. "Was he in pieces when you put him in the box?"

"No, you moron. It's a long story. One I don't want to get into, but now he's out of the box, Darwin. How could Isabella let that box get away from her?"

"Marcella?"

"What?"

"I need you to move at a slower pace. I'm fighting a mind that thinks turning your Mr. Peabody into a Mrs. is going to garner her at least a buck over minimum wage per hour. Who is Isabella?"

"My sister." God, she missed Isabella. They'd been so close until she'd married that bastard and he'd kept her from everyone she held near and dear.

"You had a sister, too?"

"Again, I didn't just hatch. I had a husband, a sister, parents, a house, a—" She bit her tongue. "A very real, rather ordinary life with all the things real, ordinary people have in it."

"Did your sister hack your husband up and put him in the box?"

"No, Darwin. *He* wasn't in the box. His soul was in the box. And now it's loose and running around somewhere. I have to find that scumbag. If I don't . . . Oh, God. What if I don't?" It was unimaginable. Unthinkable. Un-everything-able.

"May I remind you, I'm a simpleminded hooker? And take no offense. I'm certain there are oodles of hookers who have an IQ the size of seven continents. This just isn't one of them, and her thoughts stray; they muddle. Thus, it's hard to focus while I fight her desire to hit Harvey's Hut of Hanky-Panky, where business is good this time of night. So explain slowly. How did you get your husband's soul? That makes no sense. I can't articulate why, because I'm hampered by a limited vocabulary. But take my word for it, it makes no sense."

Marcella's mouth thinned to a line of hatred. "I killed him. I nailed the motherfucker when he wasn't looking. Then I summoned his black soul and I put it in the box. A locked box no one was ever supposed to figure out how to open."

"Oh. Of course you did. I mean, *ordinary* people kill their husbands every day and summon their souls so they can put them in a box—that's locked. Film at eleven."

"Forget it. You wouldn't understand. All of that doesn't matter now. What does matter is he's out. Free to roam. That cowardly fuck."

"So I finally know how you became a demon. Murder is frowned upon. You know, that crazy commandment about thou shalt not nail the motherfucker?"

No. No, that wasn't it at all. But she didn't owe Darwin or anyone else an explanation. She couldn't speak of her reasoning behind killing Armando because it hurt so much it made her physically tremble. "Right. Look, that isn't the point. The point is Carlos let him out of the box. I don't understand how he got his hands on the box, but he has it, and it's been opened. I sealed that myself and made Isabella swear she'd bury it where no one would ever find it."

"So this sister of yours, she's some slacker, huh?"

His dig fell by the wayside due to Marcella's terror. "Something must have happened to prevent her from burying it. She knew how important it was. She knew Armando had to be stopped. I told her. Begged her."

"Did she believe you?"

Marcella frowned. Isabella had never believed entirely. Not in the afterlife, and certainly not in demons or the supernatural. But the day she'd gone to Isabella and begged her to bury the box, surely her hysteria was enough to convince her that Armando's soul could never escape that box. Would her sister have ignored her last wish? And even if she had, how in the name of all that was holy had Carlos gotten his hands on it? "Isabella wasn't a believer in Heaven and Hell. She didn't believe in my gift of sight, and she definitely didn't think Armando could hurt anyone after he was dead."

Darwin scrunched his face up. "Whoa there, girlie. You had the gift of sight? What else did you have in this 'ordinary' life?"

So many things, she couldn't speak of them. Her head nodded with a slow bob. This was more than she'd ever shared with anyone since she'd chosen Hell, and it was like having her teeth pulled one by one without aid of anesthesia. "Yes . . ." She blew the admission out with reluctance. "When I was alive, I had medium abilities."

"Astonished" wasn't a word she'd use lightly when referring to Darwin's tone. "So you knew there was another side?"

Hoo, boy, had she ever. "Yes. I knew."

"And you chose Hell? I always thought you were a bitch, but not a dumb one." He clucked his tongue with scorn.

Hold up there. Anger fused her brows together and narrowed her eyes, but her words were measured and hissed from between her teeth. "*Fuck you, Darwin.* Fuck you, you judgmental asshole. You know what?—go away. Go now before I wrap my hands around that thick neck of yours and squeeze until your Mr. Peabody turns itself inside out without any help from a surgeon's knife. You don't know me, Darwin. You don't know a damned thing about me except for what you *think* you know. So take your trashy ass on outta here. I asked for your help because a little boy's in danger. An innocent little boy. It isn't for me. I'd rather be banished to a place a million times worse than Plane Dismal than ask for help for me. Just go away. Better yet, I'll go away. And stay away from me from now on, or I swear, as I stand here in front of your freaky ass, I'll figure this ghost thing out, and when I do, I'll make being run over by a big ole Lincoln seem like cake and ice cream."

She didn't give him the chance to defend himself before she floated as far away from the park as she could, because, knowing Darwin, he'd be happy to offer up more of his pious views on her life before death.

Rationally, she knew he had nothing else to go on but bits and pieces of a story that involved her killing her husband and locking his soul in a box. With the little she'd shared, he certainly had every right to judge. But she'd been judged for more years than she cared to count, and now it was all coming to a frothy head, bubbling over in angry splashes of guilt and secrecy.

She'd reached a point of no return, the point where the criticism and jabs at her morality had become too painful to keep hearing. What once had been an easy task, hiding her past had now become the ultimate in lies and deceit.

The very things that had left her where she was to begin with.

And now Armando was loose.

Her dirty deed had come full circle.

Skulking into the store, she stayed hidden in the shadows for a moment while she watched Mrs. Ramirez gather a sleepy Carlos and his things and head out the door. Closing her eyes, Marcella stood in the hushed, dimly lit silence and breathed.

There was no explanation as to why Carlos's grandfather had given him the box or where he'd gotten it. Isabella must be long dead. Marcella had never verified that, though. When she'd become a demon, she'd stayed far away from her family and anyone she'd known in her life so they'd never be tainted by her choice. That had been the deal when she'd signed on the dotted line. She'd serve Satan. He'd leave her family and friends alone. But Isabella couldn't still be alive. At the time of Marcella's death, Isabella was thirty-five, ten years her senior.

She had to tell Kellen what had been in the box. If she was careful, the explanation didn't have to involve anything other than Armando and his hateful soul.

Because the rest of her tale . . .

Shaking her head, she fiercely pushed away the day she'd sold her life and focused on coherently giving Kellen an explanation that would satisfy him. He was too smart to fall for her tripping over her words with a half-assed story.

"Sheee's baaa-ack," he crooned from behind her shoulder, husky and easygoing.

The sound of his voice, the sweet tendril of the thrill it had always given her, circled her intestines, drawing them in a tight knot. Marcella turned to face him with a solemn exterior. "She is."

"Carlos is gone, and Mrs. Ramirez managed to get Solana out of the slammer."

"What a mess."

"A mess that somehow involves that box?"

Her eyes found the floor in guilt. "Indirectly, yes. I guess it does."

"The way you ran out of here earlier means this box can't be good. You ready to tell me about it?"

"Is this multiple choice?"

"Nope."

Resignation set in as she formulated her plan. She'd just say it. Period. It didn't make her a slut for once having a husband. "Okay. The box. My dead husband was in the box."

Silence in all its painful accusation greeted her ears.

Her eyes avoided his.

Apparently, Kellen wasn't going to allow that. Tilting her chin upward, he forced her gaze to meet his, and while there was no condemnation in it, it wouldn't last. "Someone was married to *you*?" When he asked, the emotions in his eyes were hard to read. She wasn't sure if what she saw was disgust that anyone could ever be married to her, or a hint of jealousy mingled in with all that surprise.

"I knooow," Marcella cooed playfully. "It's like finding out Hannibal Lecter was once a silly schoolboy who had a major crush on his biology teacher, right?"

His eyes hardened when he shoved his hands back into the pockets of his sweatshirt. "Very close. Now stop with the smart-ass."

"Okay. Yes. I was married back in 1934."

"To?"

"A man."

"Yeah. What man?"

"Armando Villanueva. Ring any bells?"

"Not even a tinkle. But your last name is Acosta."

"It's my maiden name. I didn't want to keep Armando's after . . ."

"How long were you married?"

Just long enough to provide . . . "Just a little over a year."

"And how does that explain the box?"

She was stringing him along, she knew it. He knew it. But if she hoped to keep at least some of her secrets, she had to keep it simple. If killing someone were simple. "Armando was in the box."

"Do you mean his ashes?"

Only if you wanted to split hairs. Technically, that had been all that was left after she'd knocked him off . . . "No."

"Okay, you lead, I'll follow—how the hell did Armando get in the box?"

Looking him directly in the eye, her lips thinned to a sneer. "I killed that spineless, stupid, bastard pig and put him in there."

"So I'm guessing the two of you weren't in the throes of connubial bliss?" he quipped.

"Mensa's holding a coveted spot for you right now."

Kellen's face almost broke into a smile, until her earlier words obviously hit him again. "You killed him." The question wasn't asked; the answer was stated, flat and monotone.

Murdered, knocked off, whacked, capped his ass. Yep. "I did."

"Finally an explanation about your demon origins." His disappointment was so evident, so palpable, it was almost as if he'd been waiting to hear otherwise, and she'd blown him out of the water by telling him she was a killa.

Arrogantly, her head lifted. "Seems that way."

"Wanna tell me *why* you killed him?"

"Not particularly."

"Right, because you don't do explanations. But you can't just drop a bomb like that and not have something to say for yourself. Some sort of defense."

Her seesawing emotions stopped on angry. Lately, it was like spinning a wheel to see where her next emotion would land. "I don't have to defend myself to you or anyone, but in the interest of our new policy of sunshine and goodwill, I killed him because he was a bastard who deserved to die." So chew on that.

And here it came. Marcella saw it in the stiffening of his spine and the thought he put into his next words. "Lots of people probably deserve to die. It doesn't necessarily mean you have the right to kill them."

"Well, if you're married to me, you forfeit your rights."

"When did he die?"

"In 1934." In a blaze of fucking glory while she spat on his still-warm body, but not before she'd clubbed his cowardly ass to death.

Kellen paused. "You died in 1934, didn't you?"

"It was a good year."

The snort he gave was sarcastic. "Some coincidence, huh? You killing your husband and then kicking the bucket yourself? Or maybe it was divine justice?"

That'd work. "Divinity at its finest. Always on top of things up there, they are," she said, allowing the sarcasm of her words to ring clear.

Kellen made the external effort to avoid the bait she dangled by blowing out a sharp breath of air before responding. "What could he possibly have done to you to make you want to commit murder?"

Backing away from him, she threw up her hands in question. "Why does there have to be a reason? Maybe he was just a shitty husband who never called when he was going to be late for dinner. In fact, that son of a whoremonger never, ever took out the trash, and getting him to mow the lawn was like asking him to relocate Mount St. Helens to the Caymans. You know what he used to call me when I complained? His *cheeky wench*. After all my nagging, I decided I'd reached my last straw, and one night when he was late for dinner—I did what any wife with an overgrown lawn, overflowing trash, and a cold meal would do. He was late once too often. Tipped me right over the edge and I whacked him. I guess I showed him what cheeky was all about, huh?" She tacked on a sly smile to enforce her blasé attitude about murdering one's husband.

Kellen wasn't amused, not by the grim set of his mouth or the tight set of his teeth. In fact, if she were to lay bets, she'd say he was clinging to this newfound happy-clappy attitude toward her. "Lay off the bullshit and tell me why you killed him."

Her emotions took another wide swing while she watched him try to fight the disappointment in his eyes because it was like a wound on her heart. She wanted him to fight with her. She didn't want him to fight with her. Good God, she was like the Three Faces of Eve.

But would it really hurt to tell him part of the truth? If only so he'd stop looking at her like she'd been responsible for Chernobyl, the *Titanic*, and Hiroshima combined? Her face grew apprehensive, her words strained. "Armando was a Lucifer lover. Much like your half brother, Vincent, he'd signed a contract with Satan. His soul was due to him upon his death. I just sped up the negotiations."

A quick flash of understanding passed over his dark, hard face, lightening it a bit. "He served Satan in life."

Hoping for cocky, she kept her explanation simple, but as off-hand as possible. "Yep, and I found out about it. I was deeply religious, and divorce wasn't something that happened as easily as it does in this day and age. So I saved myself some money and a buttload of court appearances and killed him."

He fought a smirk, then straightened because this was Kellen, and they were talking murder, and his sense of morals just wouldn't allow him to see the good she'd done by knocking off Armando. "And put him in a box . . ."

But first I burned him to a nice Original Recipe crisp. "It was all the rage for husband killers back then."

"If his ashes weren't in that box, explain how he got in the box."

"I summoned his soul and put that in a box. Not him per se. That's not the point. The point is Carlos has the box—which means Armando is free. Somewhere." She couldn't hide the shiver of fear that knowledge wrought from her. "So the first question is how the hell did Carlos's grandfather get that box?"

"Hang on. Do I want to know how you knew how to summon a soul?"

She shrugged her shoulders. "I dunno. It's purty skeery," she joked.

But Kellen wasn't laughing, and he wasn't done looking for answers. "What did you do with the box after you, you know, put his soul in it?"

Marcella measured her words. "I gave it to someone who obviously didn't heed my warnings that no one should ever find it."

His interest grew in the arch of his eyebrow and the purse of his lips. "And that someone was . . . ?"

"Someone who obviously didn't do a very good job of getting rid of it. That's not the point right now. The box is here. It's real. A very, very malicious freak is loose because of that box!"

Kellen's dark head shook with disbelief. "I don't even know what to say. There's this huge chunk of your past, a pretty important one that you never shared with us, that involves murder. Why didn't you ever tell anyone? At the very least Delaney? She's your best friend."

Her shoulders lifted in a disinterested shrug. "No one ever asked, and now that you know what happened, it should make you feel like you're walking on air. My explanation definitely justifies your superior moral construct. Which means we can get back to business as usual and you can stop behaving like you've communed with God himself in a field of buttercups and he gave you a direct order to love thine enemy."

Though he said nothing, she saw the wheels of his razor-sharp mind turning.

Marcella's sigh was weary. Telling this tale twice in one day had sucked her energy points right out of her. Darwin's disappointment had hurt, as much as she hated to admit it. Kellen's would be worse when he finally got around to the absorption stage. She hoped to avoid that by getting the information out and leaving before she had to physically see how disgusted he was by her.

"Look, Armando was a monster in life. In death, I'd bet he's the Son of Sam times a million—especially after exile for seventy-six years. We have to find him and stop him. And if he goes near Carlos, I'll find the fuck and whack him all over again." She paused at her big words. How she'd whack him was still pending. "So call up your gal pal Catalina and tell her we need to get on this shit now. We need contacts in Hell, something I don't have anymore." Her rising hysteria showed in the strain of her voice as it hit an octave of panic she didn't know she was capable of.

"Whoa," he chided, his eyes surprising her by distinctly revealing sympathy for her plight. "Hold on. I get your panic. You killed him. He'd probably want revenge for something like that, but it's something he can't wreak on you because you're no longer a demon. You're afraid of him. That's understandable, but do you really think if he wanted Carlos he wouldn't already have hurt him? Carlos did set him free, that's true. But Carlos didn't mention anyone being in the box, and he knows enough to at least tell us if he'd encountered something like he experienced yesterday here in the store. I think he trusts us enough to tell us. So right now, your husband's not any different from any other demon."

Marcella shook her head, wrinkling her nose to show her displeasure. "Never call him my husband again. It makes me want to yark, and I think that would be too easy. I wish I could take comfort in the idea that Armando would just go on about his demonic business like all the rest of Satan's minions, but something terrible is going to happen. I feel it in my gut, and it involves Carlos. I can't disregard my contact's warning that 'they want him.' Whoever *they* are. Carlos and Armando are connected. From what I've gathered when we talked this afternoon, he's too young yet to understand the ghosts he's seeing need his help. So he hasn't crossed anyone over that might have been eluding Lucifer—which as we both know was what set Lucifer's balls on fire with Delaney.

That's the only grudge I can see Lucifer could hold. I don't know how or why Carlos's gift of sight is so important to Hell, but it seems as though it is. We need to know why."

Kellen was reaching for his cell phone at the insistence of her words, his face determined but not yet showing the signs that what she'd done to Armando had sunk in. "So I call Catalina."

Yay. Let's do call Miss Hades 2010. Woot.

Gnawing on her ragged fingernail, she fought the onslaught of memories Armando's existence brought in hateful, vivid colors. How she'd ever been so stupid as to fall in love with a man so hideous . . .

She'd ignored the warnings from the other side because she'd been so infatuated with Armando's dark good looks and charm. Charm that oozed from his every pore all while he'd wooed her, but she'd been nothing more than a tool. Back in the day, at twenty-five she was no spring chicken when it came to marrying. Her parents said she was too strong-willed, too opinionated for a man to want to lock horns with her for life. Until Armando had come along. He was the kind of man who'd encouraged her will of iron like none of the others who'd offered their hand, and she'd fallen blindly—head over heels.

He'd incited her on more than one occasion with his opposing views. On everything from politics to religion Armando had made her think. He'd challenged her. He'd brought more than just the idea that she was going to end up a marital doormat to the table.

And then he'd betrayed her.

In the sickest, most fetid of ways.

Kellen ran a finger along her upper arm, disrupting her long-buried memories. "I got her voice mail, but I left her a message and told her it was crucial she call us back."

Marcella's gut churned in anxious worry. "So we wait."

"We wait," he confirmed with a half smile she had to look away from in order to avoid returning.

And now she could escape his heavy disappointment at her killerlike tendencies. "So I'll go, and if you hear anything, see anything, you just dream me up there, big boy. I'll come running."

Kellen's hand, callused and lean, clasped her arm. "Where do you go when you leave here?"

"Shopping, silly. Can't you tell by my new dress?" She held up the ripped edge of it and curtsied. What sucked sweaty balls about that was she could touch the dress, feel the fabric between her fingers, but she couldn't take the damned thing off. It was like some eternal curse.

"You can stay here, you know."

How thoughtful to offer her the opportunity to see him in all his glorious muscledness while he strolled through the house in his Calvin Kleins. She'd rather wear this dress for eternity than be subjected to his House of Fabulous. "I'm good. I know your life is jam-packed with Discovery Channel marathons and figuring out global warming. I wouldn't want to intrude."

"You could watch with me."

Her head cocked to the left at his quiet request. "Aren't you supposed to be calling me a murderer and, like, reading me scripture so I can atone for my sins?"

He regarded her with cool eyes. "If Armando was anything like Vincent, then he must have deserved to die."

What. The. Fuck? What was going on with him? It was like the Dalai Lama had possessed him. "Hold on there, Mr. Self-Righteous, Law-Abiding Citizen of the United States. Did I hear you just condone my murdering someone?" She made a slicing motion across her throat. "Because I did him in but good. Very gangsta, by this day and age's definition. In fact, maybe you should just call me killa from here on out." That she was working so hard to get a rise of distaste out of him plainly showed her insecurities. She wanted his approval—longed for it—and she'd take it any way she could get her unmanicured mitts on it. So she was seeing how far she could push him, testing him to see if he'd walk away. Self-loathing rose in a swell of disgust.

"I'm not condoning it. I'm just offering understanding. Had I known what Vincent was, what he'd done to my mother and Delaney, I'd have killed him myself. Seeing as you won't give me the full story, and I just know there's more to this than you're letting on, I'm opting for the lesser of two evils." He said the words with no haughty arrogance to them. Simple and clean.

"Oh, Mother Teresa—you've been sorely missed."

Kellen's chuckle was deep. "And my new body's rad, don't you think?"

She tried not to think, though it had become a chore, with him looming all up in her personal space. "There's supposed to be a thank-you in here somewhere, right? My groveling is rusty. Refresh me."

"Nope. C'mon. I'll drink a beer, you won't. I'll probably fall asleep, you'll be wide awake—but we'll be doing it together. It's gotta be better than being alone."

She threw her shoulders back and gave him her best smoldering stare, kittenish and seductive. "Are you inviting me to sleep over, Kellen Markham? You playa, you."

"I'm inviting you to stay here until we figure out how to get you back to the other side. It has to beat wherever you go every night. C'mon, you know you don't want to miss *Project Runway*," he coaxed, holding out his hand in invitation. A hand of temptation.

She was skipping down a path of self-destruction. There were plenty of warning bells clanging in her head, telling her not to do it. It would only make leaving harder. They went off like DEFCON 5 in her head, chiming in loud, raucous warning.

But it *was Project Runway*. Marcella teetered between the cold, hard bench of the park where her thoughts and guilt were all she had to keep her company, aside from the occasional drunk, or Kellen and the warmth of Delaney's old apartment in the back of the store. The comfort of memories.

Giving him a haughty grin, she asked, "This is your last chance to back out. I mean, aren't you just a little afraid I might take you out in your sleep if I stay here? It doesn't take much to get me all riled. I did kill my husband for leaving the lawn unkempt."

"So much so, I might need some No-Doz and three pots of coffee. But then I remember you can't pick anything up—at least not yet." He grinned, and it was like a cool balm, blanketing her heart. She knew enough about him to know he was giving her acceptance, acceptance for her dastardly past. Part of that acceptance came from knowing what a man was capable of when he walked among the land of the living, yet had sold his soul prematurely to Satan. Vincent had taught Kellen a thing or two about evil. But she sensed something else in his silent approval.

And the sticky-sweet warmth it garnered was dangerous.

Hot and dangerous.

She placed her hand in his extended one, savoring the light caress of his thumb on her knuckles as he pulled her back into the living room, where Vern and Shirley slept in a ball on Delaney's old couch and the call of an almost normal evening awaited.

Marcella floated behind him like a helium balloon.

Though, she reluctantly acknowledged, her hand, wrapped in Kellen's, had she been a mortal girl at this very moment, probably would have made her feel like she was floating anyway.

How incredibly high school.

nine

Somehow, after episode three of *Project Runway*, Kellen had landed headfirst on her shoulder, snoring so loudly she was certain the afterlife felt the tremors. His heavy weight slumped against her in a not-so-unpleasant way. Little by little, she'd been able to accomplish small things like sitting on furniture, though picking things up still eluded her. Earlier, she'd just been grateful to have the ability to sit beside him.

Now, with her hormones in four-wheel drive—not as much.

She shifted, hoping to avoid disturbing him, only to find his lips precariously close to her breast. Warmth flooded her. Just a sixteenth of an inch more and he was going to be where she'd fantasized many a night away. Her breathing hitched on the way out of her lungs when he mumbled something she couldn't hear, but vibrated against her nipple.

A low groan threatened escape, a moan of pleasure she'd never be able to take back. Placing her arm on the back of the couch, she attempted to inch away from him, only to have him settle in deeper, tightening an arm around her waist and pulling her to him.

Her pulse skittered sideways when he muttered, breathing out a sigh.

If she hadn't been clear about the man upstairs shunning her before, this cinched the deal. If He were merciful, He'd never have allowed her to put herself in this position. This was the scenario of all her dreams come true. Kellen hadn't come this close to her ever, and now he was suddenly comfortable enough to slap up against her like they'd always done this. In fact, she'd be super-duper pissed that he was taking liberties, if the liberties weren't so damned liberally nice. She grew angry at how easily she was accepting his turnabout. Why now, when she was about as mortal as a vampire, had he decided to take a liking to her? Why not when she'd been, if not of the living, at the very least able to wear cute dresses and heels?

She warred with the urge to burrow beneath him or drop his ass flat and hightail it out of the apartment.

Kellen stirred. "Marcella?"

"Mmm-hmm?"

"My head seems to be buried in your . . ."

"Boobs. Go ahead. You can say it."

"Boobs."

"Freeing, right?"

"No doubt. But this presents a problem."

"Or two, maybe three. We should tally them. I'll get paper." She made a move to get off the couch, but he gripped her tighter, forcing her to arch her body into his.

"Do you know why this presents a problem?"

"Because I'm a killer, and no good, morally sound man should have his face in a killer's boobs?"

"That wasn't where I was going."

"Where are you going?"

"This presents a problem because I *like* having my face in your boobs."

Madre santa. Words she'd waited a decade to hear, now said, were more powerful than she could have ever imagined. Fireworks shot off in every direction behind her closed eyes. "If it makes you feel any better, you're not the first man to find himself in a dilemma such as this."

"That didn't make me feel better."

"Apologies."

"Accepted. So here's the thing—what are we going to do about the fact that I *like* having my head in your boobs?"

"Move my boobs?"

Marcella felt his grin against the thin, torn material of her dress. "Let's not be hasty."

"Right. Proceed with caution."

"Question? Just off the cuff."

"I'm on pins and needles."

"Do you like me having my face buried in your boobs?"

To the millionth power, baby. She fought a squirm at how direct his question was. To confirm would be to show her cards, and she wasn't sure if she'd had the chance to catch her breath at his change in attitude toward her yet, let alone express her darkest fantasies. Her response was noncommittal. "It isn't unpleasant."

"Would you venture to say *you* like it?"

She bit the inside of her cheek. "I wouldn't say I hate it."

He snickered. "It's good my ego's healthy."

"Everyone should have an ego as healthy as yours."

Kellen cleared his throat. "So the problem."

"Yes. The problem . . ."

"I really don't want to move my head."

"Maybe that's because it's been a long time since you had your face in someone's boobs and any boobs'll do? Even a killer's?"

"I'd like to chalk it up to that, but in truth, I was seeing someone a few months ago."

Jealousy clawed at her tongue, making her want to say hateful things. But she refrained, ever the lady. "And she didn't like your face in her boobs?" *Twit.*

"She didn't seem to mind, but her boobs weren't your boobs. So I called it off."

A warm glow fluttered over her ego. "You broke up with someone because she didn't have my boobs?"

"No, not exactly. What I'm saying is her boobs weren't as . . ."

"Nice as mine. I understand. I have been gifted as racks go."

"Modest."

"Honest."

"How about we do this," Kellen said, still unmoving. "I'll tell you where I'm at, then you can tell me how you feel about it."

"Are we going down the path of the warm and squishy?"

"I can't say for sure. I'd settle for honesty."

She nodded her agreement. "I'm in."

"There's always been tension between us."

"An understatement if ever there was one."

"True that. We've fought many a battle."

"Like fierce warriors," she agreed.

"We haven't always been pleasant in word or thought."

"You had unpleasant thoughts about me?" She pretended astonished disbelief.

"Several that involved various degrees of manslaughter."

A wince made her lips pucker. "Harsh."

"Truthful."

"We have a checkered past. If I seem shocked by your sudden

generosity of spirit toward me, and I credit that to your just wanting to wonk, I don't think that's unfair," she offered.

"So we're clear, I'm not the kind of man who'd ignore his morals just to boff."

Gallant. "I'll take that under consideration."

"Anyway, that very tension also translates into something else we
both know exists, but haven't ever acknowledged because I despised
your demonic origins and you despised me for despising you."

"Interpretation?"

"Some of the tension has to do with your attraction to me—"

Her eyes rolled. Truth or not. "Modest."

"Honest. It also has to do with *my* attraction to *you*."

Yeah, tha'ssright. He'd said it. Her hormones shook their pom-
poms. If she still had her heart, it'd surely shifted farther left of
center.

"I've denied it for a long time. I've told myself it was only lust,
because, let's face it, you're not exactly ugly," he teased. "And screwing for that purpose alone isn't really my thing. But I don't feel that
way anymore."

"That screwing for screwing's sake isn't your thing?"

"No, Marcella. That my attraction to you is based solely on
lust."

"What's it based on now? And be careful what you say—your
face *is* in my boobs. It'll be hard to believe you're not just trying
to get to first base with me."

"What I'm saying is I like you."

"Do you still have your class ring?"

"Why?"

"Isn't this the moment where you give me your letter jacket
and class ring so I can wear it around my neck?"

"I think you're way too far past high school to hope for a class
ring."

"Ow."

When Kellen's head lifted, he wasn't smiling anymore. His eyes flashed dark in the glow of the television, serious, and above all, with sincerity. It was stark and crystal clear. Pulling her down beneath him, he took her chin between his fingers. "I like you, Marcella. It's been easier to get along with you finding that out. I'm not sure when it happened, but it did. I don't know how long you'll be here, so I'm going to skip the bullshit we slam each other with and cut to the chase. More than that, I want you in a way I can't put into words. But that presents a problem."

And the screwing just kept on coming. "Because I'm a ghost," she said, fighting the deflation her heart felt.

"That and we don't know how long you'll be here on this plane."

"And you're afraid you'll be so much fabulous I won't be able to get over you when I go back. That I'll spend the rest of my eternity mourning you while I ignore personal hygiene and wear dark clothing?" She'd laced it with a hint of her usual sarcasm to ward off the truth to her words.

Kellen stared at her for a moment, deep and penetrating. "No. I'm worried, if we do this, I won't be able to get over *you*."

There weren't many moments she could recall, in all the time she'd been around, that words escaped her. Yet at this very particular moment, when she was finally hearing what she'd spent pathetic night after pathetic night longing for, she was suddenly in the red with her word-bank account.

Kellen's declaration, such a severe contrast to the heated words they'd snarled at each other over the years, was almost too much. The crash of her heart, the catch of her breath, the rush of her pulse didn't help facilitate communication.

His dark eyebrows rose. "You're surprised."

Like that word even remotely defined how she felt about his

confession. She fell instantly into the mode she was most comfortable with. Defensive and catty. "If this is just about getting into my Victoria's Secrets, it's not necessary. I don't need pretty words and promises. As you so enjoy telling me, I've been to the rodeo. I know how to ride the horse without getting thrown off. You don't need to woo me all right and proper." Because it would only haunt her for eternity. If he just wanted to get it on, honesty would be premium right now.

"I'm not making promises, Marcella. I'm stating facts."

Damn him and his sincerity. "Or feeding me a line of crap so you can get in my panties when you know full well you won't have to eat those words because I can't stick around to make you."

Leaning toward her, he brushed her nose with his lips. "Don't be hostile. It's not how you really feel about me."

She swatted him away, ignoring the desire to sever all communication via her mouth plastered to his. "Do you find it at all coincidental that this revelation's occurring while you have a very noticeable condition pressed against my thigh?"

"I see your skepticism," he offered magnanimously while repositioning himself against her so they were clear on why she was skeptical.

"Good, then how about we don't talk feelings anymore? It won't change what will eventually happen to me. It might just make it worse. I've had enough of worse. How about you?"

"I just want my thoughts on the subject clear."

She made a bold move by reaching down between them and pressing the heel of her hand to the cause of her buttload of skepticism. "So I won't think you're the kind of man who's capable of a one-night stand?"

Running a thumb along her jaw, he whispered, gravelly and low, "No, so you won't think I'm capable of a one-night stand with *you*."

When his finger traced her lower lip, she grew skittish, afraid now that the barriers between them were tumbling down, she'd never be able to survive it. "So you're capable of a one-night stand with someone else?"

"I've had my share of encounters—not all just one-night, no, but there were a couple." He placed a light kiss on her forehead, leaving his lips there to linger against her skin. The security that represented, the overwhelming bliss it brought her soul, frightened her.

Kellen had just been a sexual fantasy. Or so she'd thought. The mistake she'd made was believing that was her *only* fantasy where he was concerned. She'd thought leaving behind his rock-hard abs and teacherlike, sexy appeal were all she'd mourn.

Yet, lying here, circled in his embrace, the warmth of his breath on her skin was so intimate, it physically hurt.

Freaking out was in order.

"Kellen?"

His lips moved against her forehead. "Yes?"

"Snap out of it, right now!" She gave a shove to his chest to dislodge him from her. He didn't budge.

"Is this the part where you freak out as a defense mechanism against my admission of like? Before you do that, I just want you to know, it's perfectly natural. I read in a medical journal that some react—"

"Psst!" She put her fingers to his lips. "I don't want a scientific explanation for why I'm freaking out. I just want a good, old-fashioned shot at it. Now get off of me. This can only lead to bad feelings. What would Delaney say? Omigod. She'd be so hacked off if I slept with you. She's my best friend. Best friends don't sleep with each other's brothers. Ever. Now move."

"Delaney has no say in what I do. I'm an adult."

"Yeah. That's not what you were saying when she was crying over me and my predicament, pansy-ass."

He smiled down at her, infuriatingly so. "I can promise you, she won't cry if we sleep together."

No, but I might. Because as of late, if producing tears was a job, she'd be head crier. "We shouldn't do this. It'll only make everything worse. Sex shouldn't be our primary focus. Helping Carlos should."

"He doesn't need our help right now. He's safe at home."

"Spoken like a man whose little head has the reins."

Kellen yawned then grinned. "I don't think I've ever seen Marcella Acosta so rattled. I like it. It makes me feel a little superior."

Crossing her arms over her chest, she said, "As if you didn't always feel that way."

Pushing off from her, leaving her lying on the couch sprawled out like a fish out of water, he grinned again. "You're right. I behaved badly. I suck. Now, I'm going to suck while I sleep. I have to open the store early tomorrow. I say we go to bed. I'll keep your side of the bed warm. No pressure. We can just snuggle. I'd bet that appeals to the girl in you." Turning on his heel, his sudden change in direction obviously amusing him, judging by the grin on his smug face, he headed for the bedroom.

Just snuggle . . . she snorted to herself.

Spite kept her ass on the couch for a long time after Kellen had turned off the light.

Curiosity made her waffle.

She consoled herself with the notion that she'd done the right thing by turning him down. Call it crazy, but after her demonic life of excess, living day to day on mostly impulse and her selfish need to gather material things by the ton, the only thing she had done right was that she'd done right by Delaney. That was one line, no matter the coup, she would try not to cross. Delaney wouldn't want Kellen involved with her. She'd want someone who was innocent, earthy, tofu-loving. Sweet, considerate. Not some hard-assed demon jaded by decades of the demonic high life.

But that wasn't bringing her the kind of comfort his arms had.

Maybe, if she just slipped in beside him while he was sound asleep, he'd never know she was there. She didn't sleep anyway; if he woke up, she'd slip back out.

Floating to the bedroom, she passed through the wall and hovered at the end of his bed. He'd been true to his word. He'd saved the other half of the bed for her.

Clenching her eyes, she pushed the doubts that plagued her to a dark closet in her mind. There'd be plenty of time for her misgivings to eat a hole in her heart when she was back on Chez Drab.

For now, impulse clutched her, dragging her to the other side of the bed. Climbing in beside him, Marcella lay down next to the man who'd been the object of her desire for years and closed her eyes, realizing Kellen was no longer just a desirable object.

He was a man she wanted to snuggle with.

Preposterous.

The shift of the covers made her lips twitch when Kellen lifted them, tucking them around her shoulders, and rolled into her, wrapping a strong arm around her waist.

Making her smile.

"Marcelllaaa."

A wet nose buried itself in her neck. Blech. Maybe choosing not to sleep with Kellen hadn't been so whacked after all. Swatting at the intrusion, she fought to rediscover this place of apparent rest she hadn't been able to find since she'd become a ghost.

A snort, low and grunting, tickled her eardrum, as did a tongue, slimy and warm. In retrospect, that she'd passed up this kind of sexual prowess brought only relief that she hadn't allowed herself to become carried away last night. The morality police cheered in her head. *Way. To. Go!*

A heavy weight settled on her chest and began licking her cheek. Breath, not unlike that of a Dumpster, wafted beneath her nose. God in all his mercy. How had she missed the stench of Kellen's breath last night?

"I know you're in this bed, Marcella, and I just want you to know, I'm supportive of this—this—afterlife love connection with my brother. I know you've always thought I'd be against it because you were a demon. You know, the whole Hell thing, but I don't feel that way at all. I know, despite your—your displays of va-va-voomishness, and all the airs you put on, that you're a good person. And I know you hate that I know that. And, omigod, I'm so glad the two of you are getting along that I'm all weepy. Now all we need to do is get you earthbound again so you can marry Kellen and make babies," a voice, not unpleasant or unfamiliar, whispered, rushed and rambling, in her ear. "So get up, ghost, because I have some exciting news."

Married. She heard nothing else but that word. A filthy word if there ever was one. She'd been married, and now, he was dead. Maybe married wasn't a skill in her wheelhouse. Her eyes shot open to find her best friend almost staring at her, but missing her mark by just a half inch to the right of her face. "Delaney?"

Kellen sat up with a rumble, dragging the covers off her.

Marcella looked down. Delaney's dog, the one with the BeDazzled diaper, burrowed into her chest, making himself a comfy place to settle. She couldn't remember what number he was. Delaney didn't have names for her dogs, only numbers. Whatever his number, it was up, as far as she was concerned. Though, clearly he could see her, and touch her, and he liked her boobs as much as Kellen had. She gave him a narrow-eyed gaze. "Get off of me, you beast. I don't have much of a dress left. I definitely don't want it to smell like dog," she growled.

He growled back, sinking his BeDazzled butt further into her chest.

She raised her eyes to Kellen. "Help."

His sleepy, rumpled, sexy self reached over, lifting the dog to settle him by his side.

Delaney eyed the two of them from the end of the bed with a fond gaze that made Marcella squirm. "So—I don't want to jump to conclusions, but I'm guessing you've, ah, made nice," she teased with a smile, crossing her arms over her chest, allowing the flowing fabric of her shirtsleeves to drape over her belly.

"It's not what you think, D," Kellen said, running a hand through his tousled hair. "And how did you know Marcella was here anyway?"

She pointed to dog number 222, or whatever. "They're otherworldly sensitive, remember? And whether Marcella liked it or not, they adored her. Especially if she had panty hose on. Besides, her perfume's everywhere. Now both of you get up. I have some exciting news."

"News?" Marcella asked.

Kellen stretched, his toned muscles flexing and rippling beneath copper skin. "Marcella wants to know what news."

Delaney gave him a smugly arrogant look. "I know how to get her earthbound again."

Now Marcella sat up. "That's impossible. There is no way to come back from the dead unless you're a demon or a vampire. Period."

Kellen eyed her. "You know vampires?"

"If only you knew who I know," she said dryly.

"Both of you pay attention. Marcella *can* become earthbound again."

Marcella was stunned. But it was impossible.

"How?" Kellen demanded with a gruff bark. His sudden interest brought back their conversation from last night, leaving Marcella more skittish than ever.

Delaney gave him a hesitant glance as though she were reconsidering sharing her thoughts, but then her face changed and she went for it in a rush of words. "Well, here's the thing, and this is just on the fly. It might need tweaking—revisions—something. So I was on my way over here to see how you two were getting along, because, well, you don't get along. Imagine my surprise when I found you not only in the same zip code, but in the *same bed*. Never mind, that's neither here nor there. I stopped to get some coffee on the way, and while I waited, I was counting my blessings and then I remembered what happened with Clyde. So here's what we have to do. We have to find a freshly dead body. Now, before the two of you balk, give me a minute. Marcella's basically just a soul, wandering free. If we found someone who's dead, like maybe only a minute or two, just long enough so we can be sure that person's soul has crossed over, she could technically jump into the body and inhabit it." She finished with another smug smile, obviously rather pleased with her solution.

Marcella's mouth fell open. "Have the burbs given her brain damage? Maybe it's hanging out with all those housewives and their whole-food organic bullshit. I've always told her it's okay to have cow every once in a while to keep your immune system strong."

"I think it's too much *Ghost Whisperer*," he muttered out of the side of his delicious mouth.

"She's insane."

Delaney caught Kellen's eyes. "She's calling me insane, isn't she?"

"She is and so am I."

Delaney's hands fluttered in the air. "Don't you see this could work? Clyde did it. He got back into his body just as it left this Earth!"

Marcella shook her curls with a fierce bob of her head. "Tell her that, while I love her, I'm not afraid to also tell her she needs to stop sucking on all those weeds she's so fond of. They've addled her brain. The hell I'm getting into some poor dead person's body."

Kellen slid to the end of the bed, pulling his jeans from the floor to slip them on, running a hand over his forehead before he spoke. "D, Clyde was getting into *his* body, not someone else's, and he was doing it so he could cross over. If Marcella did it, she'd be violating someone else's body, and jumping into someone else's life. That person would have family, friends, maybe even kids. Marcella wouldn't know who they were."

Delaney's enthusiasm waned—big. Marcella watched as she searched for yet another solution. "So we find someone who has no family or friends or a job or . . ."

Kellen kissed Delaney's forehead and forced her to look at him. "You do know that'd be almost impossible, right?" He spoke the words with gentle admonishment, gripping her shoulders with his tanned hands.

Marcella's heart constricted when she saw Delaney's crestfallen face.

Delaney sighed. "Okay, so I didn't think it entirely through, but it still could work," she mumbled. "I have nothing else. I can't find a single thing in any of my books to help get her back here with us. I've been up day and night, trying to find anything that will help. I can't sleep for the worry. There's boatloads of info on rein-carnation, which I thought might lead us to at least a clue, but there's nothing. It seems when you're a ghost, you're a ghost, and

if you don't have the light as recourse, that's how you stay." Her
words held such defeat, Marcella winced. "I just want her back
here with us. Do you hear me, Marcella?" she called out into the
room. "I'm not giving up, you pain in my ass. You saved Clyde
and me. You deserve better!"

Marcella rose from the bed to float to Kellen's side. She gave
Delaney a sympathetic smile her friend couldn't see, forcing her
next statement from her lips. "This was what I was afraid of. That
she wouldn't let this go, and instead of focusing on her new marriage and house, she'd waste time trying to find a way to get me
back here on this plane. And I don't want that. It's impossible anyway. Tell her I love her for trying. Now stop. Please. Let it be."

"No," Kellen replied with a measure of defiance to his tone.

Marcella's eyes widened. "What did you say?"

He put his hands on her shoulders to hold her in place as she
wafted upward. "I said *no*. I'm not going to tell her to give up.
In fact, D showing up saves me a phone call. I'd planned to call
her to see if she'd figured anything out. Now that she's here, I'm
going to tell her what we know about Carlos, and then I'm going
to suggest we put our heads together and figure out a way to get
you back to this plane." His hazel eyes, flecked with gold, fired off
a challenge.

Fear gripped her heart. To hope they could find a way to keep
her here was to beat the proverbial horse. It was unfair even to ask
her to consider that she could resume her old life. Not only that,
it infuriated her.

Knowing it was also unfair to condemn them for caring about
her didn't stop her from behaving irrationally.

Floating to the doorway, she threw Kellen a hard look. "I said
I want you both to let it alone, God damn it! Why won't you two
get it through your thick skulls? Fuck-all, I don't want to do this
anymore! I don't want to keep being left behind. Jesus, how hard

is that to understand? How would you feel if you had to live eternally and watch the people you love die off one by one?" Tears thickened her throat, and that was when she turned and fled.

Because that was the crux of the matter. Even if she could regain her earthbound privileges, she probably wouldn't be human when she did. She'd let Delaney in once, and though she'd never regretted befriending her, she'd known it would hurt when it was her time to cross.

And now there was Kellen—who she'd almost let in. Kellen who was dreaming up a future that could never be.

A future she didn't deserve because she'd done something unforgivable.

Nothing could ever fix that.

What about *nothing* didn't everyone get?

ten

Hours passed as Marcella sat in her old apartment, drifting from room to room, longing to touch her things, her clothes, her shoes. Her lease wasn't up for another three months. Maybe she could just stay here until whatever was going to happen to her finally did.

It hadn't occurred to her earlier, in all the turmoil and chaos, to come home. She'd figured, much as her earthbound privileges were gone, so were her apartment and everything with it. But curiosity, and the need for the creature comforts of one's home, had called to her.

She'd come back to New York fifty years after she'd left, having spent those fifty of her demonic years as far away from her hometown as she could. The once painful memories of Armando and the doomed marriage she'd left behind were replaced by the inviting memories of her childhood growing up right here in this very apartment. Sort of. In 1934, it had been a small house that she, her mother, father, grandmother, and older sister, Isabella, had shared.

When she'd realized a development company had built co-ops where her old house once stood, she'd conjured up some cash and leased it. It was to her advantage that ownership changed hands regularly, and so did the name on her lease. In order to stay in the home she'd once loved, she'd had to continually reinvent herself to management, but it was worth the memories.

The cool colors of her apartment, pale green and ice blue with oyster accents, had once soothed her. Now all of her vases and paintings did nothing but frustrate her. She couldn't touch them. She couldn't run her fingers along the smooth tops of her walnut-stained furniture or sit on her precious off-white Ethan Allen couch with the Pier 1 throw pillows.

Floating to the kitchen, she closed her eyes and called up the image of her grandmother in their old kitchen, rolling tortillas and humming while her mother, a seamstress, worked on hemming pants for her father's tailoring business. A new batch of tears floated her eyeballs until she couldn't see anything but the blur of her recollections. The only regret she had about selling her soul was losing her family. Her mother and father never would have understood *why* she'd killed Armando. Though deeply religious, they never quite believed in her gift of sight. No one did. Only her grandmother had believed, and she'd warned Marcella of the dangers of revealing her gift. Her parents would have had her at the Vatican as fast as a boat trip could get them there. It was Grandma Rosa who'd taught her how to deal with the constant intrusion of the afterlife in her young world. It was her grandmother who'd warned her about Armando, too.

From the grave.

In a way, she was almost grateful they didn't understand what she'd done by marrying Armando. Why she'd had to kill him . . .

Her father had fought enough in the way of battles by marrying her mother, someone his family hotly disapproved of. The shame of his daughter's indiscretion would have killed him.

There was enough guilt to go around—more would only have left her with an eternity of deeper depression to deal with. Back then, Xanax wasn't an option.

Eyeing her fridge, she longed to lay her face against the cool, silvery exterior and mope some more. But there was information about Carlos to be found, and that sex kitten in work boots Catalina was due to call.

Steeling herself to stop this whine she'd become so gifted at, Marcella bolted through the door of her apartment without looking back. Surely some of her old contacts would be at the bar she'd once frequented when getting information was of the utmost importance. They might not be willing to talk to her, and some might not have the ability to see her, but she still had ears. Why she hadn't considered it sooner than this could only be chalked up to the emotional turmoil her afterlife was in.

If this thing with Carlos was a hellbound fact, someone would be yucking it up and taking pleasure in the coming mayhem.

If hitting her old hot spots didn't work, she'd dig Darwin back up out of some boozer's body. She was going to figure out what this all meant for Carlos. Her anger with Darwin was unfair anyway. She'd reacted in a very un-Marcella-like way to a response that was only reasonable, considering she hadn't shared the entire story of Armando's death.

Apologies were probably in order—which would blow the rest of her image all to shit, but Darwin didn't deserve her newly found joy in a good, crying hissy fit.

First, some of her old haunts.

Skipping in virtually unnoticed, Marcella floated to the back of the Sin Bin, owned by Satan himself and operated by his slimy pricks. Scanning the interior of the dank, greasy hole, she cringed at the memory of her last visit to this abyss of iniquity and desperation. But it had yielded information that had saved Delaney. She was almost of a mind to pray it did the same for Carlos. But she'd forgotten how to pray. So she'd instead hope for the kind of luck she'd once found in this dive.

Ears pricked, she headed to the farthest region of the black and deep purple bar where most of the action happened. Beaded curtains covered the back rooms where the supreme order of filth played. Sultry music thrummed from the speakers along the walls. Low rumbles of laughter mingled with groans of pleasure whispered along the maze of corridors to her right. Smoke, thick and hazy, wafted in clouds of gray throughout the air.

Tawdry scenes awaited her, scenes involving the most decadent of Satan's followers—alive and dead. Gagging, she fought the impulse to run. Instead, Marcella peered through one red and purple beaded curtain.

"Oh, Marcella. I knew you'd come home," a voice, black and silken, slithered in her ear. "Come give your old pal Satan a big stinkin' hug."

Whipping around, she found herself eye to eye with the Prince of Darkness. Her stomach churned bitter acid. Lucifer held out his arms, open wide, but she backed away, finding a doorway to hover in, cocking her eyebrow in a familiarly arrogant expression. "So, how's tricks?"

He threw his head back and laughed a deep, resonating vibration that shook the walls. He wore stonewashed jeans with a hole in the knee and under his open jacket a T-shirt that read "I Put the 'Cute' in 'Execute.'" It stretched over his skinny chest when he planted his hands on his hips. "Oh, Marcella. I've missed you so. Tell me, see-through one, have you missed me, too?"

"Like a seeping boil on my ass," she replied, coolly. God, it felt good to be in control. Where it had come from and why wasn't as important as that it had. Kellen and Carlos had left her bobbing in a sea of alien emotions, but this—what she felt for Satan—this she knew. Welcomed. Luxuriated in like a silky bath full of perfumed beads of soap.

His sharply angled, bony face cracked a smile filled with malevolence when he thumped his chest with a slender, pale hand. "The pain of rejection. So deep it cuts," he mocked.

Marcella's lips fastened together to ward off a snarl.

"Tell me, are you miserable on that plane riddled with wishy-washy souls?"

"As if you care."

Holding up his hand, he curled his fingers around something imaginary. "This is my 'care cup.'" He gasped when he looked down with an exaggerated pair of wide eyes. "And look, it's empty. So, how's our friend Delaney? Still full of homespun sugary goodness?"

No thanks to you. A ripple of more fear slithered up her spine. If he wanted backsies, he could still seek vengeance on Delaney and, without the gift, she'd have no recourse. "Delaney's not your concern."

Satan ignored the implied warning in her words and shot her a jovial grin. "So what's new? How's life treating you? Does it utterly and completely suck living out your eternity roaming endlessly with all those whimpering losers?"

Rolling with his jab at her spectral state, Marcella sought calm. He hadn't been her target, but who better than El Diablo to get the inside scoop? "I need a moment of your time."

He bobbed his head with a cheerfully knowing glance. "Yeaahhh," he rasped. "I guess you're here to beg for your hellbound privileges? Can't say as I blame you, cupcake. You're a hot mess." His lean fingers swept the length of her dress.

Marcella's chin lifted just like in days of old. In defiance, and without warning, she felt the surge of hatred rise up to lie solidly in her chest. "Please, you puke. The day I beg you for anything is the day we're all doing triple axels in Hell."

Lucifer mock shivered with a shake of his reed-thin shoulders. "I love it when you're spicy hot! It's ssspunky. That you don't want to revisit the shelter of my protective wings breaks my wee little heart. I haz a sad." He let his lower lip tremble before it fell back into his vile grin. "So what brings you to the Bin if not the longing for my loving arms?"

"First, a question?" Caution was the better part of valor, and testing the waters was not only wise but imperative before she got herself into something far worse than she was already in.

Lucifer arched a pointy eyebrow in anticipation.

She purred at him, smoldering her eyes and throwing on her flirtatious pout. "Let's say I wanted to come back and serve— what's the skinny on that?"

His beady eyes glowed with loathing. "You'd be wearing cute, rhinestoned leotards with frilly skirts on them and sharpening your figure skates. But even if you wanted to, or better still, *I* allowed you to, you couldn't come back. That pathetic simpleton Uriel interfered—he had the last word. That means you're his, lollipop. Too bad, so sad."

Note to ghostly self—when you have some extra time on your hands and you're not crying over something ridiculous like a commercial for that show Intervention, *find out who in all of fuck Uriel is.* Marcella grinned in response. His statement meant there was nuthin' to lose. "With that settled, I want to know what you know about Armando Villanueva."

"Who?"

Satan's apparently genuine surprise startled her, but there wasn't much he loved to do more than toy with someone who was at their lowest. She wasn't falling for it. "Stupid doesn't suit you."

"Oh, never mistake me for stupid, Marcella. You've done that once before, and now look. Anyhoodles, I have no idea who you're talking about."

"You know exactly who I mean. He's the filthy prick I killed. You know, the one I became a demon because of?"

"Marcella, Marcella. Grudge, grudge. Sooo unhealthy, fruit cup. You know that's not entirely how you ended up under my command . . ."

Her eyes went hard as granite. If he dared to speak the name, she'd—*what, Marcella? You are one loose cannon, here, chica. You got nuthin' but your mouth working in your favor. So shut it.* Reason settled back in, voiding her irrational response. "Where is Armando?"

He paused for a moment, reaching into the pocket of his bomber jacket and pulling out his iPhone. "Refresh me. There are so many of you fallen, it's like corralling greased cats."

"Dark, Hispanic, bottom-feeder, died in 1934."

"Sold his soul before or after death?"

She gritted her teeth. "Before."

"Oh, right, right. Well, my iPhone app tells me he's inactive. Pity, too. He was one evil dude, according to his stats. Could have been a brilliant protégé."

"I have a problem."

"The first among which is your dress," he responded dryly, shooting her a wink.

Enough with the damned dress, already. "He's not inactive. I locked his soul in a box. That box is officially open. Where is the fuck?"

"Considering a tearful reconciliation?"

"With candles and chilled champagne. Surely you can see my anticipation? *Where—is—he?*"

Lucifer waved a disinterested hand. "I have no idea where Armando is. If he's no longer inactive, he hasn't come forth to say as much. I don't mind telling you, I'm very disheartened that he hasn't. It's downright painful when my babies desert me."

"Which means he's rogue . . ." she baited with a satisfied tilt upward of her lips. There was nothing Lucifer liked less than a demon gone rogue—especially a demon as vile and willing to do anything as Armando had been. The very notion that someone might try to usurp his throne, no matter how ludicrous, made Satan a cranky-pants.

Yet his reaction was composed. Clucking his tongue, he tsk-tsked with a forlorn sigh. "You know how much I despise that, don't you, Marcella? It makes me so uptight and tense. Hits me right here." He reached behind him and thumped the middle of his back. "So do dish. How did Armando get out of this box?"

Shit. Cornered. "Someone let him out."

"*Who*, sugarplum?"

"A kid," someone cackled from behind the curtain of swinging beads. "Name's Carlos. Don't know what that freak Armando wants with him, Boss. Just heard the rumor."

Suck-ass demons.

Marcella fought an outward cringe and the urge to bitch-slap the fuckwit. She'd hoped never to mention Carlos's name, thus keeping him out of Hell's potential clutches and off the radar.

Lucifer peered over his shoulder, aiming a malicious eye at his cackling minion. He went from glacially cool to maniacally hot in the course of a nanosecond. "*Yooou!*" he roared. "Better have some answers for me as to how Armando's been left unaccounted for—or the pit will seem like Candy Land."

Silently, she saw Lucifer flip through his iPhone again.

"Carlos . . . there's no Carlos on my roster. Not to be collected or wooed to the dark side." His face was placidly blank, then evilly menacing when it became clear he'd realized Armando might have something he wanted. "So," he purred, low and grumbly, "whatever do you think Armando wants with this boy? What does he have that Armando wants? I'm ever so curious."

And it was the kind of sick curiosity that made Marcella's knees tremble and her mouth go dry. "I don't know."

Satan cocked his head to the left and pouted his lips. "Ah, this isn't really about your dearly departed, heinously murdered husband. This is about a little boy. So interesting. I'm all atwitter."

"Leave the little boy alone."

The expression on his face said his interest was growing. "Relax, girlie. Don't get all hinky on me. I didn't even know he existed until mere moments ago."

"Good, then forget you heard his name," she hissed, displaying her hatred for him with a flash of her green eyes.

"Come now. I can't do that. What kind of supreme ruler would I be if I didn't investigate? If he's of interest to Armando, and you're in the mix, I feel some bloodshed coming on, and I want in!"

Her temper, the one that usually created nothing but trouble, went ahead and created trouble. "You fucking pathetic bastard. You leave that little boy alone or I'll—"

"What, Marcella? Do battle with me by using your very scary floating skillz?"

"Fuck. You."

Satan tilted his head, placing one finger under her chin and thrusting her higher in the air. His glance was thoughtful. "How did I ever underestimate you in all the years you served me, cookie? You're so full of vim and vigor. It's stimulating. I'd venture to say it's even invigorating, though sadly classless. I should have paid closer attention to your potential for growth. But alas, you slipped through the cracks." He shrugged his shoulders. "It happens. Despite myth, I really can't be everywhere."

Her lips thinned, her jaw tightened so hard it trembled. She had no power against Lucifer. But by all that was sacred, she'd find a way to keep him from Carlos. "Leave the little boy alone. Do whatever you want to me. Take me back as your minion and I'll serve you in the pit, but leave him the fuck alone."

Dragging a finger along the tops of her breasts, now spilling from her torn dress, he smiled with insidious knowing. "Haven't you done this before? You offer up your soul for a loved one, live a tortured half-demon life, flying on the down-low, and all the while mourning your losses? Blah, blah, blah. Boooring. What is it about you and self-sacrifice that go hand in hand? Didn't you learn your lesson the first time?"

Ignoring the bait he dangled in front of her face, Marcella spat out, "Leave him alone."

His sigh was playful, disdainful when he dropped her. "Oh, Marcella. Always with the blame. I think I've mentioned once or twice that I'm rather put upon. I can't tell you the things I'm accused of. If I were able to create the kind of constant havoc people declare I wreak, I'd be due for a very long vacation in a room with lots of padding. Even I have my limits. However, I'm pleased to inform you, this thing with that child has nothing to do with me. Do I get a cookie for being a good boy now?"

Moving in closer, she jammed her face in his. "Everything ultimately comes down to you, you fuckwit. You call the shots—*you* can fix this."

"Uh-uh-uh." He shook a chastising finger under her nose. "No name-calling. It's unpleasant and only makes for bad feelings between us. We have enough of those, don't we, honeybunch? Now, to set the record straight. I know nothing of this Carlos, and I have no idea why he's been targeted by Armando. I set my minions free to do my bidding. How they do it, why, or when is completely up to them. I pride myself on being an equal opportunity employer and an exceptional delegator when it comes to doling out workloads."

He was lying. He had to be. Next to nothing escaped him. "Then find out, because the next motherfucker who scares the living shit out of this kid is on my hit list," she ground out. *Big words there, Marcella. What the fuck is it about you that just won't allow you to get a grip on your mouth and back down when the backing's good?*

Satan gave another mock shiver and winked at her. "Ohhh, how imposing. I just know everyone in the bowels of my kingdom of evil has left a puddle beneath their wee webbed feet because Marcella Acosta's made a threat. Scary, scary *you*." He punctuated the last word with a bony finger between her eyes.

Frustration, infinite anger, pure rage surged through her body. Launching herself at him, she screamed, "If there's ever a way, ever the slightest, remotest opportunity, I'll find a way to make you pay!"

He yawned, using one clawed finger to swat her away, sending her to the ground with a hard jolt to her limbs. "Yeahhh. Like that threat hasn't been made a thousand times before you by far more competent foes. And look who's still standing. Scurry on now. You're no longer my concern. Surely you have a house to haunt." His giggle was low, taunting, shrieking through her ears as he set his minions on her like a pack of dogs with nothing more than a nod of his head.

They dragged her to the front of the bar and chucked her out of it like day-old bread—which was when levitation wasn't as much annoying as it was handy.

Marcella's mind raced. Satan was a lying, thieving scumbag. Yet, he'd looked none too pleased that Armando was loose, not to mention completely unaware. So if Satan didn't want Carlos, and the rumor in Hell was that Armando did, what the frig was the connection between Armando and a little boy?

She had to get the information to Kellen. Maybe he'd heard from Catalina and they could piece something together.

Catalina barreled into the store while Kellen fought images of Marcella in his head. Summoning her via his visuals would only ruffle her already ruffled feathers. Her upset earlier made it clear she needed space. He wanted to give that to her. He was gritting his teeth trying to give that to her while determined to figure out a way to keep her here. Catalina stormed toward him, her work boots making clunky, wet footprints and dragging sodden leaves in behind her.

Facing him, she crossed her arms over her chest. "So, how big are your feet?"

"What kind of a question is that?"

"Just answer it," Catalina demanded.

His eyes grew wary. "Is this about my phone call?"

Placing a hand on the counter Kellen leaned against, she narrowed her gaze. "Just answer the question."

"Eleven."

Catalina pursed her lips and shook her head. "Oh, that'll never work."

"Is this some kind of code we're talking in?"

"No, I was just checking to see if your foot would fit in your mouth."

"I know there's an explanation to follow, so let's not beat around the bush."

Her sigh was ragged. "My friend, you've fucked up big. So big, you'll be kicking yourself into several reincarnations."

"Where are we going with this?"

"Marcella. Is she here, by the way?"

"No. You're clear. What about Marcella?"

"I have information. It's not a lot, but it's gonna hurt."

His stomach sank, and he found himself hoping he hadn't placed faith in Marcella that was misdirected. His feelings for her were changing, deepening, and it had nothing to do with his former lust. "I can take it."

"She's not who you think she is—was. She didn't end up in Hell because she sucked at humanity."

"She said it was because she'd killed her husband Armando . . ."

Her eyes went wide in shock then narrowed. "Oh, she definitely did that, but do you know why she put some nails in his coffin?"

Kellen's stomach shifted. "Because he was a dirty prick?"

"There's that, but there's more."

"Do I want to hear the more?"

"Depends on how well you deal with the idea that your judgment sucks balls."

He gave her a wry, sheepish smile. "I've grown comfortable with that particular assessment of my character's flaw."

"Good. Maybe you might want to sit. It's a shitwreck."

Kellen clenched his fists. "Just tell me."

"She ended up in Hell because she was probably one of the best people you'll ever know, Kellen. She definitely made the choice to be a minion, but it was for a whopper of a reason."

Kellen's head swirled. "Tell me," he demanded with a tight jaw.

"She had a son. A son her freak husband wanted for his own disgusting purposes. I don't know the deets, but I do know for a fact, she sold her soul to save her kid. A. *Baby*."

The air thinned; the room tipped and rocked, then righted itself. His breath left his lungs, then returned in a rush of too much air. "That's insane," he finally rasped.

Her eyes, hard and hawklike, scanned his. "Is it? I don't think so, Kell. What wouldn't a mother do to save her child? What length wouldn't she go to? Marcella went to the farthest length there is. To Hell and back. And you, pal, owe her an apology that just goes on and on. In fact, I think you should just say you're sorry whenever you're with her at least every twenty seconds, and still you won't be able to make it up to her. You blow chunks, and I think I speak for every demon who's ever been pressured to make a choice that in some eyes is unforgivable, when I say that you're all a bunch of self-righteous, black-and-white fucktards! It takes a strong woman to do what Marcella did, buddy."

Her defense of Marcella was so vehement, so impassioned, it made him take a step back. Catalina's anger was palpable, but he was too focused on what she'd just revealed to delve further. Marcella had had a child? His head was going to explode. "Are you sure? Are you sure your sources are right?"

Catalina's mouth formed a sour smile. "You mean because my sources are demons, right? Don't continue on the path of asshole, Kellen. I looked it up myself. I took great pleasure in stealing Marcella's file from some dimwit named Clyve—with a *v*, as he so vehemently reminded me. So, yeah. I'm sure."

The crash of reality roared in his ears. He felt like he'd just been kidney-punched. "Why the fuck would she keep something like that from us? From Delaney? Why wouldn't she just tell us what happened?"

Catalina barked a bitter laugh, jamming a hand into her hair. "Would you have believed her? How could she have proven something like that, Kellen?"

"I don't know!" he roared, unjustifiably angry with Marcella for keeping a secret so dark. It explained so much . . . He clenched his fists then flexed them to relax, softening his tone. "I don't know. But she never gave us the opportunity, did she?"

Cornering him, Catalina gave him a simmering, pointed glare. "Don't you dare turn this around on her to justify your behavior, Kellen! *Do. Not.* Marcella has her reasons. I'm sure most of them have to do with protecting her son, who, for all we know, is still alive. But you never asked her either, did you? The only person who didn't assume anything was Delaney, and that's because she was probably sensitive enough to know something horrific made Marcella do what she did all those years ago. She didn't pry because she knows a sore spot when she sees one. She accepted. You, on the other hand, are a judgmental caveman. So don't even think about blaming Marcella for your bad behavior. The demon world is full of secrets, some best left protected and definitely best left alone. Whatever Marcella did, why she did it, isn't for you to judge."

Kellen held his hands up to convey he got it. Relief that she hadn't revealed Marcella was a serial killer had begun to settle in. Now all that remained was question on top of question. "You're right, and it's obvious she and I have to talk. I'm also understanding her motivations a lot better where Carlos is concerned. Speaking of, did you get my message? Did you find anything else out?"

Catalina's lips fell into a sneer of revulsion. "Not a frickin' thing, but I've got all sorts of feelers out," she remarked, an odd, faraway look shadowing her face for a moment then clearing. "I'm not at all afraid to say I think Carlos has something Armando wants and he doesn't want anyone to know he wants it. He hasn't checked in to Hell after his imposed sabbatical. Satan doesn't like that. Means he's rogue. So wherever he's hiding, you can bet once Lucifer gets hold of this info, it'll be an all-points bulletin."

Shit, shit, shit. Just what they didn't need. "Have you seen anything strange going on at Carlos's place?"

She snorted. "Just his mother. I hate saying it, but what a piece of shit."

"Meaning?"

"What kind of mother stays out all night and sleeps her boozing off all day? She's been dropped off at that apartment by more slime than you could fill a maximum-security prison with."

Kellen's concern jacked up a notch. "Mrs. Ramirez said something was going on with her since the death of her husband. Something she didn't understand because, according to her, Solana's a good girl. Grief can do that to a person—change them." He knew that firsthand since his mother's death and the chaos with Vincent.

"Uh, does it turn them into whores?"

He winced in sympathy for Mrs. Ramirez. "Harsh assessment, my friend."

Catalina slapped her hands against her thighs. "I speak nuthin' but the truth. I don't see her during the daylight hours at all, and when I do see her, it's only her back end because she's on her way up the stairs after a night of boozing. I can't say I've even seen her up close, she's gone so much. My focus is Carlos. I can tell you, she spends more time plastered up against the side of a building, with some man feeling her up, than a bricklayer. I don't know when she has time to even bother with the kid, but I haven't seen or felt any suspicious activity in the way of the supernatural. Though, I feel like shit for the kid."

"So we're no further along than we were when this started. Fuck," he muttered, dragging a hand over the stubble on his chin.

"That we are, and I gotta blow, but do me a favor before I hit it."

"More bat shit?"

Catalina chuckled. "No. No more bullshit. Lay off Marcella, and if you confront her about this, do it without stomping all over the situation with those size elevens. She hurts. Even after all this time. You can trust me on that."

Kellen fixed his gaze on her, hoping to stare out of her what she wasn't telling him. "That sounds like it comes from experience."

"Never mind where it comes from. Just take heed. Later," she whispered low, wiggling her fingers to vaporize into the now darkened store.

Kellen sat on a stray chair and ran his fingers over his hair. He'd been so brutally wrong about Marcella, it left him exhausted just thinking about the energy he'd expended behaving like a total shit to her.

Marcella had once had a child. A baby. His chest tightened at her sacrifice. Going back over some of the words he'd snarled at her, the shitty things he'd accused her of, made him want to go back and eat every one of them. But there were no do-overs.

Why hadn't she ever told them?

Would you have believed her? He heard Catalina's succinct, cutting question ring in his head. God, he'd been a fuck of the worst order, and he had to make it right, but first he had to hear the words from her lips. Not only that, he had to find a way to keep her here.

With him.

Just yesterday and totally out of the blue, that notion had hit him like a Mack truck. Kellen Markham wanted Marcella Acosta to stay here with him. He wanted to know the person she'd been hiding with all of her sharp words and the flirtatious sway of her hips. Because she was a hell of a lot deeper than she was letting on.

And he wanted in.

"You rang?"

Kellen's head popped up when he heard Marcella's voice, smooth, weary. Definitely weary. He'd added to that burden. One so heavy, he felt the weight of it. Now it was time to ease some of it.

Rising, his legs moved like lead as he held out his hand to her, his expression solemn. "Yeah. I rang." Reaching for her, he pulled her to him, curving his hands over her back, smoothing away the tension while she floated in his arms. Marcella's first reaction was to tense, but he figured she sensed the change that had overcome him, and she relaxed.

It was time to clear the air between them. She was fiercely proud. She wasn't going to like admitting why she'd sold her soul. But the time had come.

Let the games begin.

eleven

Kellen gripped her as if he would never let her go, with a force that was both gently forceful and determinedly persuasive. Closing her eyes, she forced herself to breathe before she tried to push away from the delicious pressure of his hands on her back, but he remained firm in his hold. "Are we hugging something out I'm unaware of?"

"We need to talk." His words were quiet, calm.

Her defenses went on high alert. Talk. No one ever wanted to talk to her. Suddenly she had a line of people wanting to talk that was longer than a line to get into an *Oprah* taping. "I'm not here to talk about finding a way to keep me here, if that's what you're interested in. Or didn't I make that crazy clear when I stomped off like a teenager who couldn't talk her dad out of the keys to the Maserati?"

"That's not what I want to talk about." The hushed tone to his words, the firm but gentle ring to them, made her bristle.

Anxiety clenched her rapidly beating heart. She fell back, resting her waist in the circle of his arms and her hands on his thick biceps. "Is it Carlos?"

"That has something to do with what I want to talk about, but there's something more important. Here's the deal. I want you to promise me you'll hear me out."

Kellen's eyes frightened her—so intense—so full of something she didn't understand. Why had he changed so much in just the course of a couple of days? She didn't understand this Kellen. "Okay. I'm listening."

"I know why you killed Armando, and I know it had to do with your child. What I don't understand is why you never felt comfortable enough to tell even Delaney you had a child to begin with."

Immediately, she was irate. Fear sprung her into action. "Who told you about my son?" It was a struggle to keep a spray of spit from accompanying her words.

"Does it matter?"

"You're goddamn right it matters. It's no one's business but mine!"

He rubbed his thumb against the corner of her mouth. "Look, I get why it would be painful to talk about, but it's been a long time, Marcella. A long time since this went down. Didn't you ever want to at least let some of it go? Wouldn't talking to Delaney about it have helped?"

"What will ever help *this*, Kellen?" She swept her hands in the air with helpless defeat. "Telling someone what happened won't change what is. It wouldn't change the fact that I was a demon—it doesn't change the fact that I'm now a ghost. Ask yourself this: would you, Mr. Pious, ever have believed how I'd become a demon? I doubt it, Kellen. I don't know what's suddenly changed your mind about me, but if I'd come to you and Delaney with my heart on my sleeve, before all the stuff with Clyde went down, you'd have been the first one screaming bullshit." Her resentment for a persona *she'd* created became a whirling dervish of hot anger.

Kellen cupped her cheek, brushing a light kiss against her forehead. "You're right. I was wrong. I was an asshole. But I'm trying to make that right, and I'd really like to understand. Just talk to me." His perplexed look said he wasn't sure where to start. "So let me get this straight. You sold your soul to the devil for your son?"

Bitter resentment welled in her gut. Yeah. That's exactly what she'd done. "I did." And she'd done it without pause—with no hesitation—and she'd never regretted it.

The momentary silence he took made her fidget. She wasn't sure if he was winding up, or letting his brain wrap around what she'd just admitted. "So it's really true?"

Her eyes swayed toward the floor. "What's the point in lying now? I gain absolutely nothing from lying, Kellen. Yes, I sold my soul to save my son, who was nothing more than an infant at the time."

Kellen's hands stopped moving on her back. "Why would you let us—"

"Believe that I was nothing more than a greedy, vacuous, bedhopping good-time demon?" Her shoulders shrugged. She was too tired to keep it in any longer. The exhaustion of seventy-six years of secrets was becoming a mind fuck she was no longer up to.

Scrunching her eyes shut, she ran a finger over them to ease the tension. "By the time I met you and D, I was probably bitter more than I wasn't. I didn't get attached to humans because they die and go away. Delaney was the exception to the rule. She *made* me love her, invited me into her world. I don't know why I was compelled to keep coming back to the store. God knows I wanted to yark every time she ate wheat germ and spewed her holistic views, but she just wouldn't take no for an answer. I realize that if I'd been human, death would have been a part of my world anyway. But the hardest part about being a demon is eternal life, knowing I'd never die. I just couldn't get over how fucking unfair it was that I had to live forever with no escape.

"So I spent a good many of my demonic years having a mid-unlife crisis. There wasn't much that wasn't available to me—so I decided I'd just enjoy the material things earthbound privileges had to offer and bury my pain in shopping trips to Paris. I'm sure you have some scientific reason for why I did that, but the emotional reason is, I just wanted to forget. And yes, I did it to the extreme, but if you took those things away, it wouldn't crush me. Losing someone I loved would—has."

Kellen brushed a strand of her hair out of her face with a gentle finger. "I'm sorry. For all the time you missed with your son, I'm *so sorry*. There really are no other words, are there?" The solemn depth of his tone made Marcella fight to catch her breath. His eyes held years' worth of regret she just couldn't handle.

Madre santa, the tears again. With a deep breath, she smiled. "It's no big deal. I can't grudge on you for being disgusted by someone like me, Kellen, when I'm the one who nursed your opinion of me to begin with. I mean, really, when you're a demon, how do you change the myth behind what they're associated with? It just seemed like one more battle I wasn't up to. So I stopped fighting it and went along for the ride."

Cupping her cheek, he caressed it with a callused thumb. "Because you were tired."

It felt so good to finally admit it that she felt boneless. "Yeah. Really tired. It's work to convince someone not all demons made the choice to join Hell's ranks for nefarious reasons. Years of bad press don't help, either."

His gaze was thoughtful, penetrating. "But not so tired you couldn't save Delaney and Clyde?"

Waving a hand at him, she dismissed that night. She wasn't in this for a pat on the goddamned back. "Delaney has a future that has limitations. I didn't then. I did it because I think maybe somewhere in my subconscious I just wanted to stick it to that fuck Lucifer for all the misery he creates. In sticking it to him, I almost hoped there was some way out I knew nothing about. That maybe there was a loophole I'd missed and in taking alliance with Delaney, I'd end up anywhere but still kicking."

"You risked the pit, Marcella."

"Guilty."

"I'm an asshole."

"Do you want me to argue that point?" she teased, hoping this wouldn't go any deeper. Having feelings that you actually had to share out loud was fucking work.

His face held such regret, it hurt to look at him straight on. "Nope. That's just the truth. I didn't bother to get to know you because I lumped you into the pile with that sick fuck Vincent. I just didn't get Delaney's friendship with you. I didn't understand how she could possibly befriend someone who represented the bottom of the barrel, especially after what happened with Vincent. I never saw the gray in your situation. I just judged you. Which just goes to prove Delaney's a far better person than I'll ever be."

Marcella shook her head. "Vincent was a horrible person in life and in death, Kellen. You had no reason to think any other demon wouldn't be the same."

"But I didn't bother to ask."

"Neither did Delaney," she reasoned.

"Ah, but the difference is she didn't need to. She believed, and she's never stopped," he somberly shot back.

"She was a good friend to me."

"And in the end, you were a good friend to her."

Looking down to the floor, she fought the myriad emotions plowing through her. The cleansing understanding that forgiveness brought her rocked her core. "It's over. Now you know the truth. It's all good."

In a sudden gesture, Kellen pulled her to him, not in the heat of the moment the way he'd done earlier, but in a tender embrace. It felt so amazingly good to rest her head on his muscled shoulder, to feel the warmth of his skin beneath his old college sweatshirt. "No," he whispered huskily. "It's not good, Marcella. None of this was good, or fair, or right."

She'd speak, but words wouldn't come. To have this man she'd yearned for, with an ache, offer her absolution, in his arms no less, stole anything she might be capable of articulating. But more than just the ten years she'd known Kellen welled up inside her. Decades of frustration, of fear, of loneliness swept over her, and she was unable to escape the sob that fell from her, lips unbidden and deep. Burying her face in his shoulder to savor the moment for when she'd have no moments left, Marcella fought the rain of tears and sucked in more air.

Hookay. No more weepin' and wailin'. Pushing off his chest, Marcella found the resolve of steel she'd once worn as her overcoat. "No more. What's done is done, and there's no taking it back. Though, maybe now that you understand who I am, we can at least try not to yank each other's short hairs, which you suck at lately, BTW, and we can try to figure out what's happening to Carlos and why."

But Kellen wasn't letting go. It was crystal clear in the determined set of his mouth. "You still haven't told me the details about why you sold your soul."

Her resolve shook. *No. No. No.* "And I'm not going to. It's something I just don't want to relive out loud."

"Are you afraid to tell me? Does it have to do with a pact you made with the devil to protect them? I'll kill that fuck." His protective tone, the one she'd heard used before only concerning Delaney, made her heart thump faster.

"No!" she yelped then took a breath to calm herself. "No," Marcella repeated with purposeful steadiness. "It has to do with me not wanting to relive the kind of pain you feel when you hand over your child to someone else to raise. It's the kind of pain you can't express when you think about all the things you'll miss. I just . . ." Her head fell to her chest and she squeezed her eyes to fend off the anguish so tight in her belly it wanted to explode. "Please, could we not do this? I can't—*can't* . . ." And suddenly, she really couldn't. She couldn't hide the heart-wrenching agony of losing David.

Oh, Jesus, just thinking his name ripped another hole in her heart, constricting it until the flood of tears she'd been fighting won, falling down her face in batches of salty drops.

Everything.

She didn't want to, but she remembered everything about him as though what had passed had happened only yesterday. His sweet smell after a bath, the joy he'd given her with his gummy smile. The fist he jammed into his mouth when he was fighting sleep. The dark thatch of hair on his head, silken and springy, pressed to her breast while he fed. The way he'd wrapped his hand around a length of her hair while she rocked him to sleep in the rocking chair her parents had given her upon David's birth. His deep green eyes, so like her own, wide and alert, smiling up at her when she'd held him for the last time. Trusting. How he'd gone so willingly, innocent and beautiful.

And knowing.

Knowing she'd never see him again. Never touch him. Never press butterfly kisses to his rounded belly while he giggled. Never knowing who he'd grow up to be.

Never.

Marcella's hand went to her chest when she doubled over. Sobs so deep they hurt to expel wracked her, ripping her apart. The years fell away and a once dull ache tore open, fresh and oozing unspeakable pain.

Kellen grabbed for her, finding a chair and pulling her to his lap, cradling her. Rocking her while she sobbed at the injustice of losing David. The long nights when she'd done just this—cry herself to sleep. The nights when she'd longed for her baby with an actual physical ache. The endless years of fighting the yearning to find him—tell him who she was and end their parting. The battle she'd fought with herself to keep from just taking one peek at him to reassure herself he was all right. The kind of trust she'd had to hold on to, praying she'd placed him in the right hands.

The fear.

Oh, Christ, the fear that he'd be found. That Armando would get out of that damned box she'd put him in and find David.

Kellen murmured words that meant nothing and everything. A jumbled mix of soothing endearments laced with his deep consoling tone. "I'm so sorry, sweetheart." He cleared his throat against the top of her head. "So sorry," he rasped.

Hours passed or maybe it was only minutes, but they left her bereft. Bone dry, yet the ache, the infernal ache, burned brighter. Marcella kept her cheek pressed to his chest, hearing the steady rhythm of his heart, letting it ease her grief.

Kellen's sweatshirt stuck to his chest, and she wiped at it with a weak hand, but he caught it, bringing it to his lips to press a kiss to it. "Just rest," he whispered, low, soothing.

Scooping her up, he carried her to the bedroom, where he drew back a blanket she still couldn't totally get a grip on and laid her down. Tugging the covers up over her, he turned to leave, but she called to him in a hoarse whisper. "Stay. Please. Stay with me" was all she could manage. She was raw, vulnerable, needy, and for the first time in a long time, she let the hard shell of her misery crack just enough to let someone in.

Kellen didn't hesitate. His face flashed one emotion after the other as he walked to the edge of the bed, folding his long, strong body to climb in beside her.

Marcella pulled him close, so grateful that if she could touch nothing else, she could touch him. She needed to cling to something solid, life-affirming, even if she had no earthly identity of her own.

Wrapping her arms around his neck, she buried her face in his shoulder, breathing in the scent of the skin she'd craved for so long. His hands found her waist, fitting her to the lower half of his body, letting his fingers skim her hips, her back, moving in slow circles until she could no longer bear not to have him touching her.

Everywhere.

Marcella sensed his hesitance—the touch of his hands sought answers to his questions. Yet, she was fragile, chafed with the rash of memories dredged up from a place she'd hoped to keep buried. Her pride fell from around her like a cloak falling to the ground when she took matters into her own hands.

Damn the pain this might bring her when she was gone and left with nothing but memories. Damn the pride that had kept her from revealing her past. Damn the fact that they'd never have a future.

There was only now.

Her heart quickened in her chest, thumping hard against her ribs when she pulled his hands from her back and placed them on her breasts, arching into his lean fingers when they kneaded her.

Kellen's eyes met hers, dark, sexy, full of more uncertainties. She answered the question by giving him an easy smile.

His groan, hot, sultry, uneven, made her nipples harden to sharp tips. Marcella lifted her hips, grinding them into his, reveling in the thick outline of his cock straining against his jeans.

Hands fumbled with the zipper of his jeans, but couldn't grasp it. Feeling her inability to remove his clothing, he did it for her. Rising from the bed, he kicked off his sneakers and tugged off his shirt.

His chest, broad, hard, sculpted to within an inch of its life, gleamed in the moonlight streaming in from the bedroom window, making her mouth dry. When he jerked his jeans over his hips, lean and angled, she wheezed a sharp intake of breath. The thick muscles of his thighs flexed and bulged as though they'd been molded in granite.

The glimpse of his cock, straight, wide, long, had Marcella fighting a squirm of unashamed anticipation.

She attempted to remove her own clothing, but failed. Why could she touch it, but not take it off? Her eyes sought Kellen's for help. He sank back onto the bed, and his own eyes, dark, delicious, took her in with brazen curiosity when he lifted her dress over her head.

If this was a bust, at least she didn't have that horrible dress on anymore.

Marcella lay back on the bed, openly displaying herself to him. She was far from ashamed of her body, and she wanted him to know that not a single inch of her was going to regret this.

Parting her legs with forceful, hurried hands, he sank between them, letting his cock lie against her belly. She heard the moan escape her lips and didn't attempt to fight it. Laying herself bare was right. All the emotions, yearning, need that went with the desire she'd felt for him for so long wouldn't be quelled.

Reaching up, she curled her fingers in the hair at the nape of his neck, running her nails along his scalp, writhing beneath him when he groaned in her ear as they rolled their lower bodies together.

Kellen's lips moved to hers with painstakingly slow, measured nips to her ear, her jaw. Marcella beckoned him, dragging his mouth to finally meet hers.

The contact was exquisite, delicious, as they lay with their lips pressed together, semiopen, unmoving until Kellen took his first swipe along her mouth with his tongue. He circled it, teasing the outline, nipping it, creating a moist heat low in the pit of her belly. When he finally took possession of her lips, she jolted under him, raising her hips in response to the decadently sweet taste of their joined mouths.

His kiss was fierce, possessive, wrought with something she couldn't claim to understand, but identified with just the same. Kellen's hand swept along her naked hip, draping the tips of his fingers along the curve, running them down along her thighs.

Marcella followed suit, kneading his thickly muscled back, drawing her hands along the firm globes of his ass, raising her hips, whimpering her need to have him take her.

Kellen pulled back, but Marcella refused to let him go. The rest could come later. At this very moment, all she wanted was him inside her, driving into her, erasing everything but their bodies panting for each other.

Intuitively, he understood, parting her thighs, wrapping them around his waist, poising at her entrance, positioning himself. Yet before he took his first stroke, he cupped her cheek and demanded, "Look at me. When I make love to you, I want you to see me."

His gruff tone, the strain of his muscles, the demand in his tone made her shiver with the force of her pent-up desire.

Lifting her chin, Marcella met his eyes—sinfully hot.

He stroked his hands over her belly, smoothing the skin before dipping into the heat of her sex with fiery fingers, dragging them over her clit, eliciting moans of need from her lips.

Parting her, he took the head of his cock in his hand—their eyes locked.

And then he drove into her, fiercely, deeply, plunging into her and stretching her so deliciously, it left her breathless.

Her nipples tightened, aching to feel his mouth on them when he dipped his dark head to take one between his lips. She hissed her approval, bucking upward, accepting his thick cock with a near scream of ecstasy.

Kellen's tongue laved each sensitive nipple with rasps of his lips, inhaling and tugging at them until the pleasure/pain left tears in her eyes. Another plunge and he was deep within, driving a slow, hot path to her core.

Rising up on her elbows, she marveled at his dark head against her skin before she pulled him from her breast and bracketed his jaw with her hands. He needed to be closer, deeper. She wanted to absorb him, melt into his heavy weight until they were one. He took her mouth again, ravaging it, slicing his tongue in and out of her mouth, pushing her back to the bed.

Using his feet, Kellen upped the ante by plunging harder, rocking them against one another, their hips crashing as they rode this hot wave of need. Sweat formed a slick glide on their skin, sensuously easing their back-and-forth motion.

Her hands clawed at his back, slipping beneath his hard arms and clutching at his shoulders as she met him stroke for stroke. Wet heat spiraled low in her sex, throbbing, pulsing until she thrashed her head from side to side.

Kellen hiked her legs up higher, driving, seeking, pushing her until she could no longer stave off the flood of white-hot orgasm.

She came with a howl, rearing up against him, their flesh slapping in a decadent rhythm, shuddering against the wide shelter of his chest. Her neck arched and Kellen buried his face in the sensitive spot just above her collarbone, every muscle in his body straining, tensing until he threw his head back and roared his release, husky and victorious.

His orgasm spilled into her, filling her, washing her with a satisfaction she hadn't ever achieved in any other encounter.

Their breath was jagged, splintered by the wheeze of the fight to bring air to their lungs. Boneless, Kellen collapsed against her, sweat glistening on his forehead, leaving a glow on his ruddy skin.

Her emotions ran high as she fought for breath. This—what they'd just shared had been fiery hot, passionate, but there had been a need she couldn't define. A hole inside of her that had just been filled with something she was afraid to examine. She wanted to run away from it—hide—skulk off somewhere to dissect it. This had been so much more than just a fantasy realized.

So much more.

Marcella stiffened beneath him, but Kellen slipped his hands under her waist and pulled her closer. "Don't. You can't run away from what just happened, from what you feel for me."

"I don't run. I float," she replied, knowing it was sarcastic, yet stupidly wanting it to hurt him.

"Then you're not floating away, either. So tell me, Marcella Acosta, are you always this cranky after you make love?"

Her eyebrows rose in a familiar expression of boredom. The one she'd used time and again when it was time for a lover to hit the bricks. "I've never stuck around this long to find out. In fact, your two minutes are up. Get off me."

He grinned. Damn him. He was grinning. "Oooh—big, bad demon. Well done. But forget it. Again, I revert back to the article I read in a medical journal about defense mechanisms and the brain's reaction to them. Your defense, when someone gets too close, is to run away. You don't want to get in too deep because you've been sorely disappointed so much in your life that you're afraid to be hurt by something that has as much impact as what just happened between us did."

"How much do you charge an hour?"

"For?"

"Your psych evals."

"Consider this pro bono."

"For charity cases like poor, little me?"

"For ex-demons who're wussies and won't own their real feelings." He grinned again, wide and delectable. Just for good measure.

"And this is owning yours? We just slammed the shit out of each other. Sometimes, the brain's reaction after bumping uglies is to be all warm and fuzzy. It's the release of all those hormones and they're usually all wonky, Mr. Science Teacher, and I don't need some silly medical journal to tell me that. Maybe you might want to sleep on it," she retorted, purposely being cruel.

"Ah, now this is the part where you say things you don't really mean because you want to push me away. It's okay. I get it. Go on. Hurt me."

Run. She desperately wanted to run. "Why are you doing this?"

"Because it's far past the time for you to stop running away. That wasn't just sex we had, Marcella. You know it. I know it. Own it."

As though, because Kellen Markham had said it—it should be deemed so. Hah!

Shoving at his heavy weight, she scoffed. "I'm not running away from anything. We had sex. People have it all the time. In fact, I'd bet there are at least a million people who're making each other's eyeballs wobble as we speak. So what?"

"Nah. We didn't just have sex. We made love. Love, love, looove. Suck that up, Buttercup." He chuckled, clearly pleased with himself, but only further infuriating her.

"Get off of me, you beast. Jesus, what did you have for lunch? You're heavy."

"I had a tuna melt on wheat with American cheese. My favorite. In case you ever can actually hold a frying pan again. Oh, and I don't like ketchup on my fries. I love these things called Choco-Bliss, could eat 'em by the box, and if you ever tell D I said that, I'll lie to her face. I'm not a fan of fish unless it's a stick or fried and buried in tartar sauce. My favorite vegetable is green beans. I read comic books for fun, but if I'm honest, I like *Popular Science* just as much. I'm a sci-fi nut and there's nothing better than watching NASCAR with a beer because you can nap between laps without missing much. And funny, you weren't complaining about my weight when we *made love*."

Kellen liked Choco-Bliss? Oh, to have a box of those fuckers right now. Her chest tightened, her throat right behind it. "This isn't *Love Connection*, Chuck Woolery. I don't care what you like."

With a nod of his head, he smiled and said, "Yes. Yes, you do."

Her eyes turned pleading. "Can't we just leave this alone? Take it for what it was, and let it be?"

"It was *making love*. And sure, we could do that, but if we did that, we'd only regret it later. And I'm not so much into regrets anymore."

"I have no regrets." Which made her a liar.

"You will if you run away from me now. I'm a fine specimen of man. Loyal, honest, maybe a little pigheaded, and once very judgmental, but those days are gone. You're a smart girl. Why would you want to miss out on all of this?" he teased.

Because all of *this* would be taken from her. When or where, she had no clue. But it would. That was just a fact, and she finally admitted as much. "Because all of you will be here and all of me will be back on Plane Drab."

His gaze became tender but riddled with determination. "Well, here's the thing. I'm not going to let that happen. I don't know how I'll stop it, but I will. I'll find a way. I'll pay better attention to my otherworldly contacts. I'll sit with them all night and listen to their gibberish with pleasure if it means figuring this out. Don't you worry your pretty little head, Marcella Acosta—you're not going anywhere." Planting a kiss on her nose, he tightened his grip, obviously knowing his admission was a surefire way to scare her into flight, er, float.

Whatever.

But it was impossible to deny how much she wanted his words to become a reality. How much she wanted to let go of the reality and hope right along with him, if only just for a little while. "I'm too afraid to hope for that."

He cocked a dark eyebrow. "Ah, an admission of fear. Now we're getting somewhere. Look, I know it seems impossible, but I have faith there's a reason you can't get back to where you were when this began. I don't know what it is, but there is one."

Well, yeah. It was because she'd skipped the class "Plane Jumping without a Parachute" due to one of her extended pity parties. "I think you're placing way too much faith in karma, destiny, whatever. I think I can't get back simply because I didn't pay attention when they were teaching me how to get back. I was moping."

"You're due a certain amount of moping."

"Thank you for granting my wish, Moping Fairy."

Rolling over, Kellen pulled her on top of him, pressing her sensitive nipples to his chest. "We need a plan."

She eyed him skeptically. "You need your head examined."

"No. I need you to cooperate."

"I'm not important. Carlos is important. If you're going to summon up the afterlife, do it for him. Not me."

He stared at her for a long time. "I just can't understand how I missed this quality in you."

"What quality?"

"The selfless one. Your fear for Carlos is much bigger than even your desire to stay here."

"I wouldn't lay odds that if someone offered me the chance to shop for a new damned dress, I wouldn't give him up like a bad habit."

Kellen's chest rumbled with laughter, sending a sweet thrill of ridiculousness throughout her body. "I would." He kissed her then, long, slow, toe-curling. "I think we should take Delaney up on her offer to have a séance and see who we can contact."

"Did you tell her about Carlos?"

"I did, and she said the best way to find something out is to summon the spirits and see what we can see."

"I saw Lucifer today."

Concern laced his glance up at her. "Stay the hell away from him, Marcella. I mean it. I'll kill him if he touches one pretty hair on your head. I realize he's got a whole army of minions who'd probably rip me to shreds with their whacked mojo, but he'll remember who I am before I go down."

That protective tone he was showing off made her go all gooey on the inside again. "He can't hurt me anymore, Kellen. I'm not under his rule, and believe me, he was thrilled to tell me so."

Kellen's eyes turned to granite. "So what did the prick have to say for himself?"

"He claims he knows nothing about Armando, but you can bet your ass now that he's gotten wind Armando's rogue, he'll want to know what's up. If nothing else, that might work in our favor."

"Do you believe him? He's not exactly known for his honesty."

"I can't explain why I do, but yes. I believe him. So let's forget him and focus on what Delaney said."

"She's convinced we can find help for Carlos. The problem is she's not so convinced they'll talk to me instead of her."

"Well, you aren't exactly Melinda Gordon."

He grabbed a handful of her butt and squeezed it playfully. "Hey. Neither was Delaney."

Marcella's eyes went soft. "But she had a way with them that I can't describe. She joked with them. She cajoled them into doing what she wanted—which was for everyone to have a happy eternity. Celebrities showed up by the dozen for her. And speaking of, have we considered what Joe and Maurice said?"

"Right now it means nothing to me. It doesn't add up to anything significant. I did look up Joe and this 'monkey business' he keeps referring to. It's a title from one of Marilyn Monroe's films, and could have a million different meanings. There's been plenty of monkey business going on. Though I think the 'how can you mend a broken heart' and 'jive talkin'' referred to you and what happened with your son." He said it tentatively, letting her mull the information.

Indirectly, it made sense. She had done a lot of jive talkin', and she'd certainly had a broken heart that needed mending. "That's very true. Either way, they're not giving us the kind of information Delaney was able to get from them. I don't know what it was, but all of the afterlife loved her." Her admiration for Delaney had always been next to iconic. Time and time again, when she'd wanted to throw her hands up and flip whatever ghost had come calling the bird because they were interfering with their lunch date, Delaney'd hung tough.

Nipping at her lower lip, Kellen said, "She deserves to know about your son—about you. Who you really are."

"Delaney knows who I really am." Her voice hitched. She'd always known—somehow. Delaney had placed trust in her more than any other human being. Delaney knew who she was better than anyone else.

Nuzzling her neck, he nodded. "You're right, but I know she'd want to share your grief—your heartache. So that your burden isn't quite as heavy, because that's who Delaney is."

Letting her head fall to rest on his, Marcella took a deep breath. "Okay. Let's tell her."

"What was his name, Marcella? Your son?"

Shudders, silent yet so painful, rippled along her body. Swallowing, she closed her eyes, clenched them, then opened them to look down at him. "David. His name was David."

Pulling her down to the comfort of his chest, Kellen tucked her beside him, cradling her head in his hand, stroking her hair. "Tell me about David, sweetheart. Tell me all about him."

And she did.

Long into the night while he held her, letting his hands and words bring her solace.

For those few hours, the world stood still. There was no afterlife or ghosts and demons. There was no angry past between them. There was no fear. There was no other shoe waiting to drop.

There were simply two people—learning each other's quirks—laughing—whispering intimacies—discovering every facet of one another.

By night's end, there were also two people who were falling in love.

By the time one of them realized it—it was too late to dig in her three-inch heels and kick and scream the entire way.

twelve

The raucous pounding on the store's door jolted Marcella awake.

Awake.

What a wonderfully earthly thing to be.

Running a hand along Kellen's arm, she gave him a slight shake while admiring the view the sheet that had fallen to just below his waist allowed. "Somebody wants in."

His hazel eyes popped open, bleary from their long night, but when they fell upon her they smiled, making her heart shift and shudder.

The pounding grew insistent. "Who the hell?" he muttered, reaching to the floor for his discarded jeans. Marcella smiled sleepily, watching the tug and play of his muscles as he threw on a shirt and ran a tanned hand through his rumpled hair.

Her heart did that jumpy thing again, making her breathing choppy.

Vern and Shirley stretched beside her, kneading her thigh with unsheathed claws and purring their contentment. Marcella reached an absent hand down to stroke their backs, forgetting she couldn't touch them.

The sun, weak and mottled with clouds, tried to shine in through the bedroom window. If not for the crashing fist on the storefront's door, this day would almost be normal, a day like any other day in a human's life.

Except, Miss Afterlife, you're not human.

Last night she and Kellen had been able to set those differences aside. Let them lie dormant while they entwined their fingers, talked, laughed, made love again—this time with slow, purposeful intent. They'd done all the things any normal couple would do when they discovered one another intimately for the first time, and it was good, right.

But she wasn't normal.

Yet she longed to be with a heart that ached.

She wanted to get up every day at the same time. Make coffee, eat breakfast. Take a shower, get on the subway and go sit in some cubicle for eight hours a day, then come home and share her dinner with someone other than Mr. Yin at the Seven Dragons Diner. Maybe watch some TV. She wanted to do it without floating, or shooting fireballs and summoning locusts while Lucifer breathed down her neck.

She wanted to do that with Kellen.

Hope. He'd made her hope there was a way out of this impossible situation, and she didn't know whether to be grateful or angry.

Kellen's head poked around the door's corner. "We have a problem."

"We have so many problems, what's one more?"

"Carlos is here. Mrs. Ramirez claims this daughter gone bad

of hers hasn't come home, and she's determined to find her. She said she's going to start in all the neighborhood bars."

Marcella's eyes went wide. "My dress. Can you help? We can't let her go alone, Kellen. I'll follow her. She's not cut out for some of the places in this neighborhood."

"And you are?"

"I know, I know. I'm transparent, but I can at least follow her and try to watch out for her. You can't go. Who'd watch Carlos? You can't leave him here with me—the ghost sitter. Mrs. Ramirez might buy that Carlos has the gift, but she'd never buy me."

Pulling her from the bed, he planted a kiss on her mouth before dropping her dress over her head. "I've got Delaney on the way. She's in the city to have lunch with Clyde anyway. No way am I letting that cute little old lady hit the bars alone."

Relief flooded her. As much as she'd like to think she could handle whatever came Mrs. Ramirez's way, she couldn't exactly do much when she couldn't even walk on solid ground. "Thank God. Where's Carlos?" She wanted to poke her head around the corner. Talk to him. *See* him. With a compelling urge she had no explanation for.

"In the living room, wondering if you're going to come play Rock Band with us again."

She giggled and her insides melted to that soft butter consistency she'd become accustomed to.

"Mrs. Ramirez!" Delaney's voice, so welcome to Marcella's ears, sounded from the tiny kitchen. Kellen turned to greet her with Marcella hovering directly behind him.

Delaney wrapped her consoling arms around Mrs. Ramirez, squeezing her with a warm hug. "Tell me what I can do."

Her dark hair was in disarray and her full cheeks were red. "Oh, Meess Delaney. I am so worry for my baby. I tell you, this is not like her," Mrs. Ramirez whispered with hushed words. "She never, never bad. Not even when she was in high school. I do not understand nothing anymore. Everything is crazy!"

Delaney patted her shoulder. "You go do what you have to and keep Kellen close by, okay? We'll talk when you get back." She thumbed away an escaped tear from Mrs. Ramirez's pudgy cheek. "Go." She motioned to Kellen with a swishing hand. "Carlos and I will be fine."

Kellen planted a kiss on top of her head. "Thank you."

Delaney tugged him down to her level. "Is you-know-who here?"

He gave her a sharp nod and a wink. "Right behind me."

Delaney's eyes twinkled. "Suhweet. Give her a kiss for me. Oh, but wait. I'm assuming you've already done that."

Kellen's smile was evasive. "Keep your cell on. I'll call you to keep you updated."

Delaney peeked over his shoulder and wiggled her fingers at Marcella. "Way to get your man," she whispered. "Now go."

Kellen ushered Mrs. Ramirez out the door with Marcella fast on his heels.

Mrs. Ramirez marched down the sidewalk with determined steps, her purse swinging rhythmically as she went. Kellen grabbed hold of her arm to slow her strides. "Any clues as to where to begin?"

She grunted her disgust. "I hear her, Meester Kellen. I hear her talk to her friends on the phone. I hear the names of the places." She stopped short in front of a dilapidated brick building. The sign that had once glowed OPEN in pink neon hung at an awkward angle and was officially O EN, if it could be trusted.

Marcella wrinkled her nose at Kellen. What a dive. Paint peeled off the front door Mrs. Ramirez stomped through, letting it swing behind her so hard, it slammed in Marcella's face.

She floated through the steel and rushed to catch up to Kellen, who squinted in the smoky gloom of the bar's interior, scanning it. Marcella leaned in and spoke in his ear. "Jesus. She's a force to contend with. Don't lose sight of her. This place is foul."

The bartender's head rose when Mrs. Ramirez dropped a fist on the sticky surface, jarring a bowl of peanut shells. "Where is my baby?" she bellowed.

The bartender, scruffy, unshaven, and underfed, eyeballed her with apathy.

"I say, where is my baby?" Her anxiety was mounting. Not good.

Kellen placed his hands on her shoulders to calm her and spoke to the bartender. "We're looking for a Solana Vega. She's about . . ." He leaned over Mrs. Ramirez's stout shoulder with a quizzical glance. "What does she look like, Mrs. Ramirez? In all this time, I don't think I've ever met her."

Tears filled her coal-colored eyes. "She is beautiful. She has dark hair—black. So black. About dees—*this*—tall," she said, holding up a hand that just touched the top of Kellen's shoulder and, had Marcella been human, would have skinned her nose. "She has green eyes—" She choked, stopping short to wipe furiously at the tears that slid along her rounded cheeks.

The bartender hitched his scruffy jaw at Kellen. "You a cop?"

"Just a concerned friend. Look, have you seen anyone even remotely like her in here—last night?"

"I don't see nuthin'," he spat with a tight mouth.

"What he needs to see is a bar of soap," Marcella said, wrinkling her nose.

Kellen pulled his wallet from the pocket of his jeans. "How about I just leave you my card, and you give me a call if you do see her?"

He snatched the card from Kellen, looked at him with pointed distaste, and ripped up the card with slow precision.

"You are a pig!" Mrs. Ramirez shouted, banging her chubby fist on the bar. "You disgusting *cabrón*!"

"Hookay, she's swearing in Spanish. It's time to go," Marcella said from behind Kellen, whose jaw clenched, leaving a pulsing tic.

"C'mon, Mrs. Ramirez. Let's go." Tugging at her arm, he peeled her away from the bar with gentle force.

"Jesus Christ, Mother. What are *you* doing here?"

All heads swiveled in the direction of the bathrooms behind them.

But only two mouths fell open.

"Did you hear me, old woman? What the hell are you doing here? Shouldn't you be watching my son or making tortillas?" The woman strode across the littered barroom floor with seductive, ass-swishing steps. The sway of her hips, encased in a red micro-mini, was cadent. Her shoulder-length dark hair fell in soft waves around her face, her bangs just brushing her forehead, and her flashing green eyes glared their disapproval at her mother.

Kellen looked to Marcella.

She looked back. Eyes wide.

Holy, holy shit.

Mrs. Ramirez visibly shook with anger and upset. "Oh, Solana! You come with me right now! This is filthy! Why you behave like this? Carlos, he need you."

The clack of her heels stopped when Solana confronted her mother, one hand on her rounded hip, the other curled around a tumbler of amber liquid. "Carlos, Carlos. All you ever do is talk about that kid. What about me? Me, me, me!"

Mrs. Ramirez jerked as though Solana had slapped her.

What a selfish brat. How did such a disaster have a great kid like Carlos? Marcella might have considered attempting to pick up something again—something big—and whack this bitch just for being so disrespectful to her mother, if not for the fact that she could barely process what she was seeing.

"And who are you, hottie?" she cooed at Kellen, flashing him a seductive wink.

Before Kellen could answer, Mrs. Ramirez grabbed her daughter's hand, pulled it to her lips, and kissed it, tears falling along her cheeks, leaving wet tracks. "Please, Solana. You come home. We fix this. We get help. Whatever we need to do, we do."

A deep chuckle escaped her throat. "Fix what, Mother?" she responded, mocking Mrs. Ramirez's accent, then exhaling a sigh that had enough alcohol in it to pollute an entire army of men.

Leaning into Kellen, Marcella said, "Do me a favor?"

His eyebrow rose in question.

"Slap this silly bitch for me. That's her mother. You don't talk to your mother like that. Ever."

"This! We fix this!" Mrs. Ramirez swept a shaky hand around the room. "This is a place for *putas*!"

"Oh, Mama. You're such a cheeky wench," she cackled, tweaking Mrs. Ramirez's cheek with fingertips painted in slashes of deep red.

A warning tingle skittered along Marcella's arms, spreading to her stomach and settling there like heavy lead. Chills of terror broke out on her skin.

Oh, sweet mutha.

Oh, Jesus God.

Oh, no.

No, no, no.

Marcella's head reeled. Her hands went clammy; her knees melted like caramel in the hot sun. How could . . .

Suddenly, everything made sense. Carlos, the box—all of it. And then her eyes narrowed in Solana's direction with fury spewing from them. Fury Solana couldn't see, but if looks were deadly—Carlos's mother would burn in the deepest pit of Hell. *"Dios condenada folladora madre, inútil hija de puta! Dios condenada folladora madre, inútil hija de puta!"* Marcella spat.

"Delaney always said to watch out for you when you reverted to your native tongue," Kellen said out of the side of his mouth, his eyes never straying from Solana while Mrs. Ramirez continued to beg her daughter to leave with her.

Fear screamed up her spine. "Kellen, pay attention to me. We have to get her out of here!" How had this happened?

Kellen clearly hadn't gotten over his shock, but Marcella had.

They had to get the fuck out of here and take Mrs. Ramirez with them. ASAP. "Kellen, get her the hell out of here now," Marcella reiterated from between clenched teeth.

He shook her off, his eyes wide, his jaw still scraping the floor.

"Kellen, listen to me. Get her out of here now. Get her away from here. Trust me when I say, do it *now*!"

Kellen shook his head and his eyes cleared. He placed a hand on Mrs. Ramirez's arm. "Let's go, Mrs. Ramirez. You've done what you came to do. You know she's safe. Let's go back to my place and not make a scene. Carlos needs you."

"Yeah, Mother. Carlos *needs* you," Solana echoed mockingly with a growling tinkle of laughter.

But the older woman shook her head in an oppositional manner with vigor. "No. I no leave until my baby come with me!"

"Get out of here, Mother. Go away and leave me alone, you nagging shrew!" Solana shrieked, her laughter bordering on insane.

Mrs. Ramirez began to cry in earnest, but she allowed Kellen to pull her from the bar.

When they hit the door, Marcella gave one last glance back at Solana. One last hard, long look.

Her brain wanted to deny what her eyes were seeing, but there was no denying what was right in front of her.

She shivered.

Holy doppelgänger.

Delaney sobbed into a tissue with one hand and held Kellen's with the other. "God, Marcella. I wish you'd told me. I'm your friend. I love you. I would have listened. I would never have judged you. Most importantly, I would have *believed*."

Knots of tension tightened in Marcella's stomach. It was only fair Delaney know, but reliving her grief three times in a row, explaining herself and her motives over and over, was like being overcleansed. "Tell her I know she wouldn't have, but the memories . . ."

Waving a hand at her brother, Delaney said, "You don't have to say it, Kell. I know what her response is. It hurt too much. I can't even imagine what you've suffered. But I knew, Marcella Acosta, I *knew* you'd been unfairly judged, and it makes me that much more determined to keep you here with me." She slapped a hand on the table for emphasis.

Marcella fought a sympathetic BFF sob and stayed focused on the task at hand. "We have bigger problems than that now. Carlos is in some serious danger. So is Mrs. Ramirez. Send Delaney home, Kellen. Please. We can't afford to have her involved."

They'd decided not to tell Delaney about what had unfolded at the bar, other than that Solana refused to come home with her mother. Delaney might have had plenty of friends in the afterlife, but she had enemies, too. If Delaney knew what they'd just witnessed, she'd be hell-bent on helping, and they couldn't risk that. Letting her focus on a way to keep Marcella earthbound was far less risky because, at this point, it seemed impossible.

Kellen gave her that look again. The one that still screamed he couldn't believe what he'd just witnessed.

The doorbell jingled and Clyde, tall, handsome, glasses crookedly propped on his nose, entered the kitchen. His eyes fell immediately on Delaney with gentle sympathy. "Hey, honey. Been a long day, huh?"

Delaney was up and out of her chair, hurling herself at Clyde's hulking form. "Take me home, Mensa Man. I need babying after what I heard today." She snuggled against him and for a moment, Marcella felt a stab of envy for that thing called normalcy.

"What happened?" he asked, lips pressed to the top of her red-gold head.

Kellen gave him a brief overview of the day's events, ending with Marcella's confession, to which Clyde responded by whistling long and sharp. "So my woman's been right all along about Marcella?" He clapped Kellen on the back.

Marcella gave Kellen a smug smile. "Yeah. She has."

"She's here, by the way." Kellen tilted his head in Marcella's direction.

Clyde looked out into the kitchen. "I'm sorry, Marcella, for your loss. I wish there were something I could say, but what could lessen the pain of losing a child?"

Clyde's words were so spot-on, so accurate, she swallowed hard again. Marcella had to look away when she responded for fear she'd cry again. "Tell Clyde I said what would really make me feel better is if he and Delaney would go home and make me an auntie."

He reached out a hand to her, clasping her fingers between his, and laughed. "Marcella said go home and make babies. She wants to be an aunt."

"Will you two be okay?" Delaney's concern riddled her eyes.

"We can't do anything but wait now anyway, D. Carlos isn't

the immediate problem right now. It's Mrs. Ramirez's daughter, Solana. And what else can we do other than be here for Mrs. Ramirez when she needs us? I promise I'll call you if anything else happens."

Delaney reached up and kissed Kellen's cheek. "I feel so bad for Mrs. Ramirez. Whenever she talked about her daughter, she made her sound like such a wonderful woman, a great mother. I guess grief has many facets. What a mess for her and poor Carlos."

Kellen shook Clyde's hand and smiled. "I promise to call if anything happens. Get some rest."

Clyde chuckled dotingly. "Like she'll ever do that until she finds a way to get Marcella earthbound again. Do you have any idea how difficult it is to get all romantic with a woman who's passed out on the couch with her nose buried in a book?"

Kellen laughed, giving Clyde a slap on the back and sending them out the door.

Silence fell between them.

"I—" They spoke simultaneously.

Silence came again—words had become laborious.

When Kellen finally spoke, his voice was still laced with his confusion. "I think I've said this about a hundred times since this thing with Carlos began—I don't get it."

"That makes two of us."

"Solana looks *exactly* like you, Marcella, with the exception of her shorter hair."

"And her shitty attitude. Oh, wait. I have one of those, too," she joked, to lighten the dark turn meeting Solana had brought on.

He ignored her joke. "You're identical in every way."

"Ya think? I think my boobs are better."

"This is serious, honey. Could we try to treat it as such?"

"Okay, you're right. I think I'm just freaked out. They say everyone has a twin . . ."

"Did you have a twin?"

"No. I had a sister, but she was several years older than me. She looked more like my father."

"So how is it that this woman looks exactly like you? I've been telling you there's a connection with you and Carlos. I think we might have found it. Maybe you're related. It's entirely possible, honey. You've technically been dead a long time, but you did leave family behind, right?"

"Just my parents and my sister. And, as far as I knew, my sister was barren." She'd never forget the look of love on Isabella's face when she'd handed David to her sister and made her swear she'd hide him. It was as though she'd given her the greatest gift in the world.

"Maybe things changed. Infertility's a funny thing."

"Maybe, but Isabella's married last name was Lopez." Marcella shook her head. "Carlos's last name is Vega, and Solana's family name is Ramirez. I don't know anyone with the last name Ramirez but Carlos's grandmother."

"Okay, so maybe Mrs. Ramirez's maiden name was Acosta. Maybe your sister had a baby and that baby was Mrs. Ramirez. Though, I'll admit, Solana and Mrs. Ramirez look nothing alike. You know, this is an easy fix. I'll just call her and ask what her maiden name was." While Kellen grabbed his cell and dialed Mrs. Ramirez, Marcella paced—or floated back and forth—across the room.

The shock of seeing Solana had dulled—but the explanation for their uncanny resemblance gnawed at her. Carlos had said she looked like his mother with longer hair, and that was no fabrication, but he hadn't said they could have been twins.

But there was more than just the trouble with her lookalike . . .

Caught up in her fear, Marcella was taken by surprise when, from the corner of her eye, she saw a flutter of movement by the children's story area.

Kellen clicked the phone shut and grabbed her by the waist. "You're right. Mrs. Ramirez—Juanita—was a Gonzalez, not a Lopez. Could she be the child of a second cousin?" He leaned in to kiss her with a bone-melting swipe of his lips. "I dunno. I say we keep looking. Until then, I think you and I shouldn't be vertical," he teased, skimming her lips with his tongue.

Wanting only to wrap her arms around him and find comfort in his embrace, she couldn't ignore the presence in the story area. "We have company."

Kellen turned with a sigh and frowned. "Familiar?"

Marcella rolled her eyes at him. "How could you not know who that is?"

"Because I'm seventy-six years younger than you?"

The man in the corner winked at the pair and tipped his black fedora at them, then straightened his tie with a smile that was infectious.

"Hey, I was twenty-six when I bit the big one. That's younger than you are right now. And does 'Luck Be a Lady Tonight' ring any bells? 'Summer Wind'?"

"Didn't Nirvana do that?"

Marcella giggled. "Frank Sinatra. You know, Ol' Blue Eyes?"

"Oh, yeah. Part of the Rat Pack, right?"

"Right." Frank sidled up to them with a soft shoe and moved his lips.

Marcella squinted right along with Kellen. "I'm beginning to sound like a broken record, but I don't get it. I can't make out what he's saying."

Frank extended a hand to Marcella, bowing in front of her. She took it, letting him whirl her around while his lips moved incessantly. "Okay, Frank—slow down and answer me this. Does whatever you're trying to tell me have to do with the title of one of your songs?" she asked.

He winked, dipping her and muttering the same words; pulling her back up, he spun her again, letting her go free from his arms to point at his wrist.

Marcella righted herself. "So it's a title of a song? Jesus, Frank, you've got a million songs. Oh, '*My Way*'!" she shouted.

Frank scowled from beneath his hat and shook his head.

"'Night and Day'?"

His head moved back and forth, his glare impatient.

She shook a finger at him. "Cut me some slack, would you? It was a long time ago. Okay, wait. I'm just going to yell out titles and you nod yes if I get it right."

Frank smiled his consent.

"'Almost Like Being in Love.' 'Moon River.' 'The Way You Look Tonight.'"

Frank had stopped moving, his look of disapproval growing.

"'I Left My Heart in San Francisco'!"

Kellen made an irritating buzzing noise and followed it with a pleased smile. "Survey says: wrong answer. That was Tony Bennett. My mother loved him."

"That's helping how?"

Kellen made a zipping motion with his fingers to his mouth.

Frank grumbled, his image beginning to shimmer and fade.

"No! Wait!" She held up a hand to keep him from leaving. "Don't go. I never liked Tony anyway. What about 'That Old Black Magic'?"

His ghostly outline waffled and wavered, displaying his displeasure.

"Shit! I can't think of any more. I sucked at *Name That Tune*! Ohhh! Hold up—'*I've Got You under My Skin*'!"

Just before he began to make his exit, Frank nodded in the affirmative, tipping his hat gallantly at Marcella.

"Oh, suuure, *now* you tell us? You know, Frank," she chastised his disappearing form, "you could have dropped by much sooner with that information!" She blew out a breath of air. God, she'd forgotten how exhausting this could be.

"Does that make any sense to you at all?" Kellen asked.

"In fact, it does." Perfect fucking sense.

"Wanna share with this piss-poor excuse for a medium?"

No. Actually, she was dreading it. "When we were in the bar, do you remember what Solana called her mother?"

"Truthfully, I was so busy internally getting my freak on that it's hazy."

"She called her a cheeky wench."

"And that means something?"

"Not to Mrs. Ramirez, but to me, it means something."

He dragged her to him. "Can I tell you how goddamn frustrating it is to always be in the dark? Shed some light, would you?"

"Armando used to call me a cheeky wench."

Kellen snickered. "I hate to agree with the asshole, but 'cheeky' isn't an adjective I'd dismiss when it comes to you, honey. Even if a little outdated."

She gulped, placing her hands on his shoulders. "Outdated is right. Know why?"

"Gimme the hundred-watt explanation."

"I think we have a much bigger problem than either of us could have imagined. I think Armando didn't just get out of the box . . ."

Kellen frowned just seconds before his eyes went wide in realization. He was a smart man—clearly, where they were at had clicked. "No. Jesus Christ. Is that even possible? I mean, I've heard, but . . ."

She'd seen Darwin do it. "Oh, it's definitely possible. I've seen it. Plus, it explains a lot about Solana's sudden bad behavior."

"Do you really believe . . ." It was obvious he couldn't comprehend what they both knew. His throat worked, but the words wouldn't come, so she said them for him.

"I think the spirit of my dead husband, Armando, has taken possession of Solana Vega's body."

Cue spooky music.

thirteen

Kellen slumped down on the couch. "Christ, this is bad."

"This is badder than bad."

"Let me be clear. Armando's possessed Solana's body, but what does that mean for Solana? Does that mean she's dead—or alive—or . . . how does that work?"

Marcella's shoulders moved upward. "I don't know. I do know you can possess a living host. I've seen it. But I don't understand possession well enough to know the signs when the host is . . ." Swallowing hard, she exhaled a ragged breath as she plunked down beside him. *"Dead."* She sent a silent prayer that would likely go unheard, but she sent it nonetheless, that Solana was alive. For Carlos's sake.

"So Armando got out of the box and possessed Solana? What the hell for? He'd already signed his soul over before he was ever dead. Why wouldn't he just go collect what was promised to him when he made the deal?"

Because he's a cagey fuck. "That's what scares me. He should have gone directly to Hell without passing go. In order for him to stay here, without the benefit of Satan knowing where he is, he had to possess a body because his demon skills are limited—especially at the newbie stage. It's up to you whether you hone your skills—which was why mine were so limited. That means Armando needs a host to stay on this plane so he won't be caught and punished by Lucifer for being rogue. If he's hiding in Solana's body, no one would ever be the wiser. Well, with the exception of those who love Solana. Obviously, she's doing some things that are uncharacteristic."

"She's—he's—whatever—is jeopardizing Carlos's well-being. Damn that bastard."

"I have to wonder if he knows."

"That some demon's in his mother's body?"

"Yep. He's got the gift—he's otherworldly sensitive. Maybe Armando's communicated with him. I'd bet my bippy Armando didn't count on the fact that Carlos can see the dead. If Carlos did see him when he got out of that box, Armando's more than likely threatening him. I think we both know that bastard's not above it," she choked.

Kellen ran a fingertip along the slope of her cheek. "This guy you married, he was a real nightmare, huh?"

Worse than any ever filmed on Elm Street. "I had no idea. I swear if I'd known . . . Back then, women married for very different reasons than they do today. I was destined to end up someone's arm candy, but I'd never be allowed to have an opinion or a hand in anything except cooking, cleaning, managing a household, and bearing children. He was different. Armando was a challenge. He was so unlike any other man who'd offered for my hand. He didn't expect me to be some mindless twit. He loved a good argument. He encouraged them. He claimed to love to hear my opinion," she scoffed. "But he was a lying piece of shit. In the end I found out I was nothing more than a vessel. A cheeky one, is what he called me just before I . . ."

"Killed him. That's the one part in all this I do get." Stroking her hair, he pulled her back to sit with him. "How did you find out about Armando's pact with the devil anyway?"

One more secret well on its way to being exposed. "My grandmother."

Kellen stiffened, reading her body language. "You're hedging again. How did your grandmother know?"

"Because when she told me, she came from the other side to do it."

"She was already dead?"

"I had the gift of sight when I was alive."

There was that silence again—pensive, hesitant—hellish.

Sitting up, she faced him, but her eyes had trouble meeting his. "Here's the deal. My grandmother had the gift of sight, too. If not for her, I don't know what I would have done. She guided me. She taught me how to deal with the spirits. My parents and my sister weren't believers in the afterlife being anything other than dead. End of. They were deeply religious, but to believe ghosts were showing up and hanging with their daughter would have been like telling them Lucifer himself was coming for Sunday lunch and bringing dessert. My grandmother warned me they didn't believe, and until her death, she protected me from nonbelievers and taught me how to be very cautious. When she came to me about Armando and told me he'd sold his soul several years before we met—when she told me about the . . ." Bile rose in her throat, and she choked it back before continuing. "The things that he'd done to women—to . . . in the name of Satan—I had to act, or he'd use my baby for his selfish, foul needs. I couldn't allow that. I *wouldn't*."

"He wanted to raise David to become a follower." Kellen's statement was filled with his disgust.

Her eyes flashed with the anger, the helplessness Armando's memory brought up. "That's exactly what he wanted. There was no way I was going to let that happen."

"So here's something else that's been troubling me—how did you die? Did you . . . you know . . . in order to save David." He winced when the words left his mouth.

That awful visit from her grandmother came back to her in her mind's eye in Technicolor. It had been cold, colder than a witch's tit, as Armando had once put it. Armando was off on one of his late-night business ventures, as he'd dubbed them, and she'd been trying to keep the fire burning unsuccessfully while cursing him for being so late. David slept soundly in a wooden cradle her father had made for him by hand, his fist curled around the blanket Isabella had knitted for him when he was born.

When her grandmother appeared, she hadn't been at all shocked—only grateful, relieved to know that she was safely on the other side and happy. Then there was the fear that she'd been wandering restlessly since her death, but her grandmother reassured her she was with Marcella's grandfather again, making Marcella smile. Yet her reasons for finding her way to bring Marcella a message held no good news, and there'd be trouble to be had if anyone found out she was passing the message on because it involved toying with fate.

Yet her grandmother was a willful woman—willful and protective of her family. Her father had often compared her and her grandmother and their strong, stubborn determination. When Grandma Rosa revealed not only David's potential fate, but hers as well, and after the initial horror had settled—she'd taken action. If she died, Armando could raise David freely. Not on her watch. "If what you're asking is did I emo out and kill myself? No. My grandmother didn't just come to tell me about Armando's deceit—she came to tell me about my death."

Ba-dump-bump. More silence that chilled her bones.

But Kellen simply tightened his grip on her. "So you knew you were going to die? Jesus Christ. I think I had a much better deal when I was just a plain old science teacher."

Oh, the irony of that statement. "Uh-huh, and in order to keep the wheels of fate moving according to plan, I had to let that happen."

Kellen whistled low, scaring Vern and Shirley off the back of the couch. "You are one tough broad."

His admiration was evident, but she brushed that aside in the interest of clearing the air—totally—finally. "Anyway, when my grandmother told me about Armando's plans for David, she explained that if I offered up my soul as a bargaining chip for my son's safety, David would be protected and he could never be touched by Satan. His soul would never be in jeopardy, but Satan would be given mine in a sort of barter, meaning no loss on his part."

"And then you killed Armando."

She blew out a pent-up breath of air. "Then I killed him. I don't know that I would have if my death weren't on the table. Maybe I would have taken David and run away, but there was no way that son of a bitch was going to live *and* destroy my son, too."

"Can I ask a sensitive question?"

"Ask away."

"How did you die?"

"You'll laugh . . ."

His face said otherwise. "How could I laugh at something so fucked up?"

Oh, he said that now . . . Her expression was sheepish. "Because looking back, it is a little funny."

"I have my doubts I'll laugh."

"I slipped in Macy's and hit my head on a rack of hats."

Kellen's lips curled inward in an effort to keep a straight face. He shoved his hands under his armpits and turned his head, but his shoulders began to shake. And then he snorted through his nose. Long and obnoxious. His laughter was like a sneeze you try thwarting by pinching your nose, but only end up making worse because your eyes tear up. His cackle began low, turning into a high-pitched wheeze.

Knocking his shoulder with hers, she said. "Hey, I said it was a *little* funny." Though she had to admit, the irony of death by fashion for someone like her was worthy of a snicker.

He gasped for breath, wiping his eyes with his thumbs. "I'm sorry. It's just—I mean—you dying . . . that's bad . . . but cracking your head on a . . ." He cleared his throat and forced his face to relax. "I'm sorry. What a horrible end to someone who likes clothes and accessories as much as you do. So did you know when and where it would happen?"

Shaking her head, Marcella looked down at her hands. "No. I just knew it would be within a week of the visit from my grandmother. I was better off not knowing or I might have been tempted to try to escape a destiny I shouldn't have even known about."

Kellen's palm smoothed her hair. "So knowing you were going to die, you killed Armando so he couldn't get his hands on David. Where did David end up? With your parents?"

"My sister Isabella. Like I said, she was barren. I knew if she did nothing else, she'd take good care of David. When I went to her after Grandma Rosa's visit and told her about my fate—about Armando—she didn't believe me. I think I mentioned she wasn't a believer. It took a whole lot of convincing not only to get her to agree to raise David, because she didn't believe I was going to die, but to get her to promise to bury that goddamn box with Armando's filthy soul in it."

"So she knew you'd killed Armando?"

Marcella would never forget bringing David to Isabella, her hair tangled and matted, her eyes wild with fear, clammy sweat her constant companion. "I told her everything. Up to that point, everyone believed that Armando had run off with someone. I heard them whisper about it while I pretended to be a wronged wife. Isabella hated Armando to begin with, but she never would have condoned his murder if it had been anyone other than me. I was younger than her by quite a few years. My mother worked long hours at my father's tailoring business. Isabella was more like a second mother than she was my sister. She would have done anything to protect me, and I manipulated her love for me to keep her from going to the police. I was sick over it, but David had to be protected."

Kellen's expression darkened. "So your sister was the last person you know for sure had the box? What did she do with it?"

That panic was back again, burrowing into her gut. "I swear to you, I thought she'd buried it. She was the only person I could trust to do it. My parents would have had me exorcised before they'd ever believe I'd put someone's soul in a locked box."

"Then how the hell did Carlos's grandfather get his hands on it?"

She'd begged her sister with sobs of agony constricting her throat to bury it the moment Marcella left her. "Isabella made no bones about the fact that she thought I was out of my mind. The only thing I can think that would have kept her from doing what I asked was that she just didn't believe what I told her about Armando."

"Why didn't you bury it yourself?"

Massaging her temples, she bit the inside of her cheek before answering. "I was under a lot of pressure to take care of things, is my only defense. The week before my death, I don't think I slept more than three or four hours total. Killing Armando was . . ."

How did you describe the hideousness of murder—no matter the reasons behind it? "I'm no cold-blooded killer. His murder took thought—summoning his soul involved a lot of brain cell usage and energy. It was the most horrific thing I've ever done. Though I swear, as I stand here, I'd do it again. Top that off with my fears for David, knowing I'd never see him again . . ." Her voice grew weak, clogging with more tears. "I just wasn't thinking straight, or I would have buried it myself and none of this would be happening." She clenched a fist of frustration in her lap.

Kellen took her fingers between his, massaging them, easing the tension. "You couldn't have possibly known the box would show up, Marcella. Don't go where you're going."

She might as well go—Christ knew, she'd gone to plenty of places in the last few days that she didn't want to go to. "But this is my fault, Kellen. My mistakes have led Armando to Carlos. We have to find out what he plans to do and stop him." At all costs.

"And we will. I still don't know how, though Christ knows I'm tired of saying that, but we will. I'll find a way—*we'll* find a way. For now things are quiet. I've got another call in to Catalina with this new information. I'm hoping she'll have some answers—something."

It was getting harder and harder to hate Demonic Barbie. She settled back against the couch in the crook of his arm and sighed— cleansed—unburdened—washed exhaustingly clean.

"I just thought of something."

She was sitting back up with a shot. "That could help Carlos?"

Pulling her back into his embrace, he shook his head. "No. But I was wondering about selling your soul."

"You in the market?"

"Hah!" Kellen barked his answer. "Hell no. What I'm wondering is, because you essentially broke a commandment, wouldn't you have gone to Hell anyway? How could you barter your soul for David's if your soul was already marked? Or are the Ten Commandments something we've interpreted to suit our needs over hundreds of years?"

She gave him a grin that was smug. "That took a little fancy footwork on my part. I'm happy to say, some demons are dumber than others. I got one of the lamest asses evah. He had no clue I'd committed a sin."

Kellen grinned deliciously and winked. "Nice work."

"That stunt was hardly work."

"But wouldn't Satan want revenge because you pulled a fast one?"

"Satan just loves souls. He doesn't much care how he gathers them. Some are definitely more important than others, and I guess if he'd ever found out how I toyed with a minion, he might have sought revenge. But the beauty in this is a minion isn't likely to report his mistake for fear of punishment. It became our little secret. Satan probably would have cheered my deception, but for sure, his lackey would have paid with time in the pit."

Drawing her into his lap, Kellen positioned her to face him. "You're something else, Marcella Acosta."

"Let this be a lesson to you—do not bring my wrath down on you. It promises a shower of shit," she teased.

He grinned, the corners of his eyes crinkling, deep grooves forming around his mouth. "I've held an umbrella up under several of those."

"We've come a long way, baby."

"Wanna go longer?" His hand cupped her ass suggestively, and he wiggled his eyebrows.

"Oh, Mr. Markham. Only you would want to boff a chick that had just confessed to not only murder but deception of the highest-ranked officer of evil. You're a real edgy guy."

"Who says I'm not an assload of fun?"

Cuddling closer to him, she let her breasts rub against his shirt, shivering at the immediate response her nipples displayed, and gave him a look of astonishment. "I can't imagine anyone ever labeling you like that. How unfair."

Chuckling, he scooped her up in his arms and carried her to the bedroom. "I know. Penance is due."

"Ohhh, penance. Sounds serious."

"I take my penance very seriously," he said with a leer, throwing her onto the bed and dropping down on top of her.

"So what kind of penance are we talking here?"

His look was of mock seriousness. "*Naked* penance. I mean, it was a serious offense."

Letting her head fall back, she gave a throaty laugh, carefree and unrestrained. "I suppose this will involve my nekidity."

He toyed with the torn front of her dress, raining kisses along her jaw that made her melt with anticipation. "Well, you are the one who sinned."

"Then you'll have to do the honors," she said with a smile, lifting up her arms for him to remove her dress, unashamed of her desire for him.

"That reminds me. Hold that thought." He jumped off the bed and went into the small walk-in closet that had once been filled with Delaney's things and came back out with a pink bag she recognized from one of her favorite boutiques. "I figured it was about time. I'm not sure if it'll work, but let's give it a shot." Kellen opened the mouth of the bag for her to see inside.

Fuck-all if tears didn't fill the corners of her eyes. Again. "When did you have the time to get this?"

He dumped the bag on the bed, holding up the contents. "I didn't. D did. When I told her about your dress, she was assholes and elbows to your favorite boutique. Wanna see if you can try it on?"

Fighting more tears, she rose off the bed, hovering in midair in front of him. He'd bought her a dress. A new dress from Sinclair's. "You shouldn't have. Sinclair's is pricey."

His eyes were warm when he said, "It's a good thing I sold some fine Texas bat shit this month then, huh?" He tugged her old, torn dress over her head and tossed it on the floor, scanning her length with eyes that approved before he slipped the new dress onto her.

Marcella held her breath until she felt the cool cloth float about her skin. Her hands shook when she touched the front of the smooth, red fabric, tugging at the empire waist to make sure it fell around her knees properly. The capped sleeves brushed against her hair; the round neckline accentuated her breasts. It was as though it had been made for her.

Delaney might have shopped for it, but Kellen had bought it. Such a simple gesture seemed so magnanimous.

And woo to the hoo—here came more tears.

Kellen let out a wolfish whistle. "I'd say Delaney knows her stuff. You look great."

Putting her hands to her face, she covered her eyes to hide her latest sissy-fest. "Thank you," she whispered. "I—no one's ever . . ."

He peeled her fingers from her face. "Well, someone just did. And there's more. Shoes. Delaney says they're cute, but you won't need those, or this," he said, dipping his fingers into the neckline of her dress with a grin that was full of his wicked intent and made her heart hammer inside her chest.

Her arms went around his neck and she arched her body into his. "About that penance . . ." she murmured.

Kellen's mouth found hers with a chuckle. "Yeah. You have some work to do." With a whoosh, he pulled the new dress back off her and threw it at the end of the bed. Circling her waist, he hauled her against him hard, cupping her breast to thumb her nipple to a stiff peak.

Moaning into his mouth, she ran her hands over his chest, his arms, bulging with sinewy muscles. Kicking off his shoes, Kellen took his own clothes off, parting with her lips for only a moment before he was naked.

Their bodies pressed together, skin to skin. His was flush with heat, hers cool on the outside, but tending a raging fire on the inside. Mouths connected in a molten hot kiss, blending, melting into one another. Their tongues meshed, dueled, tangled in silken strokes.

Settling them on the bed, Kellen's dark head bent to her breast, clamping his hot mouth around it, pulling her nipple with decadent swirls. Her thigh lifted automatically, wrapping around his waist, pinning him to her.

Arching upward, she pushed her breast against the ecstasy his tongue brought, panting her pleasure. Kellen's lean hands, big, strong, swept along her ribs, brushing back up along the undersides of her breasts, moving across her lower abdomen.

Raging white-hot flames licked at her, leaving an aching tug and pull between her thighs. His hair brushed her skin as he trailed moist kisses against her flesh, leaving not an inch untouched. He nipped, licked, taunted until she realized his hair swept against the skin of her inner thighs.

Gripping his head between her fingers, Marcella held her breath when his teeth grazed against the inside of her leg. His moan of pleasure as he drew closer to her core made her writhe with an aching need. He used his tongue to part her moist flesh, rasping it apart, laving it with long, slow strokes. Her legs fell apart, her neck arched at his deliciously hot breath against her clit.

Slipping his hands beneath her ass, he pulled her flush to his wet mouth, teasing the swollen bud until she thrashed under him. Electricity shot pinpoints of pleasure to her belly, fanning out, making her nipples harden. Marcella gripped his head, latching onto his hair and bucking against him until she could no longer fight the tidal wave of sticky hot orgasm.

Rising up on her elbows, her head fell back as she screamed her release, letting it take over, letting the pulsing ache build then ebb until she was nothing but boneless and limp. Each muscle in her body tensed tightly like a bow, then flexed as climax after climax ravaged her.

Kellen nipped at her skin, finding his way back up to her mouth where he consumed her lips. She tasted herself on his tongue, and it was heady, sinful. Marcella's hands roamed the hard planes of his hips, the crisp hair on his thighs, the thick muscles of his back. When she'd gathered her breath, she slid beneath him, leaving him straddling her chest.

His thick cock, ramrod straight, hot and pulsing, brushed against her lips. He groaned, low, husky, the muscles of his thighs clenching when she braced her hands on them.

Inch by painstaking inch, Marcella enveloped his shaft between her lips, running her tongue along the heated skin. He bucked when she cupped his ass with her hands, drawing him fully into the hot cavern of her mouth.

She let him adjust before she moved, reveling in the jagged breaths he took that filled the air of the bedroom, rife with their lovemaking. Kellen's hips began to move in circles, slow, measured, each movement making him hiss a moan.

Marcella dragged a hand up along his hip, down between his legs, and enveloped his testicles, massaging them with a gentle motion. Moving her other hand to his cock, she pumped him, laved until he was slick with her tongue's moisture. Her passes grew heated, faster, as her mouth worked along his thickness.

Kellen's hands dug into her hair, tangling in the curls as he pushed her mouth around his cock, driving in and out until he pulled back with a sharp tug. Leaning back on his haunches, he let his head hang low, fighting for air.

Then he lifted it, his eyes dark, molten hot with desire for her. So intense, Marcella caught her breath. There was no mistaking his need when he caught her up in his arms with such force it made her nipples pucker as they scraped against his chest.

The room shifted then righted itself when he rolled with her, placing her on top of him, settling the tip of his cock at her entrance.

Their eyes met—their hands entwined.

The world stopped for a mere moment.

And everything changed.

Love, tender, sweet, fast, furious, welled inside her.

Love.

The realization stole her breath to think that the night before had only been her falling. Now, she was in. All in.

In this very moment, Marcella knew no matter when she was taken from this plane, from him, she would know what it was to want to spend an eternity with Kellen. This wasn't like the immature love she'd thought she'd felt for Armando. It was so deep, she felt it burrow into a space in her heart she'd thought was forever locked.

The place where David was.

Would always be.

The place that Kellen now would be, too. A place she hoped to visit when she was gone. A place that would bring her joy when time had healed the raw hurt of leaving him.

As he lay before her, the hard planes of his body highlighted in the moonlight, the slim taper of his waist with her hands upon it, she gulped with her revelation.

Lifting her hips, she decided all she wanted was to be filled by him, consumed by his hardness, taken so she could be only in this moment. Kellen didn't question her aggressive move when she thrust herself down onto him. Instead, he encouraged her, lifting his hips to meet the crash of hers, moaning his pleasure at the slickness of her entry.

She braced herself, using her hands on his chest to rock against him with a fierce rhythm. Grinding into him, she felt his crisp pubic hair rub against the swollen bud of her clit. It sent wave after wave of rippling pleasure between her legs.

Kellen's hands circled her waist, pressing her frenzied thrusts down onto his cock with force, stealing her breath. He drove upward, matching the frantic pulse of her desperate need to be one with him.

Her hands fell behind her to grip his thighs, lifting her breasts upward so that Kellen cupped them in his hands, thumbing the hard peaks of her nipples, then moved to her clit, massaging it until she thought she'd explode from the pleasure. An agonizing spiral of white-hot heat threaded along her veins, pushing, driving, until she bit the inside of her lip to keep from crying out. Tears stung her eyes when she thrust downward for the final time, clenching his thighs so hard her nails dug into his flesh.

Kellen's final plunge upward made the cords in his neck stand out, his grip on her waist ironclad. He grunted his release long and low, his lips drawing back over his teeth when he hissed his orgasm.

Marcella fell to his wide chest, her cheek pressed to his damp skin, her limbs boneless from exertion.

Cupping the back of her head, Kellen stroked her hair, brushing it from her cheeks.

She couldn't raise her head to look at him for fear he'd see what she'd discovered during their lovemaking. It would only make things harder if he knew she'd gone and done something so out of character.

It would only make leaving him more painful.

"So," he mumbled, his voice a sexy rumble beneath her cheek, "I think we're in love."

Marcella almost giggled at how reasonable that sounded. Then she froze, lifting her eyes to meet his. Tugging her by her upper arms, he dragged her along his body until they were nose to nose.

"Go ahead. Freak out. I'll hold you down."

To say it out loud would only make it more real.

"You're afraid if you say it out loud it'll make it a reality."

Thank you, Amazing Kreskin. Her tongue refused to work.

"It's okay, honey," he soothed. "There's been a whole lotta nice with you lately and it's foreign. I get it. You need time to adjust. I'll wait." He looked at the clock on the bedside table then back at her. "Was that enough time? Or do you need more?"

Before she had the chance to speak, before she could actually come up with an answer, she was sucked from his arms and he was gone.

Instead, she was back in the park.

And good Christ, she was wearing her torn dress.

Whoever'd dragged her here had better have a credit card.

With a really big limit.

Atonement and some new shoes were due.

fourteen

"Marcella?"

She cocked her head, tilting it into the harsh winter wind as a tall figure came into view. Hackles rose on the back of her neck when the bulk of his form moved closer. A very round, wide man, in a dark suit and clunky shoes, tromped toward her. Hair as black as midnight with only a hint of gray at the temples shone under the heavy, buttery moon. He cracked his knuckles as he approached, making her jump.

"It's me, Marcella. Little Ant'ony." He paused, shaking his thick head of hair. "God damn it. I mean, *Darwin*." His Bronx accent was thick. "Pardon my language."

She looked around at the park, bewildered and irritated. "What the fuck am I doing here, Darwin?"

He smiled, though the face of the wise guy that did the smiling for him had a crafty hint to his grin. "I thought ya up. It was easier dan I tought—uh, *th*ought. Woulda friggin' done it yesterday if I'da figgur'd it out sooner."

Marcella flicked his pinstriped arm. "It's a friggin' good thing I don't know too many people who think about me, then. I was in the middle of something." Deep in the middle. Of revealing her raw, exposed heart.

"I apologize, but I had to talk wit ya."

She hadn't forgotten their last meeting, and though she knew her own doing had skewed his perception of her—it still hurt. "You mean me, the *bitch*? The dumb one?"

His pudgy face, or rather Little Anthony's face, revealed such sadness at her sarcasm. He held up a hand with thick fingers attached to it. "Bear wit me fer a sec while I get Ant'ony to quiet down." Turning from her, his body shuddered as though he were waging an internal battle. He muttered a string of threatening words like "local," "precinct," and "downtown," and finally, "confessions that would make the feds' eyelashes curl" if Anthony didn't pipe down. When he faced her again, his eyes remained steeped in uncensored sorrow. Clearing his throat, he said, "I called you here first to apologize, Marcella, and second to tell you something you must know."

Looking down at her dress, she nodded then glared at him. "You definitely should be apologizing. I had a brand-new dress I should be wearing—a perfectly gorgeous dress—but you had to go and think me up in this one, you buffoon."

He bowed his greased-back head. "I've been many things, Marcella. Buffoon, ass, judgmental."

Her eyes narrowed. "Is the end of the world slated and you know the date?"

"Why would you ask that?"

"Because not only are you apologizing to *me*, but you're agreeing with me. Should I take cover?"

Taking her hand in his thick one, he squeezed it, his diamond pinky ring casting a prism of light on the pavement. "Let's not beat each other about the head and shoulders with our words, Marcella. Not tonight. Just listen and let me tell you how sorry I am for my ill-perceived, misinformed ideas about you. Truly, from the depths of my soul, I humble myself at your feet."

This was a startling turn of events, and it left her uncomfortable. Every steadfast quality in the people who surrounded her was changing and it had begun to freak her out. She'd only just started to adjust to Kellen's change of heart, her feelings for him, and now Darwin was asking her for something he shouldn't have to ask for. He'd called her a bitch. Okay, so she'd taken it badly. She'd told him to leave her alone—she'd done that at least a million times before in their relationship as frenemies and they'd always found their way back to each other, like it or not. "Go humble somewhere else and knock it off, Darwin. You dragged me away from something very important. Besides, what do you have to apologize for?"

"Because I *know*," he said, his tone low and hushed.

"Know?"

Darwin's thick red lips expelled a sigh. "Stop, Marcella. Stop pretending you don't know what I mean. I was so unfair to you, I don't even know if I can stand to be in my own skin, er, even if it's Little Anthony's. I can only say, I didn't know the details. I never would have guessed."

Marcella sucked in a breath of cold air. Would this part of it never be over? Reliving losing David and everyone's shock over what she'd done was wearing her down. "So you know about . . ." Though she'd been so cleansed at this point she should have nothing left to clean, the residual of her confessions still ached.

Darwin's head bowed, his eyes grave. "Yes. I know everything. I know about David. It's all over Plane Dismal. I can't apologize enough."

Marcella tried to dismiss it. "Yeah. I've heard that once or twice in the past couple of days. Look, Darwin. I didn't do anything to give anyone the impression I was anything other than Party-All-the-Time Barbie. It's not your fault. It's no one's fault but mine."

Clinging to her hand, he shook his slick head. "But I didn't look any deeper, either. Not even after you saved Delaney and Clyde. I judged you so heinously. I helped you get here and consoled myself with the justification that it was for Delaney, my once beloved mistress, never in a million years thinking you actually deserved help. I coaxed you back to this plane to ease Delaney's fears for my own selfish purposes, and as a result, I doomed you. I've talked to everyone to try to help get you back, so at the very least you can find some modicum of peace, with no luck, and now you're all wrapped up in this thing with Carlos and Armando."

Wrapped up. Invested. Involved. All words she'd once banished from her vocabulary. Now it was all she thought about, and once more, the helplessness of her situation pierced her heart.

"That brings me to what I have to tell you. This Armando, he's bad news, Marcella."

Her head hung low to her chest as she stared at her floating feet. "I was married to the bad news, remember? I killed him so there'd be no more bad news. So believe me, bad news I know. We're like this." She crossed two fingers together.

"There's more. He's possessed that little boy's mother. I have confirmation. And more importantly, I know *why* he's possessed her."

Fear sizzled in her gut. She'd been almost one hundred percent sure when she'd told Kellen her suspicions about Solana. To have confirmation set her into motion. "I knew it! Damn that piece of shit. Now I have proof. I have to go, Darwin. So apology accepted and all that good stuff. Go tie cement blocks to someone's feet, and I'll see ya when I see ya."

But Darwin clung to her hand, holding her in place. "Wait! You have to listen very carefully to me, please. Not just for your safety, but for the boy's."

More anxiety, more panic. So much, she shook. "Tell me what you know."

"Armando knows you're here on this plane. The only time he can't see you is when he's in that child's mother's body because really all he's doing is utilizing her limbs, but he has informants everywhere. He knows you gave him up to Satan."

Marcella blanched, but recovered when she realized something very important. "So? He'd have been found out eventually, and there's nothing he can do to me anyway."

"Don't underestimate the kind of anger a man locked up for seventy-six years is capable of. He wants revenge, and the kind of power he's honing is toxic. If he gets his hands on you . . ." His shoulders shuddered.

Please. "There's nothing he can do to me, Darwin. I'm a ghost. Like you said, he can't even see me. I know that to be fact."

"No! That's not true. He can see you if he leaves Solana's body and takes his demon form. And Jesus, can he ever hurt you. If he finds a way to capture your soul, he'll drag you off to a place that hands-down beats even the pit. But it isn't just you he can hurt. He can also hurt others." Darwin's beady eyes shifted downward.

Rage took the place of her anxiety. "If he touches Carlos or Kellen or Delaney, I'll find a way! I'll make his first murder seem like he took a Royal Caribbean cruise!" she shouted into the roaring wind as if Armando were standing right in front of her.

Placing a hand on her arm, Darwin squeezed. "He knew you'd been banished to roam restlessly for eternity. He was the one responsible for planting your image in Carlos's head, Marcella. He wanted Carlos to summon you. He wanted you to become involved with the boy."

"But why? For Christ's sake, why?"

Darwin motioned to the bench. "Sit. Please."

She shook her finger at him. "Oh, no, Guido. When you tell me to sit, it means there's some serious shit about to go down. I'll take this standing up, floating. *What-ever*. Speak."

Darwin hedged, gnawing on his thick lower lip.

Grabbing his meaty shoulders, Marcella couldn't take it anymore. *"Just say it!"*

She watched his wide neck work, his jowls tremble. "Carlos is your great-grandson, Marcella. Your granddaughter was Carlos's mother, Solana. His grandfather is your son, David."

The wind picked up with a howl, whipping her dress about her knees, the strap of her torn sandal flapping in time with it. Dead leaves bristled in the harsh gusts, crisp and brittle. The elements were all motion, yet she remained motionless, the air drained from her very lungs.

Darwin pulled her to the bench, pushing down on her shoulders to seat her, dragging her hand into his pinstriped lap, covering her fist with both of his hands. "I'm sorry. I . . . there was no other way . . . talk to me, Marcella. *Please*," he urged, his unibrow scrunching together.

Her throat was thick, her heart bursting with fear. It all didn't add up. No. Darwin had to be wrong. No, no, no. Moments ticked away while she fought to put her questions together. "This can't be. How can this be? Carlos's grandfather's last name is Ramirez! You're wrong, Darwin. I don't know who fed you this load of bullshit, but you're wrong!" Oh, God. *Please* let him be wrong.

His strong hand gripped hers harder, the bristling hairs on the back of it chafing her skin. "No, Marcella. I'm not wrong. Listen carefully to me. I made it my mission to be clear on what happened with David when I found out what you did for him. Your sister, Isabella, and her husband took David and moved as far away as they could from New York. They changed their names. They changed *David's* name. If you check with Carlos's grandmother, you'll find that David's name is now Juan."

She felt dizzy—disoriented, like a cloudy blanket had fallen over her thinking skills. "*Why?* Why did they change his name?"

"Because of a threat from one of Armando's supposed colleagues. He was convinced your sister knew where some large amount of money Armando had stolen from him was. He was a despicable thug who terrorized Isabella and her husband, Luis, with his clan of evildoers until they feared for their lives. They feared for David's safety—so they took your parents and your son and moved to California with the help of Luis's family and hid. They changed their name to Ramirez, Marcella. Juan Ramirez *is* David Villanueva."

She bent over at the waist to stop the spinning. Oh, sweet Jesus. Carlos. He was her great-grandson? David was still alive? She shoved a fist in her mouth to keep from screaming her rage, her anguish. Almost as quickly, she sat back up. "Does Armando know I know what he's done? That he's taken possession of Solana's body?"

"No—he only knows you're here on this plane. It's why he planted the image of you in Carlos's head—for confirmation."

There was always a way to bargain. Always a deal to be had. She'd make one. No matter what it entailed. Armando was a greedy pig. She'd find his weak spot and pluck the motherfucker dry. "Tell me what Armando wants. Tell me, and I'll give it to him. Does he want to see me writhe in the pit? I know he wants revenge, so I'll let him have whatever he wants and bargain for Carlos." With what or how, she couldn't even begin to consider.

"No, Marcella!" He gave her a hard shake, but his eyes still held sympathy. "Listen carefully. He definitely wants revenge, but he wants to make your eternity far worse than any pit in Hell could ever be. He wants the child. Armando knows who Carlos is. He plans to take him from his grandparents, and there isn't a thing they can do because he's in that child's mother's body."

It had come full circle.

Armando would make her pay by way of proxy. By way of a small child. A child who was *familia*—family. Her son's offspring. David. Oh, God, *David* . . . "I—I . . ." And Armando knew there wasn't a damned thing she could do about it. She was a useless ghost. She couldn't stop him. Who could stop him? How could they convince anyone that her ex-husband was holding Solana Vega's body hostage? Just the thought was insane, even to someone who'd grown accustomed to the supernatural.

"Do you know what happened to Solana?" Marcella asked, her question littered with hesitation, her voice scratchy. "Is she . . . ? I mean, is she alive? I don't understand possession well enough to . . . if that dickless motherfucker hurt her . . ." So many idle threats, so little time.

Darwin looked down at his knees. "If there's any consolation in this, it's that Armando didn't kill Solana in order to possess her. He was just in the right place at the right time. When he was set free from that box, Solana had already passed."

Jesus, God. Carlos's mother was dead. Her granddaughter was dead. Grief gripped at her heart like a vise. "How do you know your information is accurate? *Who* told you this?"

His deep-set, beady eyes grew wet. "Solana. She's on Plane Drab, Marcella. Just as you left, she arrived, and she's not crossing over until she knows Carlos is safe. It isn't just Carlos who needs your help; Solana does, too. She absolutely must cross, but she refuses until she knows Carlos and her parents are safe."

Marcella's mind raced with recklessness, almost unable to process the enormity of how tangled this had become. "How did Solana die, Darwin? Are we sure it was an accident?"

"That much I'm sure of. She'd had a particularly hard day and was missing her husband, whom I assume you know passed. While bathing, she'd consumed too much wine and fell asleep. She drowned."

Pain clutched at her heart. "Oh, God. Carlos. Not only has he lost one parent, but now two?"

Darwin clucked his tongue. "Without a doubt, the boy has suffered epic tragedy as of late. Which makes me all the more anxious to keep him from any more."

Defeat battered her entire body, making it slump.

But Darwin was beside her, shaking her out of her pity. "Don't give up, Marcella. I can feel you giving up. Don't. It's just one more battle in a string of many you've waged. I know you're tired. I know it seems like there's no end in sight, but don't give in. I'll help you. We'll find some way to protect Carlos."

She threw her hands up in a gesture of pure helplessness. "How can we protect him from that freak—especially seeing as he's in Solana's body? He has all the control, Darwin! That miserable fuck knows it, too. We don't have the resources—the kind of power it takes to thwart Armando's rage. I just know that's what he's been doing while he's been wandering around in his own granddaughter's body, honing his demonic skills. He makes me want to gag. Damn it. I don't know where to go from here. I'm lost, Darwin."

"Then let me help you find your way."

Her chest tightened into a fist of anger and other rebellious emotions she hadn't felt since she'd saved her son's soul. "Isn't it funny how no one wanted a thing to do with me, despite the fact that I was a pretty decent demon who never really caused any trouble? I mean, the most damage I've ever done is to a Visa card. But now, because you all know the truth, you're all in love with me? I'm still the same old beyotch I always was. What I did wasn't anything any other mother wouldn't have done if she had access to the kind of afterlife resources I did."

He wagged a chubby, hairy-knuckled finger at her with reprimand. "That's not fair. You hid, Marcella. You hid your sacrifices. Saving your son's soul is the ultimate sacrifice."

Marcella's scoff held disgust. "So if I hadn't saved someone's soul, I'd still be a dirty, rotten bitch? I sort of resent that. I wasn't a bad person while I was a demon. I might not have been out saving the world, but I didn't hurt anyone. I shopped. I didn't cultivate my evil. Yet still, it wasn't enough."

Darwin gave her a sideways glance chock-full of disapproval. "Please. Let's be honest here, you were the crankiest, snarkiest demon in three-inch heels and a tight tee. You wanted us to believe you were heartless because it was easier than convincing anyone of the truth. Did it make people love you? No. Had we known why you were so godforsakenly horrifying, we might have cut you some slack."

She sighed, her anger vanishing, helplessness returning. "That's fair."

He gave her a hard shove with his shoulder. "C'mon, Marcella— get mad at me. Call me a kibble-loving ass licker—*fight back*!"

"With what?" she screamed into the wind. "Jesus Christ, you canine catastrophe—fight back with *what*?"

Now Darwin slumped back, too, his beefy shoulders pressing against hers. Settling beside her, he narrowed his eyes. "I don't know, but by all that's holy, I'll find out. We'll find out. We'll end this cyclical hell once and for all. Delaney and Clyde's situation seemed helpless, but they found a way out. We'll find one for Carlos, too. But I beg you, don't give up. We will find some way to help him. I won't have it any other way."

Fat tears began to form in the corners of her eyes. Here came the whine. "I'm just so tired, Darwin. The running from the truth, the hiding, it's taken its toll, I think. I don't know that I realized how exhausting it would be until it all came crashing around my ears. Lately, I'm either crying or crying. It's pathetic."

Pulling her to him, Darwin pressed her head to his shoulder. "That's because you've stuffed this so far down inside you that it became a ticking time bomb. Letting it go, talking about something so horrible, so life-altering, is exhausting, Marcella. You need to mourn properly instead of shoving it aside. But there's hope now. You have a great-grandson who needs you. I suspect, with all the time you've been spending with Kellen, he needs you, too."

She fought another wretched sob against his linebacker's shoulder.

"Ah. It's as I suspected. Kellen knows about David?"

She nodded, mute.

"Things have changed between you, haven't they?"

Words were impossible.

"You're in love."

Marcella choked on a whimper and another nod of her head. "I didn't mean for it to happen. I thought it was just a stupid fantasy, but everything's changed."

"That's so peachy. So damned peachy," he replied, gruff and husky.

Coughing, she sat up and sputtered, "How is that peachy, Darwin? I'm a ghost. He's mortal. There's nothing peachy about my loving someone I can never be with." She hiccuped.

"But you're with him now."

"But for how long, Darwin? How long will I be here before I get sucked back to that shitty plane with a bunch of people who don't know what they want? I *know* what I want!"

"Kellen," he stated with directness.

"Yes! Yes! Fuck-all, I want Kellen and Carlos and normal. I want to be like everyone else. I want to do the same things every day. I want to live a dull, monotonous, boring, insignificant-as-shit life until I get old and die the *normal* way. I want to go to the grocery store, not shoot fireballs from my fingertips. I want to goddamned well clean the toilet and not float while I do it. I want to walk out a door, not through it!"

The look he gave her was grave, and she knew what it meant. Knew it in her core. It was time she expressed it out loud. Let it roll off her lips so that she could just come to terms with it. "There is no way, is there, Darwin? There's no way for me to become earthbound again?"

"No," he said with a hitch in his rough voice. "Dear God, Marcella. I've talked to everyone—anyone who'll listen, and I—I—"

"It's okay," she said, cutting him off. She couldn't bear to hear just how helpless this all was again. She did that enough in the confines of her mind. *"It's okay."*

Darwin shook his head. "I can't apologize enough for what I've dredged up, Marcella. Nothing will ever be enough."

She patted Darwin's knee, summoning the will to focus. "You were thinking of Delaney. You were right. I owed her peace of mind."

He snorted. "Oh, I'm positive she lays her pretty head on her pillow every night and rests easy knowing you're stuck here without a body. I've only made things worse. And you know something else? Did you ever wonder why I never crossed?"

Marcella's eyes fell to the ground again. "I have. I just figured it was personal, and you didn't want to talk about it."

Crashing his fist down on his thigh, he yelled, "Because of Delaney. Because I adored her when I was her dog. Because I never wanted to leave her. I wanted to watch her live a long, happy life, then cross with her. Now all I do is watch her suffer, and in the process, I've made you suffer, too. *Bra-vo.*"

Marcella's smile of acknowledgment was bittersweet. "You love her. I get the kind of devotion she inspires. I love her, too," she whispered.

The wind whistled between them in long gusts while they sat and pondered. In that silence, Marcella had a vague flicker of a memory that halted her breath.

And time was ticking away, precious time that could be used to keep Carlos from that monster. "Enough. We don't have time to feel sorry for ourselves. So let's figure this out." If she kept her goal set on keeping Carlos from Armando, she could force what she knew she had to do from her thoughts for the moment.

"Maybe there's some kind of spell or something we could use to stop him. If you found one to capture his soul, there must be more. But nonetheless, I'm in. *Whatever* you need, I'm in."

She looked away to keep her eyes from revealing how close Darwin was to the truth. "Well, Brain, the problem is, we're not exactly a force to be reckoned with." She held up a transparent hand. "Or I'm not, anyway. You can't go this alone. He'll massacre you. We have to catch him by surprise."

Darwin sat up straight with such force, he shook the bench. "That's it. By hell. That's it!" He jumped up, pulling her with him and bouncing his round body up and down.

Her head bobbed while she bounced, too, utterly confused. "What's it?"

"I know exactly what we need to do. So listen up, Marcella Acosta. We have a rogue demon to catch."

Marcella knew exactly what she had to do, too. At this precise moment, she knew it. Tasted it. Felt it in every pore of her body.

She could save Carlos from Armando. There was a way.

It just wasn't a way that would leave happiness in its wake.

But unfortunately, for all of Darwin's bravado, for all of his motivational speeches, there was no way to change what she was. What Kellen was.

She was a ghost.

Kellen was a human.

Never the twain shall meet.

"If this woman doesn't kill me with her mouth, she'll kill me with worry," Kellen ranted to Delaney, who'd come the moment he called. It had been hours since Marcella had vanished. His worry that she'd been sucked back to that plane grew with each second that ticked painfully by. He sat with Delaney and Clyde around his small kitchen table, coffee cups with stone-cold liquid in them littering the surface of the chipped Formica.

"Have you tried thinking about her in her, well, you know . . ." Clyde asked, looking down at the table. "That was how you got her here the first time, right?"

Kellen's nod was curt. All he could do was think about her. "I have, and nothing seems to be working."

"So she just disappeared into thin air?"

"Yep. We were . . . uh. Yeah." He halted, forcing his face to remain unreadable. "She just disappeared."

"Damn," Clyde commented with a grin that was all male, all knowing. "In the middle of, you know, the whoopee?"

Delaney swatted his arm and frowned. "That's none of our business. But seeing as you brought the subject up—are you and Marcella—you know, slammin' the—"

"A gentleman never tells." But his eyes took a break from worried and became warm and uncharacteristically sentimental against his will.

Throwing her arms around his neck, Delaney squealed, but just as suddenly dropped her arms, a frown forming on her face. "Why couldn't the two of you have figured out that you were hot for each other before she became a ghost? Talk about shitty timing."

Kellen's gut twisted in a knot. "Still nothing in the way of ideas about how to keep her here?"

Her sigh was that of frustration. "Not a blessed thing. I'm still wondering how she's managed to stay as long as she has."

Kellen decided to throw something out there that he'd given much thought to in the hours since Marcella had disappeared. "Why couldn't she just stay here as a ghost?"

Clyde's and Delaney's heads both popped up. "What kind of life is that, Kell? For either of you?"

His response was quiet, yet deadly serious. "It's better than none at all."

Delaney's mouth fell open. She clasped Kellen's hands between hers. "You're in love with Marcella."

He didn't answer. His chest grew too tight to acknowledge it with words.

Pressing Kellen's fist to her forehead, Delaney bit her lower lip. "I want to jump up and down and cry all at the same time. You two couldn't have done this five years ago? Even six months ago? You know, the two of you are the most stubborn, pigheaded fools I know! When you finally come to your senses, everything's gone to shit."

Kellen gripped her hand harder. "We have to find a way to keep her here, Delaney. But not just that, we have to find out for sure if that's really Armando in Solana's body." When he'd explained what Marcella suspected, Delaney went from mortified to angry to ready to take action. According to her, all they had to do was summon Armando's soul and draw him out of Solana's body. It was dangerous because an angry demon was a vengeful demon. A million things could go wrong that Delaney staunchly refused to voice, but made her face go chalk white.

Delaney rolled her shoulders and sat up straight. "Okay, first things first. While we wait for Marcella to show up, Clyde and I will go hunt for some of the things we'll need to get that son of a bitch out of his host's body. We'll work out the when and how when I get back, because, if nothing else, we have to have a plan. A solid one with backup." She rose from the table, holding out her hand to Clyde. "So call me if you hear from Marcella. And tell her I said if she found a way to hit the mall, the least she could have done was ask me to come with," Delaney joked, clearly attempting to lighten his dour mood.

Thumping Kellen on the back, Clyde said, "I know your worry, friend. So I won't say something absurd like don't worry. Just sit tight till we get back." He followed Delaney out the door, leaving Kellen in abysmal silence again. He sat back down and fiddled with the handle of his cup, unable to stop the visions of Marcella that swarmed his mind's eye. If that motherfucker Armando had touched a hair on her head, he'd hurl a case of fucking Morton's at him right before he made his eyes bleed by dangling prisms over his head.

"Could I wear something crazy like footie pajamas and a scarf when you think me up? It's cold outside."

Kellen's chair scraped the linoleum, his head whipping around to find the corner she hovered in. "Jesus Christ, Marcella! Where the hell did you go? Is it Carlos?"

Marcella brushed his arm with her hand, her nerves frazzled for what she was about to do—lie—stall—lie, lie, lie. "No. I just had a sudden urge to take one last shot at the Pier 1 semiannual sale. Alas"—she held up her hands—"nothing. Still can't pick a damned thing up." She smiled up at him.

He grabbed her shoulders and gazed down at her, smoothing the tension in her arms. "Okay, now let's be serious. Where did you go? Did Carlos summon you again?"

She couldn't look him in the eye, her throat tightening to the point of uncomfortable. "No. I just needed to think." This was the right thing to do. To go on believing she'd ever be able to give Kellen all the human things he so wanted, whether he'd admit it or not, was delusional. But it didn't make the right thing to do any less painful.

"About?"

How to cap that motherfucker Armando. *Again.* How to walk away from a man she'd fallen desperately in love with and wanted to be able to watch *The Bachelorette* with, every Monday night like clockwork. How to do it without crying like the total sissy-ass she'd become, and do it convincingly. "This whole thing. You know, you, me . . . what's happened between us."

Crossing his arms over his chest, he gave her his most intense gaze. "I'm ready."

"For?"

"The freak. You're pulling away. I can feel it."

Her heart thumped against her chest with hard slaps. Summoning up the Marcella of old, she hardened her face, letting her body language convey the necessary mood. "Ask yourself this, Kellen. Do you really believe there's a chance I can stay here on this plane? Like, really stay. *All of me.* Do you really believe we can ever have a normal, average relationship the way things are now? Because you're kidding yourself," she scoffed.

His jaw tightened. "There was never anything average or normal about you, Marcella."

"And there never will be. I was a demon. Now I'm a ghost. You're a human. How do you bring your see-through girlfriend to the softball games you play once a week with the other teachers? How do you have a family and do all the normal human things families do, with a woman no one can see but you? You can't, because it's ridiculously sentimental and stupid. We aren't the Ghost and Mrs. Muir."

Kellen's stance grew rigid, the gorgeous planes of his face determined. "I told you I would find a way to keep you here, Marcella, and I meant it."

She gave a snort, dripping with derision. "Right, Superman. You do that. In the meantime, I'm out. This can only end badly, so I'm ending it before we get in any deeper. We'll have nice memories, smile fondly about them someday. Now go off and get that cute blonde wife you've always wanted. Get married at the local VFW hall, have a couple of kids, and do Fourth of July picnics with Delaney, Clyde, and their twelve hundred orphans from Somalia, okay?"

Grabbing her by the arm, he shook his head, his teeth clenched. "Blondes were never my thing."

"Well, a woman who doesn't float and can change her own panties all by her big-girl self is. Or will be—*should* be. You'll only become defensive as time goes by due to a situation I can't change. If you thought you hated me before, imagine how much you'll hate me when I can't attend PTA meetings for the children you'll never have. Besides, who knows how much longer I can stick around anyway? For all we know, the next time I disappear, it could be for good."

"Or things could remain just as they are." Kellen's answer to their dilemma was stoic, but oh so solemn.

That he was willing to make that kind of sacrifice made her heart clench so hard, it felt as though someone had their hand wrapped around it. Yet a sacrifice of that magnitude could only lead to heartbreak. "You know what?"

"What?"

Marcella decided to turn the tables on him. Play the selfish man card. Whatever it took to discourage him from a relationship that would only become strained from its limitations. She knew ruthless. She understood anger. It was crucial that she rediscover those emotions if she was going to do this right. "Do you realize how selfish it is of you to ask me to stay here with you? Have you given any thought to the idea that someday, you'll die? You'll hit those pearly gates with the kind of joy that *should* be associated with crossing over. Me? I'll be peeking through them from the outside looking in. I'll have to face an eternity alone. I think I've done my time, Kellen, and I'm not doing any more. Not even for *you*." If there were any way, if she believed there were even the slightest possibility she could find a way to become earthbound again, she'd grab it and never let go. But they both knew that was impossible.

"You're running away again," he taunted, pulling her in closer, drawing her to his chest, enticing her with the security of his arms. Arms she wanted to never leave.

And she couldn't let that happen. Carlos was at stake, and there was no way she was going to let Kellen in on that. If he knew Carlos was her great-grandchild, there'd be no stopping Kellen from trying to protect him. If Armando found out how important Kellen was to her, he'd see him dead just so he could revel in her anguish.

She'd begun this cycle of vengeance—she'd end it all on her own—without anyone else's well-being in the mix. Too many people had been hurt by what she'd done so long ago. No. More.

Pushing from him, she winked a saucy, flirtatious eye, just like she'd always done, a million times before. Though her teeth clenched together and her heart crashed against her ribs. "And you can watch my cute ass as I do it." And then she softened, because looking at him was going to be her end. "So please, Kellen. Just let me go," she whispered, planting a gentle kiss on the lips she so wished to linger upon forever. "Tell Carlos, no matter what, I didn't just ditch him. I know he won't understand why I'm leaving, but someday, please explain." Marcella turned from him then, swallowing hard, fighting the temptation to float right back into his arms and stay there.

His warning was gruff, raspy, tearing at her from the inside out. "Don't walk away, Marcella."

She wasn't walking. She was floating. Right out the fucking door and away from the kind of pain that she'd have to live with for an eternity.

fifteen

"Her?" Marcella asked, pointing to one of two women who leaned against the high desk's counter. One woman, all of maybe twenty-five, stood with her hand planted saucily on her voluptuous hip, while the other hand busied itself twirling a strand of thick, dark hair with flirtatious zeal.

Darwin leaned in to Marcella. "Well, if honesty's playing a part in this body hunt, you have to admit, she's certainly a close facsimile to you. You know, big breasts, small waist, bodacious ba-donk-a-donk. Admittedly she falls to the trailer-park-ish side of things, I'll grant you, but close enough."

The idea here was to find a host body for Marcella to possess so that catching Armando while he was still in Solana's body would be two against one. She at least needed working limbs to be able to pick up something heavy and brain that bastard over the head—hard.

Ah, déjà vu.

Marcella eavesdropped on the conversation the two women were having at the End of the Rainbowl Bowling Alley and Brews. The one with the long dark hair and legs that should be illegal in a pair of Lycra biking shorts gave her not-quite-as-striking gal pal a little shove. "Go ahead, Margie. Gawwwd. You've been givin' him the once-over all night. Just go do it." She hiked up her bountiful round C cups with a wink and a giggle.

Margie, shorter and dressed like she'd just left her local VFW's annual pig roast slash clambake, was pensive. Scratch that, she was downright green. She tightened the knot on the ice blue sweater precisely thrown over the top of her shoulders and played with the strand of pearls around her long neck. "But it's so forward, Pat! I can't," she moaned with a cry, clucking her tongue while she waffled.

"Oh, I dunno, Darwin," Marcella muttered, hanging back. "I don't know if I can do this. I didn't pay attention in possession class. I didn't pay attention in any class."

Darwin nudged her. "But I did. Obviously." He spread his arms wide to encompass his host's stout body. "It doesn't have to be her, per se. I just concluded you would be simpatico with that particular breed of woman. So possess what you know and all. You can certainly possess whoever you want as long as they're young and healthy and their limbs function. Just do it so we can get this over with. Anthony's getting restless." He turned his head and gave it a good shake before muttering the words "maximum security" and "life without parole."

Marcella bit the inside of her lip. "What if I screw it up?"

His chubby face screwed up. "Stop behaving like you're afraid of a good challenge. There's no doing it wrong. You just do it. Do you want a physical body to best Armando with, or do you want to slink off without putting up a good fight? If you have a host, you stand a far better chance of walloping that no-good bastard's behind. Once you have a body, all you have to do is clunk that pig over the head and summon his soul again. You've done it before, killa. I have every faith you'll come through again. Then you lock him back in a box, but this time, we throw the bloody thing in the Hudson instead of leaving it with a pair of nonbelievers."

Darwin turned Marcella back toward the two women and pointed. "Look, it's easy. First, be open to the possibility—loosen up. Then all you have to do is shove your way in. I know you're stronger than a pair of Lycras and an overstuffed Frederick's of Hollywood bra. Once you're in, you use that fresh mouth of yours to quiet her down, and we go get that maniac before he takes off with Carlos. *Carlos* is at stake, Marcella."

Carlos. Her great-grandson. And David. Juan. Whoever. What would her son suffer if he lost his grandchild to that monster? He'd hurt until his dying day. And Mrs. Ramirez. Hadn't she suffered enough at the hands of Armando's brutal tongue? The hell she wouldn't do whatever it took to stop him. Even if it meant possessing a woman who thought Lycra was fashion forward.

Marcella shook out her hands, hoping to ease some of her nervousness. Two men had joined Pat and her friend Margie. This would be the perfect time to just slip right in—while they were distracted by beefcake.

Margie fluttered her eyelashes at man number one—a lot, and so obviously that, had Marcella a physical body, she'd have smacked her in the back of her head to make it stop.

Novices.

This was no way to get a man.

Man number one, blond and lean like a runner, in a pink polo shirt with the collar turned up and khaki Dockers, didn't appear too impressed. In fact, his face was rather flushed when he looked down at his snazzy bowling shoes.

The white ones with the pink striping.

Man number two, larger and in a similar outfit, rolled his eyes at man number one, heaving a sigh of aggravated impatience.

Oh, good gravy. These broads were barking up the wrong sexual preference tree. It was just as well she was going to kidnap the bodacious Pat's body. Not only could she try to save Carlos with it, she'd be doing some community service in the process.

As Marcella hovered, she listened to the attempts of man number one, whose name was Rick ("don't call me Dick") Short, to fend off the awkward Margie while Pat wet her lusciously glossed lips and eyeballed Rick's friend.

"So, do you guys come here often?" Margie squeaked, her face turning various shades of crimson.

Pat winked and leaned back against the counter, to ensure her breasts were properly displayed.

Darwin moved to the opposite end of the counter, pretending to talk on his cell phone. "I said just do it! Jesus, Petey. We don't got all friggin' night."

Licking her lips, Marcella hedged. Bowling balls crashed against pins while '80s music invaded her ears. The scents of beer, sweat, and French fries filled her nostrils. And then Darwin again: "Petey, for Chrissake. If you don't fuckin' do it, I will!" he barked.

Flustered by Darwin's nagging, she turned in time to see his meaty hand with the hairy knuckles out of the corner of her eye.

Just before he gave her a good, hard shove.

Right into Rick "Don't Call Me Dick" Short's body.

"Darwin?"

"Dick, er, Rick, uh, I mean, *Marcella*?"

"When all is said and done, I'm going to give you a good what-for, mister," she said with a hissing *s* in "mister." She paused and rolled her shoulders, shoving Rick to a place that was deep inside her, and put on the sternest expression she was capable of. Marcella cleared her throat. "I mean, I'm going to beat the living shit out of you, kibble king."

He snarfed. "Okay, fancy pants. But until then, we have a demon to catch." He handed her a bat from the trunk of Little Anthony's car.

"If you'd have just left well enough alone, I'd have jumped into that Pat's body all on my own." Which would have been far more suitable, according to Rick's disgruntled moan sashaying around her brain.

"If I'd have left well enough alone, we'd still be back at the bowling alley watching Margie make the big moves on Rick. Which was agonizing, to say the least. Not only did we spare Margie endless heartache, we saved Rick from having to explain the difference between heterosexual and homosexual to that Pat creature."

"But Pat's body I understand, you fool! She's a woman. This"— she waved her hands around the slender frame of Rick—"I just don't get."

He turned from the trunk and began trudging down the sidewalk, his big feet taking long steps. "Surely you're reveling in the chance to have *real* testicles, Marcella. Metaphorically speaking, all these years, that's really all you've been missing."

It was the strangest sensation ever—to possess someone else's body. Not to mention his man parts. Everything from your depth perception to using the appropriate facilities (she imagined) was awkward. Odder still, the ability to finally be able to touch things and walk on solid ground. "Can you slow down a little? I'm having trouble getting my feet under me."

Darwin guffawed. "That's because you have pink shoes on."

Yeah. A superior shade of pink, if she did say so herself. "Aren't they just fab?" she preened with a gushing sigh, stopping to admire them in the light of a store window. "Got them on sale at this cute little place on the Internet."

"Marcella?"

"Yes?"

"Beat that bitch down, would you?"

She rolled her eyes with exaggeration. "Easy for you to say, big boy, but Rick's very, very vocal and he's not too happy about our little adventure."

"Tell him to shut it. Now."

"I'm trying, but you know, I think Rick and I could be friends. He's got the most fantastic fashion sense, and he knows hair product like I know—"

Darwin interrupted with a grunt. "Marcella! Focus, for the love of . . . Tell Rick to pipe down. You'll give him back full control when we've taken care of business and not before. Dig deep, find the rip-roaring bitch that lives within, and get it together."

Marcella stopped in midstride and took a deep breath, rolling her head on her neck. Rick protested—vehemently. He wanted to go back to the Rainbowl Alley and bowl his team to V-I-C-T-O-R-Y. Marcella pushed that thought out of her mind and fought to gain control, bargaining silently with Rick in her mind.

"Think Carlos, Marcella. Just keep him on the brain," Darwin coached.

Squeezing her eyes shut, she popped them back open, catching a glimpse of herself, uh, Rick, in the store window. How utterly bizarre. Possessing a body was like having the strings to a live marionette in your hands. She held up a foot in Darwin's direction. "Well, you do have to admit, these shoes are pretty fabulous, and this jacket? Light and easy movement, but warm and snuggly."

His sigh was aggravated. "I'll admit no such thing. And you've never used the word 'snuggly' ever. Get. A. Handle on this." Darwin paused, running a hand along his tie. "Now do we have things under control?"

She cocked her head. No Rick rattling around in her brain. There was only silence and her desire to open up a can of whoop ass on Armando. "I think so."

They rounded the corner of Carlos's apartment building, her feet growing heavier and heavier. Jesus. For such a small guy, he had feet like twin cruise ships.

Darwin leaned in to her. "So here's the plan. Armando's witching hour is almost up. You wait behind that tree in the shadows. Just as he hits the corner of the street, nail him as hard as you can with the bat. I'll pull Anthony's car around and we dump him in the chest in the trunk. Then we summon."

Marcella's eyes cast Darwin a worried glance.

"You do remember how to do that, don't you?"

"It's fuzzy," she mumbled. And it was. Fuzzier still, the spell she'd need most to keep Armando from the people she loved. Hard knots formed in her stomach—for which Rick suggested Tums. Quietly, subtly. She frowned and sent him an internal message to can it.

Darwin snapped his fingers to catch her attention. "Marcella, we can't afford to flub this. You do know that, don't you?"

"Of course I know that! It's been a long time since I used a spell as powerful as a summoning. I've only done it once, and that was over seventy years ago. I'm rusty, but I'm good under pressure."

"Speaking of pressure . . ."

"Now what?"

"A little something that slipped my mind."

Her eyes narrowed. "Like?"

"Be very careful with Rick's body."

"Because?"

"Because you have to remember, while your spirit may not be susceptible to death, Rick's body is. Damage to the host is frowned upon in all afterlife circles."

Marcella planted her hands on her Dockered hips. "Darwin?"

"Yes?"

"Rick says you're a heathen, and I have to agree. If we get out of this in one piece, I'm going to poison your kibble and coat all of your pig's ears with arsenic. Rick says he'll help. How could you have forgotten to share something that important with me? Jesus." She ran a hand through Rick's highlighted blond hair in frustration, his fingers, though lean, feeling cumbersome compared to her smaller ones.

"Just be careful with him. Now get over there and watch for Armando," he demanded, pointing to the tree.

She shot him a dirty look then slunk to the big maple, standing behind it, her eyes peeled.

Waiting.

"Kellen? Hey, where are you?" Catalina shouted from the front of the store.

The frantic tone to her voice had all three of them running. "What's going on?" he asked, worried by her stricken look.

"I need you to listen to me very carefully. That phone's going to ring any minute and it's going to be Carlos's grandmother."

"*What?*" three voices said in concerned unison.

"It's Carlos. That son of a bitch is taking Carlos!" she barked, jamming a hand into her long hair, pulling it back from her face to tie it into a ponytail with a rubber band. "That Armando you left me a message about—he's going for Carlos, and there isn't anything anyone can do because he's running around in a body that everyone thinks is legit. I swear to Christ, if I get to this motherfucker, I'm going to make him wish he'd stayed in that box."

Kellen's stomach plummeted; his chest tightened. "So it's true, then. Armando's using Solana as a host." That was what Frank had meant when he'd hummed "I've Got You under My Skin." He hadn't been kidding, and once again, Marcella had been right.

"That's right, and when I lay hands on his pathetic minion ass, I'm going to squeeze the demon right out of him," she gritted out.

Clyde, ever practical, held up a hand. "Hold on. How do you know Armando has Carlos?"

Catalina pounded her chest. "I can *feel* it. I get this weird vibe when a kid's involved in demonic play. Never mind that, I have to go, but before I do, there's something you need to know," she said to Kellen.

Fists clenched, Kellen asked, "Is it Marcella?"

Catalina grimaced. "Yes. It's about Marcella, and I'm not going to dick around with the info I have. So prepare." She inhaled a ragged breath. "Carlos is her great-grandson. His grandfather is Marcella's son. The one she sacrificed her soul for. It took me days and some serious beat-downs to figure it out, but I finally got a weasel who's in on this thing with Armando to sing."

Kellen felt like he'd been sucker punched. He fought to keep his head on straight. "Carlos is Marcella's great-grandson? But his grandfather's name isn't David. It's Juan. I asked Mrs. Ramirez."

Catalina's lips thinned with impatience. "I don't have time to explain the details, just trust me when I tell you Carlos is Marcella's flesh and blood. Here's what we're faced with. Armando has Carlos. He wants revenge on Marcella. He didn't get his son the first time around. His plan is to take Carlos away from his grandparents and raise him to be a minion. A sort of payback for what Marcella kept him from all those years ago. Carlos sees the dead. Do you have any idea how many souls he can steer Satan's way if Armando can talk him into it? Feasibly, with a host's body, he can legitimately take that kid.

"When Armando got out of that box, he knew almost instantly who Carlos was. He also knows Marcella's on this plane, and he wants vengeance on her for stealing his son, killing him, and locking him in that damned box. He knows she'll come to try to help Carlos. He made sure Marcella would know what his intentions were by spreading it all over that plane she was ditched on. The plan is to trap her, by luring her with Carlos as his hostage; capture her soul; and dump her in a place I might reconsider dumping even Satan in. If you think the plane she's been banished to now blows, I promise you, it's like a trip to a day spa in comparison to where he plans to unload her."

Delaney gasped, her face pale, making Kellen search her eyes. "Oh, God, oh, God, oh, God. There's a plane that no soul can ever leave. It's desolate and barren and she'd be alone. She'd roam restlessly *alone* for eternity. Oh, Jesus. Catalina, is that the plane Armando means?"

She nodded sharply. "That's the plane, and he's got a band of ass lickers to help him get ahold of her."

Kellen held up an impatient hand, his gut churning hot acid. "But he can't even see her. We saw that for ourselves when we found him in Solana's body in that bar," he barked.

"But that's only because he was *in* Solana's body. When he

ditches that body for his demonic form, and he will, because it's no longer useful to him, it's on."

"But what about Solana? What happens to her?" Kellen asked, the bulk of his fury becoming a slow, simmering boil.

Catalina's eyes cast downward. "Unfortunately, Solana's dead."

"Armando killed her?" Delaney squeaked, wide-eyed. "But I thought demons couldn't actually take a life. I thought they could only conjure up frightening images and coerce you to take your own."

Catalina nodded her head. "That's true. But Solana's death was merely coincidental. The problem is, it coincided with Carlos releasing Armando from that box. The rest was cake for him."

"Jesus," Kellen whispered with a harsh breath.

Delaney gripped Kellen's arm, fear riddling her pretty features. "We have to find her. What Catalina says is true. The plane Marcella's been on is nothing compared to what is in essence no-man's-land. I've heard talk of it from some of the spirits I've dealt with in the past. If he gets her there, she can't be summoned, Kellen. Not by any medium—ever. We have to find her and warn her." Delaney searched his eyes. "Have you seen her since we left earlier?"

His nod was curt, the wound of her giving up on finding a way to keep her here still fresh. "Just after you and Clyde left. She gave me the big kiss-off. The afterlife's version of 'let's be friends.'"

Catalina smacked her lips in time with Delaney. They cast each other knowing glances.

Both Clyde and Kellen shot the women confused looks. *"What?"* Kellen demanded.

Catalina ran her hand over the silver gun at her waist. "She's going after Armando, and if her past is any indication, when she finds out what he's planning, she's going to offer herself up as a bargain to have Carlos returned to his grandparents, for all the good it'll do her. Nothing will appease that prick, and why should it? He holds all the cards. He can have Carlos and see to it Marcella spends the rest of eternity alone and in the dark about Carlos's safety. And as sure as I'm standing here, she dumped your ass because she didn't want you to know what she was planning or have to worry about the risk of you getting yourself killed."

Delaney nodded her agreement, her eyes wide with worry when they captured Kellen's. "Because she loves you, too," she whispered. "And she'd rather never see you again than take the chance you'd be hurt. But here's what worries me. When you said Marcella summoned Armando's soul, I got to thinking . . . So I read up on it . . . summoning souls. It's in the books I left in that big box in the hutch . . ." Delaney stopped short, her face pale white, her hands trembling. "Oh, God! I know what she's going to do. Oh, Jesus! She isn't going to bargain with Armando—she's going to bind with him!" She covered her mouth, her eyes wide with horror.

Clyde paled with her. "Honey, explain."

"I'd bet my ovaries Marcella's going to bind her soul with his so he can never be free of her. In fact, I'd bet all my vital organs on it. It's a surefire way to keep Armando from ever getting away from her and hurting anyone else. She'd, in essence, be his keeper. We have to stop her."

Kellen's stomach jolted again, bile rising in his throat. "Where did you read this?"

Delaney shook her head. "I've got bunches of books, Kellen. On the afterlife. On witchcraft—all sorts of stuff because of my gift of sight. You know that." She ran to the hutch, dragging out the box and pulling out a dusty, moth-eaten book, flipping through the yellow-stained pages. "Here!" She pointed to the page. "Second paragraph. Marcella can bind her soul with his, according to this. The hell I'm going to let her do that! The hell."

Catalina moaned, rubbing her temples. "Jesus. This just keeps getting better and better. Souls, summonings, possession. It's like a supernatural extravaganza."

Kellen ripped the page from the worn book and shoved it in his shirt pocket and looked to Catalina. "So what's next?"

"Next is," Catalina said, grim determination all over her face, "I'm outta here. I have a rogue demon to cap, and if I don't hurry it up, I'll miss my informant. He knows where Armando's headed with Carlos."

Kellen stood in front of her, blocking her exit. "Not without me." There was no way in hell he was going to let Catalina go into this alone. There was no way in hell he was going to let a small child suffer the wrath of vengeance gone beyond sick and twisted. There was no way in hell he was going to let Marcella leave this plane. No way.

Catalina glanced up at him with amusement flickering in her eyes. "You do know that's ridiculous, right, human? You'll only get in my way. So move, and let me do what I do."

Kellen remained where he was—solid, unmovable, his resolve unshakable.

"Kellen? I'm not bullshitting you. Stay put," she ordered, a vein in her neck becoming prominent with her anger.

"I'm going."

Without warning, she let her head fall back on her slender shoulders and laughed, leaving a bitter resonance. "Love makes you do the stupidest shit. Trust me, I know. You could get yourself killed when you have a perfectly good demon to fight your battle for you. Yet still, you're dipping those big size elevens in the deep end."

Kellen narrowed his eyes. "If I have to, I'll find out where he's taking Carlos, some way, somehow. I'll summon up the entire afterlife to do it, too. Either you let me go with you willingly, or I get there on my own steam. Your choice."

Catalina pursed her lips, clearly giving thought to Kellen's determination. "Here's the deal. You stay behind me, and if I tell you to bail, you'd better damn well do it, or Satan will seem like your best friend compared to the kind of shit I'll hurl at you. You're human. I'm not. I can take a serious pounding. You, despite all that Neanderthal running through your veins, can't. So let's not lose perspective. Got it?"

"Got it," Kellen confirmed through stiff lips.

She dug into her backpack on the floor, pulling out a silver gun with a long butt, and tossed it to him. "This won't kill the bastards, but it'll hold them off. Use it."

Delaney rolled up her sleeves, with Clyde right behind her. "We're in, too," she stated as if there were no other option.

"Oh, hell no. One human is plenty to keep track of. I'm good, but I'm not that good," Catalina crowed with the shake of a finger.

Kellen pulled Delaney into his embrace, giving her a hard hug. "Mrs. Ramirez will be calling. She'll need you, D. Both of you." He gave Clyde a man-signal with his eyes that said Delaney would need *him*. "I need someone to be here for her. I'll bring them back. I promise. We'll bring them back."

Delaney tugged his sweater, swiping at a tear with her thumb. "You'd damned well better. Be safe. Keep Marcella and Carlos safe. *Please.*"

Kellen took the gun from Catalina and shook Clyde's hand. Clyde pulled him in for a shoulder bump. "You keep her here with you *no matter what*," Kellen murmured.

Clyde pushed his glasses up on his nose. "You worry about

Marcella and Carlos. Go get your woman." He slapped him affectionately on the back before drawing Delaney to his side.

Kellen followed Catalina's lead to the front of the store, rage and fear and steadfast purpose creating a sour cocktail in his gut.

And then, just as Catalina had predicted—the phone rang.

sixteen

"Where the hell is he, Darwin? It's been longer than an hour!" Marcella whisper-yelled from her post behind the big maple tree. They hadn't seen a single sign of Armando. The apartment building was silent but for the screeching wind, rocking a creaking swing on the huge playground to their left.

He shook his head, clearly bewildered. "Solana, I mean, Armando's like clockwork. He should have been here by now."

Pent-up frustration made her sigh. "Damn it, he'd better hurry it up. Rick's getting antsy. He needs his eight or he's just a bear in the morning, and he has a latte date with this cute guy Kevin from his office before work tomorrow. He wants to be fresh and rested," she moaned, unable to stop Rick's words coming from her mouth. Rick was turning out to be a stronger personality than anyone could have bargained for. And he didn't like anything, or, more precisely, any *ghost*, toying with his finely tuned schedule.

"For the love of all that's holy, Marcella! Tell Rick he should be grateful to you. This has to be the most excitement he's experienced since they took *Queer Eye for the Straight Guy* off."

Movement from the apartment's entryway silenced Marcella and Darwin simultaneously. Her hands wrapped tighter around the bat, cold with Rick's clammy sweat. The dome light above the stairwell that led to the apartments boasted a large shadow, lurking.

Darwin's eyes were glued to the figure coming out of the entryway. Solana looked up toward the light. Marcella held her breath when Darwin caught a clear glimpse of her. She saw his surprise when his wild, confused eyes sought hers. Shit. She'd forgotten to tell him that she and Solana could be twins. She held a finger up with a quick press to her lips to keep Darwin from reacting.

Solana's partially hidden form came into view, revealing she wasn't alone. She had Carlos in her arms. Turning, she sniffed the air and scanned the street. Her eyes swept the shadows, then honed in on Marcella, stuck in Rick's body crouched beneath the big maple.

And Armando smiled.

Sadistically.

The smile so much like her own made Marcella shiver.

Fuck. They'd been made. How could he know it was her?

Though he, too, was in someone else's body, Marcella knew those hard eyes. Solana's were green, but Armando's black spiteful malevolence burned in them—fiery, angry. "Marcella, *mi corazón*," he called into the harsh wind, his light accent sending a shiver of revulsion up her spine.

He held up Carlos like a sacrificial offering, limp in his arms, the light from the entryway shining down on them with the harsh reality. "Look, pet. Look what I have. Our great-grandson! Come out and we'll have ourselves a reunion. Could we have hoped for a better-looking boy, Marcella? All this time I've waited and look at my reward! Oh, my beautiful, sassy wife—come count our blessings with me before I take him far, far away where you'll never see him again!" he crowed.

Darwin shook his head with visible force at her, pressing his stubby finger to his thick lips. She knew what he was telling her. Not to take the bait.

What Darwin didn't know was that *she* was the bait.

At all costs, she had to keep him from completely understanding what she was going to do or he'd try to stop it.

But at all costs, it had to be done.

Catalina slunk her way through the shadows on the playground, her mouth a thin line of fury. "That spineless *hijo de puta*," she muttered, stopping short when she saw the movement at the front of Carlos's apartment building.

Kellen followed her eyes to Solana and Carlos. Waves of anger attacked his better judgment, leaving all of Catalina's warnings in a dusty heap of forgotten words. He bolted forward, wanting only to see the motherfucker dead.

Catalina lunged for him, tackling him with the force of any NFL linebacker. They crashed to the ground in a whoosh of dead leaves and cold dirt. Grabbing him by the hair, Catalina hissed her words in his ear with a harsh whisper. "Did I tell you to stay behind me? What about *this* is behind me?"

Rolling her, Kellen disentangled himself from her iron grip, but it wasn't easy. "He's got Carlos, God damn it," he gritted out.

She gave him a sneer. "Yeaaah. That's why we're here. You listen to me. The shit you might see tonight is gonna be freaky-deaky double Dutch. I don't know if Delaney's given you the low-down on what dealing with something like this is like, but it's baboon-butt ugly. *This* is nothing. Now, if you want to help, aim for keeping the kid out of harm's way when I get him away from that prick. But pay close attention; do not interfere or get cagey. Again, me demon. You? Not even remotely close, ghost whisperer. I know you want to be a hero and save your woman, but don't be a dumb-ass hero. I can't be taken out like you, Kell, and if you want to live to see Marcella again and keep Carlos safe, stop doing stupid shit! One wrong move, and we're toast. Now, if you don't knock it off, I'll make sure you walk with a limp for a very long decade."

From the bruise he was sure was forming on his right shoulder, he didn't doubt it. He held up his hands. "Okay. I acted rashly. Seeing him, her, what the hell ever, with Carlos makes me insane."

Catalina's eyes squinted toward the apartment building, keeping a hawklike gaze on Solana and Carlos. "Do you see Marcella anywhere?"

Kellen's heart shifted in his chest, his hands clenched in tight fists. He peered into the gloom of the night, scanning the front of the apartment building. Bitter wind whipped at his hair, seeping under his parka. "No. Damn it. Where the hell is she?"

Catalina rose from the ground, brushing the leaves from her jeans. "I don't know, but you give me a heads-up if you get a glimpse of her. If we get lucky, maybe she's been detained and she won't show up at all." Stooping, she pulled open her bag and dragged out the biggest gun Kellen had ever seen. Next came a flask she had attached to a rope. She threw it around her neck with a grunt.

"Do I want to know what's in that?" he asked, pointing to the flask.

"It ain't Texas bat shit," she joked.

Jamming his hands into his jacket, he remained silent, his mind torn in a hundred different directions. Worry for Marcella seeped into his bones. Had Armando already gotten his hands on her? He'd choke the very demon out of him if he'd touched her.

Catalina gave him a sympathetic smile. "I promise I'm going to do everything in my power to help Carlos and Marcella. Though it would definitely help if I could see her. So you be on the lookout."

But activity by the side of the apartment building had caught Kellen's attention. "Who the hell is that? One of Solana's cohorts?"

Catalina's head whipped around.

They both tipped their heads at the sight of a slight, blond man, dressed in pink and white, rushing Solana while another portly, well-dressed gentleman swung a bat around like he was swatting at invisible flies.

"Amateurs," Catalina muttered, cocking the barrel of her enormous gun.

Deciding Darwin, who hadn't been spotted yet, was in a better position to nail Armando, Marcella made a snap decision.

Waving her hands to signal to Darwin to catch the bat, she hurled it at him, then mentally called Rick a girl for such a weak pass.

The bat clamored to the ground in a ruckus of metal and clanking, but Darwin scooped it up.

Marcella tripped just as she rushed Solana's knees, hoping to knock her down while Darwin scooped up Carlos. Instead, she crashed into the side of the brick building, hearing Rick's voice in her head remind her he was no athlete, sister. No one ever picked Rick Short to be on the dodgeball team, he declared. But he'd made a damned fine cheerleader, thank you very much.

She came to a clothes-ripping, tearing halt just as Darwin missed the back of Solana's head. Solana's body crumpled to the ground at an awkward angle and Armando's body emerged from her lifeless shell. Strong, tall, dark, handsome, and sure. He took off, running, toward the park, Carlos's short legs slapping over the edge of his brawny arm, his evil leaving a vaporous trail behind him.

Marcella willed Rick to get up off his bony ass, clawing the bricks to haul herself upward.

Darwin shot off into the dark after Armando, moving with agility she wouldn't have thought Little Anthony possessed.

She squinted into the darkness, heading for the playground, but couldn't see a bloody thing. Rick assured her that was because he'd left his glasses at home because, really, who wants to date a four-eyes?

With a full-bodied shake, Marcella fought to keep control of Rick's body. She clenched her teeth. "Just give me a few more minutes and I swear, you can have your body and all its pink accessories back!"

Rick stilled again, allowing her the opportunity to assess the landscape of the park from behind the cover of the slide. Hunkering down, she peeked around the corner.

The cold metal of something unfamiliar touched the nape of her neck.

"Who the fuck are you?" someone growled, low, soft. Someone not so unfamiliar.

Shit, shit, shit. What was Big-Breasted Barbie doing here? Marcella fought a scream of frustrated worry by jamming one of Rick's knuckles in her mouth. Catalina had to go. Marcella didn't know her origins, or her skill level, but it'd never match that of Armando's enraged fury.

And then, big hands were grabbing her by the back of her jacket, hauling her upward while Rick squealed his protest, so sharp, and so girlie, in her mind, it made her wince. "*Who the hell are you?*"

Kellen, oh, thank God it was Kellen, she thought with a mixture of dread and relief. Marcella threw her arms around his neck and planted a kiss smack-dab on his lips that not only surprised him, but left him sputtering. "Oh, God, Kellen. Thank God it's you," she cried against his neck while Rick purred appreciative thanks in her head.

Kellen pulled his head back while she clung to his neck, his face a mixture of shock and disgust. He ran the back of his hand over his lips. "*Who are you?*" he demanded.

Catalina held the gun directly at Marcella's forehead, sniffing the air. "For sure, he's not demon," she said to Kellen, her eyes filled with suspicion.

Marcella shook her head, pushing the barrel of the gun away from her with impatience before looking up at Kellen. "Put that thing away! It's me. Marcella! Look, long story and not a whole lot of time for deets. I possessed this man's body. His name's Rick. He says it's a pleasure, by the way—especially pleasurable to meet the big guy here." Her hand, with a will of its own, patted Kellen's hard shoulder.

Marcella stopped, shaking her head again. "Sorry. It's hard to keep Rick quiet. This is what happened. Armando has Carlos. He has to be stopped. I needed a physical body to do that. So Darwin showed me how to possess a body. Unfortunately, while I hedged on who to possess, he shoved me into Rick's. But it's me, I swear it."

Both Catalina and Kellen shared a glance that screamed disbelief. "Who's Darwin? Delaney's dog?" Kellen asked.

She bit her lip. "Another long story. Just trust me, he's a good guy." Her worried glance went to the pitch-black portion of the playground. "Look, we can't stand around. Armando has Carlos!"

"Answer me one question," Kellen demanded, holding up a hand to Catalina. "Where's Marcella's favorite place to shop?"

Rocking back on her heels, she smiled, cocky and confident. "Pottery Barn." Marcella gasped in outrage. "It is not, Rick. It's Pier 1. Shut up or I swear to God, I'm going to ram one of your damned bowling shoes right up your ass!"

Kellen scooped her up and swung her around so swiftly, it jarred the breath right out of her. "Oh, this is definitely my Marcella," he confirmed with a soft whoop then dropped her back on the ground as hastily as he'd gathered her up, looking around to see if anyone had caught his overly exuberant hug. "I'm sorry, honey. It's just like I told you, blonds aren't my thing."

Catalina eyed her while she circled the area, clearly still wary. "You do know you can harm the host's body, don't you?"

"Yes! So tell this madwoman to give it back to me! I want to go home!" Rick yelped.

That was it. Marcella had had enough. She didn't need a host to hunt Armando.

Just a soul.

Fighting the confines of Rick's body, she shimmied out of it, leaving him in a crumpled heap on the ground. "Put him somewhere safe, would you, please?" she asked Kellen. "I don't want him hurt because of me."

Catalina took the lead, dragging Rick's unconscious form to safety under the shelter of the sliding board, then said, "I'm going in. Remember what I told you, Kell," she warned.

Marcella turned to Kellen with eyes that were pleading as she tried to pull away. "He has Carlos."

Kellen pulled her to him, hard, running his hands through her hair, his eyes drinking in her face. "I know, honey. I know everything. I know about Carlos and that David is Juan. Are you okay?"

Her gut clenched, her eyes misting at his concern. "I'm fine. Forget me. I need to help Carlos. So please, I'm begging you—go back to the store and wait for him, because if you were hurt . . . I'll make sure he gets back to you and Mrs. Ramirez." Somehow.

His grip grew tighter, his eyes piercing. "Ah, no. I know you, Miss Sacrificial Lamb. Do you have any idea what that nut wants to do with you?"

Does he have any idea what I want to do with him? Kellen's words gave her pause, but then she shook it off. It didn't matter what Armando planned to do. He'd never be able to keep her from doing what she was going to do because he didn't know how. Anxiety gripped her. She had to get the hell gone. "I have to go, Kellen. *Please.*"

"No way am I letting you out of my sight. I know what you *think* you're going to do, and it just ain't gonna happen."

Lifting her head, she memorized his face, the sharp lines, the dimple on either side of his mouth. "You can't help. He'd kill you. I couldn't live with that. Enough damage has been done because of what I did. I have to go, Kellen. I *have* to. But I need you to know this. If I could have had things any other way, if there were a way for me to stay here, I'd do it in a second. I'd take mortality and you any day of the week. Now let me go. *Please.*"

"No, woman! Listen to me. I will not allow you to do what you plan—"

He stopped in midsentence when she tickled him at his weakest spot, catching him off guard. Freeing herself, she floated out of his grasp and up toward the top of the tree. Her heart thrashed against her ribs when she looked down on him. "Tell D I love her, and all those stupid refugee dogs, but don't waste any more foolish time looking for a solution for me." She paused, fighting back more ridiculous tears. "And I love you, too, Kellen," she sobbed, hoarse and raw with pain. "I never thought I'd say that to another man again, but *I love you.*" I love you. I love you. I love you.

"Damn it, Marcella, Get down here now!" he bellowed, the sharp planes of his face strained, his body rigid with anger.

"I love you!" she whispered into the wind before she took off deeper into the playground without looking back. Her heart would break if she looked back.

Instead, Marcella focused her eyes forward—where she'd find Armando, and together, they'd spend their eternity.

"Armando Villanueva! Olly, olly, oxen free!" Marcella roared.

seventeen

Marcella scanned the length of the playground with anxious eyes, searching for signs of Carlos.

And that's when she heard Darwin howl, "You filthy animal!"

Her eyes went directly to her right, where Armando stood, leaning cockily against an abandoned ice cream truck. A large clown head sat on top of it, leering an ugly, toothy grin, making her shiver. The wild swoops of his red hair, poking out from beneath his pointy hat dotted with multicolored circles, sent irrational fear shooting along her spine. Fighting to ignore her ridiculous fear of anything remotely Barnum and Bailey, Marcella swallowed hard.

Armando's thick, raven black hair was pulled tightly into a ponytail, making his cheekbones, always lean and rugged, stand out in the harsh glare of the moon. Crossing his legs at the ankles, he pointed upward. "Friend of yours?"

Her pulse screamed to a halt. Darwin, or the body he inhabited, floated high above Armando's head. Sweat glistened on his wrinkled forehead, his fists clutched tightly to his chest. "Marcella, run!" he warned, his breathing shallow and uneven.

Oh, no. There'd be no more running. There'd only be her and the man she planned to see gone from this plane forever. Instantly, she was beside Darwin, running a soothing hand over his forehead. "Let him go, Armando. He has nothing to do with this."

"*Mi amor*," he cackled, holding out his hand to her. "Forget him. If that's who you've employed to aid you in besting me, I wish you luck. Now, come, give us a kiss, no? It's been so long since I tasted those luscious lips." He smacked his own with a perverted slurp. "You're just as beautiful as the last day I saw you so long ago. You remember the day, don't you, *wife*? The day you murdered me in cold blood and stole my son from me?"

She put a finger to her lips in mock thought, giving him a sly smile. "Do you mean the one where I cracked you over the head, ended your miserable existence, burned your pathetic body until there was nothing left but ashes, then summoned your black soul and locked you in a box? Is that the day you mean, *husband*?" she taunted.

His smile was glacial, his raven eyebrow cocked. "Yeahhh," he said on a sigh. "I think that's the one. Oh, the heartbreak to be betrayed by your own wife. Imagine my pain. 'Inconsolable' isn't a word I'd use lightly."

Marcella let a catty smile spread across her lips. "Then, yeah. I remember it. In fact, it keeps me all warm and cozy on cold nights just like this one. I cover up with the memory while I toast the end to your vile existence with warm milk and freshly baked cookies."

Bada-bing, bada-boom. Take. That.

"How do you think your lover would feel if the same were to happen to him?"

Kellen. Her stomach dove to her toes. He knew about Kellen. Christ.

"Or what about his sister, Delaney? How do you think her Clyde would feel if she were locked in a box—*forever*?"

Her temper. Wasn't everyone always harshin' on her about her temper? *Could be that's because it gets the better of you, Marcella,* was what she thought just before she lost it. "I'll kill you, you pig! You leave them alone!"

The hard mask of his face changed just a hint, revealing what she was sure was just the tip of his anger. "You murdered me, Marcella. You murdered me and stole my son from me! You took from me and now I'll take from you!"

Marcella yawned, bored. "You murdered me," she mocked in his accent, rolling her head on her neck. "Yadda, yadda, yadda. Sooo dramatic. Whiner."

He cackled again, soft and low. "I don't think I'll be the one whining."

"Where's Carlos?" she demanded, her eyes flitting from side to side.

"Our great-grandson? He's fine. Just fine. I'm so proud of him it hurts. He looks just like me. You were the perfect vessel, Marcella, truly a brilliant move on my part, marrying you. I might have had to put up with a lot of your hot air, but it was worth it in the end. You bore me a beautiful child. Now come, we'll talk over old times." He waved a hand at the space by his feet as though he were impatient to get on with things. "You're so far away up there, and we've been far away from each other for too long, don't you think?"

"Show—me—Carlos!" she spat out, lifting her chin to scan their surroundings.

With the click of his foot, he popped open the rusty door on the ice cream truck and smiled. Carlos lay on the floor in his pajamas and, from where she floated, she could see his chest rise and fall with slow, easy breaths. Relief washed over her. "What have you done to him?"

"Just a spell to help him sleep, *muchacha*. Surely you don't want him to witness his great-grandmama's demise?"

If there was ever a time for her memory to be on point, it was now. She didn't pray often, but at this very second, looking at Carlos lying helplessly in the truck, and Darwin hanging like some parade blimp, she prayed she could remember the words to the spell she needed to end this. Until then, she'd just stall. She moved in closer to Darwin, whispering from the side of her mouth. "Hang tough, friend. This'll be over soon."

"Where's the bloody box, Marcella?" he hissed back, worry eating up the wrinkles on his forehead. "We need the box!"

"Listen closely to me, *muchacho*. He'll be too busy with me to keep you up here long. When he drops you, run as fast as those stubby legs will carry you to the car and get that box. You'll know when to lock it."

Darwin attempted to protest, but Marcella cut him off. "If ever I needed you to pay attention and do what I tell you to do, it's now. So hush, and one last thing. You're the best frenemy a girl could ever have. Now shut it. I'm begging you."

"How endearing. Are you saying your farewells, dear heart?" Armando tormented from between thin lips, gazing up at her with coal black eyes so full of hatred it took her breath away.

Almost.

"Give me Carlos, Armando. Give him to me and I'll go with you. I'll do whatever it is that you want me to do."

"Don't be such a silly goose, my heart. Why would I give you the great-grandson I intend to raise? Isn't this delightful? You, me, the child who should have been mine, all together—at last."

Delovely. "Let him go. You have no right to him."

He gave her a forlorn glance. "But you know that's not true, lover. You robbed me of the chance to raise my son—in my book I think that means you *owe* me," he said with menacing glee in his voice.

"I'll warn you one last time, Armando. *Let him go.*"

His eyes narrowed to gleaming points of light. "Or what, sweetling? You don't have the power to do anything to me. I, on the other hand, have been a busy, busy bee these last months while I inhabited our beautiful granddaughter who looks just like you. Who knew I'd be such an astute student? And I learned it all with you in mind, *mi corazón*. I *can* hurt you, Marcella. You can feel pain inflicted by me, your loving husband. The kind of pain that will be far worse than the confines of any box!" Spreading his arms wide, he heaved his chest upward.

Hoo, shit. That whole dramatic posing thing was never a good sign. Marcella prepared to duck but instead felt the stingingly hot heat of flames lick at her feet. A ring of fire encompassed both her and Darwin, climbing higher and higher until it almost shrouded her view of Carlos's small body.

"Hey, Armando," she shouted over the roar of the crackling fire, "is this the best you can do? Got any hot dogs I can roast, weenie? Oh, wait. Silly me. Of course you don't have hot dogs. Trying to get out to the grocery store to shop has to be hard on someone locked—in—a—box!"

Calm façade gone, Armando did just as she'd expected he would.

He reacted.

And not in the way some might call nonpsychotic.

His roar of rage was a piercing scream—loud with the fury of all of Hell's minions combined. Black smoke rose in slithering tendrils, twisting and turning until they took shape.

Lots of shapes.

The shapes of those Armando had summoned to help him do his dirty work.

Sissy.

The black shadows, oily and swift, flitted in the air, springing to the treetops, clanging the chains of the swings, scurrying across the sky at warp speed. Creating a raucous symphony of earsplitting sounds.

Darwin hung precariously, wobbling in the fierce wind, flames licking at his host body. Helplessly, he dangled. "Marcella, run! Get out before you get hurt!"

Distract. She needed to distract Armando long enough to get him to drop Darwin. Rising higher, she threw her head back and laughed at Armando in superiority. "Is *this* the best you can do? Fire and wind? You always were a lazy bastard! Lazy, lazy, lazy— especially in bed! Did you hear that, Armando? You're lazy! You had all this time to practice and this is as scary as it gets?"

She'd thrown down the gauntlet—given Armando the ultimate challenge. Show me what'cha got, candy-ass. She just hoped his gauntlet didn't include those damned locusts. They squicked her like nothing else.

Oh, but that crazy, eating-evil-for-breakfast Armando—he had something way scarier in mind.

For fuck's sake. Really? Like really?

From the top of the ice cream truck the clown's head began to spin, twisting furiously, its mouth opening wide to reveal teeth like ice picks before the huge head spun off the truck and headed directly for her. Calling her name in deep, demonic tones. Chills of terror raced along her spine.

God! She hated clowns. Revulsion twisted her gut.

However, in his fury, Armando had lost track of Darwin, who dropped to the ground with a crash of packed dirt and a startled yelp. "Run!" she screamed to him, ducking the malevolent clown head, fighting her terror. "Run!"

The winds picked up, roaring, tearing at her dress, dragging her across the inky black sky. Thunder shrieked in bright arcs of white and blue, screaming to the earth in volcanic splashes, cracking the ground. Deep crevasses split open the dirt, swallowing the slide, eating up the hedges along the perimeter.

Marcella saw movement from just beyond the ice cream truck, her stomach rising and falling as Armando's minions tore at her, sinking their deep talons into her arms, wrapping their fingers of steel around her neck.

And then there was water, blessedly cold sheets of it, washing at her wounds, torpedoing demons in every direction, whipping them against the trunk of the tree in screaming splats.

Catalina was below her, wielding the biggest gun Marcella'd ever seen, firing water upward into the sky. "Kellen! Get Carlos!" she ordered with a bellowed demand.

Marcella's heartbeat raced as Kellen ran, head down, toward the ice cream truck. His legs pumped, muscles flexed, his jaw clenched.

And that was when Armando spotted him.

Their eyes met, Armando's with knowledge, hers with palpable fear.

Raising his finger high, he pointed it at Kellen, directing all of his finely honed skills at his back.

"Kellen!" Marcella screamed with a hoarse sob. "Get out of the way!"

Catalina looked up then, her eyes wide in startled surprise, as though she could actually see Marcella, and then she yelled upward. "Marcella! Move!" With the strength of a track star, Catalina ran, hurling herself at Armando's back, clawing at his hands, gripping his ponytail and yanking it with such force his neck bent backward.

Panic made Marcella react to the fireball Armando had aimed, heading straight for the ice cream truck where a sleeping Carlos lay. She zoomed in toward the opening just as the ball of fire screamed forward, praying she got there in time to take the hit.

A roar, long and primal, erupted as Kellen sliced through the air, knocking her out of the way as Catalina, her foot atop Armando's chest, hosed the flames.

Armando twisted beneath her, flexing his wrist to reveal long talons. He swiped at Catalina's leg, making her howl in agony with a hard fall to the ground.

So it was now or never. May her penchant for memorizing every style of shoe Jimmy Choo ever made have kept her memorization skills intact.

"Get Carlos!" she yelled to Kellen, pulling free from him and rising once more to float above Armando. Kellen barreled toward the ice cream truck, hauling Carlos to him, but he didn't run for cover. He deposited Carlos under a covered seating area then tore something from his pocket.

But her attention was called away when Darwin, in his torn suit, sweat glistening from every inch of exposed flesh, waved his arms in the air from the corner of the playground and pointed.

He had the box. The top was flipped open. In that moment, she'd never loved the Kibble King more.

Her heart crashing in her chest, her hands shaking, Marcella called her husband out. "Armando Villanueva, *eres un sucio acólito de Satanás*! I bind with thee—" she screeched, only to stop in midsentence when she heard someone else echo the same words.

"Armando Villanueva!" Kellen roared, glancing down to read some piece of paper in his hand with a frown. "I bind with thee!"

No, oh, my God. Noooooo! "Kellen, noooooo!" she screamed. What in the love of fuck was he doing? Her heart raced in time with her mind. She couldn't remember the spell, but Kellen had it written down? "Come—come—" Oh, fuck. Was it come thee be mine? No, come thee and bind. Shit! She couldn't afford to get this wrong. Horror seared her gut; fear raged in every cell of her body.

Bad. This was very bad.

Catalina dragged herself from the ground, looking upward, and bellowed, "No, Marcella! No! Don't do it!"

Darwin's face went from panicked to stricken as he realized what she was about to do. Kellen stopped reading the passage and looked to him, confusion at this new player in the evil game. Darwin shook his head. "Marcella—no! Kellen, stop! You're binding your souls to Armando's—for eternity!"

Well, duh.

Except there was this one little problem with the whole binding thing.

You kinda had to remember the words to do it, and Kellen had them written down.

Oh, ginkgo. How you've failed me.

eighteen

Catalina surged across the sky, tackling Kellen, who clutched the paper in his hand like it was the Holy Grail. They went down hard, but Catalina was on her feet in an instant, thrusting Kellen's hand between her knees and prying his fingers free of the paper with a warrior cry.

Relief flooded Marcella as she began to once again focus on the spell, her mind turning over words that didn't mesh.

Armando rose up, growing to grotesque proportions, looming over Marcella in all his foul demonicness. His demon form in full view, he opened his mouth wide, tilting his head back and screeching a wail so violent, so infuriated, Marcella shuddered as the sound went straight through her.

She faced off with him, hair soaking wet, eyes wild, dress clinging by threads, ready to suffer his wrath.

Or at least until she could remember the damned words to the spell.

Armando's clawed fingers reached out to wrap around her neck, squeezing, his laughter filling the dark night. Kellen was below her, Catalina's retrieved gun in hand, eyes dead and cold, ready to pull the trigger.

The silence pulsed as she hung from Armando's grip. Ugly, thick, and pulsating with vengeance.

Just as Catalina made her move, leaping at him as though she was the Bionic Woman gone demonic, a voice roared from behind, shaking the playground with a thunderous tremor. "Armandooooooo!"

Armando deflated like he'd been popped with a pin, dropping Marcella from his steely grip.

Catalina stopped virtually in midair, slamming to the ground, landing on her feet with a jarring crash in the middle of the playground's debris. Surprise shadowed her face, her eyes wide and round.

Kellen fell to the ground, running to where he'd left Carlos and gathering him protectively to his chest. Marcella floated to them, kneeling beside them, running her shaking hands over Kellen's soot-covered face.

A man, seriously the size of a redwood, stomped forward; his eyes, cobalt blue and filled with hostile fury, honed in on Armando, piercing him with a glare so overflowing with fire, Marcella cringed. Each step he took boomed, making the hard muscles of his thighs ripple and flex then tighten through the material of his black jeans. One fist, wide and sinewy, clenched into a ball, then unclenched just as quickly when he yanked Armando upward by his ankles, using just one hand.

His blue-black hair gleamed in the glare of the streetlights, as slick and shiny as the skin of an orca, falling to just beneath the collar of his black sweater. His wide shoulders nearly blocked the view of Armando entirely as he raised the demon high in the air, like a prized fish he'd just caught.

To say he was seething would be to understate the infuriated vibe he virtually oozed from every available point of flesh on his body.

But for a moment, something caught his attention, and when he stopped to take note, the breathtaking planes of his face, angled sharply, sculpted in granite, gave him the appearance of something only Rodin himself could create.

Marcella cringed, prepared for this beautiful man to take note of them and hurl all that pissed-off glory their way.

Instead, what had caught his attention was Catalina.

Catalina lifted her chin in defiance at the man's apparent discovery of her. Crossing her arms over her chest, covered in muddy dirt and soaking wet leaves, she stuck it out in a gesture that dared anyone, even this giant redwood, to take her to task. Her full mouth thinned to a line of pure hatred; her eyes flashed a message clearly only the two of them understood.

Their eyes met—Catalina's seethed; his glimmered with sparkling blue amusement. It was then that he winked at her suggestively with a slow downward tilt of his long-lashed eye. They faced off in silence, neither speaking a word before his eyes dismissed her to return to his prey, dangling limp and helpless. "Armando Villanueva?" he asked, but it was clearly a mere formality. "How dare you attempt to usurp Satan's throne?"

"No!" he protested, squirming against the steely hold. "I was bringing the child to my lord and master," he insisted, fighting for strength in his tone but crumbling miserably under the glare of this man's disapproval.

"You've shamed my rule, Armando." He paused, then smiled, flashing a set of perfectly white teeth while pulling a sniveling Armando upward to eye level. "Would you shame me more by deceiving me?"

Armando shook his head, his long, black ponytail quivering. "No, no!"

"Good to hear because, I gotta tell ya, I don't much like it."

"But the child—he's—he's—"

"*What?*" the stranger bellowed. "Are you telling me something you think I don't know, rogue? I'd be really pretty tweaked if that were the case. I pride myself on running a tight ship. Speaking of ships and tight, mind telling me where you've been since 1934?"

"It was her!" he yelled in Marcella's direction, sweat dripping from his forehead as he pointed an accusatory finger. "*She* locked me up in a box, Dameal. I only just got out. *She* kept me from serving you."

Marcella rolled her eyes. Wasn't that just like a man? Blame, blame, blame. And Dameal . . . who the fuck was this Dameal?

Dameal's dark head tilted to the right as he gave Armando an exaggerated look of disbelief. "Are you telling me a woman kept you from your duties? A *woman?* Funny, the rumor is that you're rogue. *Rogue.*" He spat out the word as though it were dirty. "And you've been out of that box for quite some time while you've been sneaking around behind my back. Everything else pales in comparison, don't you agree?"

Armando's hands attempted to grasp the steel clench Dameal's fists had on him, but only flopped helplessly back to his hanging position. "Listen to me, Dameal! The boy! He can—"

"Did *you* interrupt *me?*" He shook him hard, chattering his teeth. "Damn it all. I hate to be interrupted. Don't you know that? No, wait. You wouldn't know that because after being trapped in a box by some whiny female, when you finally get out, you 'forget' to check in with me and instead plan an uprising I neither heard about nor approved. And that makes me very angry, Armando. Very angry. So what should we do about that? How can you make it up to me?" Dameal tapped his toe, then nodded his head as though he'd found the answer. "Oh. I know. *Twinkies.* I love Twinkies. Do you think you can get your weak, simpering hands on enough to make up for the fact that you planned the demise of *Satan*?" He bellowed the last word so loud, Armando's hair fluttered about his face.

Armando's face was turning red from being held upside down. Yet he struggled in this Dameal's iron grip. "If you'll just listen to me—I have information about the boy! Important information, Dameal," he cried. "I swear, I was just underground until I got rid of—"

"*Eeenough*!" He cut him off with a howl that echoed in Marcella's ears and shot to her toes. "I've had about enough of your lies, and I'm sure when Abbadon returns from his time in the pit—courtesy of you—he'll want a word with you for that little escapade you sent him on. Dumb as a stump, that one is. Such a follower. So whaddya say we hit a Starbucks or something, have a little man-to-man? Caramel frapps on me." He chuckled, looking over his shoulder at Marcella and winking.

Marcella looked to Catalina in question, because she was clearly the only person who knew who this Dameal was, but she was too engaged in narrowing her hate-filled gaze at Dameal.

Kellen rose, hauling the still-sleeping Carlos up over his shoulder, and stepped over the demolished teeter-totter to approach Dameal, with Marcella but two steps behind him. Kellen stood in front of her protectively, putting his free hand behind them to wrap it around Marcella's hip. "I'm not going to ask any questions. I've learned in this demon game to never take anything at face value. What appears to be reality isn't always the case. So I'm just going to say thank you, and leave it at that." His words were terse, his face hard.

Dameal assessed Kellen with eyes that gleamed, not with malice, but something Marcella couldn't put her finger on. "I accept. I ask only one favor in return for taking this leech off your hands."

Though not as wide as Dameal, Kellen met him eye to eye. His answer rang with the skepticism Marcella wanted to voice, but was unable to put into words. "That is?"

"Tell the other woman present, whose name I'm no longer able to speak because she's a fiery shrew, I'll be seeing her. *Soon*. And I'm all kinds of tickled pink." With that, he strode to the center of the playground and gave one last curt nod to Catalina.

Then he grinned at her. Wide. Playful.

In return, Catalina flipped him the bird—in stereo.

As Dameal's laughing outline began to shimmer, indicating he was making his exit, another appeared, stopping only to circle Dameal's form, cocking his head in obvious question. Dameal sent a clear, silent message to the image before nodding and disappearing.

Marcella sucked in gulps of air. What a mind fuck.

Kellen approached Catalina, who'd come to stand by them, giving Carlos's hair a ruffle with her fingers. "Wow. I think he deserves an explanation. So who's Dameal?"

Catalina's face instantly changed. "A demon. A lying, cheating demon," she fairly spat out, with a heaving chest and tight lips.

"That lying, cheating demon just saved our lives," Kellen reminded her in his calm, no-nonsense tone.

"Please. I had it. He shows up at the last minute like the Green Lantern because he's a show-off. I'd have nailed that asshole balls to the wall in another second or two." Her indignation so obviously a cover for how close they'd all really been to being killed.

Kellen clearly sensed how one-upped Catalina appeared. His words sought to appease, but he wanted answers. The ones that just wouldn't let him leave well enough alone. "No doubt, you're a force, Catalina. But I'd still like to know how you know him. Because it looked like you knew each other."

"I don't know what you're talking about," she offered with blandness to her tone, avoiding their eyes. Yet Marcella recognized it for what it was. A purposeful guise of disinterest to hide whatever she felt for Dameal. For whatever their history, and there was history between them, might be.

Like a man, Kellen stomped his size elevens all over a delicate situation. "Oh, c'mon, Catalina. It's obvious he just saved our asses, but if you could have willed it, he'd be so much shit on the bottom of your shoe. So what gives?"

Her hands clenched at her sides. "I said—"

Marcella stepped in with a finger to Kellen's lips. "Kellen? Hush. It's none of your business. Or mine. Even if I'm dying to know who he was and why he didn't help Armando annihilate us all. At this point, I'm so tired I don't care about anything other than we're all safe—especially Carlos. So leave Catalina alone." She knew this thing between Catalina and Dameal. It had to do with volatile emotions only another woman as hot-tempered and passionate as both she and Catalina were to understand.

"Take your girlfriend's advice," Catalina warned.

Kellen held up a hand in resignation, then cocked his head. "Wait. You can see Marcella?"

Catalina nodded, gathering her backpack. "It was the craziest frickin' thing. She was just there. I looked up, and bam. I'm as surprised as you are. So, Marcella"—she stuck out her dirty, bloodied hand—"nice to finally meet you."

Marcella gulped, thankful Catalina never heard the horrible things she'd said about her. "You, too." *You, too.*

She gave Marcella a vague smile. "And now that everyone's safe and sound—I'm out."

Planting a hand on her shoulder, Kellen smiled his thanks. "Catalina, I owe you—big. Whatever you need. Say it."

Clearly, warm emotions made Catalina uncomfortable, giving Marcella the sense that she didn't save children because her goal was to redeem herself. Her reasons were deeper, and maybe someday, if their paths ever crossed again, they could talk. Really talk. She knew what it was to keep your pain buried so deep it ate you up. She'd read Catalina wrong. For that, Marcella was remorseful.

Catalina offered an offhand remark. "Forget it. It's what I do. All you owe me is making sure this little monster gets back home safely. I'll be around. Good Texas bat shit's hard to come by. Be good to each other."

Before she disappeared, she placed a hand on Marcella's shoulder and gripped it in silent thanks. Marcella reached up and gripped it back with a squeeze before watching her disappear.

"Only a child could sleep through that kind of godawful noise," Marcella mused, her eyes fixed on her great-grandson. The one who was alive. So fantastically, beautifully alive.

"Only an insane woman would do what you were going to do tonight. Do you have any idea how crazy that was?" Kellen gazed at her with clear admiration.

"Um, excuse me, but wasn't that you reading the same damn spell I couldn't remember, from a *piece of paper*? Are you out of your mind?"

He grinned. "It reminded me my Latin sucks."

"Why did you try to translate it, you idiot? Do you have any idea what you were about to do?"

"I don't know why I tried to translate it into English. Shit got a little crazy there for a minute. And I do know what I was doing. I was summoning and binding, or some combination thereof."

"Why would you do something so foolish?" she chastised.

But Kellen's face went serious. "For the same reasons you did."

And those words, the words that meant he'd been willing to give up his life for her and Carlos, left her without breath and a heart that filled to overflowing with love.

Dragging her to him, he pressed her close to his side, resting his lips on her forehead. "Don't *ever* do that again. Ever," he whispered fiercely against her skin. "I would have lost you to that maniac if you'd bound yourself to him."

She placed a hand on his chest, feeling the steady rhythm of his heart against her palm. "I doubt it'll be a problem. I mean, I did forget the words to the spell, and the same goes for you, you fool."

His laughter was deep. "That's because you're old. The seniors at the center complain all the time about memory loss."

"Hey, respect your elders."

"So, wanna tell me why you didn't tell me all those oh so important details about Carlos and his relationship to you?"

"So you wouldn't do something stupid like show up and throw yourself in front of me to save me from a wall of fire that can't touch me, the ghost, but can singe you, the human, and your ball hairs, too? Oh, and then there's the sacrifice-your-soul-for-mine thing. I'm a ghost, Kellen. There's nothing that can be done for me. You're a human, with family and friends and hopefully a teaching position you can go back to when things calm down a bit."

"That was rash, huh?"

"And impetuous and stupid. Jesus, Kellen! I think my entire life flashed in front of my eyes in those seconds."

"Oh, c'mon. Let's be honest here. It had to have lasted at least a full two minutes. You've had *a lot* of life."

Burying her face in his neck, she tweaked his earlobe. "Lay off the *old* jokes. I'm still damned cute for a senior citizen."

Grabbing a handful of her butt, he chuckled his agreement. "So now we have a bigger problem."

Marcella frowned, some of her happiness evaporating. "Now what?"

Kellen dipped his head in Carlos's direction. "Him. Got any thoughts on how we're going to explain Solana's disappearance to Mrs. Ramirez?"

"I got that, dude," a voice, youthful and warm, reassured them.

Their heads turned in unison to see a young boy, bare-chested, in a pair of loud red-and-white-flowered swim trunks, approach them. "So heeeyyy, wha's uuuup! I'm Uriel. Coolio to meet ya." He extended a hand with a gleaming smile.

Marcella's ears pricked. Uriel. "You're the one—"

He winced when he cut in: "Who dropped you on what you call Plane Drab. Totally innovative on your part, BTW. Rad name for that joint. All us archangels laughed and laughed over that. And, yeah. Guilty, wahine. It was the safest place I could think of, and I did promise you'd be safe. But I was doin' my pal Delaney a solid. She's some kinda friend to have, huh?" He pointed skyward. "We love her up there. She's a slice of awesome pie with some awesome sauce. Miss her crossing over souls like crazy."

Rad. Marcella backed away from Kellen and Carlos, fear in her eyes. Archangels and former demons somehow seemed like a Molotov cocktail of ass-whoopin' just waiting to erupt.

But Uriel was quick to offer more reassurance with flapping hands and a gentle smile. "No, no, dudette. It's righteous. I'm not here to take you back. But we do have to confab." He gave a nod to Kellen. "You, too, brah."

Marcella's throat dried up. Archangel plus wayward ghost equaled game over.

This was the part where he took her from the people she loved and dumped her back where she'd started. She'd known all along someone would come calling. Marcella held up a hand. "Can you give me a few minutes to say my good-byes? I won't give you a hard time. I know I've been here longer than the average ghost, but I didn't know how to get back. I would have gone back if I could have. I swear." She knew her voice was watery, but there was no stopping the tears that filled her eyes.

Kellen's jaw was tight, as though he were trying to remain respectful when he said, "You're not saying good-bye to anyone." He grabbed her hand, pulling her close to him. "I know about you," he said to Uriel. "Delaney told me what you did for her and Clyde."

Marcella flashed a confused look at Kellen.

Kellen squeezed her hand with a gentle smile. "Uriel's the one who granted Clyde the opportunity to stay here and start over. He missed picking up Clyde's soul—Clyde ending up in Hell was a mistake."

Uriel chuckled at the memory. "Dude. Like, mon-do. My supreme bad. But all's good with Delaney now, right?"

Kellen nodded with the hint of a smile. "She's very happy. Both she and Clyde and all the dogs."

The archangel's smile beamed as he became lost in a private moment of reverie. "Such awesomeness."

However, Kellen was clearly in the here and now. "I mean no disrespect, but if you're here to take Marcella back, I can't let you do that. I *won't* let you do that. She stays. With me. And I don't care what it takes. There'll be no more good-byes."

Marcella gave vague thought to the idea that it was ludicrous to get all up in an archangel's business, but she was so sickly touched by the idea that anyone, and of all people Kellen, was defending her, that it physically hurt. She let her head fall to her chest in tearful awe.

Uriel's expression was that of surprise. "Good-byes? Naw. You're golden, Marcella. Me and the Big Kahuna had a long sit-down a little while ago. Carlos's mother brought this Armando to our attention."

"Solana?" Marcella asked in disbelief.

"Yeah." He bobbed his head full of sun-kissed hair. "That's her. The coolest lady, like, evah. Sick with worry over her little guy, too." He ran a hand over Carlos's dark head with an affectionate palm, pressing light fingers to the boy's eyelids. "She told us what you did, Marcella. Why you did it."

Her chin lifted in defiance. Nothing would ever make her regret killing Armando Villanueva. Not even the Big Kahuna. Tears fell from her eyes when she gazed upon Uriel. "I don't regret it. He would have taken my son, David, and ruined him. He would have turned him against everything I believed in. I don't regret it," she said stonily, defying this Uriel to slap her down.

He held up his slender hands and smiled that beatific grin. "Whoaaa-ho, lady tiger. I get lookin' out for your cubs. You were a good mama. Now, I'm not condoning murder. Let's keep that straight up. But I can overlook stuff for the bigger picture. Armando was a dicey dude. One of those loose cannons us folk from upstairs don't much like running footloose and fancy free. Feel me? You protected an innocent child from a psycho nut. We appreciate that where I come from. So here's the deal. I have a message from Solana and the big guy for you—for *both* of you."

Marcella was stunned to silence, gripping Kellen's arm.

"Here's the skinny. Solana knows how much you love Carlos and her father. She said to tell you this is the best gift she can give her son."

"Gift?" Marcella and Kellen echoed.

"The gift of a good life with someone who'll love the little man like he's their own. The gift of *familia*, was the word she used. She wants Carlos to have a mother and, eventually, a father who'll do all the things with him that his father can't because he's on the other side."

"I—I—don't understand," Marcella stammered.

"I know this is gonna sound all kooky, but I guess it can't get any kookier than what you've already been through. So hear me out. You and Solana, you're like twins. You now know that's because she's your granddaughter. Here's the plan. You get in her body. Just like you did with that poor wahine, Rick. Only this body you get to keep for as long as it has breath in it with Solana's blessing. She wants this, Marcella. We all do. You've suffered so she could have life. There's nothing we can do to change what happened. We can't change that you lost decades with your family or that you were in total suckage as a demon. But we can change how it's dealt with. And we all agree your sacrifice has to be totally recognized."

Marcella's mouth fell open, the air from her lungs thin and shallow. Words came from Uriel's mouth. She heard them. Felt their impact. Yet couldn't respond. The kind of hope he was offering her was the kind of hope she'd never dared, not once since she'd made the choice to save David, to ever wish for. And in the blink of an eye, it could all be over. Every long night wondering, worrying, wishing, for seventy-six years was just over.

Just over?

To have that erased without a battle—without her having to sacrifice something else—was almost too vast to wrap her head around.

"Marcella? Take my hand," Uriel coaxed.

She reached out with a trembling limb, placing her hand in his. A hand that was warm, soft, and encompassed everything good and right. Her breath hitched at the comfort it brought, the peace it gave deep within her. He brought her fingers to his cheek with a whisper of skin against skin, leaving her light-headed with surreal joy.

"Do you want to stay, Marcella? I didn't ask that. I just assumed."

Yes. Yes, yes, yes. She wanted to stay. For as long as she could.

Kellen craned his neck around the pair to look at Marcella with warm hazel eyes. "Under normal circumstances, your mouth in the closed position would be something akin to nirvana for me, but your timing's off. Answer the nice archangel, honey. And no pressure here, but I'm a little nuts about you. Take that into consideration when you finally find that sharp tongue." He chuckled, rocking Carlos in his arms.

Her heart swelled with a stinging jolt. "Yes," she managed, failing at hiding her sob of gratitude. "I want to stay. More than anything, I want to stay."

Uriel winked. "Coolio. So come with." He gave her a gentle tug toward Solana's body, lying peacefully where Armando had so casually dumped it.

"I just get in?" she squeaked. Her legs trembled, her stomach flip-flopped.

"Yeah, dudette, that's what I'm saying. Go on, jump in," Uriel cajoled with a smile of encouragement.

Marcella held a shaky hand up. This was all going so fast. Too fast. She scrambled for a reason to slow this down. "Wait. How old is Solana? I mean, look at me, right?" She waved an abstract hand around her body. "I couldn't be the equivalent of more than thirty human years, at best. But I'd settle for twenty-five."

"Marcella?"

Her eyes sought Kellen's, bleary and red from battle, but warm and loving when he looked at her. "Yes, Kellen?"

"Get in the goddamned body or I'll throw you in there myself." Then he frowned, looking toward Uriel. "Sorry. Bad choice of words."

She gave him a coquettish smile. "Have I told you how hot it is when you make demands?"

"Have I told you how completely bat shit you make me?"

"There's been a heated occasion or two."

"Get—in—the—body—now."

She took a deep breath, trying to assimilate. "Wait, and I'm being very serious when I say wait. This seems so wrong—so—I dunno, like I'm violating her." She turned to Kellen, her eyes wet with un-shed tears. A huge surprise. "There isn't anything I want more than to be with you, Kellen—with Carlos, but this was his mother. She knows things about him I never will—the little things mothers know. Like what his favorite toy was when he was a baby. When he lost his first tooth. What he likes on his hot dog. I can't be her. She was my *granddaughter*, for God's sake!"

Kellen began to speak, but Uriel held up a hand with a com-forting smile to quiet him. "That you care enough to worry about those things makes you one rad wahine, Marcella. You made a crazy sacrifice all those years ago—to save Carlos's grandfather—your son—and you took it like a warrior. All the years you were forced to let everyone believe you were someone other than who you really are is hard-core loyal. But the way I look at it is Carlos needs a mother. Little man's been through some roughage. It's gonna take a long time to get his head back on straight and help him deal with what's gone down. I can erase some of it, but I can't stop the afterlife from paying him visits. He is what he is. A con-duit to upstairs. A special, rare one at that. You could be the one to help him do that. You and Kellen."

Her lips trembled. "But what about what Armando did while he was in Solana's body? What about all those disgusting men he . . . And oh, God. He was so awful to her mother. Mrs. Ramirez'll have me locked up in the loony bin just like that." Marcella snapped her fingers, her heart torn.

Uriel nodded his understanding, but his next words soothed. "I got your back. The only thing you have to do is jump, Marcella.

Tomorrow when you wake up, Carlos and his grandmother won't remember anything but that his mother's hard-core cool and she's going to start dating a guy they both think is pretty awesome. What happens after that's up to you two."

She was being given this enormous gift, and it was almost too much. It left her overwhelmed, humbled beyond repair. The domino effect for a gesture so magnanimous floored her. Not only could she be with Kellen and Carlos, but her son. David. After so many agonizing, worry-filled years apart. He wouldn't know who she really was—she'd in essence be his daughter. Yet that didn't leave her with regret. Just to see him, be near him, talk with him for however long he had left on this Earth made inexplicable joy bubble up inside her.

Uriel placed a hand on her shoulder. "This is a lot, right? Like, all at once because everything's been such a struggle for so long."

She was slow to nod. "I'm afraid that I'll screw it up—that it'll all . . ."

"Be taken from you," Uriel finished. "Not this time, Marcella. I'm always lookin' out for the good guys. You won't see me, but you'll feel me." He cupped her cheek, wiping away the tears that fell in fat, salty bubbles.

She looked to Kellen. "But what if you don't like Solana? I know we look almost exactly alike, but we must have differences that you'll notice when . . ." She snapped her mouth shut, shooting Uriel a guilty glance. Only she could bring up a fear as inappropriate as the humpety-hump in front of an archangel.

Kellen spoke then, gruff, his voice hoarse when he planted a kiss on her forehead and held her close. "I love you. *You*. Who you are. How you became who you are. The rest is inconsequential."

She laughed a watery giggle. "I bet you wouldn't be saying that if I had a lumpy ass."

Tilting her chin up, his eyes honed in on hers. "No. You're

wrong. But I look at it this way—someday, whether you like it or not—you will have a lumpy ass and that's just life as a mere mortal. And even then, I'll still love you."

She threw her head back and laughed. "What am I thinking? Leaving my spectral body has its disadvantages."

"Honey?"

"Uh-huh?"

"Get in the body. *Now*."

She touched her lips to his briefly before looking to Uriel. "You promise Carlos won't be scarred by this? I need to know that."

Uriel held up two fingers. "Archangel's honor."

"You'll get Little Anthony and poor Rick home safely? Can you do the mojo thing to them, too? You know, so they don't remember?"

Jamming his hands in the pockets of his shorts, he rocked back on his bare heels. "You betcha."

"And Darwin. Oh, God. What about Darwin? I won't be able to see him anymore. I never thought I'd shed a single tear over that meddling half-breed, but if not for him, I never would have survived this."

"Who is Darwin, honey?"

"I'll explain later. Promise," she said to Kellen, then touched Uriel's arm. "You know who I mean, don't you?"

"Yeah. I got it covered. I can't say when or where, but you'll see Darwin again. That's a promise."

With a deep breath, Marcella knelt before her granddaughter, marveling at the uncanny resemblance to herself. Wanting to tell her how endlessly grateful she was for this chance to be with her family. To share with her how much she would have liked to have known Solana the child, the woman, the mother she'd become. She wanted to whisper soothing words at the loss of her husband as she rocked her. To tell her she herself knew loss and how devastating it could be. She wanted to bid her *vaya con Dios,* safe passage as she crossed, but all she could manage was "Thank you" in a trembling whisper and then her eyes sought Uriel's once again. "You will thank her, won't you? For me. I'll never be able to say that enough," she choked out.

Placing a hand on her shoulder, Uriel whispered, "You got it," just before he gave her a slight nudge, sending her tumbling into Solana's prone form.

The transition wasn't anything like possessing Rick. It was as though she hovered on a cloud for a moment, weightless and lighter than a feather. Then the cold ground was seeping under her thin shirt and her hands were touching her face.

Kellen knelt beside her, setting Carlos, still sound asleep, on his knee. Instantly her hands went to Carlos, running them over his silky hair, trailing a finger across his freckled nose, bringing his hand to her lips. She kissed the tip of each finger. To feel his skin near hers, to touch him made more tears flow from her eyes. Pulling her up to his chest, Kellen invited her into the circle of his arms.

Strong, confident arms that held Carlos and now her. Grateful tears slid down Marcella's face, soaking the shoulder of his jacket.

Uriel bent at the waist and placed his palm on Carlos's head. He closed his eyes, then popped them open and smiled. "So I'm out, peeps. You stay hard-core, Marcella, and, Kellen, give this gift-of-sight thing some time, dude. Once you catch the wave, it'll be a rad ride. Promise."

Just as he rose to leave, Marcella gripped his hand. She had no words. Nothing flippant or funny to say in the way of the kind of thanks she so wanted to express.

Instead, she let her eyes meet the archangel's before she closed them and held her face skyward.

In deep appreciation.

Uriel's lips brushed Marcella's forehead and he whispered, "Safe journey, wahine." With the sign for hang loose, he was gone.

They sat on the steps at the entryway to Carlos's apartment for a long time, fingers entwined, Carlos safely wrapped in her arms, Kellen's jacket around her shoulders. In silence. In thought. In awed reverence.

When Kellen finally spoke, his voice was scratchy and filled with emotion. "So, I've been thinking."

"Do tell."

"We'll have to take this slowly. This thing we have going on."

"Because of Carlos and Mrs. Ramirez."

"Your daughter-in-law, uh, mother. Yes. Because of them."

She smiled. "Absolutely."

"You do know there's nothing more I'd like to do than have my way with you right here on the steps, right?"

Her grin grew wider. "I'm right there with you." Then she sighed with a forlorn exhale.

"But Carlos has been through a lot. So we do this the right way—for him. Set a good example on how to woo the woman of your dreams."

"You mean the way two *normal human* people do it?" Marcella couldn't even imagine it, but she was willing to try. Willing, willing, willing.

"Yep. All normal-like."

"I'm down. Sooo down."

"Good to know. So, Marcell . . . uh, Solana Ramirez, I'm Kellen Markham. I think you're hot. Wanna grab a burger? Maybe catch a movie? Make out?"

There was nothing—nothing that sounded more heavenly. Giggling, Marcella gathered Carlos in her arms and rose. She kissed Kellen on the lips she hoped to kiss for as long as she had life in her. "That's so average. Is this how you plan to wow me, ghost whisperer?"

Rubbing his nose against hers, he chuckled. "Do you think you can forgo floating and possession in favor of average?"

Eyeing him, she said, "Have I told you how much I love a big juicy hamburger with onions?"

"That's a pretty average thing to like," he teased with a husky chuckle.

"Well, I'm a pretty average girl."

"You're anything but average," he murmured, taking her lips in a possessive kiss she returned, but had to reluctantly pull away from if they were going to get the average-dating thing right.

"So tomorrow night at seven?"

"Can I bring Carlos?"

He grinned. Delicious, wide, heart stopping. "You'd disappoint me if you didn't."

"Then tomorrow at seven. I'll pencil you in." With the heavy weight of Carlos in her arms, Marcella turned to head up the stairs. To her new surroundings.

To her family.

To her new life.

epilogue

Marcella Acosta Solana Ramirez sat on the bench of the playground, keeping a watchful eye on the most precious gift she'd ever been given while she waited to share a peanut butter and jelly sandwich, her specialty, with her other precious gift. Delaney sat beside her, enjoying the cool, early fall afternoon. As a pair, they sat in quiet harmony. To this day, every now and again, they'd glance at each other—sharing the knowledge of just how precious this gift they'd both been given was.

It had been over six months since that night on the playground. Six months filled with so many wonderfully rich, utterly normal events they'd be countless if Marcella didn't purposefully count every last one of them.

These past few months had been an adjustment period. A time that involved Marcella stumbling around in the dark while she parented Carlos (and he sometimes parented her) and learned how not to burn a box of good macaroni and cheese, to throw a baseball, do fourth-grade math, and play video games. It had been a time of quiet evenings on the front stoop, coffee in hand, with her son, David, who filled her with stories of her sister, Isabella, and his life as a young boy, completing the pictures Marcella had created in her mind, bringing them to life with colorful words.

It had been a time of much laughter, the kind that made tears stream from your eyes and your stomach hurt, such as when Mrs. Ramirez, uh, her mother, had attempted to teach her how to make tamales. It had been a time of bittersweet irony, such as finding out that Solana's middle name was Marcella due to Isabella's mysterious insistence. There'd also been the relief when Kellen explained he loved the name Marcella so much, he was going to call her that from now on because he secretly kept screwing it up.

And there was Kellen, who indeed took things slowly, courting her the way any respectful suitor would. With flowers, with a box of those chocolate-covered cherries she loved so much, with nights filled with predictable things like dinner at six, and the weekly TV shows they watched like clockwork—holding hands on the couch cuddled under a blanket. The long, smoldering kisses good night on her front stoop while they waited the proper amount of time to consummate their relationship.

Which had ended up feeling like forevah, but was in reality only two months.

They'd found a routine—a niche—a joy in the simple things life had to offer.

And it was bliss. The kind of bliss Marcella had once thought involved only jet-setting and shopping.

"Hey, Aunt D?"

Delaney looked up with a warm smile from the stroller she rocked with a lazy foot that held her and Clyde's newly adopted little girl from China. "What's up, little man?"

Carlos held a cat in his arms, scraggly and matted. "I found him over by the lady with the poodle from, uh . . . France. The fluffy white one who comes here every day. He says he knows you guys. His name's Darwin. Can we keep him, Mom?" He grinned.

Marcella's heart heaved, not quite as sharply as it once had when she'd first heard her new official title, but it still shivered with love. She cocked her head. "Did you say Darwin?" No. No way.

Carlos nodded his dark head, running his chin over the top of the stray cat's ears and giggling. "Uh-huh. He said he knows you and Aunt D from a long time ago and that"—he paused for a moment, clearly struggling to get the words right—"he's done the most hey-nus thing in order to be with his family. Then he said something about trading Mr. Peabody in, but I can't remember the rest. It didn't make sense." He wrinkled his young brow, trying to piece together the message from the great beyond until one of his friends called him from the monkey bars. "So I think we should keep him."

He dropped the cat in Marcella's lap in an unceremonious heap, giving it an errant scratch on its multicolored head before running off to play on the monkey bars with his new friends—of which he now had many. With the help of Delaney, Marcella, and mostly Kellen, Carlos was coming to grips with his gift of sight. He'd learned to cross souls with expertise, and he'd taught Kellen the kind of patience and sensitivity only a child can bring when handling an angry spirit. Though Kellen was still a work in progress, he was back doing what he loved, while her mother, Mrs. Ramirez, tended the store, and he'd learned to keep the spirits calm and cooperative during school hours.

Marcella scooped the cat up, her heart chugging at an alarming rate, tears filling her eyes. *Mr. Peabody . . .* was it really even possible?

"No way," Delaney muttered, her eyes wide when she exchanged surprised looks with Marcella.

"Uriel said I'd see him again. But this"—she held him up in the air to examine him—"had to be the ultimate sacrifice for him. He was a Rottweiler, for God's sake, D—a purebred. Now he's some mixed-breed cat. And, from the looks of things, a *female* mixed breed. You must be devastated, huh, Kibble King? But look what you did in order to find us." Marcella hugged him close while his legs dangled in midair. "Is that really you?" She sniffed his fur, wrinkling her nose. "You smell like the stench of a thousand rotting souls." Scratching his ears, she looked into his deep green eyes. "Where have you been? How did you get into this body? Never mind. I don't care. I'm sooo glad to see you!" She ran her fingers along the bones of his visible ribs. "You're so skinny. Wait—I have food."

Marcella handed Darwin to Delaney, who peered deeply into Darwin's eyes. "Darwin, is that you in there?" The cat gave her a haughty glance, tilting his chin up and away from her prying eyes.

"Look, Darwin," Marcella cooed, holding out her hand to him. "It's Goldfish!" she said triumphantly, shuffling the crackers in her hand.

Darwin regarded them for a mere moment before tipping his chin back into the haughty position he'd given Delaney.

Marcella nodded with a grin. "That's gotta be him. He was always such a food snob."

"Who? You can't mean me. I eat burned tamales every night for dinner and all for the sake of love," Kellen teased, reaching around his sister to give Marcella a gentle kiss and a smile that never failed to warm her from head to toe. Carlos caught sight of him and ran up to knock knuckles with him, his lips spreading into a wide smile.

Kellen returned Carlos's smile, a smile that was reserved especially for him and always tightened Marcella's heart. "Hey, bud. What's goin' on? How was that math test?"

He scrunched his face up in dislike. Much like his great-grand-mother, he hated math. "I *think* I did okay."

Kellen ruffled his hair. "Good deal. Wanna hit the books to-night after some Rock Band?"

Carlos nodded and yelled, "Deal!" before heading back to his friends.

"So who's this little critter?"

"Omigod, you'll never believe it, honey! It's Darwin." Marcella held him up in the sunlight with a beaming smile. To which Darwin responded by hanging limp and boneless, giving Kellen a look of dry indifference.

Kellen sank down beside her, wrapping an arm around her and resting his head on top of hers. He scratched Darwin under the chin. "I thought you said Darwin was Delaney's dead dog."

Leaning into him, she nodded and whispered, "He was. But I think he managed to, you know, find a host. I'm betting one that was well, you know . . ." Marcella winked.

"Ah," Kellen said, entwining his fingers with hers. "So I guess Vern and Shirley'll have to move over on the couch?"

Marcella smiled up at him and his generosity. "If he's anything like the dog Darwin, he'll own the couch." Leaning forward, strok-ing Darwin whether he liked it or not, she commented, "So I saw Catalina today. She came in to order bat shit."

"She okay?" Kellen asked.

Marcella's face expressed her worry. She and Catalina shared a tentative friendship that included nothing more than the occa-sional chat when Catalina came to pick up supplies from the store. They exchanged pleasantries, and not much else, leading Marcella to believe that Catalina felt just the way she had when she was a demon. She didn't want to become attached to anything remotely human. And Marcella understood that better than anyone, but someday, when the time was right, she wanted Catalina to know she had an ear, if she wanted to bend one. "Ever since that night when she saw Dameal, I feel like she's been hiding something. But I figure, when she's ready, she'll talk about it."

Kellen smiled at her. "I hope so, honey. Until then, I'm starving. What delicacy have you brought me today, my pretty Betty Crocker? Is it some chunky flan maybe? That's my total favorite. Wait, Hamburger Helper, right? Raw, I hope?"

Settling a reluctant and stiff Darwin on her lap, Marcella stuck her tongue out at him and reached into the portable cooler she'd brought and handed Kellen a sandwich. "Lunch," she offered proudly.

He gave Delaney a hesitant look and whispered, "Did she make it or did you?"

Marcella swatted his shoulder. "Hey! I slaved over a hot jar of Skippy and walked a full mile to school to come see you on your lunch hour, and this is the thanks I get? I think I might have to reconsider that proposal, Mr. Markham," she teased.

Delaney snarfed, scooping up little Ella and nibbling her chubby fist. "After what I went through, talking you out of that bridesmaid dress that was meant only to be worn by a full C cup and a size two who calls a breath mint a healthy meal? Uh, no. You marry him or I'll drag you to that altar by your long legs and make you wear something frumpy when I do it."

"Like she'd pass up the chance to bag *this*," Kellen joked, taking a bite of his sandwich and making mock noises of gourmet pleasure.

"So, I have an announcement," Marcella said with pride.

Kellen held up his sandwich and grinned. "You're leaving me to compete on *Top Chef*?"

Marcella tweaked his chin, lovingly wiping away a drip of grape jelly. "Guess who's going to be earning her keep starting next Monday?"

"Shut up, Kell," Delaney chastised with a grin. "So, did you get it?" She gave Marcella a secretive glance.

Kellen cocked his head. "Get what, honey?"

"A job! Guess who's Pier 1's newest employee?" Her excitement about nabbing a real, live job was matched only by the joy that she was entitled to an employee discount.

Kellen's groan was long. "Does this mean we're going to have a bunch of those foofy pillows in ten different colors and beaded lampshades?" He followed it up with a grin, kissing her lips.

Marcella giggled—something she did often these days, girlishly and filled with carefree exuberance. "This means, cranky-pants, that your fiancée's joining the workforce just like every other mortal. The whole nine-to-five thing. All normal and average."

Kellen took her hand in his and squeezed it. "You know what, future wife of mine?"

"What's that?"

"In the biggest of ways, I dig normal and average. They're the two prettiest words in the dictionary. You wear them well." He wiggled his eyebrows at her.

Smiling up at him, Marcella pressed her lips to his and kissed him with every ounce of love she had to offer.

The kind of love that was anything—*anything* but average.